HOW TO FAKE IT WITH A FAE

SEVEN SUITORS FOR SEVEN WITCHES
BOOK ONE

AMY BOYLES

LADYBUGBOOKS LLC

AUTHOR'S NOTE

Thank you for reading HOW TO FAKE IT WITH A FAE and for going on me with this journey.

If you're a regular reader of my work, I want you to know that unlike my cozy mysteries, this romance does have some steam. You can skip those parts if you wish. But whatever you do, don't skip this book, because I know you're going to love Addison and Feylin as much as I do.

Enjoy!

—Amy

1

*H*ere's the thing—when every guy you've dated dumps you for a witch who can summon a flock of doves with the snap of her fingers, as opposed to yourself, who can't even conjure one mosquito in the middle of a swamp, you tend to get a little guy shy.

However, when you've been dating someone for six months and he suddenly asks you to dinner at the best restaurant in all of Nashville to talk about something important—completely out of the blue, I might add—it's absolutely logical to think said guy is about to pop the question.

Isn't it?

You don't have to answer because I know it's true.

So that's why I'm currently shrugging on my coat and pointing myself toward the exit of Bookworm, the store where I work.

I love books.

But we'll get to that.

"Addie, there you are! I've been looking everywhere for you."

My spine snaps to attention at the familiar voice of Mr.

Roberts, one of our store regulars. I turn slowly, my gaze dragging from the door that I really want to be launching myself through to the elderly man.

His thin gray hair is coiled on his head as if he's just run his hands through it in an attempt to create the world's worst mohawk. His eyebrows match in color, and they wing upward, as do the hairs jutting from his ears, which are so long that they're currently waving at me.

Even though Mr. Roberts has hair hygiene that makes me cringe, he's a sweet old man.

He runs a plump hand down his tweed vest. "Addie, I just wanted to thank you for that last book recommendation. I loved *Remains of the Day*. Really spot on. Whenever I need a good read, I know who to ask."

I thumb the buttons of my coat into their holes, trying to be quick as to subtly hint that I'm in a hurry. "That's very kind of you, Mr. Roberts. My pleasure. After all, it's what I do, recommend books."

He pumps his brows. "Are you sure that you didn't inherit any of the magic in your family? Because I'd swear that it's magical the way you can always point me toward my next perfect read," he adds with a chuckle.

I wince at the mention of my family, but he doesn't notice. In my world, magic is out in the open—all the supernaturals are. There's no need to hide that we're different anymore, unlike the old days.

I smile. "My particular talent has nothing to do with magic and more to do with knowing a person's taste."

He stares at me a moment, drinking in the smart black coat and the peeking hem of my dress. The plum-colored dress is soft and clingy, but I butchered the tag when I cut it out, (missing half because I was in a rush), so it's irritatingly itchy against my back.

He takes in the heels on my feet before his gaze tracks back up to my face, where he scans the auburn curls cascading down my shoulders, as opposed to the messy bun I normally tie my hair into.

"You look like you've got somewhere important to be."

"I do." *I'm getting engaged!* "But I'll be back tomorrow if you want me to help you find a new book."

"Yes, certainly." His expression drops. "Don't let me keep you. Whoever is waiting for you is truly a lucky fellow."

And that's when the guilt kicks in. There's no way that I can abandon Mr. Roberts without locating his next read.

"My plans aren't more important than you. In fact, I bet you're ready for adventure after finishing *Remains*."

Surprise flits across his face. "In fact, I am."

"I knew it." I cross to the shelf and grab a hardback novel. "This is *Fallen Out*. It's by Wayne Stinnett, and is your typical murder and mayhem in paradise."

He eyes the cover before breaking into a smile. "It looks marvelous. I'll take it."

Cha-ching!

"And I was also thinking of grabbing something about the fae."

"Oh, um, I'm not sure we have anything."

"Very mysterious beings, from what I understand. They can be quite vicious and violent."

"That's what I've heard, too."

He leans in conspiratorially. "I believe they've moved into Castleview. Isn't that the town you're from?"

"It is, but I haven't been back in a while."

Which is quite true. I grab my purse off the back of a chair and smile. "Is there anything else I can help you find?"

He inhales sharply, breaking off his thoughts about the fae. "No, my dear. That's all. Have a great night."

"Thank you."

I flip my hair out from the collar of my coat, tell my

coworkers good night and march through the door into the cool autumnal afternoon that's quickly slipping into evening. With the arrival of fall, Nashville's humidity is receding, and fiery red leaves are beginning to shyly dot the trees.

My phone rings as soon as I'm on the street. I pull it from my purse, my heart quickening. I hope it's not Edward calling to cancel. Ridiculous. Why would he cancel when he's about to propose?

To my relief, it's not him.

"Hello?" The downtown streets are bustling. Commuters are beelining for their cars to return to the suburbs. Others are tourists heading for the bars on Honky Tonk Row. I wind my way quickly around a group of men gaping at all the neon signs.

"Hello?" I repeat.

"Addie?"

"Blair," I say with a soft exhale. "I didn't recognize the number."

"Nana just got a new phone," my sister tells me. "And she wanted me to call so that you'd have the number."

I chuckle. "Why didn't she call me herself?"

"Because she doesn't understand silly human things like phones."

"And you do?"

"Better than her," my sister snips. Blair is, how shall I put it, prickly. She's not mean, just simply my younger sister with a big bold head on her shoulders. "Here. She wants to talk to you."

Soft muffling occurs as the phone is handed over. The next voice I hear is my grandmother's. "Addie?"

"Nana, how are you?"

"Just fine, child," she replies in a frail, elderly voice that's drenched in all things Southern. "How are you?"

4

"I've got so much to tell you. Edward's asked me out to dinner tonight to a fancy restaurant, and I think—"

"He's going to propose?"

"Yes," I say so loudly that people turn to look. I hunch back over the phone and stage-whisper, "Yes. All signs point to yes! He's perfect, Nana. From a good magical family—the Blackwoods."

She pauses. "Addie, you know it's getting to be time."

My stomach twists tightly. "I know. I know." I'm not trying to blow her off, but I've heard all this before. "Things look promising. He's got something important to talk to me about." Goose bumps wash down my arms at the thought of Edward on one knee, his sandy hair pushed to the side, that adorable lopsided grin on his face and his teeth glinting in that magical way. *Literally.* He uses magic to make his teeth glint, though he swears it's natural. But I know the truth. I wasn't born yesterday. "So if he proposes—"

"We'll be on the right path," she confirms quietly—*too quietly.* "We miss you, child."

A knot in my chest that I didn't know existed, loosens. "I miss you, too."

And I do. The one thing I loved as a child was climbing onto Nana's lap and pressing my head to her soft bosom as she told me stories of sprites and faeries. But those days are long past.

"You need to visit," she says. "See your family. Things might be different."

My heart hardens. "They won't be. You know that."

But a proposal could actually change things. It's been ages since I've seen my family, my town, and I miss all of it. I miss *them.*

"I'm getting tired, Addie."

The tone of her voice strikes me as different from normal. She sounds weary, which makes me frown. Nana's our family matriarch. She's always existed, and as far as I'm concerned, she always will.

"I'll call you as soon as Edward proposes," I confide. "You're going to love him. He's perfect."

"Hmm."

She's clearly not as enthusiastic as I am, but she will be once she meets him. "Oh, I'm here at the restaurant. I've got to go."

Blair says, "Keep the phone on the table so we can hear everything."

"Have you been listening to our conversation?" I accuse playfully.

"You're loud, Addie. You always are when you're excited. Just be sure to send a pic of the ring," she adds, her tone softening.

"All right, all right. Gotta go. Love y'all."

"Love you," Nana says before hanging up.

When I open the door, a warm blast of air slaps me in the face. I quickly fix my bangs and spot Edward at a table in the center of the room.

My heart pounds against my chest as I approach, which is at the exact time that the scissored tag in my dress starts to scratch at my flesh.

It will pass, I tell myself. Just focus on Edward. On the amazing thing that's about to happen.

The maître d' takes my coat, and Edward stands to pull out my chair. He rakes his sandy hair from his face, and I take a moment to drink him in. He's a little taller than me and has what I'd describe as a lithe build. His eyes twinkle and his lips, which perfectly fit mine when we kiss, break into a smile.

I press my mouth to his smooth cheek and inhale his cologne—it smells like fresh mountain spring water and rainbows. I know that rainbows don't have a scent, but if they did, they would smell like Edward, woodsy and clean.

6

"Hi."

"Hi, yourself," he murmurs with a smile that makes his cheek dimple. *So adorable.*

I sit and smooth down my dress. "Sorry to be late."

Edward takes his seat and grins at me sloppily. "You're fine. Absolutely fine."

A sigh escapes me. My heart is still thundering in my ribs. The urge to leap over the table, grab him by the lapels and beg him to get to his question is overwhelming, but I manage to bite it down.

We peruse the menu and the waiter appears. I order first. "I would like the wedge salad, but instead of blue cheese, I'd rather ranch dressing, and on the side, please. I'd also like to go lightly on the bacon, and please make it extra crispy but not burnt."

After Edward orders, he smiles at me. "You're so…*you*, the way you order so particularly."

I fold my napkin into a compact rectangle and drape it over my lap. "Thank you."

We do a lot of smiling at each other as we wait for our food. Edward is perfect. He's handsome, funny, charming and a wizard, which is more than my family could hope for, considering.

After our meals arrive and we're several bites in, he places his knife atop the plate. "Addie, like I said, there's something I want to talk to you about."

This is it! I place my fork delicately beside the ramekin holding my dressing. "Yes? I'm all ears." And fingers! One in particular.

"We've been seeing each other for a while, and we've gotten very close. You're a wonderful woman."

"Thank you." It's hard not to blush.

"We have so much in common—coming from magical families and all, and you know that I'm about to go off to

AMY BOYLES

magical medical school. I should've done it sooner, but as they say, better late than never."

Edward's thirty years old, just to clarify.

"I completely understand," I say, straightening my spine. That tag is still driving me nuts. I press my back to the chair, hoping that'll ease the itch, but it only makes it worse.

"And you're adorable with the way you order food, so picky."

Why are we still talking about the way I order meals and not about getting engaged? "Well, I like things the way I like them."

"And you're very refined."

"Thank you."

Here it comes. He's giving me big googly eyes, and his teeth are supercharged. The glinting is off the charts.

"And since I'll eventually be running for office, you can imagine that I'll need a partner who's my match in every way."

That's me. *Sign me up!* "Absolutely."

"And since my family is magical and I'm a well-trained wizard, it would only make sense to have a witch at my side."

"Of course."

"And that witch must be my magical match."

My fingers curl into the napkin from excitement. "Definitely."

"Which is why I'm…"

I hold my breath, waiting for Edward to finish his sentence.

And then he does.

2

"*A*nd that's why I'm breaking up with you."

Somewhere in the background, a record scratches. "What?"

He sits back, a cocky grin plastered to his face. "You're great and all, but you can't work magic and you're so picky. You're not who I'm supposed to be with."

I completely deflate. "So you're not proposing?"

He laughs. *Actually laughs.* "I'm definitely not proposing."

It takes a moment for me to wrap my head around this news. It seems so wrong. But there's no denying the lack of Edward on his knees holding a velvet-plushed box that contains the cushion-cut diamond I've been dreaming about my whole life.

I rub the spot between my brows. "You're...breaking up with me."

"Bingo."

All around me are tables filled with people. Then it hits me. Edward's dumping me in public so that I don't make a scene.

"Look, if you had magic, that would be one thing. But you

9

and I both know that you're the one Thornrose who never got it." He sucks his teeth. "Shame."

This tag's driving me crazy. My fingers curl and uncurl as I stop myself from clawing my back.

My attention's drawn back to Edward as he pats my hand. "You look like you want to be loud and upset," he says, pity lacing his voice. "That's not who you are, is it, Addie?"

"But you said that you loved me," I murmur, still trying to wrap my head around the situation.

He chuckles and pulls his hand off mine. "Did I?"

My face is burning hot. Rage boils in my veins, and my back is on fire. "You said that you *love me*," I repeat through gritted teeth.

He looks nervous now, glancing from table to table as he palms his hair. "You aren't the sort to make a scene, right? You can either accept this news gracefully, or you can go the other way. Now, which will it be?"

My stomach coils tightly.

So, my magic never came in. On every witch and wizard's thirteenth birthday, there's the *magicking.* That's a huge ceremony where all your friends and family come to watch you receive your magic. Every kid from a magical family goes through it.

I did, but when it came time for my magic to show itself, nothing happened.

Not one thing.

My family's prominence in society made my inability to work magic humiliating. My six sisters who came behind me received theirs, but I was left hollow, a barren witch.

Worse, my incapacity to conjure magic has stuck with me —from my everyday life to the dating scene. Wizards only want to date witches, and humans are afraid of witches—they don't say it, but I know it's true.

So when I met Edward, I thought that he was perfect. I told

him right off about my condition, but he didn't care. Told me that it made me even more special.

So that was what I thought—until now.

I rise from the chair, the tag on my back irritating me so much that sweat's trickling down my spine and face. Edward's eyes are big as plates as he takes me in.

"Now, now," he replies, tugging on his collar, "you don't overreact. Think of your family," he adds, looking smug at bringing up my prominent kin. "What would they say?"

I flatten my knuckles on the table. "You said that you love me," I say loudly this time, forcefully, as if repeating the words will somehow make them true.

"I do-*ish*. But you have to understand my predicament."

"That you're a selfish pig?" People are glancing my way now. To hell with decorum. *"You said that you loved me!"*

"Addie"—he chuckles nervously—"can't we discuss this quietly?"

"That's why you brought me here—so that I wouldn't make a scene. So that I wouldn't throw water in your face."

The anger inside of me is tightening something in my stomach. I once read in an old magic book that sometimes great stress can cause a person's power to appear. Maybe this is my moment. Maybe for the first time in my life, it'll work.

I focus on the coiling in my gut and close my eyes as Edward pleads.

"Darling, please sit down."

"Don't. Call. Me. Darling."

I will all the butterflies that are dive-bombing around in my stomach, out. I push them away, focusing on the lights in the room, like I was told to do long ago at the *magicking*.

"Focus on one thing," my mother said. *"Put all your attention on it and watch what your magic will do."*

It didn't do anything then, but it will now. I see all the bulbs in my mind's eyes, I snap my eyelids open and—

Nothing.

Edward smirks. "Did you—were you just trying to work magic?"

I grab my glass of ice water and toss the drink in his face. He jerks back.

"That's for breaking up with me. You're an ass, Edward! And this tag!"

I claw at my back as the entire restaurant watches me. Frustrated beyond belief, I release a scream that a banshee would be proud of.

With my spine no longer itching and my pride completely shattered, I pick up my purse, grab my coat and march from the restaurant.

I'm outside in the cold, snapping wind within moments. Adrenaline courses through my veins. I just threw a glass of water in Edward's face!

Our date wasn't supposed to end like this. He was supposed to propose.

Oh my gods. I've been such an idiot. Did I miss some sign? But how could I have? He told me that he loved me. He said that he didn't care that I couldn't wield magic.

But the truth is that he did. Just like Ted, my first high school boyfriend who broke up with me because I wasn't cool like the girls who could use magic, or River, who dumped me in college because his friends pressured him to date a "real witch," or even Jonah, who said that magic wasn't all that, but when I couldn't even magically light a candle, he realized that he'd be stuck with a loser his whole life and he left me like all the rest.

As I walk through the crowded streets back to my apartment, I realize something—I'll never be good enough for wizards, and I'll never be normal enough for humans.

I'm not good enough for either, which can only mean one thing—I'll stop dating.

I'm done with men. Yes, at the ripe age of twenty-nine, I'm saying goodbye to romance. It's not worth the pain.

And that pain is ripping through me right now. I loved Edward; he was supposed to be my forever. But he turned out to be just like the others.

I reach my high-rise apartment building. I *love* high-rises. They make me feel formidable and tall even though I'm on the short side. When I'm standing at my window glancing down at the people who are no bigger than dots, and cars that are as long as my pinky, I feel a power that I can't grab ahold of in my normal life. It's the closest feeling I have to wielding real magic.

The doorman opens the door as my phone rings. My heart jumps into my throat. Is it Edward, calling to apologize?

I signal to the doorman that it'll be just a moment, and I step aside so that he can't hear me tell Edward that there's no way we're getting back together.

But the number flaring on the screen isn't his. It's Nana's. My stomach drops. She's calling to hear all about the proposal. She's expecting me to announce an engagement. It's strange that she didn't wait for me to call, but not surprising. She wants—or rather *needs*—me to marry. I keep telling her there's no rush, but she insists that there is.

Which makes it all the worse that I have to confess what just happened. The public humiliation's so fresh that it clings to my skin like a sweaty sports bra.

My insides tighten as I swipe my finger across the screen. "Hey, Nana. I didn't expect to hear from you so soon."

I keep my tone light. Everything's fine. It's great. I'm writing off romance forever. No big deal, right?

"It's Blair."

A gust of relief rushes from my lungs. "Oh, thank goodness. I can't talk to Nana right now."

"Addie." Her voice breaks. Blair's voice never breaks. My

AMY BOYLES

sister is void of all emotion. Not true, but fairly close. "Nana…"

Now I'm worried. "What is it? What's going on?"

"It's Nana, Addie. She's…gone."

The world spins. Impossible. I was only just talking to her. "What? This isn't funny, Blair."

"It's true. She had a heart attack, we think. She's gone. No magic could save her, and Mama tried. You have to come home. Right now."

3

*W*hen Blair says *right now*, I assume there'll be time to pack before she magicks me to Castle-view. But I'm very, very wrong.

Immediately after the words leave her mouth, a great suction grabs hold of my body, yanking me from where I stand and stretching me like a rubber band.

My feet are pulled and released, and I'm slingshotted through the air at the speed of sound. At least it feels like it. The skin on my face flaps as wind screams past me. My stomach's been left on the ground, and all I hear is a howling in my ears, and all I feel is my last meal as it pushes up into my throat.

And then, as quickly as everything started, it stops. The ground is under my feet, and I fold over, my palms scraping against wet cobblestones.

No one informed my stomach that we were stopping, however, and my few bites of dinner (along with a protein bar I had earlier) project from my mouth and splatter on top of a pair of polished leather shoes.

Oh gods. I've just puked on someone.

I swipe a hand over my mouth. "I'm so sorry."

A deep, masculine voice makes my spine tighten. "And I only just got these."

He sighs heavily and a shudder rocks through me. Should I look up and face even more humiliation? How much worse could this day get?

I close my eyes and exhale. The queasiness in my stomach subsides, and I venture a look.

My gaze tracks from the now ruined shoes to a pair of pressed jeans and up to thighs so tight a superhero would be jealous. My gaze keeps moving as my mouth goes dry, which is disgusting since the heavy taste of vomit still sits on my tongue.

The chest on this guy is so muscled it looks like those muscles made baby muscles. On top of that, his biceps strain against the sleeves of his starched white shirt. A shadow casts over a jawline that unravels to forever, and deep sapphire eyes glitter at me. This wizard's handsome on a level that should be criminal, and topping off his beauty is a royal scowl that's directed straight at me.

"I'm so sorry," I repeat. "I didn't mean to."

"Clean it up," he grinds out.

I get it. He's mad. He's had a bad day. So have I. But if there's one thing that my grandmother taught me, it's that you attract more flies with sugar than you do vinegar. And nice is what I do.

I force myself onto shaky legs and slowly unfold. Our gazes snap as I stare up at him. *Up*, yes. He's tall—a good head taller than me, and from this closer vantage point his scowl is even deeper.

But I'm not one to be deterred. I smile brightly. "Once again, I apologize. It was an accident."

"Clean it up," he demands angrily.

Who is this jerk? "Excuse me?"

16

His jaw flexes. "Clean. It. Up."

"Do. You. Have. A. Rag?" I throw back.

His gaze rips from mine in a very annoyed look. "No, I don't. Use magic. You're a witch."

And there's the rub. I don't know this werewolf or vampire or whoever this is, so I don't owe him an explanation as to my lack of magic. Also he's got my hackles up by not accepting my apology. Who does that? What woman-hating man sees what is clearly a damsel in distress and stomps on her pain?

"I'm afraid that I'm unable to do that."

His eyes flare in surprise before landing back on me. "And why's that?"

I curl my fists onto my hips. "That's none of your business. Yes, I puked on your shoes. I'm sorry. It was an accident. Wipe it off yourself."

With that, I step around him and stride forward. But my legs are still wobbly. So's my head, apparently, and I lose my balance, falling backward.

Right onto the stranger.

"Oomph!"

He catches me in arms of steel, dipping me until my back arches and my breasts lift, tugging free from the soft fabric of my dress and exposing my lacy black bra. His gaze drops to my swollen breasts for a moment so long it oversteps the awkward line, and when he finally tears his gaze away, our eyes collide.

His face is finely chiseled, and I realize that he looks like a very irked Henry Cavill, strong jaw included. His stare is so fierce that my cheeks flame like there's an inferno burning beneath my skin. Ironically it matches the smoldering heat in his eyes. They become liquid sapphires as his throat bobs dramatically, his eyes drinking me in.

The world suddenly tilts, and a tingle crawls down my head to the base of my neck, where it washes down my arms.

The sensation continues to my core, where the strangest thing happens. Lust, the I-want-to-rip-off-my-clothes-and-shove-my-tongue-down-someone's-throat lust overtakes my body, exposing me in the most basic of ways, so much so that I feel absolutely naked in front of this man.

And it feels really kind of right.

Before I get a chance to question the etiquette of shoving my tongue in a stranger's mouth (which is so wrong— I'm in love with Edward!), my senses brighten like a solar flare. I can smell the rain-drenched earth under the cobblestones. I feel pinpricks of humidity that become goose bumps on my arms. And most of all, I feel the stranger's muscles tighten—his hands, his chest, his thighs, his…you know what.

I should be grossed out by this. Like, completely. But I'm not. Insanely enough, a traitorous pressure builds between my legs, and a deep throb of want pulses.

Pretty sure my panties aren't dry anymore.

Our gazes remain glued to one another, and my throat shrivels as his hands sear fiery imprints straight through my coat and onto my arms.

All the oxygen in the world has been sucked from the earth, and in that split second it's only me and…Mr. Arrogant.

Who just told me to clean up my puke.

"Let me go," I stammer.

His fingers tighten around my arms like he wants to lay claim to me, as if I belong to him and no one else. Panic should be clawing up my throat, but all I feel is a surprising calmness as if this moment, being with him, is *right*.

But obviously I know it's so, so wrong.

The wizard closes his eyes and inhales deeply as if drinking in my scent before he pushes me up gently. My limbs are still wobbly, and my arms pinwheel as I struggle to gain my balance—and at this rate, my crumbling dignity.

Luckily I manage to catch myself before falling flat on my face.

I spin around and yank up my dress to cover my breasts, snapping my head to meet his gaze. He looks a second away from scorching the flesh off my bones, which is how I feel about him, even if my body feels otherwise.

What's wrong with me? My heart's shattered thanks to Edward. The breakup has clearly devastated me beyond the breaking point, since I'm fantasizing about some sadist who happens to look like Henry Cavill, *Witcher* scowl included.

I manage to squeak out, "Goodbye."

With that I march off, this time prepared for the equilibrium shift and compensating my body for it. I rub my arms as I walk away, the heat of his hands still warming my flesh.

I exhale a shaky breath and take in my hometown—Castleview. It's a quaint English-style village nestled in the rolling hills of Central, going on Eastern, Tennessee.

A wet cobblestone path stretches out before me. The air smells heavily of rain, but that hasn't stopped people from being outside.

A smattering of iron tables and chairs circle a fountain of a mermaid holding a starfish. A group of teen boys claims one of the tables, and one by one, they shift for each other, showing off how quickly they can transform from werewolf to their human form and back again.

At another table sits a group of teenage girls—witches by the way they're tossing up orbs of light and jabbing them with their fingernails so that they pop open. Rainbow-colored candy falls like rain into the girls' open mouths.

One girl, still chewing, whispers to another. They giggle and nod, sending an orb bobbing toward the shifters, where it opens over their heads, dropping candy on the unsuspecting boys.

Shock quickly turns to laughter as they glance over at the

girls. One of the boys nods to the others and shuffles over. The girls turn shining faces toward him, offering an invitation to join them. Within seconds the other boys follow, and young love blossoms.

I almost puke again.

To stop myself from thinking about love and my grandmother, I turn my attention to the castle on the hill—the centerpiece of our town. It looms dark and ominous in the distance, the iron spires so tall they could touch clouds.

From what my mother's told me, the castle was originally constructed as a movie set. After the production company was finished with it, the building sold and was snatched up by the tech billionaire Aaron Strickland. He's the one who created the village of Castleview years and years ago.

Unfortunately, Aaron didn't live in the castle long before he sold it. Rumor was, he was being hunted by a monster in his own home. I don't know the truth. What I do know is that after he left, other people moved in. But they eventually left too. The place was empty for years until it was recently acquired by the fae.

It belongs to them now, and as far as I know they keep to *it*, and we keep to the village.

On my walk I pass shops that flank both sides of the street. Witch lights burn outside each door, turning blue when someone approaches, signifying to whoever's inside that a customer's about to enter.

I pass Castleview Tailor and spot Daisy, a rambunctious blonde who's currently unraveling a bolt of silk brocade, displaying it to a man who smiles and reveals sharp fangs. Vampire.

I stop two doors down, the witch lights flaring blue. My breath stops and I step away from the glass, hoping my presence wasn't noticed.

My heart races, and when it finally quiets, I venture a step closer and peer through the leaded glass windows. My family's store, Castleview Books, or the Bookshop of Magic, as it's fondly referred to, houses just about any and every book imaginable. Theresa, one of my mother's employees and her friend, talks to a man and woman. Theresa's long purple dress brushes the stone floor as she takes a book from a shelf and places it atop a lectern, where she opens it. She says something to the couple, and they look at each other, smiling.

Theresa gives a nod. She taps the book, and the couple are gone—they're now inside the story, living it out Jumanji style, only without the Kevin Hart snark.

My chest constricts and I close my eyes. That should be me in there, helping that couple, magicking them into the book. But I can't. All I can do is lead someone to finding their perfect read. I can't transport them inside, because, you know, no magic and all.

I open my eyes and exhale, pressing my fingers hard against the glass. Theresa's gaze drifts up and she sees me.

I back away and move on, heading to the house that I once called home.

4

My legs are heavy by the time I reach the steps of the Tudor-style house. All the houses in Castleview are similar—stone Tudors that stretch out along the sides and back, topped with thatched roofs that occasionally house a bird nest or two, which adds to the charm, I suppose.

I climb the stairs, and the hibiscus guard-vine that winds around the top of the porch uncoils, dipping down to greet me.

An orange flower sniffs my face tentatively. "Yes, it's me. I know it's been too long." The blossom gently nips at my nose, a silent scolding. "I'll be sure to pet you a lot while I'm home."

The blossom dips in sublimation, and I stroke the soft petals.

The door flies open, and my aunt Ovie opens her arms. I turn away from the vine and sink into her, tears leaking from my eyes.

"Shh, I know. None of us expected it."

There's no telling how long she holds me, how long I sob

onto her shoulders, drenching her shirt. She doesn't seem to care, and for that I'm grateful.

It's only after my nose is stopped up and my head feels like a balloon that I take a step back, knuckling the tears away. "She knew, though. She told me tonight that she was tired."

Ovie smiles sadly. She's small like me, with a dynamo personality, almost like an extra spunky Kristen Chenoweth, witch-style.

"I'm sorry we weren't there to greet you in town," she says, pulling me inside. "No one can find it in themselves to leave."

"It's fine. The walk helped ground me."

The house hasn't changed one bit. Gray and brown stones line the walls, and a small fire burns in the hearth. A witch never knows when she'll need to brew something, so the fire's always on.

"Come on. They're in back with…her."

Ovie leads me into the bowels of the cottage. I spot Blair first. Her dark hair's long and sleek, framing her soft brown eyes as it falls over one of her shoulders. She wears jeans and a black corseted blouse that accentuates her trim figure. My sister exhales a loud sigh and rushes over.

"Sorry I didn't meet you."

"It's okay."

When she hugs me, the smell of lavender and lemon waft off her, clouding around me. I inhale her comforting scent as we both cry.

"Nana wouldn't want us getting all sloppy like this." She pulls away, eyes wet with tears, and glances over her shoulder. "Get over here," she commands my other sisters. "Addie's here."

"Addie," Chelsea says, her blonde hair hanging in loose, relaxed waves around her rounded face. "You're home."

My stomach tightens at the word *home*, because even though it is my home, I've never felt like I belonged, which isn't my family's fault. They always make me feel welcome. In fact, my parents didn't want me to move to Nashville to be with humans. But I've always felt more like a human than a witch.

"How's the city?" Chelsea asks.

It's obvious why she's making small talk. No one wants to focus on Nana. Sometimes keeping yourself busy is the best way to deal with tragedy.

Before I can answer, she adds, "Nana always said that cities were only good for two things—"

We say in unison, "Forgetting who you are and where you come from."

It *was* what she always said, and there's truth in it. It's easy to melt into the background in a big place. But Chelsea saying those words makes fresh tears pool in our eyes.

We hug and my nose stops up even more, if that's possible.

Blair squeezes my shoulder. "The city can't be all bad because you should have some news, right? Aren't you supposed to be en—"

I spin away before she can finish her sentence, and spot my other sisters hovering by the bed. "Dallas!"

The fourth sister born in our family saunters over. Yes, my mother named us all alphabetically. Nana told her that was the way to do it, so that people could keep our names straight.

Personally I think Nana suggested it because she thought it was funny.

But Dallas comes over and flings her arms around me. When she pulls back, I spot a long scratch down her arm. "How'd you do that?"

"I fell off my skillet."

Yes, we Southern witches ride cast-iron skillets instead of brooms.

I cock my head. "What? You're a great flyer. How'd it happen?"

24

Emory snorts and casually drapes her hand over Dallas's shoulder. "Oh, you know our sister—always up for a challenge. When Maddix Snow said that she flew her skillet all the way to the top of Pointy Hill and came back down without using the brakes, you-know-who had to do the same thing."

Dallas smirks. "I still think she was lying. There's no way Maddix made it all the way down without a scratch on her."

Emory rolls her eyes. "She magicked it away."

"Ugh. No good witch does that."

Emory scoffs before pulling back from Dallas and taking me in. Her gaze starts at the top of my head and flicks to my feet before trailing back up and stopping on my gaze.

"It's going to be okay, Addic."

My throat tightens. "She said that she was tired."

Emory's face crumples. The dimple in her right cheek flutters before she schools her expression. "I can take away some of the sadness."

I flick off her suggestion. "Don't you dare. I want to feel all of it."

She gives me a knowing nod. "I understand."

Finn bounds up, her fire-engine-red hair bouncing in a ponytail behind her. "Don't I get a hug?"

"Of course you do." I throw my arms around her. "And how've you been?"

"Well, I'd be doing a lot better if Blair wasn't bossing me around every day."

A laugh bubbles in my throat and it feels good. "You work with her."

Finn shrugs. "As if that's any excuse."

I peek over her shoulder and realize that we're down a sister. "Where's Georgia?"

My sisters each give me a wobbly smile. "She's with Mama," Chelsea says, slipping her hand through the crook of my arm as if to ease the blow that the youngest instead of the oldest is comforting our mother.

"Where is Mama?"

"She's taking over now," Ovie explains, stepping up. "You know that's how it goes. You won't see her for a while as she has to make sure the other witching families know that the transfer of power will happen soon, and that they'll need to refer to her as matriarch. There are meetings and friendships to keep secure."

I nod, understanding. As soon as the matriarch passes, the torch immediately goes to the next in line, and she takes up new responsibilities. Within the witching community there are alliances to shore up, as there are with any transition of power.

I inhale a deep breath because the only thing that's left to do is see Nana. It's what I'm here for, but what I'm also not sure that I can do.

Blair squeezes my shoulder. "She looks beautiful."

I swallow past a lump in my throat and step up to the bed, where she's been laid. She's lying in a black gown, her wrinkled face peaceful.

Regret and shame burn in my gut. I should've come back before this. I should've visited. A world of *should haves* prick at my mind, and I shut them out. What's done is done. I'm here now. That's better than nothing.

It seems like hours pass as I hold her cold hand and cry at her side. My sisters pass back and forth, each of them crying as we comfort one another.

It's only when the candles begin to burn low and I realize that it must be getting late, that Ovie clears her throat.

"She'll walk in a few days," she says, as is our tradition. "But tonight there's something I need to tell y'all."

My gaze snaps onto Ovie. What in the world would we

need to talk about? Nana just died. Shouldn't that take all our focus?

She wrings her hands—not a good sign for what's to come. "With your nana's passing, you know that the line of succession falls to your mother. As of late there have been…ripples in our power, fluctuations that can be attributed to one thing—"

"Bad weather?" Finn jokes, pulling her ponytail over one shoulder.

Ovie's gaze skates to her. "No. This has to do with the continuation of magic. As you know, our power survives through the primary generational line, which your grandmother was the head of. My magic came from her, and it now comes from my sister, who was firstborn. The family line must continue in order for the magic to remain strong," she says, her voice stern to stop any interruptions before they start. "Addie, I believe your grandmother had talked to you about this."

"She had," I admit.

Ovie clears her throat and slowly takes in each one of us. "What I'm trying to say is this—the six of you, seven including Georgia, must marry, or else our magic will disappear."

Deep breath.

Okay. I know this already. This was why I'd told Nana about Edward, why I was excited for the proposal. But now things are different. I've sworn off men. But this isn't the time to confess that to my aunt, who looks like a general readying the troops for battle.

Ovie pins her gaze on me. "And we'll be starting with you, Addie. You'll be the first to march down the aisle."

5

*A*ll hell breaks loose.

"I'm not marrying anyone," Dallas snaps.

"Me neither," Finn adds.

"Not even that rake werewolf, Dane?" Chelsea says, eyeing her.

Finn glares in response, while Emory and Dallas shout more protests.

"What about Nana? Don't we get to mourn her?"

"Yeah!"

Ovie throws up her hands. "That is enough! I'm sorry, but you know how this goes. I want to spend time mourning as much as y'all do, but your grandmother understood the severity of the situation. She would want us to focus on this."

I'm so tired, Nana had told me, her words ping-ponging in my head.

"The magic of this coven requires that our family line continues. That is it." Ovie's eyes narrow and tiny flames shoot from them, threatening to scorch us. We all take a step back. "There won't be any argument. Your mama has put me in charge of making sure y'all are ready for marriage, which means you must each be presented."

"Presented?" Dallas guffaws.

"At a ball," I whisper. "A *traditional* witch ball. We've had plenty of others, but this will feature suitors."

It's an old custom, pretty much unheard of anymore, just like arranged marriages are, but it does happen on occasion, like when a family needs to get rid of—I mean, *marry off*—a daughter.

Finn scoffs. "So we're to parade around like peacocks? That's ridiculous. I'd rather take part in a witch hoedown."

Ovie ignores every protest. "You will all go, but our upcoming focus will be on Addie as she's the oldest and, therefore, should be the first to marry." She pins her searing gaze on me. It's enough to make me wither. "We've already taken care of your apartment and job. Your apartment is paid for, and your employer has you on an extended vacation. So there's no need to worry about the human world."

A hush blankets the room. The hairs on the back of my neck prickle as I feel my sisters' gazes on me. I don't have magic, they're thinking. How would marrying me off help the family line?

Ovie answers their silent questions. "Sometimes magic jumps a generation, you know that. So Addie is first. End of story. There won't be more discussion."

"But Addie just go—" Blair starts.

"Didn't you hear her?" I interrupt, not wanting anyone to know that Blair was about to say I'd just gotten engaged. "We're all going to a witch ball." I swallow down a knot of sorrow at the thought of Edward. "Ovie, when's the dance?"

She takes each of us in, making sure that we're giving her our undivided attention before saying, "Tomorrow night."

Which gives me exactly one day to find a way out of this.

I MANAGE to avoid everyone as I leave the room through the open pocket doors that lead to the den. Then I wind my way back to the living room and up the narrow staircase that's butted up against the wall.

The steps creak as I clomp to the second floor and then to the third, where my old room is situated. It's technically the attic and has the exposed beams and large round window to prove it.

As soon as I step inside, fairy lights flare, bobbing up and down, illuminating my old canopy bed, the wizard pop-band posters that are still pinned to the walls, and my vanity.

Dad had magicked the lights for me when I was young. They turn on when I arrive and off when I leave or snap my fingers.

A wave of nostalgia sinks in deep, and I lean against one of the beams, drinking it all in.

"Why didn't you tell her?" Blair's voice sounds from behind me.

I sink farther onto the pole. "Because he didn't ask."

She sucks in a breath. "I'm sorry, Addie."

I flick my hand. "No big deal."

"No big deal?" A whoosh of air blows my hair off the back of my neck and into my face. Blairs stands in front of me now. "You love him." She says it like it's a demand. Knowing her, it probably is.

I lift one shoulder. "Love doesn't matter when you're a witch without powers. Just one more notch in the old belt of heartbreak." Then I smile tightly. "But it's okay. I'll be fine. I'll go to the ball tomorrow."

"No. You won't." She takes my hand. Even though Blair's my younger sister, she's always been my fierce defender, punching anyone in the face who dared make fun of my magic-less status. "You shouldn't have to go."

"You heard Ovie. We don't have a choice. Don't worry. It's going to be okay." Besides, there's still time for me to find a way out of it. "As soon as the wizards and werewolves at the ball realize that it's me who's being pawned off, they'll all turn to you."

"Don't say that."

"It's true."

With her chocolate-colored eyes and dark hair, Blair's a beauty, just like all my sisters.

"And the shop?" she asks.

"What about it?"

"Yes, what about it?"

The new voice comes from the direction of my vanity. I peer around Blair and see a familiar face grinning at me from inside the mirror.

"Elmore!" I lift my hands in glee and rush over.

He cocks his chin. "Missed me?"

"So much."

He smooths a hand over his white pompadour. "Seeing as you decided to abandon me for the human world, I should be hurt, but I've decided to forgive you."

Blair pats my shoulder. "I'll leave you two to catch up. But Addie—"

"Yes?"

"You're not doing this."

I wink. "Don't be so bossy."

She rolls her eyes and pivots on one heel. "Bye, Elmore."

"Goodbye, Blair."

As soon as she's gone, I hop onto the velvet stool in front of the antique wooden vanity. "Tell me everything."

"First, I'm so sorry about Rebecca. She was a wonderful witch and a good person."

Somehow I manage to keep my voice from trembling. "Thank you."

"Now, as for what I know, I can only tell you what I can see through my mirrors."

Elmore, for lack of a better explanation, is a wizard trapped behind glass. I don't know the exact circumstance that caused him to be imprisoned (as he's very secretive), only that his choice was either to die or live in a mirror for pretty much eternity. So he chose the mirror.

I bring my knees to my chin, stretching the plum dress over them, and beam. "Well, tell me what you've seen, then."

He puckers his lips in thought. "I'll tell you that we need your talent. Your ability to find books is perfect."

"No."

"Why such a tone?"

"The person who inherits the bookshop has to have magic."

"Maybe you should tell your mother that."

My heart stutters. "What? Is she giving it to me?"

"I don't think there's a choice," he tells me in a snobby voice. "You're the eldest and you have the ability to find books for people."

"But I can't put them *inside* the book."

"A minor detail."

I drop my knees and lean my cheek against one fist. "A detail that *can't* be overlooked."

"You know"—he leans back and studies me—"I never did believe that you don't have power."

"Stop it. We're not doing this again."

He sighs dramatically. "Have it your way. But I will say this —if you'd been around when the tragedy occurred, my guess is that it never would've happened to begin with."

My brow lifts. "Tragedy?"

"Didn't you hear?"

"No one tells me anything about the shop."

He nibbles one side of his mouth. "Hmm. Perhaps it's a secret."

"As if that's ever stopped you from spilling tea."

He considers that while stroking his chin. "You have a point."

"See?"

"Several years ago—and this is just between you and me—"

"Of course. Like always."

"A reader came to the bookshop and asked to jump into a certain book, one that was very violent, and the person on duty, who shall remain nameless, was unfortunately not as familiar with that tome, so he or she—*nameless*, remember?—they let the reader in and..."

My eyes become big as plates. "They...what?" When he doesn't answer, I gasp. "They died?"

"It was terrible."

"But...that's not possible." My mind races. Never, not in all my life have I known an accident to have occurred when someone jumped into a book. "You must have it wrong." But the look on his face tells me that I'm the one in the wrong. "Why haven't I heard about this until now?"

"Because everyone wanted it buried, especially your mother."

"Was it my mother, the one who let them in?"

"Of course not. She would've known better."

"At least that's something." My tight chest loosens. "Who was it?"

He leans in, and I know he's about to tell me. "Well—"

My aunt's voice booms throughout the house, shaking the walls and causing dust to float down from the ceiling. "Lights out! Everyone! All you girls need your beauty sleep tonight. That means no more conversations with Elmore, *Addie*."

I smirk. "Talk to you soon."

He nods. "I'll be in touch."

He disappears like a bulb being turned off, leaving me alone to plan my escape.

"And in case any of y'all are thinking about trying to get out of the ball," Ovie's voice booms, "the doors and windows are locked tight. And with that said, good night."

A heavy sigh rattles from my lungs.

Welcome to my family.

6

Feylin

The falcon soars high, casting a long shadow on the grass. It banks left and cocks its head. It's spotted the prey.

The prey in question is a small mouse that happens to be finishing a block of cheese. When the last crumb disappears into its mouth, the creature scurries, trying to dash off the box it's been set atop. It only takes a touch of my magic to freeze it in place.

"There," I whisper into Ryals's ear. "This is it. What you've worked for all week."

My cousin stands stock-still, barely breathing as he watches the falcon—*his* falcon. All week Ryals has been working with the bird, training it to retrieve a fake mouse and drop it in his hands. Practice lessons have been successful. But this isn't practice.

"I'm worried, Feylin," he murmurs, his silver eyes flashing up to me.

"Stay calm." I place a hand firmly on his shoulder and

squeeze. "Birds of prey respond to our emotions. He'll deliver the mouse to you unharmed."

Or so I hope.

The falcon sweeps over the box, snatching the mouse in one talon like a claw machine grabbing a cheap toy. The bird soars into the sky and banks right, turning toward us.

"Now," I tell my cousin. "Cup your palms."

My heart thunders as the bird closes the distance. This is it. The moment we've been waiting for. The bird's almost to Ryals. Just a few more feet and—

"Oh, that's *gruesome*," declares a raspy voice from behind us. "Didn't see that one coming."

I tilt my head to the sky and close my eyes. We were so close. All the falcon had to do was drop the mouse in Ryals's hands.

Trawick comes into view as the mouse's tail disappears into the falcon's beak. "So brutal."

I roll my eyes. "He almost had it."

"If you consider *playing* with your prey almost having it, then you're nearly right," he says, his gold eyes sparkling as he ribs me.

I pat Ryals's shoulder. "We'll keep working on it."

"It's okay," he replies, gazing up at me with eyes that have seen more hurt than I like to think about. He rubs his hands on his jeans and taps his foot impatiently, obviously tired of standing around.

"Go play. We'll get the falcon put up."

He runs off and I lift my gloved hand. The bird alights, curling its talons around my forearm.

"Why couldn't you have obeyed instead of eating the mouse?" I ask it. It blinks in reply.

The menagerie man comes over, and I gently transfer the falcon to its cage and turn to Trawick.

"Trying to teach a falcon not to eat a mouse sounds like the sort of torture that's best left to others." My best friend's long bangs fall into his face as he picks up a branch that's lying on the grass. He brushes back his hair and prods one end of the wood into the ground, testing it before putting his weight on it. "Your groundskeepers aren't doing a very good job. You should fire them."

"And where would I send them?"

He lifts the branch to eye level and aims it like a rifle. "I don't know, to live with the humans."

"Very funny." Once the menagerie man is out of earshot, I say, "Trawick, to what do I owe the pleasure of your company?"

"Come on, Feylin. We both know you'd be lost without me."

He's not wrong.

I pivot us toward the castle, and we walk across lush green grass. Everywhere I look there are fae—some trimming hedges, others mowing grass. Two are working on the fountain that decided to quit the other day.

When you buy a castle that was originally built as an old movie set, things tend to break on you more often than not.

"But really, I've come to see you."

"My company's hard to live without, I know," I say wryly.

"And hard to live *with*," he adds.

I smirk.

We reach a table, and I pull off my leather gauntlet, dropping it atop the wrought iron. A pitcher of tea and two glasses appear.

"You're drinking tea?" he says with surprise.

"When in Rome. Sit. Have a glass." I lift a brow. "You may find you like human things."

He snorts. "I doubt it. But I will sit." As I pour him a glass, his gaze roves over the grass and stops on Ryals, who's coerced a worker into fencing with branches. "You do well with your cousin."

"He needs a mother, something I can't be."

And don't want to be.

And yet my cousin *could* have had a mother, one that would have loved him as much as his own. If only she hadn't—

I curl my fingers around my tea glass so hard it cracks. Trawick glances over and I relax my grip, quickly fixing the cobwebbed splinter with magic.

My nerves are on edge today.

And I know why.

That witch from last night. She made me feel things— things I buried. Every time my eyes close, the swell of her breasts is there, her full lips are there, those deep brown eyes of hers are there. And thoughts of ripping off her clothes and claiming her *are there.*

It's excruciatingly annoying.

Trawick's voice snaps me from my thoughts. "Ryals is nearly at the age where a man's influence is better."

"I don't disagree. But you didn't come here to talk about him."

"No, I came for other reasons." He sips his tea. "Ugh. Well, actually not that bad."

"Told you."

"No surprise you'd like human things."

It's not meant as an insult. "But you've come all the way from the Northern Court."

"Yes, because—and you're not going to like this. Feylin—"

"Do I ever?"

"No. But this is worse." He unbuttons the cuffs of his shirt and folds them to his elbows. "There's talk among the lords."

"What sort of talk?"

Trawick stares at his drink.

"Tell me," I insist.

"They say you're weak, that you've given in too much to the humans."

Not this again. I flex my jaw in an attempt to temper my fury. "You know as well as I do that when the veil tore, I had no choice but to position myself closer to the humans so that we could build trust among our peoples. The other courts remain behind the veil, as they should. But how am I supposed to convince humans that we mean them no harm, so that they don't use their bombs against us, if I'm behind the veil?

"Better to be in sight of them than to live behind a wall that was already torn." I jerk my head to the grounds. "Besides, the castle was empty, and if I was going to move anywhere, it was here."

Trawick gives me an understanding nod. "You don't have to convince me, but you want trade with the humans, and our people want stability. Until your line of succession is shored up, you're vulnerable."

I groan. "Spare me."

But he's not dropping the subject. "Look, you know how brutal fae can be. Give them any reason to topple you and they will. As it is, your claim to the kingship can be challenged because there's no heir." His gold eyes flash soberly. "You need to marry."

"We've gone over this."

"This isn't about you anymore. You've got a cousin to think about—one who's human and has no magic to protect himself. If something happens to you and the fae lords fight over who becomes the next king, Ryals will be in danger. He'll be hurt, or worse if I can't get him to safety in time."

He's right.

"Do it for him, Feylin," he says quietly. "If the lords believe your line is secure, they'll stop grumbling, and any thoughts of plotting behind your back"—I flash him a look and he lifts his hands in surrender—"not that there are any, but if there were, they would quickly die if you marry and have an heir."

Ridiculous. "And who am I supposed to wed? What should I do? Pluck some woman off the street? Get on a dating app?"

He snorts with laughter. "Of course not." Long pause. "You're supposed to attend a ball."

I grind my teeth at the suggestion. "A ball?"

He nods. "There's one tonight—in town, of all places."

My eyebrow hitches with interest. "And how do you, a fae, know about a ball happening in town, among the witches, I assume?"

He dips his head and gives me a look full of mock hurt. "You wound me, thinking that I don't keep up with the social scene in your quaint little town."

I scoff. "I'm not going."

"Why not? Go find yourself a witch."

I rub my hands down my face. "If the lords didn't worry about me already, they'd think I'd gone insane to marry a witch. Besides, I ran into one last night, and she was no better than any of the others."

He leans forward. "There must be a story here if you're bringing it up."

Long pause before I finally admit, "She puked on my shoes."

He roars with laughter. "What I wouldn't have given to see that. Well, there you go right there. Any woman who pukes on your shoes is clearly marriage material."

"No, thank you." I give him a look of warning, and Trawick settles back in his chair. "She barely apologized."

"What did she look like?"

Like an angel with lips so soft that I wanted to drag her into a cave and never let another man lay eyes on her, because if one did, I'd kill him. "I don't know, reddish hair, brown eyes."

"And did she have freckles?"

An image of flawless skin flares in my head. "No."

He laughs again. "You paused before answering. She must've been pretty."

"Hard to say since there was vomit coming out of her mouth."

But my body tightens at the very thought of how she felt in my arms—small, fragile, needing protection.

And how, for the first time in years, I wanted to protect a woman. *More* than that. Every part of me wanted her. I wanted to own her completely, brand her with my body, fill her and hear her moan my name.

Have I lost my mind?

"You haven't had the best luck when it comes to love. I get it, Feylin. But that doesn't mean the past equals the present."

"But it does mean I'm not interested in it," I growl.

He pushes one end of the stick into the ground until it snaps; then he tosses the piece in his hand toward the trees. "Well, I'll tell you this, and it might change your mind. The ball's being held so that the Thornroses can marry off the oldest daughter."

Surely I misunderstood. "What did you say?"

"You heard me—the Thornroses. This could be the chance you've been waiting for. Just think of it, you can finally get what you want."

"Marry a Thornrose?" I nearly choke on the words.

He shrugs. "You don't have to marry her, but go and see what it's all about. At the very least your presence will scare the hell out of them."

"And at the most?"

"You know what."

"Revenge," I murmur.

"Just as long as you don't get attached," he adds, shooting me a pointed look.

41

"If you're worried about me falling in love, don't. That's off the table."

Wait.

The puker's a witch, which means she might be at the ball. Seeing her again, along with the idea of dragging my lips down her neck, might be worth dressing up for.

I lean back and stretch my legs in front of me. "Why're they holding a ball? It can't just be to marry off a daughter."

He smirks. "Word is they're losing magic and getting her hitched, as they say, will restore it."

This *is* news. The Thornroses are weak. *Huh.* "What should I wear?"

"A tuxedo? Hell, how should I know?"

"You're the one who brought it up."

He runs a hand down his face. "Fine. I'll find out and let you know. Does that mean you're going?"

"It means," I say, crossing one ankle over the other, "that I'll think about it."

A slow smile spreads across his face. "I know you too well. You're going. Come on. Let's see what you're supposed to wear to a witch ball."

He gets up and heads inside, recruiting Ryals along the way. Unlike Trawick, I'm in no hurry to sort through my closet for a tux.

I watch them go while tapping my fingers against the iron table. Who would have thought the Thornroses would be desperate to pawn off their daughter? This opportunity's too precious to let pass by.

It also means I can finally get what I want.

To destroy them.

7

"*W*hy is this entire dress made of lace?" I demand, plucking at the purple fabric that's clinging to my arms, throat and back. It feels like the whole thing's made of tags, and all I want to do is rip it off.

"Because," Ovie replies, her fingers smoothing the shoulder seams that refuse to lay flat against my skin, "this is what the witch who's being presented wears."

My reflection tells the tale of a woman forced to do the opposite of what she wants. My hair's pinned high on my head, with only a few strands cascading to my shoulders. The dress is beautiful—purple lace with a black sweetheart-necklined bodice underneath and a full bell-shaped black satin skirt with a slit up the side.

Beside me, Blair runs a hand over a silky lavender strapless gown that ripples like water when she walks. My other sisters are also wearing dresses similar to Blair's. Jealousy is a prickly barb that seems to be growing exponentially in my gut.

"It's only for one night," Blair says to me.

I tip my face to hers and grimace. "One night of sheer torture."

Ovie rolls her eyes. "Fine. See if this helps."

She taps my shoulder with her finger, and golden magic spills over me, wrapping me up in a shimmering cocoon before it vanishes. The itchiness immediately eases.

I exhale and my red, irritated skin calms. "Better," I confess.

My aunt smiles. She's wearing an emerald-green, high-necked dress that cinches at the waist and splits at her hips, revealing silk pants beneath. How I wish that I was wearing that.

But a minute after she spells me, the itchiness returns and all I want to do is tear the dress off.

"Girls!" Ovie claps above the chatter and rustling of fabric. My sisters turn to give her their full attention. "It's almost time to go out. All of y'all may dance with whomever asks, but remember—this is Addie's night. She's supposed to find a suitor first."

No one says anything, and I can feel the whispers inside of their heads, wondering why I should go first when, well, you know—I don't want to beat a dead horse—but the whole magic thing.

That's okay. I have a plan.

Ovie snaps and French doors open. For the ball, my family opened up the house, making it longer and taller. Oak floor-boards unfurl outside the solid wooden doors, leading to a narrow hallway lined with sconces filled with witch lights. Another set of doors opens at the end of the hallway, and from here I can see a gigantic crystal chandelier suspended from the ceiling.

Talk about pulling out all the stops.

My aunt smiles. "You have fifteen minutes, girls, and then I'll announce you. Get into places before then, outside the hall where you won't be seen." Her gaze flashes to me in warning, and I drop my head, not wanting to be on the receiving end of anger flames darting from her eyes. "Your mama will be in attendance."

My stomach drops. She hadn't shown herself all day, which makes sense given that she has her own rites and rituals to undergo in order to lay claim as the new matriarch.

But even so, she couldn't appear once to say hello?

Ovie leaves and my sisters follow. Blair starts to go, but I grab her elbow, stopping her.

"Wait."

Her eyes narrow. "What is it? Ovie'll have our hides if we're late."

I softly close the doors and press my back to them. "You're taking this dress."

Blair's eyes flare in surprise. "I'm not."

"You are. You and I both know that you're the most suitable for marriage. Any wizard with eyes would be an idiot not to fall in love with you, and that ballroom is about to be filled with dozens, if not a hundred eligible bachelors. So take the dress. I demand it as your older sister."

Blair drops her head into her hands. "Addie, I can't."

"You can and you will. Now. Help me get this thing off."

I approach and she backs away, worry bright in her eyes. "But they'll look for you. Ovie'll lose it when she sees me in this gown. She'll hunt you down."

A smile twinges my lips. "Don't worry. I already have a plan for that."

COOL AIR SLIPS across my shoulders as I make my way outside. Amber light glows from inside the leaded glass windows that are already steaming up from the hot bodies attending the ball.

Blair's about to enter, and I want to get one good look at

her before I slink away, hiding someplace where Ovie won't be able to find me. If I'm gone all night and Blair meets the love of her life, then my aunt can't be angry, nor can she drag me back inside where I'll surely be faced with my future. Or as I like to think of it, the destiny of doom.

Even through the steamy glass and the flock of men pushed against the room's walls, I'm still able to make out my sisters as they enter. They look lovely, all of them. Blair's the last one to appear and I gasp. She looks gorgeous with her dark hair pinned up and the purple dress complimenting her olive skin. No one, not even my aunt, can argue that. Yes, I've forced Ovie to announce Blair as the witch to wed, but so what? She'll find a match, which will give me time to mend my shattered heart.

Relieved that my plan's worked, I sneak past a row of hedges, making my way deep into the garden that's surrounded by a tall hedge wall. If I can climb that sucker, I'll be safe for the night.

Unfortunately there's no way to leave through the front of the house. Witches and wizards crawl everywhere—they're greeters for the event. They'll easily spot me and tell my aunt that I've gone AWOL.

So the back it is.

Fast as lightning (or, not really), I take off, darting down the path on my way to the very back of the garden.

With freedom nearly in sight, I round a corner at full speed and crash into a brick wall. Right as I'm cursing whoever decided it'd be fun to add a new wall, my feet fly up and I plummet toward the ground.

Quick as a thunderbolt, a hand shoots out and grabs my arm, catching me before my back collides with the earth. My breath leaves in a *whoosh* as I gaze up into glittering sapphire eyes.

That face…I recognize it immediately. And just as immediately, anger hardens my heart.

Perfectly arrogant lips tip into an expression that's short of a smile, and when he speaks, it's a sexy growl that sends a shudder ripping down my spine. "Ah, if it isn't the puker."

"If it isn't Mr. Arrogant," I snap back.

His expression becomes stony, cold and humorless. In contrast, his hand is warm. No not warm, *hot*. His fiery fingers hold me gently as he stares down at me. And keeps staring as he takes me in—the pulse quivering at my throat, my bare shoulders, the low neckline of my dress.

His eyes smolder, and the anger that fuels me slowly drains away, replaced with that same feeling the first time I wound up accidentally in his arms—*want*. To prove it, my girlie parts throb right on cue.

It's irritating as hell.

Every muscle, including my tongue, is tangled and tied, but somehow I manage to spit out, "Let go of me."

His gaze snaps up to mine. He blinks away the hazy look in his eyes and straightens. "You won't fall again? It's your second time crashing into me."

My response is more of a growl than actual words. Very sophisticated.

I watch him as he rights me. Moonlight slices across high cheekbones and his jawline, which still unravels to infinity. His scent's a cloud I've fallen into—amber and leather. The aroma wraps around me like a warm blanket, one I want to snugg—

"You're staring," he snips.

Oh. Right. My gaze lowers to my arm. "You're still holding me."

He drops his hand like my flesh is made of hot coals. Well, I have news for him, I am not made—

"You look like you have something you'd like to say," he says, sounding more annoyed than interested.

"Um…"

"I'm fairly certain that's not a word."

I scoff bitterly. The *nerve* of him. "I know all about words. I use them all the time."

His eyes glitter with mischief. "You mean when you're not puking?"

"That was a one-time deal. I don't normally do that. Only when traveling by magic."

"Then for the safety of us all, please keep your feet on the ground."

"Very funny. So." I cross my arms defiantly. "What brings you to the garden tonight? Wondering if the roses smell the same during the day as they do in the dark? I can tell you right now that they do."

One side of his mouth tips up in amusement. "I thought they smelled like lollipops. Don't they?"

A laugh threatens to rumble in my throat, but I squash it before it escapes. "Only small-minded people think roses smell like candy."

"You've caught me. I'm small-minded and weak-willed," he replies flatly.

If anyone's weak between the two of us, it's me. He's built like a superhero, all big and masculine, whereas I'm the complete opposite, small and soft.

He tilts his head and studies me. "You seem different."

"Because I'm not at your feet?"

"No, I think it's your hair."

I touch it only to remember that it's up. Not that I'm going to say that to him. With absolutely no intention of giving him the satisfaction of having the last word, I reply, "You seem different, too."

He lifts a brow, obviously hanging on my every word

(heavy dose of sarcasm intended). "How's that?"

"You're not demanding I lick your boots clean."

He snaps his fingers. "I knew there was something I was forgetting."

He's funny. I'll give him that. But I won't give him the smile that nearly flutters to my lips. "Now if you'll excuse me, I have somewhere to be."

I step away but his voice, which sounds like smoke rolling over a creek bed, catches me. "If you mean the ball, it's in the other direction."

Guilt starts to spiral down my spine at how I'm abandoning my sisters, but I swallow it whole. "I'm not going there. I'm headed...someplace else."

Which means that he's clearly headed inside.

I spin around and take him in. Mr. Arrogant's dressed in a black tuxedo, complete with bow tie. His clothes fit him immaculately, as if they're tailor-made to his body. Golden cuff links set with round diamonds glint in the moonlight, catching my eye. This man drips wealth, whereas I drip runaway witch with a messy bun and a clingy lavender dress.

I take him in one more time and laugh.

He frowns. "What?"

"Why are you wearing that?"

He glances down. "What do you mean?"

"No one wears a black bow tie to a ball."

"They don't?"

"No. It's white bow ties only." I scrunch up my face and look at him. "What wizarding family are you from?"

He ignores my question and taps his bow tie, which turns white. "Better?"

"*If* you're going. Have fun."

I wave him off and then stop. If he's going to the ball, then why's he outside? I gasp at the realization that—

"You're trying to run."

He slips both hands into his pockets. "I have no idea what you're talking about." There's that bored voice again.

"Yes, you do." I jab my finger into his chest. It's confirmed, solid as marble. "That's why you're out here. You're not planning to go inside."

Well, I'm not having that. Blair's entitled to meet every eligible bachelor wizard, even if they *are* hideously arrogant.

"Maybe I came looking for you," he says coolly.

My heart stutters to a stop.

Even though it's an obvious lie, a thrill zips down my spine at the thought of him searching me out.

"Oh, very funny." I laugh so loudly that the crickets stop chirping. Way to be smooth.

"Besides, if anyone's leaving, it's you."

I scoff. "I'm getting air."

"Oh, so that's why you were running when you slammed into me," he adds with an eye roll.

"I wasn't running *away*," I grumble.

"Prove it," he challenges, his eyes twinkling with delight.

It's tempting to march off, to leave his dare hanging in the air, but the superiority in his voice along with the memory of how he insisted I clean up my puke (which I would have done, if given a rag), make it impossible to leave.

"Fine." I cross my arms. "I'll prove that I'm not leaving the ball, which I have no reason to be doing anyway."

He smirks and the urge to slap it off his face is nearly overpowering. "If you have no reason, then go back."

"You with me," I grind out.

He swallows so hard his Adam's apple bobs before he slowly extends the crook of his arm. When I don't take it, he sighs heavily. "I don't bite."

My nerve endings fire on all cylinders at the thought of touching him on purpose, but we've come this far, and I plan to call his bluff, to see if he really intended to go inside. I link my arm through his and feel him jolt at our touch.

He apparently finds me revolting. The feeling's mutual.

"Shall we?" he extends his other arm, allowing me to lead the way to certain death—I mean, *the ball.*

"Sure."

But neither of us take a step. He tips his head down and hitches a brow. "Anytime now."

"Yes."

I take one step, two, and he walks easily beside me, even with our height difference. I slide my gaze to the corner of my eye and notice that my head just brushes the top of his massively broad shoulder.

His gaze darts down to meet mine, and I jerk my eyes ahead of me.

We pass hedges, and I find myself looking longingly at them. If he hadn't been here, my plan would've succeeded. I could've escaped.

Until Ovie found me and dragged me back, that was. If she didn't shoot fire at me first.

We walk in silence until glass-lined French doors rise up in front of us.

He nods slightly (it occurs to me that I don't even know his name) and the doors open by magic just as my aunt, who's standing in the center of the ballroom, spins around and pins her scorching gaze on me. That look says it all—I'm in deep trouble. My soul shrivels just the tiniest bit.

"And the first to dance," she says, biting out each word as she glares at me, "will be this couple."

My stomach drops as we step inside and a string quartet begins to play, all eyes on us.

8

*N*ot dancing. I hate dancing. I'm terrible at it.

But Ovie's staring at me to begin, and every pair of eyes in the room is zeroed in on my face, making pinpricks crawl down my spine.

Mr. Arrogant's breath caresses my ear as he leans down and says, "Shall we?"

There's barely a chance to nod before I'm swept into his arms. His left hand slides around my waist while the roughly calloused fingers of his right hand brush against the soft inner flesh of mine.

My palm's sweating so profusely I'm surprised salt water isn't dripping onto the floor.

The music begins, setting a tempo that's faster than I anticipate. My left foot stumbles over my right and I lurch forward.

But *Arrogant* compensates, stepping closer and pulling me to him before my mistake becomes obvious to our audience.

"Thank you," I murmur, glancing up into his eyes. It's the first time I've seen him inside, in actual light, and if it's possible, he's even more handsome under amber lamps than he is in moonlight.

His hair's dark as charcoal, without a hint of gray, but there's a heavy look in his eyes as if he's lived many, many lives. He seems more than a decade older than my twenty-nine years. Not that I care about his age.

And not that I care that he's touching me.

No, I don't think about how tightly he's holding me, how his fingers dig into my waist, pinning me to him, and how his touch is so scorching against my hand it feels like I'm being permanently mark by whatever evil wizard power he possesses. I certainly don't think about the heat coming off him and how a slow bead of sweat trickles down my back from nervousness. I *think* it's nervousness. It's probably anger since I clearly can't stand this man. Look at me. I can't even decipher my own emotions. His sheer presence has me all kinds of knotted up.

So instead of thinking about all of that, I focus on the music. It's enchanting.

The violin's sweet melody winds around us as he moves with fluid steps, more cautiously now that he's realized I'm not quite as good at this as he is.

Of course he's good at it. The man has to one-up me every chance he gets.

He gazes down. "People are staring. You should smile."

"I don't want to," I snap.

"Perhaps you don't know how." His eyes are begging me to prove him right. So I give him a wide smile, keeping my mouth tight. "You look like you're going to vomit, which I suppose for you is the norm."

He. Is. The. Worst. I'm so mad that I punch my heel into his foot.

Of course he doesn't miss one step, but his eyes tighten. "We've reached the physical-battery stage of our relationship, I see."

"We don't have a relationship."

"Well aware and thankful for it."

I lift my nose. "I don't date arrogant men anyway."

"And I don't date pukers."

My eyes narrow. "Everyone pukes."

"Not *on* people."

"Make one mistake and it gets held against me for the rest of my life." I think about that a moment. "Only horrible people hold a single mistake against a person. People who have no social skills and zero hobbies."

"Trust me. I have social skills."

"Compared to what? A walnut?"

One side of his mouth twitches. "And since I have no hobbies, I suppose you have extravagant ones like sailing or spelling men to fall in love with you."

"No. I read. Do you?"

"Read?" He sneers in disgust. "No."

He says it so darkly, like he actually despises reading. In my opinion, those who dislike puppies and kittens as well as nonreaders are without souls.

I knew he was soulless.

"You just haven't met the right book," I tell him.

His fingers harden slightly around mine. "The right book? There's no right book."

"Spoken by a true reader hater."

"And how would you know what the right book is?"

Before I can answer, he lifts his chin, and I'm left wondering how in the world he was blessed with such amazing genes. How could that face end up on such an arrogant ass?

The thought makes a sincere smile turn up my lips.

"Ah. She *can* smile."

I balk, feeling naked under his glittering eyes. "Given your company I'm surprised I managed it at all."

He huffs, and it's the closest thing to laughter I've heard

from him. For some crazy-strange reason, the sound warms me, and my skin flushes all the way to my ears.

As we continue dancing, he turns me with an ease that's surprising. Now I've gone to a lot of witch balls, and no, I'm still not a great dancer, but none of my male partners were ever as good as him. All those wizards used magic to keep their steps in time, but I sense no magic from him. Yeah. Even though I can't work it, I can feel it.

"I'm curious," he murmurs as his gaze scans the crowd of magicals—men and women combined. No, my sisters and I aren't the only females present.

"Curious about what?" I keep my gaze pinned on his shoulder so he doesn't see the flush that still clings to my skin, which is thankfully going away, but not as quickly as I'd like.

"Why are you here? Isn't this supposed to be a ball so that a family of witches can find husbands?"

I tilt my face upward and he glances down. Silver flecks constellate the sapphire of his eyes. "Who says I'm not looking for Mr. Perfect?"

"You certainly don't act like it. Attempting to escape."

My voice rises. "I was not—" I drop my volume and glance around to make sure no one heard my outburst. People murmur to one another, barely watching us. The coast is clear. "I wasn't doing that. Just like *you* weren't doing it."

"I already said why I was outside."

I tap my fingers impatiently on his shoulder. "Right. Looking for me—supposedly."

He sweeps me to the right, and I follow, becoming liquid mercury in his arms. "You didn't answer the question."

"Why are *you* here?"

"Brilliant deflection."

"I'm a master," I retort.

"What if I told you that I *am* here to find a wife, and from

55

the look of it"—he nods—"there's the creature of our celebration right there."

I gaze to the right as he turns again, following his sight line and spotting Blair, who stands at the head of the room, a flock of men lining both sides of her. She's talking to one—a blond-haired wizard I don't recognize. And she's smiling.

My heart constricts. She looks happy. So very, very happy, while I just got dumped and am stuck dancing with Mr. Arrogant, who obviously thinks Blair's beautiful, like everyone who sees her does. Otherwise he wouldn't have pointed her out.

"You should meet her," I say, feeling an unexpected twinge of jealousy.

"Why?"

"If you're here to marry, she's a great option."

"Maybe." His gaze drops to my lips before it slowly skates back to my eyes. "Maybe not."

A flush starts to work up my neck again, so I quickly glance away and greedily scan the throng for my parents, but I don't spot them.

Mama's still probably doing things that need to be done because Nana died.

Nana.

Before sadness overcomes me, I pivot the conversation again. "They say the fae moved into the castle on the hill."

"Ah, the mysterious fae." His thumb glides softly back and forth over my finger. It's distracting. "And why are you concerned with them?"

"I'm not." I shrug. "But if I were—are the rumors about them true?"

"What makes you think I know anything about fae?"

"Just making conversation."

His fingers tighten on my waist slightly. "What have you heard?"

"The usual"—I flick the hand that's resting atop his shoulder—"they're ruthlessly cruel, sponsoring games that lead to vicious deaths. You know, they think blood sport is entertaining. They also hate witches."

"But witches hate them, too."

"Then I guess the feeling's mutual."

He leans down and presses his lips to my ear. My belly quivers as he whispers, "I've heard their king is worse than the rumors you know."

My throat suddenly jams up. "King?"

"Mm, and a billionaire at that. One who likes to drink the blood of virgins on moonlit nights, but only after they've competed against one another in a fight to the death."

I blanche before pulling back and seeing his mouth twisted wickedly. "You're teasing me."

He straightens. "Never."

"I should've known better than to attempt a conversation with you." I sigh. "I wonder if the bloodthirsty king's here tonight."

"If I see him, I'll introduce you."

My jaw drops. "You *know* him?"

"We have certain things in common."

"Arrogance," I reply.

He smirks. "You're certainly opinionated."

"As if you know me."

"I know a few things about you."

I roll my eyes. "Puking doesn't count. But anyway, I've never seen a fae, and I wonder if they look as coldhearted as they're rumored to be"—I shoot him a scathing look—"virgin-blood drinking and all."

"Worse," he says with a wink.

"Worse than you?"

He sighs. "Your high opinion of me is truly mind-altering. I don't know how anyone's going to put up with me, or my ego for that matter, after your skillful stroking of it."

I tamp down a laugh. "That's nothing. You haven't seen what I do best."

"And what's that?"

"Pick your perfect book."

"Books again," he mumbles. "But the fae, from what I understand, keep to themselves. They stay in the castle, and the witches remain down here."

"Why move to Castleview then?"

"So many questions."

"So many answers," I parrot.

He takes in the crowd before dropping his gaze to meet mine. "Supposedly they moved here because, with this being a magical town, it's neutral ground for them to reach out to the humans and initiate peace."

"That's almost noble."

His brow lifts in amusement. "Careful or someone might think you're giving a compliment."

"And what if I am?"

"It sounds good on your lips," he purrs.

The music comes to a stop, and we stand there for a beat, his hand on my hip, my hand on his shoulder. With a deep breath he releases me as if the spell that brought us together has suddenly popped like a soap bubble. It's only when his hands fall away that I realize how blazing hot he is, and how chilly the ballroom air is as it cloaks me.

"I didn't catch your name."

"That's because I didn't throw it at you," I retort.

His lips twitch, but he doesn't walk away. He waits.

Is he interested *in me?* No. Not after how I've treated him. Besides, my heart's too damaged, too tender to even think about pushing it into someone's hands so that they can carve it up like a steak.

But that doesn't stop me from telling him. "It's Addison."

"Addison," he repeats.

He says my name like he invented it. Like he created the way those sounds work together.

My gaze grazes over his warm eyes, the wavy charcoal hair that's cut short, the sides just covering the tips of his ears. A foreign sensation stirs in my belly. It feels like a bolt of electricity sparking, sending flares pulsing to my toes.

"Thornrose," I add.

The warmth in his eyes instantly vanishes, and his gaze turns icy. His shoulders tighten before he turns on his heel and walks away.

Rude.

But before I can wonder why he did that, a hand grips my arm and drags me off. My aunt gives tight smiles to the crowd as she yanks me into the belly of it, and more dancers take their place on the marble floor.

"Addie, just what were you thinking?" Ovie snaps in her dramatically Southern way.

"I, uh, I'm…I'm sorry for leaving."

"Not leaving, what you were *just* doing."

What is she talking about? "I don't under—"

"What are the chances that I'd see you here, Addison?"

Time stops at the sound of that voice, *his* voice. The world tips and my knees threaten to buckle, but I keep my spine straight as I slowly spin around and see Edward.

All the blood drains from my face. He's standing before me, his sandy hair in a high pompadour, the hair on the sides of his head freshly shaved down. He smiles, and his teeth glint.

"What are you doing here?" I hiss.

He waves his hands theatrically. "I'm doing what everyone else is doing—picking a bride from one of the Thornrose sisters."

He steps back and cocks his head toward Blair, who, to my

absolute horror, is standing beside him. He leans forward and whispers, "Let's not make a scene, shall we?"

Not make a scene. That's what he told me when he dumped me literally a day ago. *One day.* And now he's here at my family's ball, trying to win over my sister.

"From what I hear, she has quite a bit of magic."

Blair gives me a worried smile. She's probably wondering why I'm not over the hedges and long gone. How I wish that I'd just ran off instead of feeling the need to challenge what's-his-name. What *is* his name?

"Good seeing you again, Addison," Edward says flippantly, clearly blowing me off before turning to speak with Blair.

Oh no. That's not going to happen. So I say very loudly, "Edward, are you looking for that magical woman you so desperately want?"

His spine snaps tight, and I swear that the hairs on the back of his neck rise to attention.

Lucky for him, I'm not done. "The Thornroses are the perfect family to marry into if you want a wife who's ripe with power. Don't you think?"

He laughs nervously and turns back to face me. "Now Addie, you know as well as I do that—"

"You dumped me," I say cheerfully as if my crushed heart isn't a bleeding, pulpy mess. "Isn't that what you did?"

People are staring now. My body burns with anger. Or is that embarrassment? It's embarrassing to cause a scene, but more embarrassing to let Edward woo my sister.

He chuckles as his gaze zips around nervously. When it swivels back to me, his eyes are hard as flint.

He drops his mouth to my ear and whispers so that only I can hear. "We both know that no man here, no wizard worth his salt would marry a witch without power." Then he pulls back and adds loudly, so that now *everyone* can hear, "No man would marry you, even if you are a Thornrose."

A fire erupts in my belly, fanning inside me like an inferno. I don't know what causes the next words to spill from my mouth. Maybe it's the crowd. Maybe it's how my family's gaping at me for causing a scene. Maybe, just maybe, and most likely, it's the superior smirk that's slapped across Edward's face.

No matter what it is, nothing can stop me from saying loud enough for witches three towns over to hear, "I've got news for you—it just so happens that I've already been picked."

His brows lift as he chuckles in disbelief. "Is that so? And who, here in this crowd, would propose to someone as *unmarriable* as you?"

Oh crap. He's called my bluff. But since I've come this far up shinola creek, I better keep right on paddling. "In fact, the man who wants to marry me is—"

My eyes rip from Edward and rove over the room until they land on *Arrogant.*

No no no no no no.

Not him. Anyone but him.

But before I can protest, Arrogant steps up and slinks his hand around my waist, sending a shudder raging down my spine.

"To me," he tells Edward. "She's engaged to me."

9

*A*s soon as the words leap from his mouth, magic unfurls. It's hot, dangerous power, coiling around me like a snake. It sears into my flesh and spears my stomach, sending a tremor through my limbs.

The power moves through me, and as it leaves, my spine snaps, pressing me against the near stranger at my side. I try to break away, but the magic holds me fast.

Then just as quickly as it all started, light bursts from my skin and the magic melts away, soaking into the floor as the marble drinks it up.

The crowd has taken a step back. Even they can feel that this magic is different, stronger, more potent and, yes, dangerous.

My gaze snaps to Ovie, and her mouth is wide, her eyes filled with an emotion that I can't place. Maybe it's fear. Oh yeah. That's what it is. This can't be good.

After the magic vanishes, Edward eyes me coolly. "Then let me be the first to congratulate you both."

He stalks off and I gaze up, seeing only jawline until *Arrogant* looks down.

"What was that?" I ask.

Ovie storms over. "Come with me. Now."

She claps her hands and the ballroom vanishes. I'm standing in the den, where my grandmother's body had been just the day before. But now it's been moved to the funeral home as she prepares for her final walk.

Arrogant stands beside me, his hand still on my hip. My mother's here. Her blonde hair hangs softly around her face, and her dark blue gown shimmers like satin.

Where did she come from, and why does she look so worried? My father's here as well, and he's doing that thing with his lower jaw that he does when he's thinking. His sandy hair's graying but still has a lot of its natural color. He's wearing a tuxedo with a white bow tie, and the pair make a striking couple.

My mother sighs and that's when I remember what just happened. I really don't see what the big deal is. I shy away from *Arrogant's* grasp, and this time I'm able to. Words rush from my mouth like a geyser.

"I only said what I did so that Edward would leave me alone, y'all. I'm sorry," I apologize to everyone. "We were dating up until yesterday when he very suddenly dumped me, so I guess I was looking for revenge. Oops."

An embarrassed—and if I'm being honest, shameful—giggle bubbles from my throat. No one looks amused. My aunt and parents are giving me excruciatingly sad looks that I don't quite understand. But that's okay. We can fix this!

"It's fine. No big deal." I turn to *Arrogant,* and even though I can't stand him, he did me a solid and deserves thanks. "I appreciate you coming to my rescue. You didn't have to do that. But now that you have, it's done and over with and we can go about our lives. And Edward's probably gone now. He can't stand being shown up, and in an hour everyone at the ball will forget about me and focus on Blair."

I dismiss this whole crazy fiasco with a wave of my hand. "No biggie."

My mother glides over, wrapping me in a hug. The circles under her blue eyes suggest that she's tired, so very tired dealing with her new responsibilities.

"Addie, you don't know what you've done."

My father glances behind me, at *him*. "Did you do that on purpose?"

What are they talking about? I look over my shoulder as the man, wizard, whatever, answers. "I didn't know it would happen."

My mother stiffens. "Where do we go from here?"

"We all say it was a mistake, the spell gets broken and we move on with our lives," my aunt announces with a clap that's so loud it's thunderous.

Antique plates attached to the walls rattle. The exposed wooden beams above our heads quake, sending dust spilling to the floor.

My father scowls at Ovie. "Using magic doesn't help the situation. That's what got us here in the first place. Besides, it's not that easy, Ovie."

"It is to me, Phillip," she says through clenched teeth.

"For now, there's nothing we can do," my mother adds, her voice tender but loaded with worry like a baked potato from Cracker Barrel.

I ease from her arms. "What's going on?"

"The magic," the wizard grinds out, "has been ignited. On accident," he adds in a stony voice, while glaring at my family.

Perhaps everyone should settle down. There's no need to be stressed. This can be solved. "Yes, I felt it. But what is it?"

A shadow falls over his jaw, and ever so slowly he drags his gaze from my family back to me. "It means we're joined."

The last word becomes a growl, a warning—to my family? And a shiver skips down my spine.

"Like at the hip?" I joke.

My father's face drops with sadness. "More than that. Explain it to her," he commands.

Arrogant looks at me with such intention that the world shrinks, and it's as if no one else exists. Which is very weird, considering he's my least favorite person on the planet.

"It doesn't always happen, and what I stated wasn't a formal declaration." His eyes darken as they rip from me and land on my family. "But it was enough."

"Enough for what?"

His gaze shifts back. "Enough for us to be formally joined."

"I heard you say that, but I don't understand what that means."

"Addie," my mother says softly, "do you know who this is?"

I thumb toward him. "This guy? Well..." Though I'm tempted to make a joke about how he's my new arch nemesis, the worried looks on their faces stop me. "No, I don't."

My father shuts his eyes tightly. "Maybe you should tell her."

Now I'm curious. I tip my face toward the mystery wizard. "Who *are* you?"

He takes a deep breath, and it seems like his shoulders widen, like the room shrinks around him. "My name is Feylin and I'm a king."

Every ounce of moisture in my mouth vanishes. "*King?*"

"Addie," Mama whispers, "he's the fae from the castle on the hill."

Oh crap.

Well, the one upside is that I'm not a virgin, so he can't drink my blood.

10

*M*y mother's words soak into me and I frown. "You're fae? You don't look fae."

Ovie scoffs, which makes me guess that's not the most important detail in this conversation.

As if to prove it, Feylin doesn't reply to my statement. Instead he says, "When I said that we were engaged, an ancient fae spell was ignited. *Accidentally.*" Ovie starts to protest, and he shoots her a look so dark that it could scorch the hair right off her head. "That spell hasn't been triggered in generations. So you understand I didn't think it would be cast now."

Thick tension fills the room. It's charged with magic that's leaking from my family. They're upset about this, so upset that magic is literally spilling from them and landing in small golden drops onto the floor.

"We'll break the spell," Ovie declares. "Tell us how."

He gives a slight shake of his head. "There's no way to break it. It must be seen through."

"Seen through? As in, I'll marry you?"

His jaw flexes and his dark eyes flash on me, but his words

are directed to my family. "May I have a word with Addison alone?"

"No," Ovie snaps.

He tips his head slightly toward her. It's a small movement, but in his eyes there's *power*—magic that he's restraining. I don't know why I didn't see it before. Maybe he was keeping a tighter leash on it, but in this room it's obvious that he could snap his fingers and an inferno would leap from the floor. The magic inside of him is, for lack of a better word, intimidating.

And he knows it.

Mom squeezes Ovie's shoulder. "We'll let you talk."

They don't bother marching from the room. Instead my mother nods and they disappear one by one in spirals of smoke.

As soon as they're gone, I whirl on him. "There's no way that I'm marrying you. First of all, I don't even know you, and what I do know, I don't like."

Shadows jump on his jaw. "This is less than ideal."

"Astute observation."

"But we can both benefit."

I throw up my hands in frustration. "From being married?"

"No, from being *joined*."

He shifts his weight to one hip, which doesn't seem very fae-like. I always think of them as standing upright, never moving, sort of like vampires. Though with my limited knowledge of their kind, I'm pretty much making up any and all details about them.

I fold my arms. "How can this be beneficial?"

"Your family needs the line to continue, and let's just say there are those who want to see me joined as well."

"Yes, but my family's magic relies on the line of succession to *actually* continue. It relies on the bonding of two lives."

"And is that what you want for yourself?" When I don't answer, he continues. "You were escaping tonight. Don't argue. You're a terrible liar. You don't want to marry any more than I do. This could be your way out—at least until your sister finds a mate. Which, from the line of suitors tonight, will likely happen sooner rather than later. You have a choice —play pretend with me, or jump back into that ballroom and face a hundred men looking to marry you. Some possibly with sincerity, while others are only interested in gaining advantage from your family's position."

I gape at him. He knows so much about my family, about me, about what I think about those men. How is it possible?

Ugh. It's probably some stupid fae mind-reading talent.

But still he has a point. Being with him would free me from endless balls and being forced into marriage, an idea that makes my heart throb with pain. It would also force Ovie to focus on Blair.

Blair—who actually wants to marry.

And Feylin is offering me a way out.

It's the best of both worlds—my family's magic will remain strong when Blair marries, and I won't have to swap nuptials with anyone.

But still, there are the fine details to hatch out. "My family's magic won't survive unless there's a union."

He takes an intimidating step forward, shadows falling over his shoulders. "Then return to the ball and find someone to marry—perhaps the man who announced that you're *unmarriable* has changed his mind."

Right. Okay then. Maybe Feylin's way *is* the best.

But before I make any decisions, there are still unanswered questions. "So what is the joining? What magic did you unleash?"

"The spell was created to ensure that couples in arranged marriages learned about one another before the wedding. It was a way of bonding the two."

"How?"

He glances away. "By making them inseparable."

This doesn't sound so good anymore. "Inseparable. Can you please elaborate on that?"

"We can't be far from each other, if I remember the spell correctly."

"Far from each other? Like, how far?"

His gaze scans the room as if he'd rather look anywhere but at my face. "I don't know the limits."

"Try to know them."

He shifts his weight again, this time sighing like I'm a nuisance. *Me.* I'm not the one who ignited some weird-ass spell from centuries long past.

"Perhaps forty yards is the limit."

Forty yards? Panic claws up my throat. This is why my family's so upset. This means that I'll have to be with him, night and day. I don't know him. I don't even like him, and now we're about to be joined at the hip? This is not the trivial spell that I imagined. This is real.

My knees quiver, but I will not show weakness. I haven't shown him any yet, and this won't be the first time that I do.

Besides, if this minor inconvenience is what it takes to give me breathing room, it's worth a shot. "But we won't marry. Right?"

"Not if I can help it," he replies, sounding as uninterested in that idea as I am.

Well, at least we're on the same page when it comes to nuptials. "So what does this mean in terms of logistics?"

"It means"—those dark eyes flash on me, and I'm barely able to swallow the knot jamming up my throat—"you'll have to come with me."

"To where?" It's a stupid question. I know the answer, but I want to hear him say it.

"To the castle, to my realm."

Sweat sprouts on my forehead. I swipe it off and notice his

skin's perfectly dry. He's not sweating about this one bit. "I'm supposed to go to your castle."

"Yes."

"I've never been to a castle."

He flicks his hand, gesturing to the room. "It's like this, but bigger."

Somehow I doubt the castle's filled with mismatched bricks, a fireplace scorched with burn marks and colorful crocheted blankets that cover literally every chair and couch. "And are there servants?"

"It's a castle," he tells me dryly.

"I take that to be a yes."

Good grief. I don't know how to act in a castle. I don't have servants. How do I talk to them? I'm a regular person, not a princess, and here, standing in front of me, is a king. Of the fae. A billionaire king at that.

Holy crap. I might faint.

"How long will I be gone?"

"I don't know."

I'm to go with him.

I'm engaged but won't marry.

Too many thoughts are swirling in my mind. I can't think clearly. Pacing helps me sort things out, so I start crossing back and forth in the room.

"There are things that I need to do here, in town." I shoot him a look. "My grandmother's funeral."

"We'll go. I'll attend with you."

"And I might be needed at the Bookshop of Magic." I shake my head in frustration. "Supposedly I'm taking it over."

Not that I deserve it.

He visibly stiffens but nods. "I'll accompany you there as well."

"But not right beside me."

He rolls his eyes. "No. I'll be sure to keep a respectable

distance." His gaze catches me as I turn to walk toward him. "There are also things you'll have to do for me."

Oh gods. I am not sleeping with him. He might be hot, but there's no way I'm doing *that* with someone I don't know.

My face must reveal what I'm thinking because he says, "Not *that*."

"Good."

"Our engagement will be announced, so you'll have duties."

"Duties?"

"Ceremonies, events to attend," he replies in a tone that suggests I'm the densest person in the world. "Those sorts of things."

Fae things. Fae events. Everything fae. "Are you sure we can't get out of this—the whole distance thing?"

"How about when I leave here, I magic myself away and let's see what happens."

Relief floods every cell in my body. "You would do that?"

"To keep you happy? Anything."

"You don't have to be sarcastic."

"I thought those were the terms of our relationship."

Our gazes collide and his eyes search me. It feels like he's peeling back the layers of my soul, scanning my thoughts. The tips of my ears burn, and my gaze skitters away.

"I can't think of any more questions."

"When you do, just ask. I'll tell you anything that I know." I nod. He hesitates slightly. "I...don't want this to be any more horrific than it has to be."

There's almost comfort in his words. *Almost.* "Can my family come back in?"

"So you're agreeing."

"I don't have a choice."

"You have a choice in whether or not you'll go along with the ruse happily." He studies me with such intensity that my insides nearly wilt. "Anyone who sees us together must think we're in love, that we've come to this decision together. It can't look like we barely know one another, that we're only going through the motions. This extends to the witches and fae. No one must suspect. It's best for my people."

"But my parents..."

"They know the truth, that I said what I did to help you, but no one else."

No pressure there. "So basically I'm in a fake relationship with a fae. I'm faking it with a fae."

He exhales in annoyance. "So that you get the space you need, and I get the lords off my back."

"What about the spell?"

He shrugs. "What of it?"

"We need to break it. I can't be tied to you forever."

"I wouldn't hear of it. It will be researched."

"Just like that? With a snap of your *kingly* fingers?"

He smirks. "Yes."

I pause in pacing to peer into his eyes, searching for any hint of a lie. I don't see one. And just as quickly as our eyes meet, the outside world falls away again, dimming my peripheral vision so that only he exists. I don't know if that's the spell or just him and all his...fae magic stuff.

Either way it's distracting.

It takes hard focus to tear my gaze from him. "How did you know that my family needs us—the daughters—to marry in order to keep the magic alive?"

"Rumors fly fast in this community. It's easy to overhear what the werewolves and vampires talk about. Even the witches, though there my kind keeps our distance."

That I understand. Fae and witches have never gotten along. The relationship's strained, like distant relatives that only visit during the holidays—we tolerate the other, but there's no love lost.

And I don't know why. There aren't any comprehensive texts on the subject, at least none that I've found.

I exhale a deep breath. I'm ready. "My family can be called in."

"So you agree?"

I nod. "I agree to ever so happily be your fiancée."

Saying it makes me feel like I'm dying on the inside. Not only do I *not* like him, but I don't know anything about his culture, and what I do know isn't nice. It's full of fierce competitions, vengeful leaders, bloodthirsty rulers.

I keep my head tipped toward him in a limp attempt to prove that I can act like I love him. Feylin watches me closely before nodding his approval.

"Do you want to bring them back?"

He's offering me the chance to use magic, but he's the last person I want to know my secret. We might be in a fake relationship, but I don't trust him.

"No, you can do it."

"As you wish."

Then they're back. He doesn't wave his hand. He doesn't even blink. He simply works magic without a hint of effort.

It must be cool to be fae. Witches have to use hands or a body movement to summon power. Never have I witnessed a creature conjure magic as easily as breathing.

While I'm thinking about cool fae magic, my father and mother shoot worried looks back and forth. I open my mouth to speak, but Feylin takes a step forward to come beside me. His arm brushes my shoulder, and a flash of heat explodes down my skin. In that millisecond the urge to rake my fingers down his bare chest grips every cell in my body. The intensity's so strong that I curl my hands into fists to squash the urge to tear off his tuxedo shirt.

Get a grip.

"Addison and I have talked."

"And?" my father asks, his face red, strands of hair falling into his eyes as if he's just been running. Or yelling. Probably yelling.

Feylin looks at me and I understand. It's for me to say; otherwise my family will question whether or not this is what I want.

I clear my throat and lift my chin as high as I can to gather every ounce of strength possible. "We have discussed the spell, the joining, and have decided to continue with it."

"No, Addie—" Ovie starts.

Mama flings out her hand, shooting Ovie a look full of warning. "Hear her out."

Ovie settles down and I go on. "Our family needs the magic to continue, and I'm willing to do my part. Besides, the entire ballroom heard the announcement. To go back on it now will make me look like a liar, and our family's honor will be questioned." *As if Edward hadn't already made that happen by being such a jerk in the first place.* But—smiles! "I understand there are physical conditions to this arrangement."

"We already know," my father says sourly.

I smile, doing my best to look happy. My gaze skates up to Feylin, and he glances down, scowling. I'm quickly reminded that he thinks when I smile I look three seconds away from vomiting.

I turn back to my family. "The joining means I'll have to stay close to Feylin. But he's promised to test the distance."

Mama smiles weakly. "We'll see you as often as we can."

"It will be a busy courtship," Feylin adds.

My father's eyes harden. "She's my oldest daughter. If anything hap—"

"She'll be kept safe." The king's jaw jumps. "There's nothing for you to worry about."

"Of course there isn't," Dad says sarcastically.

"I promise you," Feylin growls.

74

They stare at one another for a long moment before my dad nods in submission.

Is there another conversation going on that I don't know about?

I frown. "We don't even know how this will work. I may not have to leave."

"There are things I need to prepare for you," Ovie says. "Clothes to pack."

"There's no time," Feylin tells her. "When a king or queen joins, the magic reverberates throughout the kingdom. All my subjects will have felt it. I'll be expected back. Now."

"What about Addie?" My mother demands. "What about what she wants?"

He pushes back his shoulders. "It is what she wants, and you may see her tomorrow. But I'm afraid my time here is over." He glances down at me and nods before vanishing.

I rush to my mother, and she hugs me, clutching me tight, and for one brief moment I feel all the loss and sadness that she suffered with Nana's passing and the added weight of this situation as it burdens her shoulders.

"Addie, there's something you must know."

"Don't worry." I curl my fingers into her arms. "He's going to see how far apart we can be. It's possible that I won't have to leav—"

The room vanishes and my mother disappears. Next thing I know, my body's being sucked down a vacuum tube, and all thoughts are wrung from my head. I claw the air while traveling at the speed of light through impenetrable darkness.

So much for believing we could be more than forty yards apart. Next stop—the fae castle on the hill.

11

It turns out that travel by fae magic is eerily similar to traveling by witch magic.

Which is unfortunate for me.

One moment I'm hurtling through the air at breakneck speed. The next, my body comes to a lurching halt atop a stone floor. My legs fall out from under me, and I drop to my hands and knees.

A wave of pain slams down my shins as vomit erupts from my mouth and splatters across the floor.

The upside is that it doesn't land on anyone's feet.

The downside is that I *feel* Feylin's displeasure before I see him. The air constricts as if it's a living, breathing thing that's fully irritated.

I wipe my mouth, and before I can apologize, the vomit disappears. A shoed foot steps beside me, and when I gaze up, Feylin eyes me steadily, his hand reaching out in an offering.

He's not smiling. He's not frowning. There's no emotion on his icy face.

Yet he's offering his hand.

I slide my palm over his and feel that same explosion of

heat radiate up my arm. Once again, a completely unwanted and nemesis-level lusty urge grabs me by the throat.

Would he moan if I nibbled his ear, and if so, how loudly?

It takes all my focus to shove that thought away.

"Sorry about the travel sickness," he murmurs.

"It's fine." Those thoughts and that heat still surge down my spine, but the moment I rip my hand from his, they both stop.

Thank you, joining, for screwing with my head.

"Everyone," he says, "this is Addison Thornrose. My fiancée."

The equilibrium shift must've really knocked my senses clean off my head because it's only then that I realize that lined up before me, on either side of a grand hall, stand two dozen fae.

Who all saw me puke.

My knees threaten to buckle again from embarrassment. Men dressed in smart black suits and women in tailored ebony dresses with white collars and cuffs all smile at me as if I hadn't just lost my dinner right before their eyes.

I don't know what's worse, that they're pretending it didn't happen or that *I'm* pretending it didn't.

Yet my shame evaporates as I drink in their presence. These people are ethereal, radiating with magic that's on a different plane than that of witches, wizards, werewolves—even vampires.

Their skin shines like they're illuminated from within. Small tips of their pointed ears slip through their hair, and their skin, which is all different hues from light to dark, glows under the chandeliers.

They smile at me expectantly and my gut clenches. I suddenly feel awkward, very much a magical failure compared to their flawless grace and beauty. It takes all my will not to scream that I'm an imposter and dash out the door toward home.

But the buzzing of Feylin's skin beside me is a quick reminder that even if I run, I won't get far thanks to the magic locking us together.

"Hey there," I say brightly to the crowd. "Thank y'all for saying hello. It's so"—my gaze travels to the arched ceiling, the skylights filled with winking stars—"beautiful here. Wow. This is amazing. You get to look at this every night? How do y'all get any work done?" They're looking at one another as if I've lost my mind. I probably have. I clear my throat and clasp my hands in front of me. "Anyway, I'm just really excited to be here."

Feylin motions with his fingers, and a bright-eyed fae woman approaches. Her dress isn't black, it's dark emerald, matching her eyes. Her chestnut hair's lifted in a high ponytail that trails down her back, and her honey-colored skin is perfectly creamy.

"Ophelia will take you to your room." He hesitates, his gaze dropping to my hand. He shifts his weight as if trying to decide what to do next, but he settles on a simple, "Take care of her," to Ophelia, and to me a slight bow topped off with, "Good night."

Then he spins on his heel and leaves, abandoning me to this hall full of his people.

Ophelia's several inches taller than me and has a wide smile. "Come, lady."

The rest of the fae murmur congratulations, to which I nod in thanks as I follow her past them and get my first real glance at the castle.

On the outside, Castleview Castle is a gloomy, gray-stoned fortress. But inside it's bright and full of life. The walls are painted a vibrant light blue, bordered with white arches that rise up to the ceiling. Potted orange and lemon trees are sprinkled against the walls, filling the hall with the scent of citrus, and great crystal chandeliers hang like heavy raindrops from the ceiling.

As Ophelia leads me up a spiral staircase, I spy gold rugs lining the stone floors and a set of glass doors that lead outside. The reflection of the light makes it difficult to see through the glass, but I manage to snatch a glimpse of a garden filled with thick hedges and a pool beyond it.

I slow and Ophelia glances back, following my gaze. "The gardens are beautiful during the day. I'm sure you'll receive a tour from His Majesty."

My stomach plummets. *His Majesty.* He really is a king. *Great.* I'm just a powerless witch who's now fake-engaged to a fae king. Talk about having a heavy dose of imposter syndrome.

We pass a painting that's lush with red and gold hues. It catches my eye enough that I pause and peer closer. It's a battle scene of fae riding horses as they mow down what looks like a field of women and men wielding orbs of power. So, witches and wizards.

Witches lay gutted, thrown over rocks while fae women raise their hands in victory. Dead and bloody wizards litter the grass, impaled by fae swords.

Good night! No wonder my parents didn't want me to come. This painting says it all—I'm in enemy territory.

My breath hitches and Ophelia stops, cocks her ear. She turns around gracefully, and her gaze skips to the painting.

Her chest falls. "It's an old scene, one that His Majesty's grandfather kept. The artist's well-known, and so it's stayed with us. Though our pasts are interwoven in violence, that isn't how we are now." I lift my brow skeptically. She smiles and glances at her feet. "Come. Your room is just here."

We round a corner and she opens a door. My jaw drops at the huge canopy bed topped with a sage-green satin comforter. There's a wardrobe, a desk, a vanity—all made of darkly stained cherry wood. There's also a bookcase but no books on the shelves.

Where are the books?

A fire crackles cheerfully in a fireplace, filling the room with the scent of woodsmoke and throwing shadows over a line of leaded glass windows. Is this place gothic or what?

Ophelia crosses to the wardrobe and stops beside it. "You'll find clothes in here. They'll fit you."

I lift my brows in curiosity. "*How* will they fit?"

"Fae magic. It's different from yours." She gestures to a door. "The bathroom's through there. It's fully stocked with shampoo, conditioner, soaps, bath bombs—most of the essentials."

When did bath bombs become essential? Never mind. Stupid question. I will take that *essential* and use it to the fullest, thank you very much.

She smiles. "If there's nothing else you need, I'll see you in the morning."

"I'm fine. Good night."

"Night."

She shuts the door, and I find myself alone in a place where I know no one, and where a painting of witches being ripped apart hangs on a wall. The castle doesn't look like enemy territory, but all signs point to yes.

Wait. *Stop, Addison. Feylin's not going to kill you.*

I exhale, remembering that he needs me as much as I need him. Right. There's a part for me to play—the happy and cheerful fiancée. This I can do. I'm a naturally optimistic person who smiles often. If there's anyone who can march into enemy territory and make it work, it's me.

First things first—get out of this dress.

I half expect moths to fly from the wardrobe when I open the door, but they don't. It smells of cedar, and the clothes inside are glossy silk and comfortable cotton. There are everyday clothes—jeans, tops, slacks and blouses in a multitude of colors, and gowns for formal occasions. Hanging in the very back is a set of pajamas—a light blue long-sleeved top and bottom that feels soft as butter between my fingers.

"Hope these fit."

They look huge, but as soon as I slip on the bottoms, magic unfolds. In a blink, the fabric shrinks and the clothes vacuum seal to my legs, tightening before loosening to a perfect fit.

"Oh!" I gaze at my reflection in the head-to-toe mirror, admiring how the pajamas fit and nearly laughing at how ridiculous it is that I'm admiring *pajamas*. These aren't even real clothes, and yet they fit perfectly. Even the feel is amazing, like I'm draped in a silk blanket. There's not one tag itching anywhere. I could get used to this. "That's some magic."

After I slip into the top and it does the same shrink-wrap magic, I wash my face and brush my teeth, the whole time wondering how I'm going to pass my time in this castle.

Even though thoughts are ping-ponging around in my brain, I'm tired, and the bed looks amazing.

As I cross the room to climb into it, I smack headfirst into an invisible wall.

"Ouch!"

I rub my throbbing forehead and decide to approach again, this time slowly. Once more I hit a wall.

"What the...? Oh no. The joining."

Feylin must be too far away. Perhaps I can climb in on the other side. I keep my hands pressed to the unseeable barrier as I move around the bed, which is of course butted up against the farthest wall in the room.

So every place that I touch, my palms meet the wall.

This must be some kind of fae torture device. Torture me with a beautiful bed and then don't let me sleep on it.

Okay, I have two options—go back outside and find

Ophelia and probably pass that horrible painting again. Also, there are no assurances that I'll find anyone.

Or I can sleep on the floor—the cold stone floor without one blanket or pillow underneath me.

My gaze skims the room and lands on the wardrobe. Who needs blankets when I've got handfuls of clothing?

I pull out the dresses, make a pallet, and somehow manage to fall asleep, where I have the strangest dream that I've sold my life away to a horribly arrogant fae king.

The next morning a gruff voice pierces my ears. "Get off the floor."

My eyelids slowly open. Standing in the doorway looking like his head's about to explode with rage, is Feylin. *Crap.* So it hadn't been a dream after all.

My brain's fuzzy in those few seconds between being fully asleep and fully awake. My gaze feels lazy, dreamy, as it washes over the deep scowl lining his handsome face.

Part of me wants to know what it would feel like to run my finger over that perfect jaw and trace those full, soft lips.

When I don't move, that same jaw jumps. "Why are you on the floor?"

I flinch. Ugh. My back kills and my legs ache from sleeping on the dresses. "Um. I just...wait. What are you doing in here? Why didn't you knock?"

"I did," he spits. Anger smolders in his eyes. "But you didn't answer. So I came in."

"You came in unannounced?"

His gaze flips to the ceiling. "You didn't answer. I wanted to make sure that you were alive."

Now I'm worried. "Do you think someone's going to murder me?"

"No, of course not. We don't kill witches anymore."

"Anymore," I repeat.

He huffs out an annoyed breath, waiting for me to answer.

But now I'm pissed that he entered and is demanding that I tell him what he wants to know, like he's some king or something.

Yeah, I know. He *is* a king.

But I'm still pissed. "What do you want?"

His dark gaze slices into my soul. "Get dressed. Eat breakfast. And then we begin."

I rub my stiff neck. "Begin what?"

"Your tutorial."

"Why so early?"

"Because the first engagement event is today. Important fae will be here."

Alarm bells ring in my head. "Today?"

"Today."

"Why not tomorrow?"

"Because once a king joins," he says as if he's explaining things to a child, "the first ceremony is completed the next day. That is today."

"What will I have to do? Smile, look pretty? That sort of thing?"

His gaze sweeps from my head to my feet where the gowns are pooled, and slowly back up. Not one fleck of emotion shows on his face, but the way his eyes linger on my body makes my cheeks heat.

"You'll not only be expected to be the doting fiancée, but you'll have to work your magic."

My stomach drops. "What?"

"Your magic. We must work magic together to prove our union is true." I cringe and he notices. "That won't be a problem, will it?"

Work *what* magic? But if I don't try, I'll be thrown back to the wolves of the ball. So I smile brightly. "Magic? Of course that won't be a problem. I can't wait."

12

*O*phelia enters a few minutes later. When she spies the pile of dresses, her eyes become big as plates.

I grab a handful. "Sorry."

"Let me do that," she says, reaching for the mound of clothing in my hands.

"No, it's okay." I smile. "It's my mess. I can clean it up."

She grabs a teal gown off the floor and shakes it. "But you're my lady."

The words *my lady* send a pang of guilt straight to my gut. She's so sweet, and I feel terrible lying to her, making her think that I'm actually going to marry Feylin.

Not in this life.

Which of course makes me clean up the dresses even faster so that Ophelia doesn't have to do it.

She serves me breakfast, which consists of buttery pastries stuffed with nuts and honey. I pick at one, and the sticky honey coats my fingers. I lick them off and grin. There are also quail eggs and coffee.

I take a bite of the pastry and moan. "Oh wow. I don't think I've ever had anything so good. Would you like some?"

She looks at the already bitten half of the pastry I'm offering and shyly shakes her head. "No, my lady."

I sigh and flatten my palms on the table. "Ophelia, if you're going to see me every day, you have to stop calling me that. My name's Addie or Addison. My last name is Thornrose."

"But—"

"No buts!" I swish my finger left and right. "You can call me Miss Thornrose if Addie's too personal."

"Yes, my—Miss Thornrose." She gives a slight nod.

"Better," I say with my mouth chock-full of nutty pastry.

"His Majesty wants to see you on the grounds after breakfast to prepare for the ceremony."

It takes all my willpower not to roll my eyes. "All right. I'll clean up and head over."

THE GROUNDS, as Ophelia calls them, is a sprawling meadow situated in the back of the castle. If Castleview proper is styled after a charming English village, then these grounds are a botanical garden set deep in the South.

Crepe myrtles heavily pregnant with light pink, magenta and lavender flowers bow deeply toward the ground. Waxy-leafed magnolias with blooms as big as soccer balls line the lawn, and azalea bushes with flowers ranging from white to bloodred sway in the breeze that lifts the hair off the back of my neck.

It might be fall in the village, but it's most definitely summer here. It's so beautiful that it fills my heart with happiness. I breathe in deeply, stuffing myself with the sweet fragrance of gardenias that I can't see but can certainly smell.

Tight muscles in my neck caused from sleeping on the floor relax, and I'm pretty much at peace. All I need is a good book and I'll be hap—

"You're here."

And just like that, my calm's shattered.

I turn to see Feylin striding over. He's wearing pressed jeans and a perfectly ironed white button-down. His shoes are highly polished, and the cuffs of his shirt are pushed up, revealing forearms corded with muscles. Can arms be sexy? Because they are on him.

Not that I care as I've given up on love and all that.

His sapphire eyes pin me, and I glance away before I can get sucked into the black hole that is Feylin.

There's a job to do and it's always best to do things with a smile, so I plaster on a big one. "I'm here. Ready to find out about the ceremony."

He scowls. "Why did you sleep on the floor?"

"And good morning to you, too."

He rips his gaze from me and stares at the crepe myrtles. "Good morning. Why did you sleep on the floor?"

I should tell the truth—that *his* arrogant ass is the reason I was forced to sleep on the cold hard stone, but the fact that he's *demanding* an answer is so irksome that I refuse to tell him —at least not right now. Obviously I'll tell him later, because I can't sleep on the floor the whole time I'm here.

I run my hand over the soft azalea blooms. "I don't see why it matters."

He swallows and his Adam's apple bobs. "Servants talk, and if Ophelia had found you this morning instead of me, then she could have told the others."

"And what would they have said? His Majesty offers her a bed, but she sleeps on the floor?"

"Exactly. They would wonder if I was forcing you to do that."

Worried about his reputation, is he? "Why would they think that unless you're a brute and a jerk?"

Scowl. "I'm not a brute."

"But you let your fiancée sleep on the floor."

"You're twisting things."

"I'm not. But anyway, what is it that I'm supposed to do besides bat my eyelashes and blow you kisses from across the lawn?"

He gives me a scorching look. "Don't overdo it."

"I'm not. I won't. Trust me, I don't want to attend any more balls. Speaking of, I haven't heard from my family."

"They'll be here soon."

"They will?"

"Yes."

"They told you?"

He clasps his hands behind his back. Total royalty stance. "I received the message this morning."

I frown. "Was it for me?"

"It was to me."

That makes my heart throb with hurt. They messaged Feylin and not me? Why? I stare at the azaleas and do my best not to feel brushed aside.

"Shall we begin?" he says, almost tenderly.

His gentle tone takes me back, and I glance up to see him watching me. He quickly looks away, giving me a view of his perfect profile.

"Yes, let's start. So. What do we do?"

He begins crossing the lawn and I follow. As we walk, servants mill about, setting up chairs and tables, using magic to throw cloths over their tops. Some trim hedges while others decorate the tables with cut flowers.

"There are four ceremonies in a fae joining, each one representing the four elements—earth, wind, fire and water. This ceremony honors the earth."

He comes to a stop in front of a small tree with bright green leaves sitting in the center of a ring of blooming cherry trees.

He gestures toward it. "That is the engagement tree."

"Engagement tree?" There is such a thing?

"Holding hands, we'll cross over the lawn, stop here and release our magic into the tree. Then it fruits."

"Why?"

His cheeks tinge red. "It's symbolic of love and a fruitful marriage."

"Babies, you mean."

He grunts in reply.

I wait for him to say something else, but he's silent. "That's it?"

He nods. "That's it."

"So we don't have to prove to the tree that we're in love or anything?"

"No, we only have to prove that to our guests."

Right. And I only have to come up with some magic.

"Should we do a trial run?"

"You mean walk over again?"

"Holding hands," he corrects in a testy voice.

Every time I touch him, that weird power surge takes over my body and impure (code word for dirty) thoughts flood my mind. "Um…"

Before I can answer, he retreats a few paces and stops, turning around to face me. "Well?"

"Well what?"

He cocks his head impatiently. "Let's call this a dress rehearsal."

A tornado of butterflies takes flight in my belly as I cross to him in the wedge sandals I found in the wardrobe. I matched them with a pair of jeans and a white off-the-shoulder blouse that I also pulled out of that thing. All of it fits amazingly.

I'm hoping when this is over, I get to keep the clothes.

When we're both facing the tree, he extends his hand.

I stare at it.

"Take. It." He glowers.

"No."

He closes his eyes and says in a pained voice, "We'll be holding hands for the ceremony."

"We'll do it then. But not now."

"Why not?"

Because every time we touch I want to throw you on the ground and lick every inch of your skin is not the answer I want to give, and the less I have to experience that feeling, the better. "Because my hands are clammy."

A shadow jumps on his jaw. "Going to be sick?"

"No, I'm not. I just prefer...not to touch you." *And to not think about you with your clothes off.*

He rolls his eyes. "We'll have to look like we love one another in a few hours."

"I'll smile a lot. How's that?" And then I smile to prove how good I am at it.

He shifts his weight from one leg to the other. "Do you want to back out?"

"No," I say quickly. "Besides, how can I? There's no way out of the joining. Unless you've found one."

"I haven't."

"Have you been looking?"

His dark gaze could scorch the hair right off my head. "Ever since I saw you on the floor."

No way am I going to let him rile me up. "The whole magic thing. We just aim our power at it?"

"That's it."

"We don't have to, like, conjure up fireworks or do anything fancy to show off?"

"Not unless you want to." He cocks a brow. "Do you want to?"

"No, no. Not at all. I'm just wondering." I clasp my hands in front of me. "Want to make sure I've got it all down pat before showtime. I like to be prepared, have all my ducks in a row, that sort of thing."

I am so rambling. He's going to know something's off if I keep this up.

But he only murmurs, "There's one other thing."

"That is?"

"Our story."

He says it so low, raking his fingers through his hair as he does so that it takes me a moment to figure out what he's murmured.

"Oh, our story! Is that what you said?"

His gaze zips around. "Yes. We need one."

An ant crawls onto my foot, so I bend over and brush it off. "Like how we met?"

"Right."

"How about the truth?"

"Do you really want to tell people that?"

Good point. "Then how about we met at my family's bookstore, Castleview Books?"

"No," he snaps so abruptly that I jump. When I stare at him in shock, he shakes his head. "You know I don't read."

"Maybe you can pretend, just this once, that you do."

"No."

Okay, so he clearly doesn't like to read. "Then how about we *skim* the truth? Say that we bumped into each other." He cocks his head as if thinking it over. When he doesn't answer I continue. "Is that what you'd like me to tell people? We bumped into one another on the street?"

He nods. "It's fine."

"Okay. Great. What's your favorite food?"

"What?"

I shrug. "I should know things like that."

"Steak."

"Easy enough. Mine's spaghetti with the sauce added after

the noodles are cooked, not all mixed up together, because then things just become mushy, and a salad with it, but with the salad dressing on the side, and I'm also not a fan of tomatoes."

He stares at me for a long beat. "That's completely unsurprising."

I choose to ignore his snark for now. "What's your favorite sport?"

"Falconing."

"Oh. Wow. Not what I expected to hear. Do you have falcons?"

"Yes."

I glance up, but there's not a falcon in sight. "I love football. I like to see men taking each other down."

He steps toward me, and his gaze falls to my mouth before slowly tracking back to my eyes. "That's shockingly surprising, given your weak stomach."

His words should be a burning insult, but there's a lusty quality to his voice, one that makes my mouth dry. Heat floods my cheeks and drifts down, pooling between my legs.

"Well, then." I take a step back. "So you'll escort me to the ceremony?"

He inhales sharply and snaps his gaze away from my face. "No. Ophelia will bring you when it's time. I'll see you on the lawn." He pauses, studies me. "You can do this, can't you?"

His eyes are so scrutinizing that sweat sprouts on my brow. He knows that I can't work magic. How could he have guessed already?

"You *can* act like my fiancée," he clarifies.

I slap the air, dismissing his worry. "Of course. This'll be a piece of cake."

13

I am so screwed.

There's absolutely no way I'll pull this off. As I watch the servants outside my window setting up for the ceremony, I realize how far I'm in over my head.

There are ice sculptures situated all around. And these aren't even simple ice sculptures. These are giant horses and bears, fish jumping out of water. Not only that, but there are a thousand tables set up and each one has golden plates on it. Plates made of *gold*. I'm not even kidding.

My family might be well-known in the witch world, but we aren't wealthy. We eat off Fiestaware.

I think I'm going to be sick.

So I take a deep breath and think. I've got to have a plan for the ceremony. Okay, I'm bound to Fcylin with this joining magic, and we're supposed to work together to make the tree do whatever it's going to do. So maybe, just maybe, if I focus on trying to summon my magic (yes, I know it's never worked before, but I've also never been spelled like this before), it'll come and the ceremony will be successful.

It's the best plan I've got.

A quiet knock comes from the door. "Come in."

Ophelia enters, beaming. "My la—Miss Thornrose, your family's here to see you."

"Where?"

"Downstairs in the sunroom."

"Yay!" I'm so happy that I could hug her. "I'll follow you."

The sunroom's just off the main hallway and is painted a cheery white and lemon yellow with tall windows that over-look the garden.

Ovie, Blair and Chelsea are seated and looking uncomfort-able. They're all dressed for fall in high boots and oversize comfy sweaters. Sweat sprinkles Ovie's brow, and she tugs at the collar of her cable-knit.

They stand when I enter and rush over to me.

"You look great," Ovie says loudly as she sweeps me into a hug. Did she think I would look awful?

We separate and I say, "Is Mama—"

"Busy," Blair tells me before pulling me into her arms. "Nana walks tomorrow, so there's a lot to prepare."

A knot jams up my throat. "It's tomorrow?"

I was just talking to my grandmother a couple of days ago, but a world of change has happened since then.

"She'll walk in the afternoon," Ovie clarifies.

"I'll bring refreshments," Ophelia says from the doorway.

I hate to put her to more work. Everyone's so busy with the ceremony. "No, that's okay."

She smiles broadly. "I'm happy to. I'll be right back."

She leaves the four of us alone. We sit and Chelsea squeezes my hand. "Everyone here is so beautiful," she says with awe.

Talk about the pot calling the kettle black. Chelsea's gorgeous with blonde hair, creamy skin, a round face and plump lips.

But she's also right. "Their good looks are a little intimidating, aren't they?"

She smoothes a hand down the herringbone braid draped over her shoulder. "I thought Feylin was handsome, but they *all* are. It's part of being fae, I guess."

"I guess."

"How are…things?" Ovie asks, eyes taking in all the scenery.

"They're good. The servants are very nice."

"It's not the servants I'm worried about. It's the high fae. They're known to hate us."

I smile broadly. "We'll find out today, I guess. At the ceremony."

"Oh, we brought your dress." Chelsea plucks a black hatbox from the floor and hands it to me. "This is what you're supposed to wear. We'll have the other dresses sent over for the other ceremonies." She leans forward conspiratorially and grins. "What *are* the ceremonies?"

"Oh, those." I peek inside the box and am greeted with a sea of emerald tulle. Great. More itchy fabric. I settle the box on the floor beside me. "I just have to prove that my magic can mingle with Feylin's."

All three of their jaws drop.

"Magic?" Blair chokes on the word. "Addie—"

I rub her arm. I don't know how well fae can hear, but I think it's close to superhero level, so I tap my ears and nod toward the door. "Yes, my *magic*. I'm all good."

I wink several times, and they get the hint. But worry brims in Blair's eyes. "Are you sure about this? About *him*? What happened last night?"

"Hasn't Ovie or our parents told y'all?"

"All they said is that you're now engaged," Blair confesses.

My gaze zips to Ovie, who's suddenly focused on a thread sticking out of her sweater.

So it's up to me to explain. "Well…" Feylin's words about keeping up the ruse bounce around in my head, reminding me that I'm supposed to be blissfully in love. "It was love at first sight," I blurt out.

"Love at first sight?" Chelsea croons, practically swooning.

A storm brews in Blair's eyes. "You were going to be engaged to Edward only two days ago, and by the way, I didn't realize that I was talking to *the Edward* until your argument. Otherwise I never would've said one word to him. You know that, right?"

I wave off her concern. "Of course I do. You have nothing to apologize for."

My aunt clears her throat to get us all back on track. "There's also magic involved between Addie and Feylin. Magic that has joined the two of them."

Blair shoots me a frantic look. I grin widely, doing my best to ignore the wrecking ball knocking holes in my stomach wall. "It was *already* love at first sight, and then magic got involved," I stress really hard, hoping they buy the story. "So we can't be far from one another. That's why I'm here."

Chelsea turns to me with surprise flaring in her eyes. "Is that so?"

"Yes, it is. We have to remain within a certain distance. So when he left the house last night, I was magicked with him."

"Oh, that's so romantic," Chelsea declares, collapsing onto the back of the overstuffed chair. "And you're engaged to a *king*, no less."

Don't remind me.

"But you're not really going to marry him," Blair tells me. It's not a question. "You can't."

Ovie shoots her a look. "Addie can marry whomever she wants."

"But not him," Blair snaps at our aunt. Chelsea frowns at

her, giving a silent warning. Blair explains. "Because it's all so sudden."

I scoff. "Isn't it supposed to be sudden? We're having balls so that we'll each be married off. This has to happen in a timely manner or else"—I drop my voice—"or else, you know what." My cheeks burn from all the attention plus the secret that I'm keeping. Time to change the subject. "What about those balls?" I take Blair's hand and give it a playful shake. "Those'll continue, right? So that you can find your husband."

Chelsea shoots an annoyed look to Ovie. "We're waiting until after you're married to start them back up."

My throat shrivels. Ovie was against me being with Feylin, so why are they waiting? As I watch her, my aunt's eyes narrow, saying it all—she wants my relationship with Feylin to end so that I can find a different husband at a different ball.

That can't happen.

"You have to keep the balls!" I shout. The three of them look at me like I've grown a second head. I smooth the hem of my blouse and clear my throat. "What I mean is—why wait? Ovie, you've said that we have to marry, so why stop because I've found my true love?"

She coughs.

I fight the urge to roll my eyes. "Y'all have to keep up the dances. Blair—you want them, right?"

Chelsea elbows her. "Not if Devlin Ross keeps showing up."

Blair scowls at my sister.

Ophelia enters and places a tray of cookies on the table along with a pitcher of sweet tea. I thank her and she nods before slipping out the door.

Chelsea picks up a shortbread square and takes a bite. She moans. "Oh my gosh. I think there's rose petals in this. It's amazing. Try one."

She pushes the plate toward me, but my appetite's dried up. "What about Devlin Ross?"

Chelsea smirks. "He showed up with a woman on each arm —twins, and then he had the nerve to ask Blair to dance."

My sister exhales like she's the north wind trying to stir up a blizzard. "If I can keep from having to lay eyes on him, I'll be happy."

Crap. This isn't the way the conversation's supposed to go. Ovie's got to be on board with continuing to marry off my sisters, which means I'll have to whittle away at her resolve until she relents.

"Won't the family's power be secured as more of us marry?"

My aunt tips her head back and forth. "There's truth in that, but even just getting one of y'all married will help."

"But two are better." She hasn't touched the cookies, so I pick up the plate and shove it toward her. "Don't you think? Two weddings, double the power?"

She studies the cookies closely before picking one with chocolate chips. "Maybe. I'll have to think about it."

"But Blair wants to marry," I blurt out.

"Addie," my sister snaps.

"Sorry, but it's true."

"Maybe she'll finally tame Devlin," Chelsea adds with a laugh.

"Never."

My younger sister smirks. "Never say never."

Ovie munches on the cookie for a moment. "We should really be focused on your wedding and not balls right now."

"But life has to continue as it should be. It has to keep on going. You can't stop just because I've been snatched up."

"*Have* you been snatched up?" Blair questions skeptically.

I love my sister, but right now my only wish is for her to shut it. "You'll see this afternoon at the ceremony. Y'all will be so amazed at how in love I am with Feylin, and how much he loves me, that you'll be begging Ovie to have a ball next week."

Blair folds her arms in a display of sulkiness, but it's Chelsea who says happily, "I can't wait to meet him. The whole community can't."

Wait. "What?"

"Yes." She sips her tea and grins. "Everyone's coming to the ceremony—the whole town. They're excited to see a witch and fae marry. It's historical, you know."

My gaze darts to Ovie. "The whole town's coming?"

She wrings her hands. "Well, probably not the *whole* town." I pin my laser-beam gaze on her and she wilts. "Okay, maybe *some* of them. You know how word spreads. Last night, as soon as Feylin announced that y'all were engaged, tongues began wagging. No one knows these people—I mean, fae. Even though they've lived here for years, they keep to themselves."

"For good reason. The backyard's climate-controlled."

"What's that mean?" Blair asks.

"It's summer out there. Be sure to wear light clothing for the ceremony. Otherwise you'll have a heat stroke."

Chelsea brushes crumbs from her mouth. "Summer?"

I grin. "With no humidity."

"Sounds like heaven."

"It is." I nibble my bottom lip. "But back to the balls—"

"Addie, can we please get through my mama's funeral before we start talking about those?" Ovie snaps.

Shame floods my cheeks at her scolding. "Yes, of course. You're right. I'm sorry. I don't know what got into me."

"Love's what's gotten into you," Chelsea announces, her voice sparkling with delight.

"Yeah, I guess so," I murmur as I stuff a cookie into my mouth.

Blair just watches me. Her dark eyes are loaded with suspicion. She knows I'm lying, that something's off.

"Just because you had that weird magic happen doesn't

mean you have to marry him," she murmurs. "How well do you even know him?"

Not at all. "That's why we're taking our time with the engagement."

She doesn't look convinced. "Ovie, is there any way to break the spell?"

"It's fae magic. When I poked at it, I couldn't feel where it began or where it ended." She shakes her head. "Only a fae can break it."

My sister frowns. "Addie, are you sure about this?"

I force a smile. "As sure of it as I can be."

Ovie brushes crumbs from her hands and rises. "Girls, we need to get going."

My stomach falls. "You're leaving?"

"I'm afraid so. We only wanted to bring the dress and see how you're doing." I hug each of them, Ovie last. "If you need anything, let us know." She holds me at arm's length, studying me. "Be careful, Addie. Here. I brought your cell phone."

Tears spring to my eyes as she shoves the cell and charger into my hands. "Thank you. Now I'm not cut off from the world."

"No, you're not."

I escort them to the front door, which isn't far away, thank goodness. The last thing I need is for my family to see me stub my toe on an invisible wall.

They leave and I take the hatbox up to my room, where I settle it on a table and pull out the dress. It's beautiful—emerald-green tulle with small flowers stitched on the skirt. The bodice is a fitted corset, shaped with bone, and the sleeves are made of more translucent tulle, flowy and relaxed. It's a gorgeous gown.

I hang it up and move to close the box when I spy something peeking out from under a slip of tissue paper.

"What's this?"

The round object's covered in multicolored beads that are glued to the top and bottom. There's a lip on one edge, and I open it to find a mirror.

A smiling face stares back at me. "Hello, Addie."

I grin. "Why hey there, Elmore."

14

FEYLIN

*W*hat the hell's wrong with me?

This entire situation feels like a betrayal—to myself, to my kingdom. It was one thing to dance with Addison, but to turn around and announce that we're engaged? I've truly lost my mind.

But no, I remind myself, *I tried to leave the dance.* As soon as she made it clear that she was a Thornrose, I couldn't get out fast enough. But when my feet touched the grass outside, it felt like my heart had been ripped in two.

Once again, *what is wrong with me?*

It was my body that compelled me to return, if only to see her once more before I turned my back for good.

Which I would have done if she hadn't been sucked into that argument. The pain and frustration in her voice sliced into my chest. Who was this man insulting her, and how quickly could I kill him?

When I finally laid eyes on the perpetrator, it took all my willpower not to laugh. This small, oafish man who clearly uses magic to enhance his looks had the balls to declare that no one would marry *her*? He's lucky I didn't kill him on the spot.

Even now savage rage ravages my veins at the thought of her being hurt. Obviously there was no choice but to save her dignity, which I did, and I wouldn't change that, even if my own actions make me sick.

She's a witch. Worse, she's a Thornrose.

One who clearly doesn't know what I mean to her family. That much was obvious when they told her who I was. Well, if they're not going to tell her, then I won't either.

But am I wrong? Will they say something? The question flits across my mind for a brief moment. No, they won't. It would only complicate things more than they already are.

And speaking of complications, now when we touch it's... *ruinous*. What has the joining unleashed? My entire body feels like it's on fire when our skin meets.

And I can't get enough.

My cock stiffens just thinking about it.

Gods, I've got to get ahold of myself. Thinking like this is doing me no good.

But I can't help it. If I could put a stop to it, I would.

Worse, what will Trawick say? He'll hit the roof, no doubt, especially because of what a joining signifies. But he won't be able to argue it. No fae can question the significance of joining magic—even if it is to a Thornrose.

I suppose the one light in this is that it's all fake. None of it's real. Just keep thinking that, and I can maneuver through this situation without a scratch.

Yet if anyone's got nails, it's her.

How would they feel raking down my back?

I shake the image of Addison, naked underneath me, out of my mind as I make my way through the castle in search of my cousin. If there was ever a time when I needed a distraction, this is it.

Ryals is sketching in my office when I find him. Sheets of white paper clutter the top of my desk, blanketing most of the documents I'd neatly stacked atop it.

He's sitting in my leather chair, neck bent, shoulders hunched. Sunlight pools on his back and the top of his head. He rotates his shoulders as if adjusting because of the heat.

I lightly tap the edge of my desk. "And what are you sketching today?"

"The falcon," he says without bothering to look up. "But this time he's bringing me the mouse."

I glance at the drawing. The detailing on the falcon's exceptional—shadows and highlights fall exactly where they should as the bird dives toward an outstretched hand, the mouse falling from its open talons.

He sighs. "I suppose you want your chair back."

I ruffle his hair and drop onto the seat across from him. "No. You can keep it."

"Thank you," he says, sounding surprised.

I steeple my fingers and breathe in deeply. "There's something I want to talk to you about."

He glances up, his brown bangs hooding the tops of his silver eyes. "Am I in trouble?"

"No." I pause. "Should you be?"

"I don't think so." He nibbles the inside of his mouth in thought. "Nope, there's nothing for me to be in trouble for."

"Good to hear. But that's not what we need to discuss."

He goes back to sketching. "What is it, then?"

I thread my fingers and hunch forward, dropping my elbows to my knees. "Well, um, there's a woman. I...you see, we..."

"Just spit it out," he tells me without looking up.

It's impossible not to smile at his matter-of-fact tone. He'll make a good councilor one day. Goodness knows whoever takes over after me will need someone strong by their side.

"I may have accidentally gotten engaged."

His pencil stops and he slowly lifts his gaze. "You mean as in engaged to be married?"

"That's the one."

His voice is thick with disgust. "To a girl?"

"Yes, but—"

"Yuck."

"Right." I smooth a hand over my hair. "I know it's gross now, but one day it won't be."

"It *will* be."

"We're engaged, but we won't be for long."

He eyes me suspiciously. "What do you mean? Because after that, you'll be married?"

Why is my throat so tight? This is an impossible situation to explain to a ten-year-old. "Can you keep a secret?"

"Yes."

His eyes are sparkling now. Every child loves a secret. "I'm only *pretending* to be engaged. You're going to hear that I'm getting married. Don't say otherwise. Just ignore it."

"Is she pretty?"

My insides tighten as an image of Addison flashes in my mind. How she looked genuinely curious to know what my favorite food is, how her dark amber eyes were filled with a question instead of the normal irritation she has for me. No one's asked anything about me in...well, I can't remember the last time. When you're a king, it's easy for others to forget you still have a heart.

Even when you don't.

"It doesn't matter if she's pretty."

"She's ugly, isn't she?"

"No, she's not ugly." *She's the most beautiful creature I've ever seen.* Wait. I've got to stop thinking like this. "But she won't live with us long, and I don't want you getting attached."

There. I've said it. I rub my forehead because this discussion makes me feel like I've been dipped in slime. Having an orphan become attached to the first mother figure he's had in years isn't something I wish to torment Ryals with—*again.*

"What do you mean, *get attached?*"

I close my eyes and slump back into the chair. "Don't talk to her. That's what I mean. Just ignore her."

"Is she mean?"

My lids pop open. "No."

"Let me get this straight." As he starts to tick points off on his fingers, it's obvious—and humbling—that my cousin's way too grown up for his age. "She's not ugly. She's not mean. You're not getting married, but I'm supposed to keep that a secret, and I'm not supposed to talk to her."

I pinch the bridge of my nose at how horrific it all sounds coming from him. "That's right."

He cocks a brow at me. "I think you're lying."

I smirk. "I'm not lying. Her name's Addison."

"Will I meet her?"

"No," I say sharply. Then I soften. "Ryals, it's better if you stay away from her. For your own good. Look. She won't be in our lives very long. It's hard to understand now, but I'm doing you a favor."

He gives me a hard look. "I bet she *is* ugly."

"She's not ugly."

He cocks his head to one side, thinking. "Is that what the party's for?"

"It's an engagement party, yes. It'll be fun."

"Parties are never fun here," he grumps.

I fold my arms and study him. "This one might be."

"There are never any kids." He returns to sketching. "It's all adult fae."

"There might be children at this party."

That gets his attention. He straightens. "Why?"

"Because the witches and wizards from the village will be here."

His eyes brighten. "They will?"

"Before you get too excited, I'm not promising anything. You're welcome to come. But like I said"—I wag my finger, and we say in unison, "Don't talk to her. Promise?" I ask, rising and stretching a kink from my back.

"I promise."

"Then I'll leave you to it."

Right before I reach the door, he says, "Feylin?"

"Yes?"

"Will you ever get married?"

My heart crumbles at the sadness in his tone. He wants a mother. *Needs* a mother. But I'm not the person who can give that to him. Once I was. But not anymore.

I slowly turn around to read his expression, but his head's dipped, his eyes hidden. "No."

"Is that the truth?"

"Was it the truth when you promised not to talk to Addison?"

He glances up. "Yes."

"Then it's the truth." I nod firmly. "I'll see you at the party."

But as I head from my office, I get the nagging feeling that instead of promising, Ryals was crossing his fingers behind his back the whole time.

15

A couple of hours later when a knock sounds, I fully expect it to be Ophelia ready to escort me downstairs.

But it's not her on the other side of the threshold. A fae woman slouches against the doorframe with an arm draped over her head. Her skin's the color of a newborn fawn and her ebony hair's piled high on her head. Her citrine-colored halter dress shimmers when she adjusts her arm.

She blinks slowly and her expression suggests that she finds most situations tedious. "So you're the witch who stole Feylin's heart," she says in a voice that matches how bored she looks.

"I'm sorry?"

"I can see why he fell for you. It's obvious."

And what am I supposed to say to that?

She drops her arm to her side. "I'm Zandra."

"Addison. But everyone calls me Addie."

"Of course you have an adorable nickname." That could be taken as an insult, but the warmth in her eyes suggests it's a genuine compliment. "Tell me—how afraid are you of meeting an army of fae?"

"Oh, uh…"

"Terrified. I knew it. Come on. I'll take you down and spill the tea about the different courts."

Who is this woman? I smooth my hands down the skirt of my dress. "Shouldn't I wait for Ophelia?"

"She's busy, so I asked if I could escort you. Come on. I don't bite unless you're male and I'm trying to bed you," she adds with a playful wink.

I slip from my room and close the door behind me.

Zandra links her arm through mine. She's gorgeous and smells of lilies. She seems to float as she walks, and I do my best to look just as elegant as we head down the stairs, but at best I resemble a clomping horse instead of an ethereal being.

She gives me a sly look. "I'll admit when I felt the joining last night, I was shocked. It woke me up."

"You *felt* it?"

"You didn't know? Let me guess—Feylin forgot to tell you. Figures. This is a thing about fae magic: if a king joins, the magic's experienced everywhere. All the high fae and even lesser fae feel it. It's like being punched in the chest. Don't look so worried. It doesn't hurt. That's how we all knew to be here today."

Ah, that makes sense. Last night he'd said that his subjects would be notified about the joining. *That's* what he meant.

Downstairs, a gazillion fae bustle around us carrying plates filled with champagne glasses and hors d'eourves that look like miniature roasted quails.

It's when we step outside that the full force of what I've gotten myself into hits me. A warm breeze slides past, carrying with it pink rose petals that dance and spiral in the air.

The hydrangeas are in full bloom, and bumblebees bob drunkenly from one flower to the next. The air smells of citrus, and the lawn's covered in fae that turn and stare when I appear.

My cheeks instantly heat, sending a rush of warmth that travels down my neck. My gaze skims the crowd, but Feylin's nowhere to be seen.

Zandra pats my hand. "All you have to do is walk around and smile. Feylin'll make formal introductions later. Got it?"

"Got it."

"Deep breath—and go."

I inhale deeply as she leads me down the steps. "All right, let me tell you about us. Assuming you don't know much, is that right?"

"Yes, how'd you know?"

She leans in and whispers, "Because I never heard that Feylin was dating anyone, so I assume you only recently met."

"That's right."

Thank goodness she doesn't ask for details about our relationship. It's all I can do to get my bearings.

"See those fae dressed in black?"

On my left stand a small group of fae wearing midnight-colored clothes. The men wear dark suits, the women, regal satin gowns. They're decked out in jewels, the women's necks dripping in diamonds. Many of the men and women have white hair and dark skin like Zandra.

"That's the Eastern Court," she explains. "It's my court. They all look very serious, don't they?"

They do. Most of their mouths are set in firm lines.

"Hey, y'all," I say as we pass.

They give snobby nods in reply.

"It's amazing I come from them," she admits. "And those fae over there are from the Southern Court."

My gaze skips to where she's nodding at people dressed in lighter clothes—linen the color of the ocean. The points of their ears are more pronounced, the tips slanting back as if to help them swim through water faster.

"They're fairly laid back for fae," Zandra says. "And if you're looking to make friends, you'll find good ones among them." She points to the right. "Over there you have the Western and Northern Courts. Can you tell which is which?"

"The ones in furs are from the north?"

"You're very good at this game," she teases genuinely. "I'm going to like you."

The Northern Court of fae are decked out in white fur that lines their dresses and the lapels of the men's suits. They're a pale people with eyes that remind me of ice chips.

"Aren't they hot in all that fur?"

"Nah. Temperature doesn't affect us like it does to you and humans."

The western fae are dressed in flowing gowns with low necklines and suits with bow ties. Their skin is sun-kissed, and they regard me with bows but no smiles.

The northern bow as well. Still no smiles.

"They don't play well together," Zandra says after we pass.

"The Northern and Western Courts?"

"All of them," she confides. "It's only because of Feylin that we tolerate one another."

A servant carrying a tray of champagne approaches, and Zandra unlinks her arm from mine and takes two glasses, handing me one.

I sip and bubbles pop against my upper lip. "How's it because of Feylin that the courts get along?"

Her gaze bounces from group to group. "When the veil fell, no one knew what to do. But Feylin said that he'd make his court available to humans in order to keep everyone else safe. He'd be our ambassador to their world."

"So he volunteered himself."

She laughs lightly. "Well as king it's not exactly volunteering, is it? Even if he *was* the sacrificial lamb, so to speak."

Feylin kept them safe. He did so selflessly, without anyone having to ask. My heart softens a bit, knowing that about him.

Yet as soon as it softens, I recall how he came to my rescue last night for his own benefit—to get the lords off his back, as he had said.

She smacks her ruby-red lips. "He's like that—caring. But I'm sure you already know."

I don't, actually! "He's your king. Of course he had to help."

She tsks. "You'd be surprised what some of our kings have been like. His father would've done the same thing, but many of the others—they would've abandoned the rest of us in a heartbeat."

"That's..."

"Very fae," she finishes for me. "After all, witches and wizards haven't been great friends of ours, either." She watches me carefully. "But maybe you can change all of that."

"Maybe," I murmur. "But what's Feylin's court, if all those other courts are sectioned by region?"

She throws her head back and laughs. "Typical Feylin not to mention it. You're in the Royal Court, the most powerful of them all."

She runs a finger over the rim of her glass and studies me with chocolate-colored eyes. She must think I'm terribly plain compared to fae beauty.

"Tell me—what do you love about him? Is it that he brings you flowers every morning?"

I choke on a sip of champagne and have to tap my fist to my chest to stop coughing. "Sorry," I croak. "He is very... attentive."

Before I have to answer more questions about my relationship, I spot my mother brushing something off the lapel of my father's suit. "Oh, my family's here. Would you like to meet them?"

She shakes her head. "You go. I want to find your fiancé and interrogate him about why he isn't here, with you. I plan to give him a piece of my mind."

A servant carrying an empty tray passes by, and I place my glass atop it, then I grin at Zandra. "It was nice meeting you."

And I mean it. If I'm stuck in this castle for a long time, having a friend'll help keep me sane.

She winks. "I'll see you soon, Addie. Good luck with the earth ceremony, but you won't need it. You're a witch. He's fae. The magic will flow," she says, lifting her arms to the heavens and gliding off.

My mama wraps me in a huge hug when I reach her. "How are you?" she asks when I pull away, her eyes searching me for any sign of…I don't know, injury?

I pull her hands from my face. Lines of worry deepen her forehead, so I squeeze her hands. "I'm fine. Really. It's good."

"And you got our gift?"

I drag my teeth over my bottom lip and grin. "The mirror's tucked safely away in my room."

She releases a breath. "Good."

I want to know how she's doing, if she's ready for my grandmother to walk tomorrow, but the words are jammed up in my throat.

"I don't see him anywhere," my father remarks coldly. "Seems the distance that the two of y'all can have has grown."

I frown, my gaze sweeping the lawn. "We're not that far from the castle. He could be right inside."

"And not here with you."

"He can't be everywhere at once," Blair reminds him.

My father's face turns crimson, so I place a hand gently on his arm. "Why don't you go look in the castle? You'd love the architecture." His eyes brighten, and all it'll take is a tiny shove for him to start knocking people over to get inside. "Go. You and Mama."

"But Addie—" she protests.

I shoo them off. "Honestly. Look around. I'll be perfectly safe right here with Blair. Hey. Where are our sisters?"

Blair points to a row of hammocks that I hadn't noticed before. "Over there looking classy."

Chelsea pushes Finn out of a hammock so that she can sit, while Georgia climbs into one that's already taken by Dallas, who tries to shove her out. Meanwhile Emory leans against a tree, watching the whole thing and shaking her head.

"One thing you can't say is that our family's a bunch of wallflowers." Blair rolls her eyes. "Y'all go on inside. I'll stay here with Addie, make sure she doesn't get eaten."

"You go, Phillip," Mama says.

My father never misses the opportunity to study a building with old-looking architecture. He loves it. It's one of his passions, along with recording the subspecies of every dragon he's ever seen. With a huff that I know is fake, he stalks off.

Mama turns to me. "How are you?"

"You keep asking me. I'm fine. Good. Everyone's nice."

"You're sure?"

I can't handle this anymore. "Where's Ovie?"

Mama doesn't answer, so Blair does. "Uncle Charlie's in town."

My stomach pitfalls. "Is he coming here?"

"I—we don't know," Mama says, dropping her chin. "But anyway, tomorrow you and Feylin will walk behind me and Dad. There'll be the traditional taking over of power, and you as the oldest will be given the bookshop."

"But Mama—"

"No buts." She glares at me. "Until you've proven that you

can't own it, it's yours. Besides, no one can pick books for a reader like you. It's meant to be yours."

"Clara!" We look over our shoulders to see my father waving at us. "Clara, you've got to come here!"

Every head turns. All the fae lords in their silk suits and the women in their satin gowns stare at my father. Distaste fills their eyes at the wizard waving his hands.

The tops of my ears burn as my mother murmurs an apology and walks off.

"Don't worry," Blair says, patting my shoulder. "Things can only go up from here."

I laugh and she joins. When our laughter dies down, I say, "When did Charlie come home?"

She sneers. "This morning, before we came to see you. Ovie didn't want us to mention it, so we kept quiet."

I fiddle with my blousy sleeve. "How long do you think he'll stay this time?"

"Oh, long enough to get money, or whatever it is he wants. Then he'll leave. Again. Like he always does, and Ovie'll be heartbroken because he didn't stay this time."

Bitterness sharpens her words, but I can't argue because everything she's said is true.

"Blair?"

She drags her gaze from my sisters frolicking at the hammocks to me. "Hm?"

"Last night, when Mama and Daddy found out about the engagement, they seemed…mad. Really mad. Like they know Feylin and dislike him. Do they know him?"

"Are you asking if there's history there?"

"Yeah."

She clears her throat. "I'm not the person to ask."

"Then who is?"

She opens her mouth to answer, but another voice cuts us

off. "Why, if it isn't little Addison Thornrose, all grown up and getting married."

Devlin Ross approaches with a woman on each arm—*blonde twins, no less*—as was already reported by Chelsea earlier today.

Saying Devlin Ross is handsome is like calling a peacock pretty—a complete understatement. He's tragically good-looking with his walnut-colored hair raked back from his face and stubble peppering his cheeks and chin. A peach-colored T-shirt peeks out from beneath his white suit, the sleeves of which are rolled up to the elbow.

"Devlin, good to see you."

He leans over and kisses my cheek before his gaze darts to Blair. His eyes linger on her, and his entire face brightens.

"Well, imagine seeing you two days in a row, Miss Blair."

"Imagine that," she mutters, rolling her eyes.

"I was disappointed that you didn't dance with me last night."

She gives him a hard look. "How could I dance with you when you were already occupied with two other partners?"

"Who? These ladies? They know to give me up when I ask."

My sister taps her foot impatiently. "Do you want something, Devlin?"

"Only to say hello and to mingle with the fae." He glances over both his shoulders. "Looks like a lot of witches and wizards have come, so maybe they're not as afraid of these people as we think they are."

"Astute observation," she grinds out, shooting him eye-daggers.

He smiles and the corners of his eyes crinkle. "Ladies, I'm going to take *my ladies* and find some refreshments. Addison, congratulations. And Blair"—his eyes spark with mischief—"I *will* get that dance."

"When hell freezes over," she mutters after he's gone. "The

nerve of him. Dating two women and flirting with me. But anyway." Blair exhales a gusty sigh before forcing a wide smile onto her face. "Where's this fiancé of yours?"

I cringe, because I don't know. But as I scan the crowd, a shadow falls from the castle doorway.

It's Feylin.

And he looks drop-dead gorgeous.

16

Feylin
Ten minutes earlier

"*J*oined, Feylin? You're *joined* to her?"

It was a terrible idea to allow Trawick into my office once I sequestered it back from Ryals. He's reacting exactly as I knew he would.

My best friend glowers at me. He drops into the chair across from mine and rakes his long brown bangs from his face. "I said *go* to the ball, not *join* with one of the Thornrose women. Gods, you didn't even join to Tess when the two of you got engaged."

My chest tightens so hard it feels like a hand's squeezing my heart. "Don't you think I know that?" I growl.

"Sorry to bring her up," he apologizes. "But back to this— how'd it happen?"

"It just did."

"It couldn't have happened unless you said it," he snarls.

"You guessed it." I lift a stack of papers and tap them

together, straightening them before dropping them back on the desk. "I said it."

"Why?"

"Because I fell deeply and passionately in love at first sight."

He scoffs. "You're a liar, and I don't understand why you're not telling me the truth."

For so many reasons. I rub my eyes with the heels of my hands, then rest them on the arms of my chair. "I went to the ball and ran into Addison. I'd met her before—"

His eyes narrow. "The puker? *She's* the puker?"

"Not that it matters."

"But yes," he replies, triumph lacing his voice for puzzling it together.

"At the ball she got into a bind. An ex-boyfriend of hers was a prick, so I stepped in."

"And declared yourself engaged?" he roars.

"Yes."

"And then the joining magic just sprang up out of nowhere?"

"Exactly."

He slumps into his chair, shaking his head and looking two seconds away from choking the life out of me. "And you want me to believe that's how it happened."

"That *is* how it happened. Believe what you want."

"I thought you would go as a joke. Make an intimidating entrance, dance with a few of the daughters." His knee bounces in frustration. "I didn't expect you to come out engaged."

"We're only pretending. She doesn't want to get married any more than I do. This isn't permanent."

"Whatever this is, it isn't good. It changes things," Trawick tells me.

"It changes nothing," I remind him fiercely. "Everything still goes as planned."

He throws his arms out. "So your great plan is to, what? Have the charade of an engagement, let all the fae rejoice, and then break things off? How exactly do you think our people will respond to a broken joining? You're going to crush them." When I don't answer, he adds, "Does she know how to *end* a joining?"

"No," I tell him pointedly. "I haven't tortured her with that knowledge."

"This just gets worse and worse." He rubs his hands down his face and drops them to his thighs "Do I need to remind you what such a bond signifies?"

Anger flashes in my eyes. "No, you don't. I'm well aware what it means."

"Does she, though?" When I don't answer, he groans. "Let me get this straight—she doesn't know how to end a joining, and she doesn't even know what such a bond means to fae."

"Right on both counts."

"You've got to tell her."

And have her hate me more than she already does? Addison only *tolerates* me now. All I want to do is crush my mouth against hers and run my hands through her hair. But every time she looks at me, her eyes scream that I'm her captor. Albeit a convenient one, but still I'm holding her here. I won't risk having her hate me more by revealing the truth. Because that's exactly what'll happen. She'll run, and I'll be left even more scooped out than I was before meeting her.

"What are your intentions with the witch?"

Trawick's question takes me off guard. I don't suppose claiming her so that no other man can touch her is the right answer.

"The same as they were before."

He shakes his head and stares out a window. "If that's the truth, have you contacted the Witch and Wizard Council? We could never move before since you had no direct link to witch blood. But by being engaged to one, you have sway. They'll have to listen to you now. They'll have no choice."

"No," I'm embarrassed to say. "I haven't contacted them."

He scowls as if to repeat, *Nothing good will come of this joining, and this is the beginning of it.* "Then I'll do it for you."

My chest constricts, squeezing my heart so hard it feels like it's going to be crushed. This is what I've wanted for years. I can't let some *feelings* for a woman I hardly know get in the way.

"Get it done," I tell him.

He nods, his knee still bouncing. "At least with the joining, no one can question your bond to a Thornrose. You should be thankful for that," he grumbles, shooting me a contemptuous glance. "Otherwise the fae would be in an uproar."

"Don't you think *I'm* in an uproar?" I tell him.

"No, I don't," he says flatly.

And sadly he's right. I should be enraged at this joining. I should be furious, but being around Addison confuses me, winds me up, guts me and makes my primal instincts prickle up and down my spine.

"I haven't heard of a true joining occurring in over a century. They don't happen anymore," he mutters. "I can't even guess what kind of magic that is between two people."

It's atomic. It's being sucked into a black hole where the only thing that exists is the other person. They're all you can see. They're your world, and their scent is your oxygen.

It's torment and ecstasy wrapped up in a pretty little bow.

"What's that look on your face?"

Shit. I must've been daydreaming. "It's nothing. Absolutely nothing."

He studies me suspiciously for a moment before moving on. "If you're sure about this whole relationship thing, then where is she?"

I glance behind me, out the window. "Probably getting ready to go downstairs, if she's not out there already."

He balks. "You're not escorting her out?"

"Fake relationship," I remind him. "Besides, I had to catch you up on what had happened." I rise and slip on my suit jacket that's hanging over the back of my chair. "Ready to meet my bride-to-be?"

He grunts out an, "I suppose."

Outside my office, we're greeted by a host of fae and witches swarming inside the castle. I nod to those I know, and head toward the back garden. The doors leading outside are open, and sunlight spills onto the marble floor. The sound of laughter drifts in from outside as Trawick reaches the doorway first.

"Which one is your witch?" he asks.

It must be the magic of the joining because my gaze instantly hones in on Addison.

I suck in a breath at the sight of her. Her auburn hair tumbles in loose curls down her back. The green dress she's wearing cups her perfect breasts and cinches at her waist, revealing a figure that makes my body stir.

She's smiling. It's angelic, and for once she keeps smiling when our gazes lock.

Then I'm falling into that black hole. The edges of my vision darken until only she exists. She's walking—I think. It's impossible to think when the urge to bury my face in the soft curve of her neck's overpowering.

A breeze lifts her hair and makes her skirt flutter behind her. Everything happens in slow motion—everything except how quickly my cock stirs.

Then I blink and she's standing in front of me. I can't rip my gaze away. All I want to do is trail my tongue over every inch of her exposed skin, see if it tastes as delicious as it looks.

Then someone clears their throat. "Feylin," Trawick prods.

Right.

I gesture to her. "Trawick, my oldest friend, may I present Addison Thornrose, my fiancée."

When Addison drags her gaze from me, it feels like the sun's been eclipsed by the moon. "Trawick, how do you do?"

He takes the hand that she offers and brushes his lips to the back of it. His eyes shine as they land on her. "I hear you're to marry our king."

She tips her face up to him and beams. Then she says in a voice ringing with authenticity, "I can't wait to be his wife."

As she tugs Trawick off into the garden, he looks back and mouths, *She lies easily.*

That should ease my mind, but the only thing it does is make my insides wither and die. Addison's only playing a role, as am I. Right?

She glances over her shoulder and shoots me a shy smile.

Don't lose yourself, Feylin, I remind myself. *You know what happened last time.*

I push back my shoulders and steel my heart. I would never forget Tess. Not for a thousand years.

But as much as I want to keep my distance from Addison, just looking at her sends a thrill racing through my body. A minute alone with her and I won't be able to control myself.

And most surprisingly, I don't want to.

17

*I*t's easier to pretend to love Feylin than I ever imagined.

Which is annoying, I might add.

Mostly I smile and nod, telling everyone who asks, how we met, how we literally ran into each other, how it was love at first sight, and that everything happened so fast—*that's* why our relationship remained a secret.

My parents sit at our table for dinner, along with Zandra and Trawick. The fact that Feylin has any friends at all is a surprise, but Trawick's nice, kind even, as he explains the details of fae food, how it's light and vegetable-based with lean protein.

While we eat, Blair keeps shooting me worried looks, but I find it easy enough to avoid glancing in her direction and keep my attention on Feylin.

I touch his arm when he says something charming. I beam up at him when his gaze lands on me. There's this one loose curl that spirals down the center of his forehead, and at one point I brush it away. Both of us shudder when the jolt of electricity passes between us.

When my plate arrives and it's chicken loaded with what looks like feta cheese, olives and tomatoes, I feel Feylin's gaze as I push all the extra stuff off the breast and cut it into small bites.

My eyes flick to him and he quickly looks away, straightening as he cuts his own chicken (he doesn't bother to push off the weird stuff on top, I notice).

He keeps my father entertained with stories about the inside decor of the castle—it came from the old one in their previous Royal Court, he explains.

My mother and father both listen attentively, but every once in a while my mother slips me a questioning glance. I only smile and admire how Feylin plays the perfect host, how everyone who talks to him seems enchanted.

Truly, it's easy to play this part.

Too easy.

And when dinner's over, he rises. The fae rise as well. All of them.

Because Feylin is their king.

Whereas I'm a nobody.

The king extends his hand, and I feel every eye land on me. "You'll have to excuse Addison and me. The ceremony's about to begin."

Everyone at the table murmurs their approval, but I freeze. My stomach ties into a thousand knots at the thought of the magic, or lack of, that I'm about to conjure. The worry must show on my face because he nods to his outstretched hand, silently willing me to take it.

Well, there's no time like the present.

I slip my palm over his, biting down against the fissure of heat that sparks when we touch, as well as the desire to suck on his ridiculously muscular neck.

Fae bow deeply when we pass them. Feylin, for the most part, ignores them as he guides us toward the ceremonial tree.

124

When we're out of earshot, I slip my hand from his and he turns to me. "It appears that our fake relationship's a success."

My stomach's coiled too tightly for me to answer.

"You've done a great job pretending," he adds. Why's he talking to me? No one's around. We don't have to perform anymore. He smirks and a dimple peeks out from his right cheek. *Has he always had that?* "You look lovely, by the way."

Does he have brain damage? Once again, we can return to hating each other.

But he did give me a compliment, so at the very least I should be appreciative. "Thank you."

This dress, for the most part, has been itch-free, but as the evening's worn on, there's a spot tucked between my shoulder blades that's aggravatingly scratchy.

I pulse my shoulders back and his brow furrows. "Something wrong?"

"No. It's just…it itches."

"Why don't you use magic to fix it?"

Because I don't have any, is definitely not the right response. "Sometimes that doesn't work."

"Here." He runs a finger across my shoulders, and where it touches, fire dances. My stomach quivers and all I can focus on is the rough pads of his fingers as they lazily drag across my flesh, leaving heat in their wake. "Better?"

Did he ask me something? Earth to brain! Are you working? When I rotate my shoulders, the itch is miraculously gone.

"Yes, much." I don't even try keeping the awe from my voice. "You got rid of it."

Red tinges the tops of his cheeks. "Sometimes we fae can do things right."

"You definitely did that right." Since he's complimented me, I feel the need to say something nice to him. "You look…"

Feylin's suit jacket fits him perfectly, accentuating shoulders that look strong enough to sit on. His collar's unbuttoned, and the white shirt underneath flares open, letting a few chest hairs peek out. His jaw flexes, making his dimple deepen, and highlighting those superhero cheekbones. His dark sapphire eyes smolder as he watches me watching him.

My mouth dries.

"You look very nice as well," I barely manage.

We're silent until we reach the tree. It looks innocent enough, just a bare tree waiting to fruit. No big deal. I can do this.

"Don't be nervous."

"I'm not," I lie. He turns back toward the people in attendance, and for the first time, I notice that the tops of his ears aren't pointed. "Your ears," I say before I think better of it. "They're rounded."

His hands fly to them. "They are? Are you sure?"

I roll my eyes.

He leans over conspiratorially, causing his amber and leather scent to cloud me. "Can I tell you a secret?"

"Only one?"

"Okay, two."

"Yes, you may."

"Ah." He wags a finger in a mocking scold. "But you didn't ask if there's a cost to those secrets."

I cock my head in suspicion. "What sort of cost?"

"A secret for a secret."

"If you tell me a secret, then I tell you one?" He gives a slow nod. It's questionable whether this trade's worth it. "That depends on how good your secret is."

He drops his mouth to my ear. "It's a very good secret," he murmurs in a voice that makes my girlie parts throb.

"I'm not sure I believe you," I reply weakly.

He backs away and shoves his hands into his pockets.

"Then don't learn the secret, and forever wonder what knowledge I was going to impart on you."

Now I *have* to know what it is. "Fine. I'll tell you a secret, but you first." He opens his mouth and I quickly add, "And if I don't think your secret's worth giving up one of mine for, I have the right to forfeit."

He exhales a mocking grunt. "You drive a hard bargain, Addison Thornrose."

I grin. "Speak. If we have time."

Feylin's gaze sweeps the meadow. "We have as long as we want."

"We do?"

"They're waiting for *us*."

Great. They're waiting for me to prove that I'm some sort of fae goddess wannabe, which makes me want to dive into the nearest bush and never return. "Even if they're waiting on us, we can't stand here all day."

"We won't. Just long enough to make them sweat," he adds with a mischievous wink.

"That's not very kingly of you."

"People want a show. I'm just giving it to them."

I fold my arms defiantly. "Okay, what have you done with Feylin? Where've you hidden him? You had me for a few minutes, but I know a double when I see one."

He chuckles, and it's the first time I've heard him laugh. It's a low, sexy grumble that makes my insides somersault. "Surprisingly we're the same person."

"Hm. I'm beginning to think you're stalling and that there isn't a secret."

"Oh, there's a secret." He frowns, which creates an adorable divot under his bottom lip. "I'm part human."

It's the last thing I expect him to say, but it makes the most sense. How else could his ears be rounded? "Oh. Wow. That's...unexpected." And knowing how much fae hate

127

witches, I can't imagine they made it easy for him, being part human and all. "Did they accept you?"

"Partly," he admits, pain flaring in his eyes. "Mostly it's been an uphill battle. Being different with the folk has it's... challenges."

The sadness on his face makes a pit open in my stomach. I, too, understand being different. My whole life I've been an oddity in my family.

I peer into his dark eyes. Among the flecks of silver floating in that deep blue sea is the anguish of a life spent trying to prove that he's good enough.

My chest tightens just thinking about the pain he's suffered. "I'm sorry."

"Don't worry. I killed all those who opposed me."

He says it so seriously that it takes a minute to recognize the sparkle in his eyes. I bite back a laugh as he slowly smiles.

And again, it's a first. If I thought he couldn't be more handsome, I was wrong. Smiling lifts his beauty to a whole other level.

"I'm not sure killing them is something to brag about."

"Trust me, it is."

He shifts his weight, and his gaze trails down my body. This dress is modest, but the way Feylin drinks me in is scandalous.

"You make it very easy to lie about us," he murmurs in what sounds like a reluctant admission.

I tip my chin toward his and study the sharp lines of his superhero face and the soft curves of his mouth. Again, the urge to trace his features overtakes me. I wonder what it would feel like to touch those lips.

I clear my throat to jog some sense back into my head. "You make it easy, too. I don't think anyone suspects the truth."

He takes a step forward, closing the distance between us.

"You play your part well," he adds as if upping an unspoken ante.

He's so close that his body's blocking my view of the sky. "And *you* are a natural actor."

Magic that I'm quickly realizing is from the joining hums between us. Body heat wafts off him and wraps around me as he bends down.

Is he going to kiss me?

But his lips only brush my ear and I shiver. "You owe me a secret."

I tilt my face toward his. "You owe me one more."

He laughs, his breath warming my cheek. "Terrible, evil witch to remember our bargain," he teases before straightening. "That *was* the second secret."

"What was?"

"That I'm impressed with how well you've fawned over me."

I use the opportunity to step back a few paces. The more space there is between us, the easier it is to breathe. "Well, I don't think that I've batted my lashes at you nearly enough. I also haven't ruffled your hair or nibbled your ear. Given that, I've done a terrible job."

"Good point. You could do better."

Don't ask, don't ask, don't ask! So I ask. "How could I do better?"

He flares out his arms. "You could start by declaring that no one's more handsome. Unless you'd rather step on my toes again."

I cringe. "Sorry about that. I didn't mean to—"

"Yes, you did."

"You're right; I did. Would I take it back?"

"I doubt it."

He inches forward. There's a silent challenge etched on his face. *How close will you stand to me?*

AMY BOYLES

I step up. *I'll see your wager and make another.* "You're right. I wouldn't take it back."

We're so close now that our lips are only inches apart. It's impossible not to stare at his—they're full and look tragically welcoming.

This is playing with fire. This flirtation—what is this? We're not interested in each other. I'm not in any shape to be interested in anyone—let alone the man I'm in a fake relationship with.

"You want me to declare that you're handsome?" I wave my hand around. "If that's all you want, then you're a cheap date."

"You're right. We need more." He rubs his chin, thinking. "We haven't kissed. How's everyone going to believe we're in love if we don't kiss?"

My breath hitches. I wait for him to laugh and say it's a joke, but the desire in his eyes suggests he's serious.

Good grief, if holding his hand makes me want to strip-tease, what would kissing him do to me?

Best not to find out. "I can't exactly throw myself at you. Who wants their king to kiss in public? That's not decent."

He takes in the crowd. "Trust me—these people don't believe in decency."

"But I do."

He pivots back toward me, and his smoldering eyes send a bolt of desire straight between my legs.

Stop it! Stop it!

"So you need a more intimate setting." He hitches a shoulder and the guests disappear—every single one. "How's that?"

"What have you done?" My gaze zips over the lawn, but it's empty. "Where are they?"

"They're still here. You just can't see them, and they can't see us." He leans in and whispers, "So that we can be *decent.*"

Decent suddenly becomes the filthiest word on the planet.

It all hits me then—not just what he's saying, but what he's done—made an entire crowd disappear with a single thought.

Holy crap. He *is* powerful.

"Um. Maybe having an audience doesn't bother me," I say past the lump in my throat.

"Throwing decency out the window already?"

"No comment."

He chuckles, and just as suddenly as they disappeared, the fae and witches return.

"Still not convinced? Then how about a deal?" he offers. "I'll trade your secret for a kiss."

He's not giving up. *What* is going on?

"You can tell me your decision after the ceremony." He extends his hand. "Ready?"

Before I can say, *No, there's no way in hell I'm going to kiss you,* his hand slides down my arm and his fingers thread through mine.

My entire body explodes with desire. All this talk of kissing isn't doing a thing to quell the deep throb that's taken up residence in my nether parts.

Worse, I'm wondering what kissing him would be like. What does he taste like? How would his lips feel grazing across my mouth? Would he just peck me, or would he want more?

Oh, he'd want more. Definitely.

This is dangerous territory, but the warning bells that should be blaring in my mind are silent.

They want to kiss him, too, apparently.

I find myself thinking that I may just say yes, that I'll give him that kiss. It's way too tempting an invitation to pass up.

"You want the kiss, don't you?" he says smugly.

"Nope," I scoff.

"I can tell. It's written all over your face."

"You'll just have to wait to find out, now won't you?"

131

A rose petal lands in my hair, and he brushes it out. "I have the patience of an elephant."

"I think you mean memory."

He winks. "Maybe it's both."

I stifle a laugh as he nods to the ring of cherry trees.

"Focus on the center," he coaxes, his voice a caress that flutters over my skin.

My head's fuzzy. It's taking all my control to harness my thoughts and saddle them down. The fire that's flowing through my veins is distracting, making it nearly impossible to focus on the tree.

Surprisingly it helps to think about something other than how warm his skin is, how strong and calloused his fingers are as their pads brush the back of my hand.

I do what I've tried a thousand times before, concentrating on finding my power and hoping that the joining magic will somehow trigger what's never surfaced inside of me.

Next thing I know, magic—glittery gold magic, trickles from where we're standing and circles the tree. The green leaves shiver, and my heart lodges in my throat.

Oh my gosh, am I doing that?

Small round bulbs swell from the branches. At first they're green, the color of unripened fruit. But as they grow, they shift, becoming yellow, then peach, until finally they deepen to plum.

Glee, absolute riotous joy, rocks through me. We've done it!

I turn and grin at Feylin. He's already watching me, a slow smile spreading across his face.

"What the…what's happening?" someone yells behind us.

My gaze slams back to the tree. The magic's stopped flowing into it, but the fruit's still transforming.

Now the purple flesh's withering, dying. My eyes widen and fear tears at my spine.

No no no no no no no!

I expect the fruit to fall, to shrivel and drop to the ground. But that's not what happens. Next thing I know—

Whoosh!

Flames erupt and engulf the tree. They incinerate it in seconds, leaving nothing more than a smoking husk. The acrid scent of charred wood fills the air as brittle branches crash to the ground and explode into dust. People wail about a terrible omen.

All I can do is watch as my lack of magic destroys the fae earth ceremony.

I turn to apologize to Feylin and suck air at the sight of him. Ebony mist leaks from his shoulders. It crawls along the grass toward me, ready to coil around my legs and drag me to the underworld, or whatever Hell is to the fae.

But that's not the worst of it.

The raging blaze reflects in his eyes, and those eyes brim with betrayal that's directed straight at me.

18

$\mathcal{I}$ can't sleep. It doesn't help that I'm lying on another pile of clothes. Yes, I'd planned to tell Feylin the truth about that after the ceremony. But you know how *that* went. He looked so mad I basically ran away so that I wouldn't have to face him. And unfortunately my pallet isn't any more comfortable now than it was last night.

Worse, every time my eyes close, I see the burning tree, hear people yelling about a bad omen and watch betrayal become etched onto Feylin's face.

His eyes were smoldering, and not with lust.

Giving up on getting some sleep, I push off my blanket dresses and exit the room. Maybe, just maybe I can find the kitchen (given I can reach it without running into an invisible wall) and warm up some milk.

I pad quietly down the stairs and head toward the belly of the house. So far so good. No walls and no Feylin.

It's when I pass an open door that I hear, "I want to talk to you."

My spine becomes a steel rod of fear. I slowly back up and look into the room.

Feylin slumps on a chair that's facing me. His forearm drapes over the arm of it, and he's loosely clutching a tumbler of amber liquid. A fire roars to the left of him, casting orange light on his shirtless physique.

Okay, he's not completely shirtless. He's wearing a silk robe that's open, and what look like soft jammy pants.

He downs the contents of the glass tumbler and places it on the table beside him with a thud.

He leans forward and every muscle in his chest ripples.

He rises and it's confirmed—there are muscles on muscles. His pecs are perfect, his abs—I can't even count them, he's got so many.

"Are you going to enter so we can talk?" he growls.

I can't run. It's not as if I can get far, and I owe him an apology, even if I don't understand exactly what happened.

I timidly step inside. I'm wearing a robe over my satin nightgown, but the chill in his voice makes goose bumps erupt over my skin. Feylin's gaze drags over every inch of me, and I feel naked even though I'm clearly not.

"I'm sorry," I start.

He holds up a hand to stop me. Then he pours a glass of whatever he's drinking for me and a small amount for himself.

I scan the room. There's a desk, chairs, the fireplace. Ancient maps made of hide are pinned to the walls. Some are so old that their edges are crumbling.

This must be his office.

He points to a chair beside him and I sit. It occurs to me that the chairs should be facing the fireplace, but they're not.

"I was waiting for you," he mumbles as if reading my mind.

"I'm sorry," I repeat. "I don't know what happened."

A shadow jumps on his jaw, and for the love of all that's good, somehow it makes him look even more handsome.

He leans back and circles his finger over the rim of the

glass but doesn't drink. His mood's so dark that I feel the need to swallow some of mine.

The whiskey burns as it slips down my throat. The alcohol content is high—maybe 100 proof. All I know is that I won't be needing any more of it.

"What happened," he says replying to my statement, "is that you sabotaged the ceremony."

"No." Panic claws up my throat. "No, I swear that I didn't."

His eyes are hard as flint as he turns toward me. "Then what did occur?"

I can't tell him the truth. Tell him that I don't have magic and he'll find a way to undo the joining sooner than I want, and I'll be thrown back into the engagement season—balls and all.

My gaze drops to my hands. "I don't know what happened. Maybe it's a weird mix of fae and witch magic—or maybe the joining affected it."

"Maybe." He rises, picks up his chair and drops it in front of me so that we're facing one another. He sits with a heavy sigh. "But I don't think it's a problem with the fae and witch magic."

"What else could it be?"

He leans forward, stopping so close that I can see the firelight dancing in his eyes. He smells of whiskey and leather. I like the amber, but I'll take the whiskey.

Our knees collide, shooting sparks up my legs. I shift to the side, but he shifts, too, pressing his knees against mine.

His gaze skims my face, stopping at my mouth. "You tell me why the tree burned to the ground."

"I've told you—I don't know what happened."

It's not exactly a lie. I actually don't know the ins and outs of it, though clearly either my lack of magic or me *trying* to work it was the culprit.

He shifts forward and adjusts his legs outside of mine so

that his thighs are holding me prisoner. Even through our clothes, my skin screams.

"Do you know what's riding on this relationship?"

I glare at him. "What?"

"The stability of my realm. Even though we won't see this relationship to the end, we don't need anyone to suspect our love isn't real. And the omen we gave them"—he gestures toward the wall—"will have every one of my people thinking this relationship is cursed."

"What's it matter if it's not real?"

"It matters because of the front we're supposed to show. It matters because my people need to think that at some point I'm going to have an heir. Otherwise they'll—never mind." He sinks back into his chair and rubs his right eye with the heel of his hand. "What was I thinking, doing this? And with you, of all people."

I didn't walk in here to be insulted. *"Me of all people? You're the one who caused this joining. You're the reason why I can't go back to my home, why I can't go anywhere unless you're there, too. Do you think I want to be in this?"*

I've had enough. I rise and start to leave, but his hand shoots out and stops me.

Feylin rises slowly, eying me as he straightens to his full height, a head taller than me. He gazes down with anger blazing in his eyes.

"We wouldn't be in this mess if you hadn't needed saving."

"I didn't need saving."

He laughs bitterly. "Oh no? Tell your ex-boyfriend that. Tell anyone else who was in that ballroom."

Why's his jaw so straight? Why are his eyes so dark that I lose myself in them? Why am I now looking at his chest?

When I glance up, his gaze is locked on my lips.

I lick them and his eyelids flare. This attraction between us infuriates the hell out of me. "You want to blame me for today, but you're the reason today ever happened. It's because of you that we're in this, and if you'd find a way to break the joining, like you said, then I'd be out of it."

Instead of replying, Feylin gently trails his finger down my cheek. My nipples tighten at the thought of his finger going lower, and lower still.

My mind's screaming for me to slap his hand away, but his touch holds me in place. Sheer *want* clouds my brain.

"I wonder," he murmurs, "what that kiss would've been like. What it would feel like now."

His finger traces the top of my nightdress, dipping to outline the V between my breasts. My nipples are so tight I'm pretty sure they're about to pop off.

"You feel this, don't you? This, that's between us."

I close my eyes and swallow. His finger runs over my collarbone. The urge to slide my hands through his silky hair's nearly overwhelming. I curl my hands into fists to keep from doing just that. Also, maybe if I don't look at him, maybe he'll go away, and all these insane sensations will stop.

But they don't. His finger trails over my lips, and a shudder rocks my spine. I open my eyes and he's smiling slightly. "Whatever you feel, I feel ten times more."

"Impossible," I whisper.

He smirks. "It's not."

I will see his wager and top it. Keeping my eyes locked on his in a silent challenge, I slowly rake my fingers down the rippling muscles of his chest.

"You're so hard," I whisper.

"And you're so soft." He shivers as my finger traces his abdomen. "I thought you didn't like touching me."

"I don't."

His mouth turns up into a smug smirk. "Then why are you?"

"I'm trying to torment you."

He exhales a husky sigh. *"Please.* Torment me more."

His flesh is silky, manly, and oh wow, do I want to feel all of it. Touching him gives me a head rush that's euphoric. It makes me feel like I'm falling into an ocean of limitless ecstasy.

And I don't want to come up for air.

It must do the same to him, because he tips his head back and moans.

So I don't stop. My fingers glide down his abs, slowly sliding to his waistband, where I make little circles on his flesh.

He moans even louder.

Okay, maybe he does feel things more than me.

When his head drops back down, lust engorges his pupils. His hands slip under my silk robe and over my shoulders. With an expert push, the robe falls to the floor, pooling around my feet.

He runs his palms down my arms, and I exhale a staggering breath. It's so much...*feeling*. All my nerve endings are alive, screaming at me to do much more than simply touch his abs.

He watches me, smiling. He's enjoying my agony.

Two can play this game.

I run my hands back up his chest. His stomach quivers, and his eyes widen with surprise. It's my turn to smile in victory as I slip my hands under his robe and push it off.

But I'm not done. I run my hands down his biceps (hard) to his forearms (manly and muscled).

When I reach his hands, he grabs mine and threads our fingers together.

Electricity shoots through every limb, shattering me. Every time he touches me it feels like I'm being shredded before being pulled back together just as quickly.

We stare at each other for one beat, two.

And that's when I can't take it anymore.

My hands circle his neck as his mouth drops onto mine. His lips are hot and soft as his mouth opens and his tongue sweeps inside. He tastes like whiskey.

My hands are in his hair. It's as silky as I knew it would be, even silkier as I twist the locks around my fingers—*hard*. He inhales with surprise, pulling back to watch me briefly before claiming my mouth again.

My tongue lunges deep, and he moans into me. I want more. I want all of him, and I want him now.

He wants me, too.

His hands tuck under my rear end and he lifts me, but this damn nightgown's so long that it doesn't have give, so I hike it up around my hips.

I don't care that I might have my granny panties on. I don't care if he sees them. All I want is Feylin. Right now he's everything, and I can't get enough.

He lifts me and I hook my legs around his waist. I'm pressed against his hard-on, and a pool of moisture soaks me between my legs.

He's walking us somewhere. I don't care where. My body's on fire, and only he can make it stop. Objects clatter to the floor, and he settles me gently atop his desk—I think.

There's no time to look.

His mouth leaves mine (no!) and grazes down my neck. "Addison." My name sounds sacred as it drips from his lips. "You are driving me out of my mind."

"The feeling's mutual."

He chuckles low, hot. "I think we're talking about two different things. I don't mean right now."

I close my eyes, savoring the feel of his mouth on my throat. "I don't even like you," I whisper.

"You get under my skin so much."

"Like no one I know."

"Plus, you puke a lot."

I pull him back to me, kissing him deeply. His tongue probes hard, and I open myself for all of it. His hands slip up my waist, and his thumbs graze my nipples, making my spine spasm.

The fire that's between us is an inferno. The only way to stop it is to quench it.

I tighten my legs and pull him so close that I can feel his length even with the flimsy clothing between us.

Feylin. Is. Huge. And I want him. There's no time to question my actions, no time to think about the fact that I hated him a moment ago, and yesterday, and will probably hate him tomorrow.

My fingers slip down his abs and curl into his waistband. All I have to do is get those suckers off and—

A crash erupts from the hallway. We each jump back and stare at one another.

Feylin's chest is heaving. Mine is, too. My heart's racing as I stare into his eyes. He blinks as if surfacing from a spell.

That's how I feel, too. My cheeks are on fire. I'm going to pretend it's from shame and not passion, because this is wrong. *All* wrong. Flirting with Feylin earlier was one thing, but this isn't real. Our relationship is fake, and I need to remember that. Because whenever I get involved with someone, it all winds up crashing and burning to the ground.

Just like the tree did today.

He rips his gaze from mine and rubs a hand up the back of his head. When he glances at me again, his jaw tightens. Mine does, too. The veil that had cloaked our anger is gone, and our true selves have returned.

I slide off the desk, barely noticing the mess of pens and papers strewn across the floor. He doesn't say a word as I grab my robe from the rug.

Relief washes over me as I head out the door. This is the right thing. Whatever that sound was, it saved me from making a terrible mistake. I pass a stack of books that had been sitting on a table but are now scattered on the floor. That's what made the crash.

I glance around, but everything's still. If we were both in the office, what could have caused the books to fall?

19

The next morning every inch of my body's stiff. I stretch my arms and groan at the twinge of pain that shoots up my neck from the kink knotting it up.

"And how are you this morning?" Elmore asks from his spot on the table.

He flashes his shit-eating grin before pumping his brows as if he knows what happened last night.

Which he does not.

"Feeling like I want to leave."

I blink and push the dresses off me. After hobbling up to my feet, I start putting them away.

Elmore rubs his chin with a flourish, which is how he does everything. "But you're living in all this luxury. It's a shame you can't sleep on the bed, however."

"Yeah, a shame," I mutter.

His eyes sparkle with mischief. "Where'd you go last night? You came back angry, kicked some clothes."

Flashbacks from my office encounter with Feylin flare bright and hot in my head. Just thinking about his electric touches sends a pulse of pressure between my legs.

I hate him so much.

"I went to look for milk but couldn't find the kitchen. Nothing important happened."

Besides, nothing *can* happen. I'm obviously rebounding from Edward. I'm sad and needy, and the joining magic's screwing with my head. So what if Feylin was nice earlier in the day? It's all an act, I remind myself. Our entire relationship's fake, and I need to remember that. It's not genuine because nothing genuine ever happens to me.

It's like my aunt Ovie's relationship with Charlie. It's not real, but she won't admit that to herself. At least one of us has accepted reality.

"It's going to be a hard day," Elmore reminds me.

"I know. I'm about to get ready."

I grab the black funeral dress my family left for me, along with a dozen other dresses they dropped off yesterday when they came to the debunked ceremony. I'd rather wear the nice clothes in the wardrobe, but witch funeral and engagement protocols demand certain garment styles must be worn at certain times.

Once I'm in the bathroom, I peel off the satin nightgown while hot water steams up the room.

This is what I need—a hot shower will make everything better.

I've just rinsed the shampoo from my hair for the second time when a familiar tug yanks me by the stomach. My brain barely has time to register what's happening before the bathroom melts away and I'm spit out of the darkness.

Water sluices down my head, my face, stinging my eyes. I blink it away and look up. Feylin's right in front of me, his eyes closed, head down. His arm extends over my head, resting against gray tile.

Tile that's different from the ones in my bathroom.

My throat shrivels to the size of a walnut. I'm in *his* bathroom. I'm in Feylin's bathroom while he's taking a shower and—

I'm naked.

He's naked.

I'm about to say something when his eyes pop open. He spots me and winces but still keeps his hand pinned to the wall.

"What are you—why are you in my shower?" he says, sounding more shocked than angry.

This entire situation's so maddening that I screech, "What do you think I'm doing here? You pulled me in! You moved too far away."

His blue eyes shine with surprise before a lightbulb of realization sparks in his eyes. He knows I'm naked.

Very naked.

"If you wanted to apologize," he says in a husky voice that makes my mouth dry, "I'm sorry would've sufficed."

"I already said I'm sorry!"

It would be just like his arrogant royal highness to make a joke while I'm humiliated.

His eyes glaze as they trail to my breasts and down my hips to my—

I clamp an arm over my breasts and a hand over my pelvis. His arm still extends over my head, and he slowly pushes off the tile, taking a step back as if willing me to get a good look.

Well, it's only fair, isn't it?

The water blurs my vision, but my gaze flicks over his chest, his abdomen and down, down, down…

I shut my eyes as soon as I spot his massive hard-on.

"Send me back," I scream. "Send me back. You did this on purpose!"

The water turns off, and a second later a towel's draped over my shoulders. I open my eyes a slit, and Feylin's got a towel cinched tightly around his waist.

I'm not sure if I'm relieved or disappointed.

He smiles gently. Last night's anger seems to have melted off him. When he turns away, I tuck the towel under my arms, drinking in the sight of his muscled back and shoulders.

Water drips from the hair curling under his ears, splashing onto his neck.

"You decent?" he asks, turning slightly toward me. That one rogue curl dips onto his forehead again, and the urge to brush it away makes me flex my fingers to give them something else to do.

"I'm decent."

He grabs a hand towel and scrubs it back and forth over his hair to dry it. "I'm sorry. It's my fault you're in here."

"I know," I reply stiffly.

He cocks his head as if trying to decide if I'm angry or not. After a moment he drops the hand towel on the counter. "Walk with me into my room and I'll return you."

I scowl so hard I'm surprised his hair doesn't go up in flames. "Why should I?"

"So that I don't send you into the middle of the servant's quarters," he says dryly.

Good point.

I pad behind him quietly and do my best not to gawk at his bedroom. It's decked out in green and gold, with dark cherry furniture. Everything's placed meticulously. There's no clutter, and there's definitely not a mess of dresses on his floor.

But even for how neat it is, there aren't the personal touches that my family's house has—pictures everywhere, horribly painted ceramic animals that we created as kids dotting the surfaces.

It's like Feylin doesn't want to have a deeper life, as if taking care of his people steals so much of his time that who he is inside doesn't matter.

What could have happened in his past to make him shield

himself like this? And is that why he was so cold when we first met? Not that he's warmed up much, but at least he smiled yesterday. And laughed. I couldn't forget the rich sound if I tried.

As if the answer will jump in front of me, my gaze sweeps up the walls where a white-tailed deer and elk head are mounted.

"Did you kill that elk?"

His gaze follows mine. "Yes, and I'm going to try not to be impressed that you knew it was an elk."

"My dad hunts, too. But I thought falconing was your favorite sport?"

He smirks and folds his arms. "They both involve hunting, and I like hunting. Ready?"

His hand twitches as if he's wondering whether or not to offer it. In the end he leaves it by his side and nods.

"I'll see you downstairs."

Darkness envelopes me, and a moment later I'm dumped into my room with the towel still tucked tightly under my arms. It takes a moment before I realize that on both the trip to his shower and back, I didn't puke.

Not once.

20

FEYLIN

*W*hy the hell can't I stop thinking about her?

This isn't real. It's what I've been telling myself ever since last night.

This relationship is not real, and it won't ever be. If Addison knew the truth about me, she'd hate me.

And maybe that's better.

But for the love of fae, would someone please tell my cock that?

Trawick drops with a huff into the chair across from my desk. "What happened yesterday?"

I rub my eyes and lean back in my own chair. "Which part of yesterday?"

The part where I wanted to rip Addison's panties off and take her on my desk, or the part where I flirted with her shamelessly?

What the hell has gotten into me?

"The part where your fiancée sabotaged the earth ceremony."

Oh, right. *That.* That was the part that led up to the near-panty ripping.

Though to be fair my first intention had been to spank her, because I was convinced she'd screwed me over on purpose.

But if she's a liar, that woman's a damn good one.

No. Addison's no liar.

"Did she ruin the earth ceremony?" I say lightly. "I didn't notice."

Trawick scowls and plucks a nut from a bowl in his lap, tossing it into his mouth. "I was barely able to convince some of the other fae that it was an accident. Feylin, what the hell happened?"

I lift my palms in a surrender gesture. "I don't know. She swears that she doesn't know, either."

"Do you believe her?"

"Yes."

He watches me, his gold eyes narrowing. With a heavy sigh, he brushes nut crumbs from his hands. "Would you like to explain *why* you believe her? Because from where I'm sitting, that family of hers put her up to it. They're trying to strike before you have the chance."

I motion for a nut and Trawick tosses one into my hand, which I pop into my mouth. "I asked her, and she said that she didn't do anything."

And then I grabbed her by the ass and lifted her onto my desk. I would've done a hell of a lot more than that if Ryals hadn't accidentally knocked over those books.

I must've been out of my mind to leave the door open for him to see us.

I *was* out of my mind—with rage and lust.

My cock stiffens as images from last night barrel into my head. Addison moaning into my mouth, how she shivered under my touch. How her nipples hardened when I stroked them.

I need a cold shower.

Good luck there—she'll probably wind up in it naked

again. And what a glorious sight that was. Her breasts with those hard pink nipples are perfect for cupping, and that stomach and waist—I was ready to worship them both, along with what lay between her legs.

I curl my hands into fists. Why can't I get her out of my head?

And for that matter, how did she wind up in my shower in the first place? She'd obviously been in her own bathroom, while I was under the water remembering how she tasted and dealing with my own hard-on.

Wait. Maybe it's not just distance that pulls her to me. Maybe there's more to it. Maybe my desire played a part. Hm.

Trawick eyes me suspiciously. "I told you this was trouble."

"It's not trouble," I argue.

"Feylin, there are whispers that your relationship is doomed, just like…"

"Just like what, Trawick?" I growl. His jaw jumps, but he won't get off that easily. "Say it."

He averts his gaze. "Just like Tess," he murmurs. "Do I have to remind you what happened?"

"No," I snap. "You don't. Believe me, no one could remember more than I."

"And you're walking right into their trap. She destroyed the ceremony," he repeats for emphasis.

I slam my hand down. "For the last time, she didn't! She doesn't know anything about me. About Tess. I know that for a fact, and before you question how, when her family introduced us and told her who I was, do you know what she said?" I laugh because it's so ridiculously sweet and quintessentially Addison. "She said, you don't look fae." I scoff. "They haven't told her, and for how much that's lacking in judgment, they believe that they're doing her a favor by not revealing the truth. They realized that it doesn't help her if they tell."

He shoots me a hard, skeptical look. "How does it *not* help her?"

"Where can she go that I won't be? Nowhere. We're stuck with one another. Besides, I promised her father that no harm would come to her."

"Physically," he snips.

I exhale a gusty sigh. "With my promise of protection, that sealed their decision. Believe me, I've played this over in my head. She knows nothing about me and how I'm connected to her family."

If anything proved that to me, it was last night. She seemed truly sorry for what had happened.

So here I am taking up for her, taking up for the one woman who's not supposed to have an effect on me. She's not supposed to get under my skin, but everything about her is clinging to me anyway. The way she smells, the way she moves. Watching her is like looking at an angel come to earth.

That proves it—I've lost my mind.

"The magic's getting to you," my friend whispers.

I inhale sharply. He's right. It's impossible to separate the magic from what's real. What *is* real?

Her showing up in my shower taking a good look at my cock was *very real.*

Which reminds me. I need to speak with Ophelia. Whether I pulled Addison into the shower with my desire, or whether it had more to do with distance, it doesn't matter. It can't happen again.

"The magic's *not* having an effect on me," I tell him lamely.

He snorts. "Of course it is. The ceremony gets ruined, and you're taking up for the one person who caused it, and everyone knows that. It obviously wasn't your magic that made the tree burn to the ground." He sighs. "Feylin, I say this as your oldest friend—don't forget what you want. Don't forget what was taken from you, and how you've dreamed of this opportunity."

My chest constricts. He's right. I've bided my time for too long to simply believe in coincidence. Addison is a stepping stone.

What we have is forced by magic.

But that's hard to remember when she's smiling at me, or when she pushed that curl off my forehead. Her every touch makes my skin sizzle. It ignites me from inside.

I exhale a gusty sigh.

It's not real. It's not real. This will end. It has to. It's supposed to.

No one—especially not her parents, would allow anything to come of us anyway.

"Have you contacted the council?" Trawick asks.

"I thought you were going to do that," I complain.

"I was bluffing. Giving you a chance to see if you'd do it. Well?"

He's eyeing me with suspicion. I wave my hand. "Clearly I've been preoccupied."

He snorts. "I'll do it for you, then. You need to get this moving if you want the bookshop shut down *before* you end the relationship." He gives me a hard look. "*If* you're going to end it."

What he doesn't say, and what he doesn't have to, is—*like you said that you would.*

"You made a promise to yourself. Think of Tess."

My words growl out. "I am thinking of Tess."

My chest tightens so hard it feels like a hand's squeezing every drop of life from my heart. What I'm doing, I'm doing because it's supposed to be done. Because it *has* to be done.

The last time I loved and lost, it nearly killed me. I'm not going through that again.

I'm not.

This, whatever this is between me and Addison, it's only magic. There's nothing else to it.

And I'll do well to remember that.

I rise. "I hate to cut our meeting short."

Trawick rises. "You have to go. And as a reminder, the water ceremony's soon."

"Things'll go better. Addison's burying her grandmother today. Whatever happened with earth, I'm sure it was because of the stress."

"Make sure she's ready. You can't risk another failure."

"She'll be ready." I gesture to the door. "Now if you'll excuse me, I have a funeral to get to."

21

It's a half-mile walk to the cemetery. I'm reminded of this because the shoes I've chosen to wear are pinching my heels so hard I'm sure to have wet blisters by the time we're done.

Nana's back and is lying in the same bed as she was when I first arrived. All my sisters are here, and Feylin stands beside me. We haven't said much to each other, but he also hasn't been an arrogant jerk, which I appreciate.

My mother takes a silver-encrusted amethyst pendant from a box and approaches my grandmother. "She will walk."

"She will walk," we repeat.

She drapes the necklace over Nana's head, and my grandmother's eyes pop open. She sits up stiffer than Bela Lugosi rising from his vampire coffin, and takes my mother's hand as she slides off the bed and onto the rug.

Her eyes are open, but they're vacant as she shuffles slowly toward the front door, which is wide open for her—for this walk.

She wears a gorgeous peacock-blue caftan and black flats. Even in death, Nana's got serious *drip*. Go, Nana.

Feylin stands beside me quietly as we follow her out the door.

Once we get outside, the sidewalk's packed. People are bunched together tighter than race cars rounding the last turn of the speedway. All of Castleview's waiting to escort my grandmother to her final resting place.

My father and mother walk behind Nana, with Ovie and Charlie beside them. Feylin and I follow with the rest of my sisters behind me.

The porch vine dips, and a blossom kisses my face as I walk down the steps. Feylin glances over, a brow lifted in question, but I just shrug.

No, we haven't talked about *the shower incident.* That's what I'm calling it. What's there to talk about? He saw me naked. I saw him *very* naked. Nothing more to say.

My cheeks flush just thinking about it.

The going's slow as we make our way through Castleview proper. Nana leads the charge. When you're dead and walking, you can't expect it to be fast.

We make our way past the shops in town to the cemetery on the outskirts. Nana knows where to go. She stops at an open plot, and my mother steps up beside her.

Nana opens her mouth wider. For a split second, recognition flashes in her eyes as she takes all of us in. Her gaze lands on me, and a chill washes down my spine.

She lifts her arms. "To you I shall pass it all."

Magic erupts from her chest, screaming out into the crowd as a great gale blows our hair and ruffles our clothes.

A blue halo buoys around my grandmother. It pulses once, a small thing, a fraction of what our power should be.

That's why we're getting married, isn't it? So that the blue halo can be bigger?

The magic slowly dissolves and fades. The spark in Nana's eyes dims as she lies down in her casket. My mother takes the necklace from her, and a wizard priest begins the ceremony.

"DID YOU SEE THE MAGIC?" Blair asks me later.

We're back at the house. While we were attending the funeral, a magical caterer was dropping off casseroles big enough to feed that giant statue of Paul Bunyan out in Oregon.

Anyway, I'm sitting on a bench beside Blair while nibbling a dish that I think has chicken, green beans and fried onions on top.

I really hope those are fried onions.

"What're you eating?" she asks.

"I have no idea, but it's not half-bad."

She chuckles as Chelsea sits down in a flurry of black lace and ruffles. "Thank goodness y'all are here. Please save me. There's a sixteen-year-old trying to get my number."

Blair's jaw drops. "At a funeral?"

"We do need to marry," I say, nudging her shoulder with mine.

Chelsea picks up a chicken finger from her plate and takes a bite. "He's a distant cousin, which means he figures he's entitled to be totally tacky."

I bite back a laugh as Ovie slides by, Charlie behind her. He grabs her sleeve and she turns. Then my uncle gives her his blue-eyed puppy-dog look and whispers something in her ear.

Blair kicks my leg, and I roll my eyes. We've seen this way too many times before.

Ovie sighs in annoyance, but then Charlie keeps whispering and she smiles and nods. She takes her purse off her shoulder, digs into it and hands him a wad of cash.

He kisses her cheek and turns to walk away but spots us.

His gaze zeroes in on me, and my skin feels like it just got coated in slime.

"Addie, I haven't seen you since I've been home. I hear you're engaged. Where's the lucky fellow?"

Charlie's a handsome man, there's no question. But he's the sort of handsome that knows he's handsome. He's got a dusting of gray in his short-clipped hair that gives him a distinguished, TV-commercial look. He's buff, built.

And a total loser.

"What's his name again?" he asks.

"Feylin," Blair says loudly. "He's a *king*."

Charlie blinks. "Wow. A king." Then he rubs his chin as if he's trying to plot how to steal the gold dishes from the castle. Which would be on point for my uncle. "You don't say."

Feylin's leaning against a wall while picking at his plate. He's successfully casting his broody Henry Cavill *Witcher* vibe throughout the living room.

"I'd like to meet him," Charlie says to my horror, because no doubt my uncle'll ask to borrow money. "Where'd you say he was?"

He turns, scanning the crowd. Before Charlie can accost Feylin, I jump up. "You can't meet him."

My uncle balks. "What?"

"You can't meet him because...he hasn't met all my sisters yet."

Not a lie. Feylin hasn't met all of them because they were too taken with the hammocks yesterday to drag themselves away before the dinner started. And since I'm supposed to be head over heels in love, they should be introduced, right? If this also happens to shove my uncle a little bit out the door—oops!

I cross to Feylin, pushing my mouth up into a smile and swallowing a huge knot in my throat. We did this whole fake-love thing effortlessly yesterday, but a lot's happened in between. I'm not sure how enthusiastic he'll be about going along with it today.

His gaze flits up as I approach. He appraises me with a hard look, which suggests that this morning's shower did little to cool his mood. Yet the steel in his eyes looks more like a smolder, which makes him resemble a god and has me forgetting my own name.

I'm just kidding.

My name's Blair.

I push up on my tiptoes and whisper in his ear, "I need you to be my cover."

He doesn't say a word as I drag him over to Blair and Chelsea, practically shoving Charlie out of the way with my elbow.

"Blair, you met Feylin yesterday."

"How do you do?" she asks.

He smiles. "Good to see you again."

All right. This is going well. I plant myself between Charlie and Chelsea and gesture to my sister. "This is Chelsea."

She extends her hand and grins. "There are a lot of us, so I'm going to make this easier on you. You can call me Charming Chelsea, and you can call her"—she cocks her head to Blair—"Bossy Blair."

Feylin's eyes dance with amusement. "Ah, alliteration."

"Yes." I roll the back of my tongue in annoyance. It kind of sounds like a purr, or like I'm trying to hack up a furball, but it works. "Since there are seven of us, it makes it easier for folks to keep us straight. Ah, here comes Fiery Finn."

My redheaded sister glances over, sees me pointing to her and drags Emory with her. "It's *the* Feylin! I need to meet you."

I gesture grandly to him. "Meet *the* Feylin."

Finn extends her hand, and he takes it (for that matter, it's the same way he took Chelsea's hand) with the backside facing the ceiling.

She pulls it to her as he gentle releases his grasp. "It's a pleasure to meet you."

Feylin smiles genuinely. "Fiery Finn."

"It's easy to remember because of the hair." She points to it. "And this is Empathic Emory."

Emory swings her blonde hair off her shoulder. "Don't worry. I don't touch you and know what you're feeling."

He lifts a brow. "You know how people feel?"

She cocks her head as if trying to decide if he's genuine. "That's why they call me Empathic Emory. Chelsea works with charms, Finn is just fiery. Oh, here comes Dallas and Georgie."

Dallas's eyes become big as plates. "Oh, I haven't met Feylin."

There's a crowd of women surrounding him now, but he's taking it all in stride. He's probably used to women hanging all over him.

It occurs to me as they talk that Feylin's never mentioned his family. His parents are both dead, so is he all alone? There weren't any pictures in his bedroom, and there aren't any in the castle, for that matter.

Yeah, it strikes me that Feylin doesn't have any family.

"Meet Daring Dallas," I say, "and Glowing Georgia. Georgia's a healer, and Dallas is simply daring. Give her a motorcycle and she'll go all Evil Knievel on you in no time."

He laughs and then introduces himself. I take the opportunity to glance over my shoulder to see if Charlie's still skulking about, but he's gone. A wave of relief washes over me. Charlie shmoozing with Feylin at a funeral would've been almost as humiliating as Edward hitting on Blair the day after we broke up.

Thinking of Edward makes my throat shrink, but the feeling's quickly replaced when Feylin turns to me. "I'm ready to be tested. I think I've got it all down."

I quirk a brow. "Are you sure? There are seven of us."

He rubs his hands together. "I've got this. Blair's easy to remember because we met yesterday. You're Charming Chelsea, then there's Daring Dallas and Empathic Emory." He points to each of them in turn, and my sisters nod when he guesses their names correctly. "Fiery Finn and lastly Glowing Georgia."

"You did it," I say, clapping. A little happiness in this somber living room takes the edge off our loss.

Feylin gives a slight bow. "But how old are you? You look nearly the same age."

"Georgia's twenty-three at the youngest. I'm twenty-nine." At the confused look on his face I explain, "Witches have a shorter gestation period, and my mom wanted a big family."

"Right away," Blair adds, her voice tense.

This whole time she's been eyeing Feylin with worry. For me, I'm sure. Of course she's worried that I'm rushing into things, which I am.

"Fae have long gestation periods," he explains. "Nearly a year and a half."

"Why?" I ask.

"No clue. Maybe it's because of our magic."

"May I steal Addie for a moment?" my mother asks, cutting in.

I excuse myself and she walks me to a corner of the living room. "Looks like y'all are getting along good."

"I introduced him to all the sisters. They were too busy exploring hammocks yesterday to be bothered with meeting him."

My mother clasps her hands in front of her. "How are you? Yesterday was—"

"A total cluster." I drag my teeth over my bottom lip. "I'm worried about the other ceremonies."

"I know." She tips her face toward me, and her lily-scented perfume cloaks the air. "What did he say?"

"He thought I did it on purpose, but I convinced him I didn't."

Her eyes flare with worry. "Was he mean? Are you okay?"

"Mean? No." My gaze flicks to him. He's still with my sisters, nodding and listening attentively while they jabber on. I zero in on his strong hands and clearly recall how they made fire dance on my skin. "He wasn't mean. We worked it out."

"Just be careful."

"You say that like there's a reason to be."

"Not at all." She watches him for a moment before directing her next sentence to me. "Addison, you'll have to come to the bookshop. You'll need to take your rightful place."

"Mama—"

"No buts." Her eyes harden. "You will be there. This is your birthright."

"How can I even show myself when I can't help any of the customers?"

"You can. You always pick the right read."

"But I can't drop anyone into a book. I'm useless."

"You're not useless." She brings her finger up between us for emphasis. "You are not useless."

"YOUR SISTER'S NICKNAMES SUIT THEM," Feylin says.

They're the first real words he's said to me all day, and it's nighttime. We're walking back to the castle. I didn't want to travel by magic, and he didn't ask, which I appreciated.

"They do suit them," I agree quietly. "Thanks for letting me introduce you, for letting me interrupt your"—I make a circle with my hand—"whatever it was I interrupted."

He kicks a pebble. "You didn't interrupt anything. I was

watching your family and the others mourn your grand-mother. She was much loved."

"She was."

Is he going to bring up the shower? I sure as hell am not. If he does, then we'll have to discuss it, and there's nothing to discuss.

An uneasy silence falls over us before he asks, "I didn't catch your nickname."

"Oh." I chuckle nervously. "They call me Affable Addie. That's the A nickname. But Blair calls me Optimistic Addie."

"It fits you better—optimistic."

"You don't even know me."

"Anyone who'd agree to be my fake fiancée has to be opti-mistic," he replies, his voice slightly teasing.

I don't stop the smile that spreads across my face.

We walk in silence the rest of the way until we're inside, where he gives me a quick "Good night," and walks away. It's abrupt, but that's all right. We're nothing to each other, so I can't expect lingering moments before we part ways.

I start to head up the stairs when Ophelia stops me. "Miss Thornrose, your room's been moved."

I halt and turn around. "Moved?"

"His Majesty moved it."

"To where?"

She leads me in the direction that Feylin disappeared, down a long hallway. She stops at an ornately carved door and grins.

"Here."

She opens the door to a room that's more lush than the last one. Golden sconces adorn the walls, throwing light onto the thick white bedspread accented with pink pillows. There's also an overstuffed chair with a white fur throw atop it, a fire-place crackling with a cheerful fire, a desk, a vanity topped with lotions and creams, and a sparkling chandelier that's so wide I wonder if I could swing from it.

This room is way too nice.

"This is my room? You must be wrong."

Ophelia shakes her head as she opens the wardrobe to show me new clothes. "His Majesty picked it out himself. He wants you near him."

My jaw drops. "Near him?"

She jerks her head toward the door. "His room is just across the hall."

Before I can utter another word, she leaves. I run my fingers over the wooden surfaces. All the furniture is carved. It's beautiful.

When I reach the desk, I stop. A cream-colored envelope sits atop it. I dig my thumb beneath the seal and pull out a small note written on cardstock. The handwriting is confident, the words written quickly but legibly.

So that you don't have to sleep on the floor.

Feylin didn't sign it. He didn't have to because I know who wrote it.

He knew, or at least after the shower this morning, he'd puzzled it out. He switched my room so that I don't have to sleep on a pile of dresses, and so that I won't be flung into his morning shower.

For someone who gets under my skin so badly, in this moment all I can process is how grateful I am.

And how, for the first time in two nights, I can finally sleep on a bed.

22

---

*E*ven with a luxurious pillow-topped mattress cradling my back and a down-stuffed duvet pulled up to my ears, I'm still wide awake.

After slipping into a robe, I pad from the bedroom with every intention of finding the kitchen for real this time. My gaze falls on Feylin's door for a long moment before I force myself to look away and head into the bowels of the castle.

The halls are silent, my slapping feet the only sound against the marble-tiled floors. Pools of light unspool from the moon and splash atop the cold stone. Everything's in shades of gray and white—beautiful but cold.

A chill sweeps down my spine as the feeling of being watched overcomes me.

My mouth twitches into a smile. Is it Feylin, following me? No, no. Certainly he wouldn't drop me in the room across from his so that he could spy?

Or maybe he did.

The quiet sound of shuffling fills my ears. Yes, someone's definitely following. That sneaky fae. He probably smelled me get up or heard me open the door and just had to know what I was doing.

How annoying.

Well, two can play at this game.

A big potted plant hugs the wall. Quick as a wink I'm behind it, ready to pounce. But the castle's too dark, and the palm leaves are so big that I can't see whoever's approaching, and if I move the fronds, he'll hear. So I have to wait.

When the footsteps are only inches away, I jump out, totally expecting to surprise Feylin.

But it's not him.

It's a kid. He's maybe about ten or so and wears dark pajamas with white piping. His eyes flare wide as he leaps back in fear.

"Ah," he gasps.

"I'm so sorry." I reach for him. "I didn't mean to scare you. I'm sorry," I repeat.

He clutches his chest, panting for a moment before cocking an eye and appraising me with what can only be described as deeply etched cynicism.

"You're her," the boy accuses in a voice rimmed with tiny authority.

It takes all my will not to laugh at how he's so insulted by my mere presence. "I'm *her*?"

"The woman Feylin's not going to marry."

I almost ignore the strange pang that erupts in my stomach when he says that. Pushing any and all irrelevant feelings aside, I bend at the waist and place my hands on my thighs so that we're eye level. "I'm Addison. How do you do?"

He takes the hand I offer. "Very well, thank you." He tilts his head back and forth before adding. "You're not ugly."

I bite back a chuckle. "Did Feylin say I was?"

"No. But I suspected he was lying."

"Did you, now?"

"Oh, I did," he tells me, incredulous. "I also suspected that you're mean, but you don't look mean."

"How do mean people look?"

He shrugs. "I don't know. They frown a lot. Yeah, and they don't eat sweets."

"That does sound like a mean person."

"That's what I think, too."

"May I ask who you are?"

He puffs out his chest. "I'm Ryals. Feylin's cousin."

"Cousin?" I quirk a brow. "I didn't know Feylin had a cousin who lives here."

"That's because he doesn't want me getting attached to you." He drops his voice and places a hand to one side of his mouth and whispers, "Because of the whole fake-engagement thing."

"Ah. Well, he's right to tell you not to get attached."

He taps his foot as a serious look spreads across his face. It's the most adorable expression ever. "Hey, do you play chess?"

"Chess?"

He nods enthusiastically. "I can't sleep, and when I can't sleep, I play. Want to come?"

"Now? It's late. You should be in bed."

"I should be, but I'm not. Same as you."

Huh. He has some wicked logic. "You've got a point. Lead the way."

He glances over his shoulder every once in a while as he talks. "I usually wake up Feylin when I can't sleep, but since I ran into you, you and I can play."

I skirt around a steel knight holding an ax. "And does he play with you?"

"Usually." Feylin gets up in the middle of the night to play chess? First he moves my room, and now I learn that he sacrifices sleep for his young cousin. My original opinion of him as an arrogant fae is slowly burning to ash. "I looked for him last night, but…"

He doesn't finish and he doesn't have to. Shame warms my cheeks. "You ran into the books and knocked them over?"

"I wasn't looking where I was going. Some weird noises came from Feylin's office and they scared me."

Please don't let him say they sounded like rutting animals. "I'm sure it was nothing."

"Yeah, Feylin said he had a stomachache."

"Something of his certainly ached," I mutter.

"Here we are." Ryals opens a door and flips on a light. This room is a child's dream. A tent that looks like it's covered in spun gold sits in the middle of the floor, surrounded by toys— old ones like Etch A Sketches and new electronics.

Ryals climbs onto a chair and nods to a chess board in front of him. When I step toward the doorway, my toe hits an invisible barrier.

"I can't come in."

He frowns, and for the first time I notice his silvery eyes. The hue matches the flecks in Feylin's. "Why not?"

"Because I can't be too far away from your cousin. There's magic tying us together."

"Okay." He gets off the chair, takes the pieces off the board and stores them in a box and then he hauls the board and box over. He settles both on the floor between us and lowers himself into a sitting position.

I mimic him and sit cross-legged on a thickly padded rug as he pulls the pieces from the box. Up close, they shine under the light and look like they're made of polished marble.

"I always play black," he tells me as he carefully settles each piece on its square. "Is that okay?"

"Sure. That's fine." We silently make opening moves, neither of us talking until I ask, "Are your parents here, too?" *Are there any more relatives hiding in the woodwork?*

He shakes his head. "No, they're gone."

Even though he keeps his gaze firmly secured to the board, there's no missing the sadness filling his eyes. "I'm sorry."

Ryals hitches a shoulder to his ear. "It's okay. It's why I can't sleep. Sometimes I dream about them."

He's quiet after that, and I'm not sure if I should ask, but my conscience tells me it's okay. "What do you dream?"

His brow narrows and the weight of the world seems to settle on this young boy's shoulders as he replies, "I dream that there's food to eat, and that they get up out of bed."

My gods. I don't expect him to say that. I barely croak out, "I'm sorry that they passed away."

He shakes his head. "They're not dead. They take pills and then they go to sleep."

My entire body sags as I realize his parents are druggies. That's why there wasn't any food in the house. They spent it all on getting high.

I plaster on a wide smile. "Well, Ryals, there's plenty to eat here in the castle. I'm sure Feylin feeds you very well."

He nods. "I'm glad that I'm here." Then he glances up at me. "I think I'm going to like you."

Tears just about spill from my eyes. "I think I'm going to like you, too."

"But we can't tell Feylin we met," he whispers. "We're not supposed to."

I mimic locking my lips and throwing away the key. "I won't tell if you won't."

"I won't." A moment later he grins. "Your knight's mine."

And so it is. "You're sneaky."

"That's how you play chess."

I lean back on my hands. "If I'm going to have any chance of winning, I'd better start paying attention."

He captures my pawn with his rook. "Yep. Looks like you're gonna need some tutoring."

23

"*A*re you ready, Miss Thornrose?"

Ophelia pins the last of my hair in place and smiles at me in the mirror. I force my lips to tip up. "As ready as I'll ever be."

"It's going to be a lovely water ceremony."

My stomach plummets just hearing her say the words *water* and *ceremony* in the same sentence.

It's been a week since my grandmother's funeral, and since then Ryals and I have played chess four times and I've only seen Feylin once.

Yes, once.

For us being tied together, he's done a miraculous job of avoiding my presence, even with the addition of us sleeping across the hall from one another.

I rise from the vanity as Ophelia turns to leave the room. "Wait."

She pivots around quickly. "Is something wrong? Do you not like your hair?"

"I love my hair. It's beautiful. It's just, I'm wondering. What are the fae saying about last week's ceremony?"

Her gaze drops to the floor. "They'd never seen anything like it."

My shoulders drop. "That bad, huh?"

"Even if that's what they think, no one can forget how special a joining is." Her eyes shimmer with happiness. "It means the relationship is blessed."

I frown, confused. "How so?"

She drags her teeth across her bottom lip. "The joining is supposed to be a sign of true love."

I nearly bark a laugh. True love? She's got to be kidding. Feylin's not my true love, and I'm not his. The truest thing we are to one another is business partners.

"But I thought the joining was created to bond those in arranged marriages."

"It was." She crosses to my bed and fluffs the pillows one by one, frowning as she thinks. "But it's also said, and believed by many, that a true joining like yours goes much deeper. That's why all of us felt it when His Majesty joined with you."

My heart throbs. True love? Me and Feylin? Impossible. Most of the time I can't stand him, and the other half I want to rip his clothes off.

Pretty sure that's not the making of true love.

If she notices me pausing, she doesn't comment on it. Instead Ophelia sighs heavily. "Miss Thornrose, it's been a long time since we've had a queen. We're all just happy that His Majesty is happy."

But he's not. "And what about you? Are you happy?"

Her gaze darts around the room like she wants to dash under the bed. I'm getting way too personal, but I see her every day. It's rude not to ask Ophelia about herself.

"Let me say this—we always knew the veil would fail at some point. It wasn't a matter of if, but when. A lot of us worried about the humans and what they'd do to us, but His Majesty has kept us safe. *All* of us. I have a young daughter."

My jaw drops. "What?"

She tucks a strand of chestnut hair behind one of her delicately pointed ears. "She's five, and all I want is to keep her safe, and that's what King Feylin has done." She gives me an encouraging smile. "This ceremony will be wonderful."

Ophelia gives a small bow and leaves while I still stand, jaw open.

"You didn't expect her to say that, did you?" Elmore appears in the open compact that sits on my dresser. His brow wrinkles in worry. "And who would have thought that fae have feelings, too?"

"Elmore," I scold. "They have feelings."

"I'm not so sure."

"Is that what my mother sent you to do? Talk smack about fae?"

"No, she sent me to keep an eye on you. If there's anything you need, just say it. I also communicate messages from her."

I turn to the vanity and dab powder on my shining nose. "Where is she? I haven't heard from anyone in days."

He grimaces, tugging down the ascot at his throat. Yes, Elmore wears some serious threads. "She's, um, busy."

"With what?"

"I don't know...things... She's wondering when you'll come to the bookshop."

A thousand-pound weight falls on my shoulders. "I can't. You know I won't be any use at that store. There's no reason for me to hurry. Unless there is." My gaze shoots to him, and he's pursed his lips. "Elmore, what's going on?"

He clears his throat, stalling. "It seems that, uh, since your mother gave up her right over the bookshop and it's gone to you, that, well..."

"Spit it out," I demand.

"It seems that it's broken."

"What do you mean, broken?"

"No one can dive into a book."

I sag onto a chair and grip the arms for support. "But then you can't even *have* a bookshop. That's the whole point of it—the magic."

"I know."

My heart flutters against my ribs, and I gulp down several deep breaths. *Get control of yourself.* Ever so slowly, my grip on the chair relaxes. "What do they think has caused it?"

His gaze washes up and down me.

"Oh no. I can't help this problem."

"Well," he says, shooting me a pointed look, "the first thing is that the magic's weaker than your mother ever thought. The second is that the bookshop must have someone from the bloodline attached to it."

"Why haven't they come to me?"

"You've been busy."

"No, I haven't. I've been playing chess and taking short walks. Ugh." I drop my face into my hands. This is all wrong. I can't help the bookshop. "Maybe I can talk her into giving it to Blair."

He flicks his hand in dismissal. "Say what you want, but your mother won't listen."

"Then I'll make her." I head toward the door. "I'll be back."

He waves. "Good luck at the ceremony. I can't wait to hear how it goes."

TURNS OUT, I don't get a chance to make my mother do anything.

People are already filling the lawn by the time I'm outside. Some faces I recognize from the last ceremony, but my family hasn't arrived yet.

"You look gorgeous, same as last time." Zandra, wearing a

red mermaid-style dress that flares at the knees, slinks up to me. She tosses her hair over a bare shoulder and grins. "Ready for today?"

My stomach somersaults. "Of course."

She tugs me toward the champagne. "You don't have to lie. I know you feel terrible about last time."

"You do?"

She tips her face toward mine and lifts a brow. "Of course. Feylin told me."

"I didn't realize y'all talk a lot."

"*Y'all.* You're so Southern. It's adorable." She grabs a flute from a silver tray and hands it to me. "Yes, we talk every once in a while. I called to make sure he was okay. The way people overreacted"—she scoffs—"you'd think it was Feylin's first wedding all over again."

The earth falls out from under me. "First wedding?"

She rips her gaze from where it's latched onto the lawn to look at me. "Yeah, first one. You know about Tess, right?"

Since I'm supposed to be marrying the *king* of my dreams, the only appropriate answer is, "Yes, of course. He's told me all about her."

"You're very different from her." Zandra shakes her head and laughs. "But then again, you're not fae. So of course you're not like her. Between you and me, a witch is a better match for Feylin anyway."

She continues talking, eyeing a wizard in a dark three-piece suit. Zandra says something about seeing what he's up to later, but my mind's spinning.

Feylin was married to a fae named Tess. What happened to her? Did they divorce? *Do* fae divorce?

What a silly question. Of course they do. But why hasn't he mentioned it? Maybe he's got her hidden in a closet all *Jane Eyre* style.

No, even Feylin wouldn't do that.

As Zandra continues to eye the wizard, it's all I can do to keep the world from toppling over. The shock vibrates in my bones. I don't know why. There's no reason for Feylin to tell me important things like he has a cousin in his castle or he was once married.

But for some reason this knowledge stings. I don't know him at all. And as much as I'd like to deny it, the fact that he's kept this from me makes my heart crumble.

"I hope you're taking good care of my fiancée, Zandra."

It's the first time I've heard his voice in days, and the dark, sexy timbre of it—like smoke rolling over rocks—makes my stomach clench. If any man's voice could immediately impregnate a woman, it would be Feylin's.

My mouth dries as I slowly take him in. He's wearing a dark green tweed vest with brass buttons and a tie the same color. He doesn't even bother with a jacket, and he doesn't need one. He slips his hands into his pockets, forcing the white shirt to strain against his powerful biceps. His face is cleanly shaven, and his hair's still damp from the shower.

The shower.

I can't allow my mind to go there.

His wavy hair's combed to one side, but that one curl bobs in front of his forehead.

Zandra bows with a flourish. "Your Majesty. I'll have you know I'm taking excellent care of Addison. I was just telling her about that wizard who I plan to jump on after this."

He smirks, which is obviously intended for her, but his gaze never leaves me. My heart slams against my chest as magic unleashes between us. I'm sucked into Feylin's gravitational pull. Zandra's saying something, but it's all jumbled because only he exists.

He offers his hand. My first instinct is to lunge for it. It's been too long since I've seen him. It feels like my body's been starved of water and now a geyser stands before me, and I'm ready to devour it. I want to press myself against him and drink up every bit.

It takes a steel wall of restraint, but I don't launch myself at him. Yet as soon as my hand slips over his, a tsunami of desire sweeps to my toes. Suddenly I'm back in his office and I want to climb atop that desk and let him do...things to me. Many, many things.

How any couple could resist the physical want created by the joining is beyond me. Every cell in my body thrums to throw Feylin on the grass and rip off his clothes.

I bite it down and nod to Zandra as he excuses us from her presence.

Not wanting the physical temptation to cloud my mind, I pull my hand from his and twine it around his bicep. As he leads me around the garden, we nod to fae who bow in return.

"How've you been?" he asks nonchalantly, keeping his gaze trained straight ahead.

"Fine. Good. Thank you for moving my room."

"I take it you're using the bed."

"Yes."

"You could've told me why you were sleeping on dresses," he murmurs, which sounds more like a purr.

"You were so demanding that it ticked me off."

His jaw jumps. "So you didn't tell me to get back at me."

I stop and we face one another. "I'm not proud of it."

We pause before each of us breaks into a smile. Our gazes collide, and all it takes is one look at him and my heartbeat is thrumming like a traitor in my neck. I rip my gaze away first and clear my throat. "So...are you ready for this?"

"The question is, are you?"

To be honest—*no*. In this ceremony our magic's supposed to conjure four water horses from a fountain. The horses symbolize the steadfastness of our love.

Or something stupid like that.

175

"I'm as ready as I'll ever be."

For the past few days I've worked on standing motionless in front of the fountain. According to Ophelia, you can't practice any of the ceremonies ahead of time, which is annoying.

We wait a little while longer for people to enter the garden. It seems forever before I spot my family and wave.

They wave back, and that's when Feylin says, "It's now or never."

I exhale a deep breath. "Okay."

"Just focus," he explains.

I can do this, I tell myself. Easy peasy. We step before the fountain and everyone, friends and family alike, surround us.

The fountain's the centerpiece of the back garden. Normally water shoots straight from the center, shifting into the colors of the rainbow as it splashes onto the pool underneath. But today the water's been turned off, and sunlight shimmers like diamonds atop the filled pool.

He cups my hand, and I drop my hold on his bicep so that we can entwine our fingers.

"Focus. Concentrate," he tells me.

I stare at the water as Feylin squeezes my hand tight. Magic unfurls from us. Well, *him.* My whole goal is to remain as motionless and empty as possible.

A golden ribbon of power flows into the fountain, and the water begins to bubble. It churns and swirls like my stomach's currently doing.

A form slowly rises from the surface—pointed ears, a muzzle, and a strong, muscled body. Four horses constructed of glistening water surface, each with front hooves lifted and teeth bared.

The crowd explodes into applause, and my heart, so heavy with worry, lightens. *I've done it!*

The motionless horses begin to paw the air as if they're restless. My stomach knots.

"Are they supposed to do that?" I whisper to Feylin.

But before he answers, the four leap off the fountain and scatter in opposite directions, crashing atop tables. Plates and food batter the ground. Porcelain and glass shatter against one another.

"Run," someone screams.

And that's when I know that the horses are not, in fact, supposed to do that.

24

---

*P*eople—witches and fae alike—scatter across the yard. Before there's a chance to say anything to Feylin, he takes a step. Magic whooshes from his body, slamming into one of the water creatures. The horse breaks apart, splashing onto the grass like a waterfall.

There are still three of them left. The creatures rampage over tables, sending people running and screaming for their lives.

I've got to do something. I can't just stand here.

I grab a broken chair and run toward one of the horses. There's a slim chance my shard of wood will do anything against the magical creature, but at least it's something.

The horse lifts its front legs, and a shrill neigh rips from its throat. Beneath it stands a wizard who's shooting magic up at it.

Wait. I know that wizard. It's Devlin.

He's throwing blades of magic that look as sharp as a knife's edge, but they dissolve into the beast, not causing any damage. Why not?

It hits me. The horses were created by Feylin; maybe only he can destroy them.

The creature stomps the ground. Where its hooves land, clumps of grass fly into the air. It's as solid as ice, but only Feylin's magic can touch it.

I whack the beast's flank with my stick, but the wood slices straight through, coming out the other side. I lunge forward, following the swing, and stumble to the ground.

The horse turns to me and rears again, both hooves above my face, ready to stomp out my life. Panic winds around my spine and yanks my heart against my ribs. But before I can blink, the creature explodes into thousands of water droplets that splatter me.

Feylin stands where the creature had just been, a dark look on his face.

Now's not the time to apologize.

He pulls me up, and his gaze flicks to the other horses. There are two left, one of which is barreling across the lawn toward town. Next thing I know, it bursts like a water balloon.

Feylin's shoulders sag, and a shadow falls on his jaw. The magic he's using, it's taking a toll on him. He must've spent a lot of it on the ceremony, and now he's wrung dry.

People are scattering like fire ants rushing to fix a broken ant bed. My family's among them. They're dashing toward the castle, to safety. Feylin runs off, searching for the last creature, who's disappeared in all the chaos.

My heart plummets. This is my fault, every bit of it. How can this possibly be made right? But I'll worry about that later. First—stop horses, then make apologies.

A scream grabs my attention. The last beast charges to my left, head down, nostrils flared. Ryals stands in its path, legs trembling.

Feylin whips around. His face contorts like he's summoning every last drop of magic he's got.

And it's not coming.

The horse's hooves are as strong as steel. Ryals will be trampled if I don't act.

I throw myself toward him, pumping my legs as fast as they'll go. The horse is bearing down, nearly to him. We'll collide. It all plays out in my head. The three of us will meet at the same time.

Unless I do something.

"Ryals," I yell.

He turns toward me, his face twisted in fear, his eyes shining because he knows tragedy's bearing down.

At the last moment I leap, replaying in my mind every movie that involves a secret service agent taking a bullet for the president.

My arms wrap around his shoulders, and we fall to the ground as the horse explodes into a mist that's swept away by the wind.

I sit up on my knees and pull him to me. "Are you okay? Are you all right?"

"Y-yes."

I hold him at arm's length and search his face for any signs of injury. My thumb brushes his freckled cheek. "Are you sure?"

"I'm sure. I promise, Addie. I'm okay."

I hug him again as a dark shadow falls on both of us. I don't have to glance up to know who it is, but eventually I do. Feylin offers his hand to Ryals, and Ryals jumps up and throws his arms around Feylin's waist. The king's head falls, and he closes his eyes tight.

"Addie saved me," the boy tells him. "Did you see what she did? She threw herself at me. It was just like in the movies."

"Yes." He opens his eyes and strokes Ryals's hair. "She saved you."

My legs tremble as I push off the damp grass. Blades stick

to my hands and knees. This dress is ruined. It's okay. Dresses can be replaced. People can't.

As I scan the lawn, my stomach drops like it's been thrown off a cliff. The damage is bad. Fae glare at me. Witches stand in shock. But Feylin doesn't notice any of it. He's still holding Ryals.

There's a knot lodged deep, deep in my throat. I've got to say something, or he'll think I sabotaged the ceremony—*again.* "I'm—"

His eyes shoot to mine, and he gives a slight shake of his head, silently telling me not to say one word. "We need to talk."

My entire body sags with the weight of the inevitable that's coming. "Yes, we do."

25

FEYLIN

*T*he lawn's finally clean after the horses nearly destroyed it. As fae pick up the last shattered plates, a heavy sigh loosens from my chest.

I step back from the office window and roll the tension from my shoulders.

"Feylin?"

Ryals stands in the doorway, pressing the bare toes of his right foot onto the hill of his left.

"Feeling better?"

He nods. "I'm tired. I wanna go to bed."

"Give me a hug."

It's when I wrap my arms around him that a weight clamps down on my chest so hard it threatens to smother me. If Addison hadn't pushed him, Ryals would've been trampled. Sorrow clenches my gut just thinking about it. It's deep, like a bottomless pit. I haven't come close to feeling this powerless since Tess died.

And I *was* powerless today—my magic spent, I barely smashed that last horse. I owe Addison his life.

And I know how to repay it.

"Good night." I ruffle his hair as he pulls away.

Ryals palms it smooth. "I just combed it."

"Well now it looks better."

"Are you joking?"

I wink. "I'm joking. Off to bed."

It's only when I hear his door close that I follow his steps and stop at Addison's room.

As soon as I knock, it flies open. Her hair's down, and the ends curl just above her perfect breasts. She's changed out of her gown and is dressed in loose pants and a cropped sweater. Her belly button peeks out above the pants, and seeing that slice of flesh makes my throat tighten.

She bites down on her lip, scraping her teeth over it. She's nervous. Her eyes are panic-bright, confirming as much.

"Let's walk," I say.

"To where?"

"To wherever we go."

Her eyes narrow for a beat, but then she nods. "Let me slip on my shoes."

I step away from the door and wait, glancing down at my own clothes. I'm still in my suit pants and white shirt, but it's no longer pressed smooth. Wrinkles crinkle every inch of the fabric.

Addison slips out the door and quietly shuts it behind her.

I lead us through the castle until we're outside, heading down the hill toward town. "Why're we going this way?"

I tip my head toward her. "Because it's neutral ground. You're not in the castle."

"It's not neutral for you. We'll be in witch territory."

"You're right. How about we sit, then?"

"Where?"

My chest tightens and a blanket appears. "Here."

She eyes me warily before sitting on the blanket and

pulling her knees to her chin. I sit beside her, stretching my legs and crossing the ankles.

Blue witch lights from the village glow dimly, and people mill from store to store. A few cars fill the streets, the low hum of their engines joining the crickets' songs.

She glances into the sky. "When I was a kid, I always wanted to see more stars, but the town lights made it impossible."

Stars do constellate the sky. I can see millions, but she can't. Fae have sharper senses than witches. But it doesn't have to be that way. I wave my hand in front of her face. She jerks back, nervous because of my closeness, and blinks.

"Try to look now."

Addison slowly peers into the sky. Her mouth falls and she gapes at me. "What did you do?"

"I let you see."

"Wow. There are so many stars."

With a satisfied—and dare I say carefree—sigh, she falls back onto the blanket and stares up. My gaze washes over her, drinking in the smile that tugs her lips, the joy on her face. My heart slams into my ribs.

Fake, I remind myself. It's better for all of us if I remember that. Not looking at the curve of her hips and the slice of skin surrounding her belly button will help, so I rip my gaze away.

I lie down beside her, and her scent trickles over me. She smells like vanilla and lemons. It's frustratingly intoxicating.

We're silent for a moment before she says, "When were you going to tell me that you had a cousin?"

"So we're starting there, are we?" I turn my head to her. "Well played."

Heat warms her cheeks. "I do my best."

An involuntary smile flashes on my face. "In that case, when were you going to tell me that you don't have magic?"

She swallows loudly. "You first."

"Honestly?"

"I think that's the best policy."

"Never."

She swings onto her side, props her elbow on the blanket and drops her head in her open palm. "Really? You were never going to tell me about Ryals?"

I shrug. "Not if I could help it."

She barks a laugh. "Did you really expect to keep him hidden for"—she slaps her thigh in frustration—"for however long we're going to do this?"

"Yes. And let me ask you—were you ever going to tell me that you'd met him?"

She gasps like I've insulted her. "Maybe."

I turn over to face her, push up and rest my forearm on the blanket. This close, the gravitational pull of the joining feels like there's a rubber band lashed to each of us. It's pulled so tight it's about to break.

"When did you meet him?"

She traces a finger over the blanket nervously. "About a week ago. I couldn't sleep, and I was trying to find the kitchen so that I could heat up some milk. He was following me."

"You were trying to *find* the kitchen?"

Her doe eyes lift from the blanket and latch onto me. She nods. "Yep."

I've been such a jerk. I drop my head. "I should've given you a tour. I'll change that. Tomorrow."

"It's okay. Ophelia showed me where it is."

"Has she shown you anything else?"

"I haven't asked."

I rub my face, disgusted with myself. "Tour. Tomorrow."

"Thank you." She walks her fingers over the blanket. "We played chess."

A laugh rips from my throat. "You and Ryals?"

She grins. "Me and Ryals. He's woken me up a few nights to play."

I groan. "I'm sorry."

"Don't be. I like him. You have a good cousin."

Our gazes lock and I'm falling, all of me, into her, and I don't care, even though I should. It's like this every time we're together. Which is why I stayed away last week. Too much Addison is not good for me.

Or my plans.

She gazes at me curiously. "He told me a little about his parents."

It's my turn to sigh. "They can't keep him. They battled with drugs off and on to the point that he wasn't safe. I found out and demanded they give him to me. They must've had a rare moment of clarity because surprisingly they handed him over without a fight." She's staring at me as if I'm some kind of hero. I rub the back of my neck, because that's the last thing I am. "Ryals is from my mother's side of the family. She was close to her first cousin, and he was her grandson."

Why am I telling Addison all this again?

"You're good to be his guardian."

My mouth curls into a smile. "Are you complimenting me?"

She rolls her eyes. "Don't get used to it."

I smirk. "I won't. And now..." She watches me carefully as if waiting for me to deliver bad news. "It's your turn. When were you going to tell me you didn't have magic?"

She drops onto her back and covers her face. "Never."

"So, the same as me never telling you about Ryals. To be fair, I had a good reason for doing what I did. I'm trying to avoid him being devastated when you leave."

My heart shreds at the mention of her leaving. It's impossible to stay in control of my emotions around this woman.

Our verbal sparring turns my blood to lava, and touching her sends waves of euphoria coursing through my veins.

Damn joining.

Even now, my skin ignites at the thought of running my lips down her stomach, breathing into her flesh, watching goose bumps flush her belly.

Gods, if I keep thinking like this, I'll wind up ripping off her shirt. *Snap out of it.*

Addison exhales and drops her hands so that they fall to her sides. "I've never had magic. I'm the black sheep of the family, the one who's supposed to have magic, the one who's supposed to be the leader of the next generation, but I never have."

She shakes her head, so distraught. The need to comfort her grabs me by the throat. "There are worse things than being born without magic."

"Not to me, there isn't." His head snaps toward me, and an electric bolt slams into my chest. "Can you imagine that every guy you date only wants to be a part of your family because they're magical, and when he finds out you don't have any of that magic, you're dumped fast and furious?"

Who are these men? I'll kill them. "It's not much different than being a king. Women want me for my status, not for who I am. Then they find out I'm part human, or they've known all along and sneer behind my back but smile to my face."

Her brows pinch and she lifts her hand, reaching out like she's about to touch me. My own fingers twitch, anticipating taking hers. But she lets her hand drop to the blanket. "That's awful."

"It's not as bad as being told you're not good enough simply because you don't have magic. I hope you know that's not true, and any man who would judge you based on that instead of how brave and selfless you are isn't worth knowing."

Surprise ignites on her face. Any man who can't see what a treasure Addison is, is an idiot and not worthy of one glance from her beautiful doe eyes.

She slides back onto her side, propping her hand under her head. "Were you ever going to tell me that you were married?"

Her words punch me in the gut, winding me. "How did you—"

"Zandra told me."

Air slowly fills my lungs. Zandra. Of course Zandra would've said something. She likes to think that she's my best friend.

"I'm sorry if I've offended you," she says.

"You haven't."

"Did you divorce?"

"She died."

Addison sits up, and I do, too. "Feylin, I'm so sorry. I'm so, so sorry. I never would've brought it up if I'd known."

"You didn't know. It's okay." No, it isn't. It's not okay. It's definitely *not* okay. But the way the words leap from my throat, there's no anger in them, no fury. Addison doesn't deserve that.

Her family does. Cold, steely anger wraps around my heart, threatening to incinerate it with frozen flames. But my anger isn't at Addison. It's at the rest of them.

When I don't elaborate on the circumstances surrounding Tess's death, Addison drops the subject. Good. I don't want to lie to her, because as soon as she finds out what happened, the game is up. It's over. She'll demand the joining be severed, and she won't like the way to undo it.

She tips her face back to the stars and sighs. My gaze sweeps her from head to toe. She's gorgeous, every bit of her —soft and supple, no hard lines, no sharp edges. Not like me.

"Thank you for saving Ryals."

She turns and gives me a genuine smile—not a smirk, like

she usually does when we verbally volley. "Thank you for saving me from being embarrassed at the ball."

"Let me guess, your ex was one of those who dumped you because of the magic."

Her moods shifts at the mention of her ex, and this won't do. I bend my right leg and drop my arm onto my knee. "Now. You and I have things to discuss."

Her face falls even more. "I know. You have to stop the joining; otherwise, your people will hate you. Did you see the way they looked at me? Like I'd made those horses go crazy on purpose."

"Who cares about them?"

She frowns and sits up. "You care about them. You told me so. You said that you needed them."

"I do, but everything's not ruined. There are still two more ceremonies to go, along with the solstice ball."

"Two more? So you're not dumping me?"

"How can I? We're still joined."

"Right."

Her gaze flicks to my mouth and I smile. Before she starts poking around with questions about breaking the joining, I lift my brows. "We need to discuss your magic."

"I don't have any."

"That's not true."

She tips her head in confusion. "What are you talking about?"

"You've got magic. It's just buried deep inside you."

Addison squints at me. "Have you lost your mind?"

"No."

I lean over and press my hand to the base of her throat. Her skin flushes crimson, and her heart thrums beneath my palm. Underneath her flesh, deep in the center of her core, there's a pulse. I could be wrong, but I don't think so.

Her eyes flare from the spark that kindles between us. I

shake my head. "I haven't lost my mind. It's in there. It's just never been unlocked."

Heat creeps up her neck to her cheeks. Addison's gaze trickles down my arm and to my face. Worry flickers in her eyes. She doesn't think she can do this. But she can.

The worry in her gaze quickly melts into lust. I should let go before we forget ourselves. But I can't. All I want to do is run my hands over her, claim her like I intended after the first moment we met.

Not real, I try to remind myself. But when she glances shyly at me, the last bits of ice encasing my heart shatter.

I am undone. There's no use denying the feelings buried inside of me. The ones I've tried to tamp down and chase away are real. This isn't the joining. It can't be, because Addison is shattering me bit by bit, and for the first time in years I'm not afraid to bear the mantle of meaning something to a woman.

And in return, having her mean something to me.

"I'm going to help you find your magic."

She laughs bitterly, the tilt of her head suggesting that I'm joking. When I don't budge, she asks, "How?"

"First agree to let me help you."

She huffs and pulls away from my hand. Her mouth quirks like she wants to say something sarcastic. It even shines in her eyes. But after a beat she drags her gaze from the blanket and pins it onto me.

"You believe in me?"

And it's the way she says it that cracks my heart in two, as if no one's ever believed in her before. But even I know that's not true—her family believes in her. They're giving her that cursed bookshop.

But maybe I'm the first man who's ever shown her that she's more than what she limits herself to.

Several long seconds pass before she swallows and a lump

trails down her throat. "Okay. I agree. You can help me. On one condition."

"Name it."

"No touching. You can't touch me, and I can't touch you. When we start…"

Her gaze drops, as does her voice, and I understand what she means. It's not only that the desire can become over-whelming; it's that she's afraid of being hurt.

"No touching," I agree. My mouth ticks up in a smile. "And here I thought I might have to beg."

"That's still not off the table."

I bark a laugh, and her eyes shine with amusement. A hammer's cracked the brick wall between us, and it shatters, crumbling to the ground.

When our laughter dies, she asks again, "How will you help me?"

A slow smile spreads across my face. "Starting tomorrow you'll find out."

26

"*T*his is useless." I heave in a breath and exhale hard. "I'll never work magic. I don't know why you're trying."

Feylin shoots me a scathing look. He's standing with one hand under the opposite elbow and his chin resting on his fist. It's a ridiculously sexy stance, even though I'm doing everything in my power to ignore the sex appeal that rolls off Feylin, King of the Fae.

He smirks. "With an attitude like that, you're right. You'll never be able to do it. Now, let's try again."

"What's the point?"

"Because I like to torture you."

I stick my tongue out and he smirks. "Be careful. I might find use for that tongue."

The hungry look in his eyes makes my ears burn. Since I certainly don't want to talk about anything of *that* nature, it's probably best that we focus on the magic.

I thread my fingers and crack the knuckles. "Okay. So, the apple?"

"The apple," he affirms.

The lush green grass of the back lawn unravels in front of me. Not far off sits an apple. I narrow my eyes, thinking this will help me focus.

"Your eyes aren't going to move it," he tells me.

"I'm focusing."

"As I said, *think* about lifting it. Not narrowing your eyes. Wrap your magic around the apple and raise it."

All my concentration is pinned on that little sucker. I grit my teeth, thinking hard, but nothing happens.

I rub the back of my neck. "We've been doing this for an hour. It's hopeless."

"You need a break."

"I definitely need a break."

He crosses to a pitcher of lemonade sitting on a table and pours me a glass. When he hands it over, I make sure my fingers don't brush his. So far he's kept his word and hasn't touched me. Even though that's made it easier to work with him, his mere presence is still a distraction, because just sniffing his leathery scent makes my head spin, and when those sapphire eyes of his land on mine, the world gets sucked away.

So I've made him stand behind me during the lesson.

He drops onto the chair and sits with a huff. I sit across from him and stare at my glass. "I told you it was pointless. There's not a lick of magic inside of me. You might as well give up."

He frowns. "Don't do that."

"Do what?"

"Sell yourself short."

My gaze shyly lifts to meet his. He's studying me, his brow furrowed and the corners of his eyes crinkled. He drops his gaze, and his thick eyelashes nearly brush his cheeks they're so long.

"I'm going to ask you something, and I want you to be honest."

"Okay."

"What makes you happy?"

"What's that have to do with anything?"

He runs his finger along the rim of the glass. "Magic isn't something you can touch, and often the only way to get at it is to free yourself, to be who you were meant to be. That means feeling something primal, like joy."

Who I was meant to be? Who is that person? "I don't know who I'm supposed to be, but what makes me happy? That's easy. Books."

"Of course they do." He frowns for half a second before slapping his thigh and rising. "Come on."

"Where are we going?"

"I'm going to give you that tour I promised, but I'm also going to show you something else."

"What?"

He grins mischievously. "It's a surprise."

THERE'S SO MUCH MORE to the castle than I ever expected. There's a hedge maze in back with a huge patio that overlooks it, and there's also an indoor swimming pool. Yes!

There's a greenhouse that grows the biggest elephant ears I've ever seen, and all the while there are fae, sweet, kind fae, who smile and greet me at every turn.

Feylin stops outside a door and turns to me, hand lifted in a stop motion. "I'm going to let you enter, but on one condition."

I fold my arms and mock-glare at him. "What's that?"

"No squealing, no hugging me, and no screaming."

I cock my head in skepticism. "You really think I would lose my senses and hug you?"

"Yes."

I grin. "Well, you won't know if you don't show me. I'm ready."

"No screaming."

"I won't scream unless you keep this room from me, and then I might scream out of spite."

"I wouldn't expect anything less." He drops his hand onto the knob. "Are you ready?"

I grunt in frustration. "I've been ready."

"Are you sure? Because I don't want to let you in and—"

"Just show me," I screech.

He rings his ear out with a finger. "That proves it. You're not ready for this. Never mind."

He starts to walk away, and I block his path with my body —which is tiny compared to his. If he wanted to, he could easily push me aside. "All this buildup is killing me. Will you please show me what's behind this door?"

He stares at me for a long moment as a slow, delicious smile curls his mouth. "Okay." He drops a hand back to the knob and watches me, his gaze never leaving my face. "One, two—"

On three, he flings open the door and moves away. I step inside slowly, feeling like Dorothy entering Munchkinland.

Light streams through tall leaded windows and falls in thick sheets onto the floor. Dust motes whirl through the air, floating in front of rows and rows of—

"Books!" I launch myself past Feylin without a care in the world. My shoulder grazes his chest, and a jolt of passion singes me all the way to my toes. I gulp it down as I race into the room.

Bookcases line the walls from floor to ceiling. Ladders are

secured to rails so that even the books on the highest shelves can be retrieved with little effort.

As soon as I reach the first case, I start scanning. "These are classics. Human classics!"

One glance over my shoulder tells me that Feylin's more interested in watching me than he is in browsing the merchandise. As he leans one shoulder against the wall, his eyes overflow with warmth and a slight smile tugs his lips. "There are fae books, too."

"Fae books?"

"Translated to English." He points to them. "You'll like them. They go over our history—witches and fae."

The entire room's steeped in the heavy smell of leather and paper. It's heaven. I want to bury my nose in all the books.

"I could kiss you," I yell.

The tops of his cheeks turn red. "No touching."

"Then at the very least I can thank you."

"No thank-you needed. Seeing you this happy is thanks enough."

His words hang heavily in the air for a brief moment as each of us digest what he's said. My stomach ping-pongs, and I divert my attention back to the shelves. "Oh, I know what I need."

"What do you need?"

"Romance and pirates—not together. Separately. Come on, help me look."

He laughs. "For romance?"

"Yes!"

When he doesn't move, I rush up and take his sleeve, tugging him down the steps and into the room. "Come on. Help me. You know your way around this library. I don't. Show me."

He rubs the back of his neck as I release my grip on him. "Okay. I'll help."

For the next hour we search through the books until I find the two I'm looking for. "Where's Ryals? This book's for him."

He glances at his watch. "Outside working with his falcon."

"Can I see?"

"Of course."

We leave the library, but before I'm completely out the door, I take one last good whiff and let the scent of paper and leather trickle up my nose. Nothing smells better than that.

"You coming?" he calls from down the hallway.

"Coming!"

I dart to catch up with him and spin around to take in the beauty of the castle (rib-cage-like flying buttresses, all that jazz) as Feylin leads me through another part, where we reach a set of doors that exit onto the back lawn.

Ryals is there with a fae who holds the falcon. He hands the bird off to the boy, who sends it up into the air. The falcon banks to one side and then returns to land on Ryals's arm, taking the piece of meat he offers.

"That is so cool. Can you teach me?"

Surprise flashes in Feylin's eyes. "You'd rather learn falconing than magic?"

"I'd rather have fun."

He smirks. "I'll show you."

Ryals smiles widely when we approach. "Addie, did you see what he did?"

"I did. You're so good at this, and look, I have something for you."

"What is it?"

I hand him the book. "It's *Treasure Island*. I picked it out just for you. It's full of pirates and adventure."

His gaze skims the cover before he grins up at me. "I can't wait to read it."

"You can start now," Feylin tells him. "Addison wants to learn to falcon."

"Don't try to teach him not to eat mice," Ryals warns as Feylin takes a huge leather glove from the fae in attendance.

"Eat mice?" I quirk a brow. "What's that about?"

"Just something we've been working on." Feylin hands me the glove, and I slip it on. It's a lot heavier than it looks, and if I have to hold my arm up too long, I'll be aching. "Now hold your arm like so."

He demonstrates and I mimic the pose. Or at least I think so.

"Not like that. Like this." And without warning he slides his hand down my arm and adjusts my stance. Then he presses his knee to the inside of my thigh and gently pushes my legs wider.

Well. I didn't expect that to be the first time Feylin was between my legs.

Lust pools in my stomach; my mouth dries to a desert and my breath hitches.

"Sorry," he murmurs in my ear as his fingers trail over my arm before taking up residence back at his side. His words might be an apology, but his eyes are dark with want.

He shakes his head and inhales sharply. "Now, this is what you do."

He explains everything, standing beside me as the falcon's placed on my arm. He watches me like a hawk, his gaze never leaving mine as he tells me when to lift the bird into the air.

The falcon's heavy, and its eyes glitter like he's searching for his next meal. Like any good predator would, I guess.

Feylin directs my attention back to him, and I listen intently to his instructions.

He's a great teacher, nodding and encouraging me as the falcon takes flight, soaring high in the sky and banking before coming back around to land.

The king hands me a strip of meat, and I lift it, waving my

arms like I'm an aircraft marshal. "Come on in! It's safe to land!"

Ryals laughs and Feylin's eyes glimmer with humor. "Usually we do things a bit more subtly."

He slips the gauntlet from my hand and slides it on his just before the bird alights on his forearm. The falcon swallows the meat he offers in one bite, and then Feylin places the blinder on the bird's head. He makes it all look so easy.

I cock my head. "Just had to show off, didn't you?"

"Only because you thought waving your arms would help him land better."

"It's what they do to airplanes."

"Huh. Last I looked, this was a bird."

"Have to get the final word in, don't you?"

He winks. "Only when it comes to you."

"Are you two finished arguing over there?" Ryals asks from where he's standing under a tree. "I could use some lunch."

Feylin nods. "Let's eat. I know the perfect place."

HE LEADS us to a pond far on the other side of the lawn. Ryals brings a fishing rod and heads over to cast his line while Feylin opens a blanket and smooths it onto the grass before resting a picnic basket atop it.

Inside's a bowl of fruit, and I grab a handful of pink grapes. A sweetness I've never experienced before explodes on my tongue when I take a bite.

"What are these? They're amazing."

"Candy grapes," he tells me. "We grow them."

I moan. "They're wonderful."

"If you like those, you'll love this." He plucks a raspberry from a container and offers it at eye level. I open my mouth and slowly slide out my tongue. He eyes my tongue like he's thinking a million things besides eating lunch, and then gently rests the berry in my mouth.

Another explosion of sweetness skates across my tongue. "Oh my gosh. I could eat fae food forever."

"Be careful what you wish for," he jokes.

Our gazes snag again, and the air around us crackles with electricity. There's no ripping my eyes from him. I'm being sucked in. In fact, I'm tipping closer and closer to him, letting myself fall into his pull. His gaze drops to my lips as we lean to one another and then—

"I got one," Ryals calls over.

I jerk back and Feylin flinches. He rubs his hands down his thighs and rises. "Time to gut some fish. I don't suppose you'd like to learn this, too."

"Pretty sure I'm going to say no to that one."

"Don't move. I'll be back."

He doesn't have to worry, because I'm not going anywhere.

27

"Who's the other book for?" Feylin asks after we've eaten.

I'm lying on my side atop the wool blanket, one hand under my head, facing him. His legs are stretched out, and he leans on one propped elbow.

"It's for Ophelia."

"Not for you?"

"No, not for me."

"That's disappointing."

I sit up. "Why?"

"I showed you the library so that you could have something for yourself."

The sincerity in his voice makes my heart rattle against my ribs. "Knowing it's here makes me happy. Isn't that what you wanted?"

When his gaze rips away from mine, it feels like the sun's slipped behind a cloud. He watches Ryals, who's hunting for frogs in the bushes. "That *is* what I wanted."

Even though Feylin's relaxed, his clothing is still miraculously wrinkle-free. "How do you keep your clothes looking so perfect all the time?"

He glances down at them in surprise. "Magic. It wouldn't do for a king to have wrinkles, and while we're on the subject —why are you always put in itchy clothing?"

I tip my head back and laugh. "It's a curse, I guess. I don't know. I think the original witches wanted to curse me, so they made sure that for every major event, the clothes are itchy."

"Hm," is all he says. The sun's high in the sky, and he tips his face toward it as if drinking up the warmth. "There's an old story about a witch and a fae. It's supposed to be the beginning of the rift."

My eyes flare. "Tell me. I don't know anything about the history. Our books don't dive into it."

He eyes me with mock suspicion. "And what should you give me, since you want this information so much?"

"Don't push me, or I'll run my finger over your collarbone. I know what that does to you."

"Sadist," he jokes.

I laugh and shake my head. "Are you going to tell me the story?"

"Only because you're such delightful company."

"I'm going to pretend you mean that."

"I do mean it," he says sternly.

Heat blotches my neck, and I can't look at him. His words carry too much meaning. "The story?"

"Yes, the story." He plucks a blade of grass and twirls it between his fingers while he speaks. "It's said that a fae king fell in love with the queen of the witches."

"We don't have a queen," I tell him, my nose wrinkled in skepticism.

He rolls his eyes. "It's a story. Are you going to let me tell it, or are you going to interrupt me?"

"Fine. I'll be quiet."

"Thank you." He watches me silently, waiting for an interruption. When he's satisfied that I'll keep my promise, he restarts. "A long time ago, a fae king fell in love with the queen of the witches."

He gives me a look that says, *well, are you going to let me speak?* I almost want to throw something at him, but when I don't argue, he keeps on. "It's said that their love was true, but blood had already been shed between the two people. The king's advisors told him not to marry the witch, and her people warned her against the union as well, but the king was persistent, stubborn."

"Sounds like someone else I know." I really couldn't resist. He walked right into that one.

Feylin scowls, but light fills his eyes. "To prove to his people that the two were meant to be in the relationship, the king threw a ball and invited the witching community and his lords. The people were wary when they realized the king wanted to unite their people, but he had a surprise for them. At the end of the night he plucked a red rose from a bush and presented it to the crowd. He told everyone that he'd imbued the flower with a spell. If he handed the rose to his witch and when she took it, it turned golden, that meant their love was true. But if the rose withered and turned black, their love was false. If it died, he told his people, then he would sever the relationship with the witch, even though he loved her terribly."

He drops the blade of grass and traces a line on the blanket with his finger. The suspense is killing me. "Well?" I finally say in a huff. "What happened?"

Those sapphire eyes lock onto mine, and it's all I can do to remember to breathe. "What do you think happened?"

"I don't know. Our people hate each other. It makes me think the rose turned black, which would be awful. But that would also mean the witch didn't really love him in return."

Feylin nods slightly. "When he gave her the rose, it turned into gold, proving their love was real."

My heart warms and I sigh. "That's so romantic. But it's not true, right?"

"No, it's true. The roses exist."

I sit up and cross my legs. "No!"

"Watch out, or you'll make me think you enjoy my company and my stories."

I swat the air. "I like this one."

There's a long pause between us as we stare at one another, and then he clears his throat. "But that's not why our people hate one another. That happened later. The fae lords couldn't stand the witch, so they made the king think she was cheating. It destroyed him, so he destroyed her."

"Ugh. Why'd you have to ruin the good story with a bad one?"

He shrugs. "You've been wondering why our people despise one another. That's why, and if I had to guess, your people don't know about it because it makes them look bad, as if they started it."

"But she was framed."

"So she was."

I place my hands behind me and lean on them. "You said the roses are real?"

"They are."

"What are they called?"

He levels his gaze on me, and it feels like he's peeling back the layers of my skin until he's peering at my soul. "They're called Golden Roses."

"Ah. Fitting."

My bones ache to ask him if lovers still give them to one another, but I don't have the nerve. There are just some questions better left unasked.

"Want to work some more?"

"Yes."

He rises and begins to pack up our lunch. "Then let's get to it."

WE WORK FOR ANOTHER HOUR, but nothing happens. By the time we're finished, I've pretty much decided I'm never going to have magic, but I keep that to myself.

I spend the rest of the afternoon in my room. But as the sun sinks in the horizon, I'm restless. Stretching my legs sounds like a good idea, and before I know it, I'm striding through the castle and out the back door.

As soon as my feet touch grass, it hits me. Feylin must be close by. But how close?

Deciding to push the boundary, I keep walking, cutting back to the front of the castle and down the hill. This is weird. I've never made it this far before.

The sun's buried in the horizon, and the witch lights in the village burn brightly. The shops are closed, and people are heading home for dinner, leaving the streets mostly deserted, with only a few people sprinkled here and there.

So I keep going.

My steps are slow, hesitant, as I wait to run smack into an invisible barrier. But when that barrier doesn't shoot up in front of me, I keep walking until I find myself standing at the threshold of the Bookshop of Magic.

How in the world have I made it this far? Has the joining magic broken? Is this some fluke?

Better not to ask questions that I don't want the answer to.

I don't know what makes me do it—perhaps it's curiosity, perhaps sadness for what the bookshop once was and now is —a place where you can't dive into the books anymore. But before I think too much about it, my fingers push on the fake brick that looks exactly like the others that make up the outside of the store, and a spring releases, revealing the hidden key.

I unlock the door and return the key, closing the brick back into place.

The store's silent when I enter. The familiar scents of paper and glue trickle up my nose. There really isn't any better smell in all the world than that of a book.

Well, maybe amber and leather. But I shove that thought aside as quickly as it drifts into my mind.

I close the door behind me and give the street a quick glance. Only a few people walk the cobblestone paths, and none of them are paying attention to me.

The place seems so barren, so sad and still without the ability to throw people (nicely) into the story of their choice.

My heart hurts like a giant hand's squeezing it. I take in the hundreds of books lining the shelves, knowing that right now, no one can jump into any of them.

I approach the far wall and lightly trace my fingers over the leather bindings.

From behind me, it sounds like papers are shuffling.

"Hello?"

Maybe there's someone in the office, but when I peer around a freestanding case, there isn't a light on in the back.

The shuffling sounds again, and this time it's easy to pinpoint. It's just a couple of bookcases over. Maybe there's a draft and it's blowing open a book.

Well, that's easy enough to fix.

I march past the shelf and turn to walk down the aisle but stop. Sitting on the floor, open, with the pages jagged like teeth, is a book.

And it's growling.

Oh *crap*. A guard book! A book that's been magicked to attack any trespassers in the shop. Like a junkyard dog, but worse if you can imagine that, because there's no bone you can throw a guard book to make friends with it.

They're savage beasts.

Which I forgot about. That isn't surprising since I haven't visited the store in forever. It's just too painful to enter this place.

Maybe I can sweet-talk the book into calming down.

"That's a good guard book," I tell it. "I'll just be going now. You don't have to get upset."

The book continues growling as I slowly backtrack. I move for the door, turning toward it.

But blocking my path sits another book. It's bigger than the first one, and it's growl is much more savage.

I swallow down a knot in my throat. I haven't brought my phone. No one knows I'm here, and these books, even though they're made of paper, could slice me up badly.

"That's a good book," I say soothingly. "You probably don't remember me. I'm Addie. Clara's daughter. I'm not going to bother anything."

The book snarls and a slice of paper drips from its jagged teeth. It's not moving.

But there's still the back door.

I slowly turn to make my way to it.

But another book blocks my path.

That's when, out from the edges of the shop, several books join that one. It feels like I'm in *West Side Story* and a gang's coming together to give me a beatdown.

"Nice books," I say like I'm talking to a dog. "Be good, now."

My only chance is to run.

I flip around and dash to the front door, but all the books beat me to it. There are at least six, maybe seven. They're hovering in the air, open, snarling, their flaps snapping open and closed in a threatening manner.

They rear back and I grab the closest weapon I can—a book that's on a lectern—as the guards attack.

I bat at them, but these suckers are organized. One takes my right sleeve. Another takes my left. Two others grab my legs, and I'm sent falling to my butt. A throbbing ache races up my spine when I hit the hard carpeted floor.

"Let me go!"

But they've got me good. Their sharp papery mouths rip my clothes, leaving long, jagged gashes. I can't beat them away. I'm pinned.

That's when the biggest, ugliest book of all hovers a couple of feet in front of my face. A long scar runs down the middle of its right page. It approaches, snarling and snapping. It's slowly bouncing up to me (they can't walk, no feet and all), right between my legs. The pages curl as it growls menacingly.

It's going to rip my face off. For sure, that's what'll happen.

I struggle to free myself, but it's no use. The books are holding me tight.

The tome rears back, readying to pounce. This is it. I'll be scarred with a thousand papercuts to the face for the rest of my life.

In a flash, all the books release me and lunge.

I scream, waiting for my demise.

The front door crashes open, bringing with it a wind so severe that loose papers (where did they come from?) scatter like birds.

Feylin stands in the doorway, his eyes narrowed in anger, his jaw jumping in rage.

The books flip toward him and attack. One grabs his arm, and he snatches it with his hand, throwing it to the floor and stomping it with his foot. It whimpers in pain, its anger deflating. Another lunges for his face, but he grabs it with his lightning reflexes and throws it across the room.

Watching Feylin is like watching Jet Li take on an army of

assassins. All I can do is stare, slack-jawed as he neutralizes every single guard book, throwing them off him and hitting them with magic until they're all lying on the floor, limp and whimpering.

That's when he turns his attention to me. I sit there for a moment, staring, shell-shocked from what I've just witnessed. Worry flares in his eyes as he stalks over. "Are you all right?"

All right? I've literally just watch an American Ninja Warrior destroy an army of guard books. I'm in the presence of greatness and can't speak.

But somehow I manage. "Yes. Thank you."

He offers his hand and I take it. He pulls me up, and I'm still staring at him, dumbfounded. His gaze searches me from head to toe. "Are you sure that you're okay? Are you hurt? Did they cut you?"

"No. I'm fine."

That's when I spot a long gash down his bicep. One book sliced through his wool coat and white shirt. Blood seeps onto his clothes.

"You're hurt."

He shakes his head. "It's nothing."

"It's not nothing," I scold. "There's a kitchen in back. Come on. I know there's a first-aid kit here somewhere."

Yes, he's fae and could heal himself. But it's because of me that he got hurt, so the least I can do is play nurse.

He follows me as I pick my way over loose papers and knocked-out guard books that litter the floor.

I flip on a light and rummage in the cabinets until I find the kit. "Take off your shirt," I command.

He complies without argument, and I take his coat and shirt, draping them over the back of a chair before opening the first-aid kit and turning to him.

My heart jumps into my throat at the sight of his muscled

chest. The dips and swells of his body are mouthwateringly beautiful.

I take in his body a second longer, which I hope isn't so long that he notices I'm drooling over him.

He sits on a chair, and I survey the wound. It's a long gash but not deep. A little soap and water, Neosporin and a bandage is all he needs.

"Thank you," I murmur, gently pressing a cotton ball to the wound, "for saving me."

"You do have a habit of getting into situations that you need saving from."

I chuckle because he's right. "You followed me. How?"

His jaw jumps when I apply ointment to the wound. "I felt it when you stepped out of the castle. I was curious where you were headed." He lifts his gaze to mine and studies me with such intensity that it's too hard to hold his stare. "And you came here. Why?"

"I don't know. I started walking and when I wound up here, I wanted to see, I guess, if I had any magic in me." I sigh. "You saw how that went."

I place the bandage over the cut and drop my hand. Feylin takes my wrist. "Don't let today discourage you."

"Okay," I say half-heartedly.

"I'm serious."

He's still holding my wrist, and warmth winds up my arm. I swallow against it, even though it feels like Feylin's a rope tugging me to him. It's so easy to get lost in these feelings.

And I was just as lost not long ago, when I was with Edward. Falling so hard for him just to have the entire relationship snatched away still makes my heart ache. I can't go through that again. And touching Feylin jumbles my feelings, and they can't be jumbled, not if I'm going to protect myself.

"I felt your magic when we first met," he says.

My eyes flare in surprise. "What?"

His throat bobs as he swallows. "When you fell and I caught you. I could feel your power. That's how I know it's inside of you."

My mind darts back to that moment, and the connection that I felt to him slams into me. I remember feeling his entire body tense, and I could sense what he was experiencing. It was brief, but it happened.

"You felt it, too, didn't you?"

I nod slowly. "Yeah. I did."

He releases my wrist and rises, stretching to his full height, heat from his shirtless body caressing my skin like a kiss. "So don't doubt yourself."

Then he dips his head, and suddenly his lips are closing in on mine. My heart slams against my ribs as that soft and pliable mouth gets closer. He's going to kiss me. Like, really kiss me, and not because we're angry and horny from the joining.

I tip my face toward his as…he reaches past me and grabs his shirt.

He smirks and takes a step back, sliding one arm into the sleeve. "Ready to head back?"

My heart skips several beats as I attempt to collect myself and not look like I was expecting to receive a kiss. So I twirl a strand of hair around my finger and act like it's perfectly normal for his lips to have been honing in on mine one minute and the next he's getting dressed.

"Sure, I'm ready. But we've got a mess to clean up first."

28

It's late by the time we return to the castle. The halls are quiet, and most of the servants are preparing for bed.

As we make our way to our rooms, Feylin pauses. "You didn't eat."

"I'm not hungry," I say as my stomach growls.

He tilts his head because he clearly couldn't help but hear my roaring middle. "You need to eat to keep your strength up."

"So that you can work it out of me?"

"Careful what you wish for," he says in a voice laced with devilish innuendo.

"I'm strong." I curl a bicep to prove it. "I can handle it."

"Come on."

"Where are we going?"

"The kitchen."

"I'm not forcing anyone to cook for us. We missed dinner. That's on us."

He gives me a sidelong glance, brow furrowed as if what I'm suggesting is ridiculous. "I'll cook for us."

"You cook?"

HOW TO FAKE IT WITH A FAE

"Surprisingly I'm not just a pretty face," he jokes.

No, but he certainly has one. "Lead the way."

Within ten minutes Feylin's got meat browning in a skillet and is tearing lettuce into bite-sized pieces. When I ask how to help, he shoos me to the other side of the big marble island and says he'll take care of it.

"So what happened back there?" he asks with his marvelously strong back to me as he grinds pepper into the meat.

"I don't know. I walked into the bookshop, and the guard books attacked. Pretty simple."

"Hm." He dips the spoon into the skillet and holds it out for me. "Here, try this."

"What is it?"

"Spaghetti sauce. I want to make sure I've got the flavors right."

I blow on the steaming liquid as he holds the spoon. When it seems cool enough, I take a bite and moan. My eyelids flutter shut.

"Oh wow. Feylin. That's amazing."

When I open my eyes, he's staring down at me, his eyes shining. "It's been a few days since I've seen that look. I could get used to it."

He's talking about that night in the study. My cheeks instantly flame with embarrassment. "Well, you won't get used to it, because..." My voice trails off as there's no good answer.

"Because why?" he asks nonchalantly, his back to me again.

"Because we aren't touching, and because this isn't real. Remember?"

His back tightens before he nods. "Right."

When Feylin's done cooking, he presents me with a salad that has the dressing on the side, and spaghetti with meat sauce, also on the side.

I almost weep from the tenderness of his offering. He

listened to me when I told him my favorite foods, and he made them. Just for me.

"Thank you."

He nods his *you're welcome*.

As soon as we enter the dark dining room, arms loaded with plates, floating candles flare to life.

He positions himself at one end of the table. I start to move to the other, but he stops me. "We'll barely be able to talk if you're all the way on that side of the room."

My head swings from the far end to where he's standing, holding out a chair for me. Decision made. I slip onto it.

"Thank you," I murmur.

The candlelight makes the whole room feel terribly intimate, and a slight tension buzzes between us, making me acutely aware of every move he makes with his muscled arms. How his jaw flexes when he pours my wine, and how his gaze lingers on mine as he waits for me to take my first bite (amazing, I confirm).

Yes, it's all terribly, painfully intimate for two people pretending to be in love.

Once we're a few bites into the mouth-watering meal (literally, Feylin is a *boss* cook), he says, "I'm sure you miss being away from your family and here with me. I'm sorry."

The tenderness in his voice plucks one of my heartstrings. "It's okay. The balls are supposed to start back. Maybe Blair can find a husband soon and we can go our separate ways."

A muscle feathers on his cheek as he drops his gaze to his food. If I didn't know better, I would think Feylin's sad, and if I'm being perfectly honest with myself, the thought of walking away from him opens a hole in my own heart.

Strange how quickly bonds can form.

Since I'm on the subject of sad things, I add, "And I miss my grandmother."

"I'm sorry that you lost her."

"Me too." I push the spaghetti around on my plate, deciding how much to say. "I knew it'd be soon, but I didn't think it'd happen when it did."

"Tell me about it."

He's sincerely asking, so I tell him how within hours of her death we were told that we had to marry.

"There hasn't been time to properly mourn her." I trace the rim of my wineglass. "She was always there when we needed her, and my tears weren't even dry before Ovie said, 'Pull yourself together, Addie; time marches on.' She didn't really say that, but pretty close." My chest aches just thinking about it. "I just wish...I wish that I'd gotten a few more days with her. But that's what we always want with loved ones, isn't it? More time."

The way Feylin's looking at me, as if I hold the moon, makes me want to dive for cover. It's exhilarating but also disconcerting to have the full attention of a king on me.

"But," I add, wanting to change the subject, "I'm glad that I'm not at the house right now."

He sips his wine. "Why not?"

"My aunt's husband is back. Uncle Charlie. You may've seen him after the funeral."

"Tall man, his good looks only second to mine?"

I half laugh, half scoff. "Maybe."

He winks devilishly. "I saw him. You don't like him?"

"No." I absently twist my wineglass in circles. "Charlie's a tornado that casually sweeps into my aunt's life when he needs something—money, usually—and then he leaves, shredding her heart every time. But she always takes him back."

He frowns as he smooths a hand over his thigh. "Why?"

"That's the question we all ask. But I wonder if I'm any better. If Edward had dumped me and then asked for me back, would I have been as weak as Ovie? I've watched her do the same thing over and over, for years. Charlie comes, she gives him what he wants, then he starts a fight, tells her he needs space and leaves, abandoning my aunt to her own tears."

He reaches over and squeezes my hand. "You don't deserve to ever be with a man who doesn't appreciate you."

I should mention the no-touching rule, but everything about this touch is right. He sweeps his thumb back and forth across my knuckles and squeezes before releasing me. My skin chills as soon as his hand's gone, and I immediately mourn the loss of his touch.

"Sometimes love can make a person do foolish things," he murmurs.

"Oh?" I cock a brow in mock surprise. "Are you speaking from experience?"

He scowls and quickly turns the look into a smile. "There are plenty of things I wanted to do when Tess died."

A surprising stab of jealousy pierces my heart. I shove it to the back of my mind. "Did you and she join?"

"No. Our marriage was arranged."

For some reason that reassures me. "And you *didn't* join?"

He levels that sapphire gaze on me, and little pulsing jolts of energy skitter down my spine. "*Ours* is the first joining by a king or queen in a hundred years."

A wide-mouthed pit opens in my gut. That can't be right. Fae must have joined before us. "You're kidding."

"I wouldn't joke about it." He takes another sip of wine. "We were friends, Tess and I. Very different, and she loved me in her own way, and I loved her in my own, but it was never an all-consuming passion."

His gaze flits to mine, and my throat shrinks to the size of a pea. I hear what he's left unsaid, *but it was never an all-consuming passion like we have.*

Or perhaps I'm imagining that's what he means.

"But her death still wounded me, like the deaths of my parents."

"I'm sorry."

"Where there is life, there is death," he states. "They died a long time ago. My mother from pneumonia. She got sick and no magic in the world could cure her. Unlike what the world believes, fae aren't immortal."

"And your father?"

He folds his hands over his plate, his elbows resting atop the table. "He died from a broken heart, and I was left a seventeen-year-old who had no choice but to learn how to wield power that I never expected at such a young age. Others tried to take advantage of it. One lord wanted me dead, and tried. But he didn't succeed." He touches a silvery scar that runs just above his collarbone. "But my father made me work hard with my magic and learn who to trust and who not to."

"And now? Do you trust the lords now?"

"I keep the ones I do close. The others know not to challenge me. They had plenty of reasons to hate me—the fact that I'm not pure-blood, that I was young when I took control."

"And how old are you now?"

"Thirty-eight." Mischief flashes in his smile. "Careful, *puker,* you're asking a lot of personal questions as if you care."

"Maybe I do." Before he can dive deeper into that, I say, "What's it like to be a king?"

Feylin inhales a deep breath before rubbing his brow with the back of his thumb. "The responsibility isn't anything that I take lightly. My people are who I think about when I first wake up and before I go to sleep. They are who I want to protect, with my life if need be. Their happiness and security are the most important things. It's why I want to open trade with humans, so that the fae learn to trust them and they learn to trust us."

I drop my elbows onto the table and stare into the light dancing in his eyes. "And what about you, what do you want?"

His jaw jumps. "What do I want?" He deflates into his chair. "No one's ever asked me that."

"They should, and often."

A smile quirks his lips. "What I want is to take the tragedy and sadness of a veil being ripped because our power isn't what it used to be, and turn that into a victory by strengthening our numbers and establishing peace."

His kindness and dedication to others makes my heart soften even more to him than it already has. Here he is, working to help me find my magic when clearly the man has more important things to do. The fact that he's choosing to focus on helping me makes my chest swell with an emotion that I can't place. Pride, maybe?

"And what about you?" he asks, taking a bite of spaghetti. "When we first met, you were traveling from someplace. Where?"

"Nashville," I reply, surprised by his question. "I live—or *lived*—there."

"You did?"

"Yeah." I wave my hand in dismissal. "My family's lived in Castleview since before I was born, but if you don't have magic, what's the point of staying? Humans aren't allowed to buy property here, and I've never felt like anything but a human."

His brow wrinkles in concern. "But not because of your family."

"No, no. Not because of them." I twirl spaghetti around my fork, looking for a distraction because what I'm about to say sounds petty and foolish compared to guiding an entire population. "It was just what I put on myself. No magic? Might as well live with humans. But it's okay," I add quickly. "I have my dream job. Or *had* is the better word. Until this whole marriage thing is done, I'll be here in Castleview. Don't get me wrong, I love this town. I do, and under any other circumstances I would gladly live here. But it's hard to want to when..."

My voice trails off, and he picks up the sentence. "When you don't feel like you belong."

I slowly nod and finally bite the spaghetti that's tightly wound around my fork. I talk after chewing. "When you're different, it's hard to belong. You were different, too. You just had a bigger burden than me. But I'm not trying to compare us."

"Don't apologize. It's true."

One side of his mouth ticks up into a smile, and I find myself returning the expression. "So yeah, the night that we met, I'd just come from dinner with Edward, who I was convinced was about to propose to me because he said that he had something important to discuss. But in reality he took me to a restaurant so that he could dump me publicly. So that I wouldn't make a scene."

"A scene," he bites out.

"Yeah." A bitter laugh slips from my throat. "For so long I thought that I wanted him, fake glinting teeth and all. But now..."

He leans forward. "But now?"

"But now if Edward appeared and asked me to marry him, I'd look him dead in the face and say no." It feels good to admit that—to myself and to Feylin. "All Edward wanted was another magical connection, a stepping stone for his career."

"You are so much more than a stepping stone," he murmurs in a way that makes my rib cage squeeze my heart so hard it may pop out of my chest. "And what about you? What do you want?"

When was the last time I asked myself that question? I can't even remember. "I had my dream job, picking out books for people, so that's what I'd love to return to, or do something similar. I just love helping people find something that's perfect for them."

He takes a sip of wine, eyeing me over the rim of the glass. "And what makes *you* happy?"

You, I almost blurt out. *You* make me happy.

Good grief, where did that come from?

"This dinner makes me happy," is as close as I can get to the truth. "And reading, of course."

He settles the glass on the table. "What's your favorite book?"

"Oh gosh. There are so many. Let's see..." I rack my brain because this really is hard. "If I had to pick just one, I guess it would be *Pride and Prejudice.*"

"Ah, the Jane Austen classic."

My entire face brightens. "You know it?"

"Half-human mother, don't forget."

"Right. Well, yes, that's my favorite book." I cock my head and pretend to study him. "You know, you'd make a perfect Mr. Darcy."

He tips his head back and roars with laughter. After several long seconds he rights himself, using the heel of his hand to wipe his right eye. "I guess I deserve that. But you realize that if I'm Mr. Darcy, that makes you my Elizabeth Bennett."

It's my turn to chuckle. How ridiculous. I'm not Elizabeth Bennett. But before I have a chance to argue, I sneak a glance at him. There's no amusement in his eyes, no laughter. He's serious. I gulp past the knot in my throat and suddenly feel very, very hot.

Wanting to shift the conversation to something besides the growing tension building between us, I decide to blurt out the first thing that comes to mind, which turns out to be, "Ophelia told me something about the joining, but she can't be right."

Yep. Brilliant way to get us off the topic of *us.*

He shifts his attention to his plate as if he's just as happy as I am for a distraction. "What did she say?"

"Something about," I say dismissively, "about it being something about love, which is silly." And now my cheeks are on fire as he watches me carefully, so I quickly toss out more words. You know, because why not? Why not dig the grave deeper? "The joining's power is so crazy. It's impossible to separate true feelings from the magic."

"Is it?"

His eyes are holding me hostage now. My brain's spinning, whirling, spiraling into darkness. "I...I don't know. I mean, how does it end? If the joining was created to bring two people together before marriage, are they stuck in this"—my hand motions up and down toward him—"state for the rest of their lives?"

"No," he says quietly. "The joining ends on the couple's wedding night."

Relief floods me. *Wait.* Why am I relieved? "But you said that we don't have to get married."

"We don't. Not to break a joining."

"Oh." I sink back onto my chair and take another bite of spaghetti. "So you found a way to end it?"

Does this mean we'll do it right now? Break the joining? But what would that mean for us, for our agreement?

He wipes a napkin over his mouth and drops it onto the table beside him. "As far as I know, there's only one way to end it."

What? Anger flares hot in my core. "And you've been keeping this from me?"

"Because you won't like it."

"I'll be the judge of that." When he doesn't reply, I push slightly. "What is it?"

He runs a finger down the side of his wineglass and murmurs as if he doesn't want to hear what he's about to say,

"The reason why the joining's broken the day a couple marries is because that's usually when a relationship is consummated."

Oh.

His gaze flicks from the wineglass to study me, and instead of looking at him, I decide to fold my napkin into tiny squares. "You mean, we have to…?"

After an excruciatingly long pause he swallows so loudly I can hear it. "Yes."

The silence in the room's so pregnant I'm surprised a baby isn't born right there. Finally I lift my gaze and meet his. Feylin's cheeks are bright red, which I imagine matches my entire body.

We must have sex in order for the joining to be broken. We have to sleep together.

As much as my body wants him whenever we touch—and I do, don't get me wrong—the idea of mixing bodily fluids with him terrifies me. This goes beyond being worried that I'll fall for him so soon after jumping off the Edward ship.

If I sleep with him, I'll be lost.

Completely.

A weak, "Oh," is all I manage to say. "Well, then I guess we'll just have to…"

Have to what? Find another way? There *is* no other way because joinings were meant to end in marriage. Rings exchanged. Vows taken.

"We'll cross that bridge when we come to it," he tells me, picking up his fork and stabbing a piece of lettuce.

His gaze is back on his plate, but the entire mood in the room's shifted. Breaking the joining means super personal contact. Contact with Feylin that would light me on fire. Can I handle that without getting burned?

Hell no.

29

For the rest of dinner we talk about everything besides the joining—how Feylin hopes Ryals will grow up to be a great councilor to the next king, how pushing trade between humans and fae is key to their longevity as a people. When I ask him why, he says that it'll build trust, because right now the fae don't trust that human weapons won't be used against them, and the humans distrust fae magic.

After that, he asks me about myself—what will I do once this is over? Go back to Nashville, I suppose. Or return to the balls when my heart isn't crushed anymore.

As we discuss it, I realize that my heart isn't as raw as it was a week ago, though I keep that to myself.

For as much as we talk that night, the one thing we don't discuss anymore is breaking the joining. Though when he walks me back to my room, a similar topic arises.

"There's to be another ceremony."

All the happiness I've been feeling deflates. "Oh, and here I was hoping we were done with those."

He smiles tightly. "There are four."

And once again, more words are left unsaid. After the fourth one there should be a wedding. But there won't be.

"Right. Four. But what about my magic?"

He sighs, smooths his hair. "I'm putting it off as long as I can, but at some point I won't be able to. I'm hoping to push it back to after the winter solstice."

"But that's a month away."

"Would you rather we do it tomorrow?"

And have it fail and his people demand he break the joining and send me back into witch-ball hell? No thanks. "After the winter solstice is fine."

"That gives us time to draw out your magic."

I sigh in frustration and drop my head onto my back. "Again with the magic."

"I'm not giving up on you."

The sternness in his tone makes my head snap back up. There's fire in his eyes, a burning so strong that my stomach coils tight.

"Okay," is all I can muster.

We've reached our rooms, and each of us pause in front of our respective doors. I place a hand on mine and glance over at Feylin.

Low lamplight slashes across his face, which holds an expression that I can't read as he watches me. His gaze flicks from my hand to my mouth and to my eyes.

"Thank you for dinner."

"You're more than welcome."

Silence ignites between us—a tense, awkward moment that can only be broken when one of us leaves.

I turn the knob and start to slip through my door. "Good night."

"Addison?"

I whirl back to him. "Yes?"

His lips tug up into a ghost of a smile. "Tomorrow morning we'll begin again."

Then he opens his door and disappears inside. Even though he didn't say good night, an unexplainable hope mingled with happiness balloons in my chest.

THE NEXT WEEKS are spent with Feylin trying to find every which way possible to draw out my magic, and when we're not practicing, we're spending time together. He listens as I read aloud the best parts of the book I'm currently obsessed with, after first catching him up on the plotline, of course. He doesn't even seem to mind when I describe in intricate detail how a romance unfolds.

He shows me how to falcon, and I eventually realize that waving my arms in the air and shouting at the bird, hoping it lands, isn't the best way to go about it.

Shocking, I know.

We spend a lot of time with Ryals, who wrangles me into fishing with him. So of course I get Feylin to join us, telling him that he has no choice.

The king grunts a lot in his broody style, but when he helps Ryals pull in a fish, there's no mistaking the happiness in his eyes.

We spend mornings lounging in the grass, eating sticky-sweet grapes and telling each other stories about our families.

I go into boring descriptions about my sisters and how different each of them are while he tells me about his parents and how his mother was a true lady.

"She would've liked you," he says one particularly lazy morning that we spend sitting by the pond.

It's awkward how my chest sings at the comment. My own family, I'll have to admit, has been contacting me. But I've done everything in my power to dodge their visits since I can't bring back the shop's magic. I'm barely even talking to Elmore, choosing to keep his mirror closed.

In the afternoons Feylin disappears to do kingly stuff. Then he reappears for dinner, cooking me elaborate meals while I watch and point out all the things he's doing wrong.

Just kidding. He doesn't do any of it wrong.

"I think," Feylin says, skimming rocks along the pool, "that I know how to make your magic reveal itself."

I lift a brow in skepticism and let the book I've been reading fall onto my lap. "And what brilliant idea do you have? Shoot me to the stars? Tickle me?"

He leans back on his heels as if he's considering it. For all the time we've spent together, we've been good about keeping our hands to ourselves. It's been freeing but also frustrating.

Because there are so many times when I want to brush a curl from his forehead. But whenever I think about it, I remind myself that I'm protecting *me* by keeping this rule.

But right now it's late morning, so while Ryals hunts cicada shells stuck on trees, Feylin's about to leave, which means we won't be doing any magic practicing until tomorrow.

So it's strange that he's bringing up the topic now.

I close the book, memorizing the page number first because only a monster would dog-ear the corner. "What are you trying to prepare me for?"

He smirks. "You know me too well."

"I spend all my time with you. I've figured out your tells," I tease. "For a king, you're pretty easy to read."

"Don't reveal that to my enemies," he jokes.

For all his talk of bristly lords, I've gathered from Ophelia that pretty much everyone loves Feylin, even if he is broody and arrogant.

Even I like him.

More than I care to admit.

"So what's your great plan?" I ask, steering us back to the conversation.

"You need to be angry."

"Angry? Like someone-puked-on-my-feet angry?"

His jaw flexes as he glances over his shoulder at me. "I had every reason to be mad that night. I thought you weren't cleaning it up on purpose."

"Now you know."

"Oh, I know," he volleys.

I toss a flimsy blade of grass in his direction. "And what do you know now that you didn't know then?"

He cocks his head to one side and folds his arms as if he's thinking. "I know that you're a kind person who would rather die than puke on anyone, even your worst enemy. I know that you love your family deeply, that you think you'll never be able to wield magic, and for some reason you believe that makes you flawed. Which it does not," he says pointedly. "I also know that you like everything in terms of food on the side, that most of your clothes are itchy in some way and that you put others first."

My mouth dries. How does he know so much about me?

"I pay attention," he says, "which is why it's surprising that it's taken me so long to figure this out."

It's my turn to fold my arms. "And how do you plan to make me angry?"

Here his expression falters, his gaze dropping to the ground. In a wink he's standing in front of me, holding out his hand.

"No touching," I remind him.

"Trust me. You have to trust me." I quirk my brow, and he nods to his hand. I take it and he pulls me until I'm standing in front of him. "Close your eyes."

I do as he says, a smug smirk on my face. There's no way that Feylin can make me angry. *Good luck, buddy.*

He releases my hand and runs his fingers up my arm, sending sparks of desire licking along my skin.

The next thing I know, his breath's tickling the fine hairs on my ear.

"You will never have this," he whispers.

What does *that* mean?

"You will *never* have me the way that you want me," he bites out.

Oh, *that's* what he means.

"No matter how much you think that I'll succumb to this desire, I won't. I never will. This is as far as it will ever go."

The full pulse of desire that's flaring from my core and pooling between my legs screws with my head while lust twists my mind into a pretzel. I want to crash my mouth against Feylin's, twist his hair around my fingers, make him moan while I graze my teeth down his throat. Even now my fingers flex, wanting to dig into his flesh.

"You can't have me, even though you want me." His fingertips leave a trail of heat across my collarbone. "All of this will be for nothing, because once you're gone from here, once we're done with each other, you'll go back to those balls."

The lust pauses and frustration circles me.

"You'll dance and you'll dance and you'll dance, giving everything of yourself, but no one will care. You're nothing more than someone to be married off, forced to help your family's magic even though you don't have any of your own. You're their puppet, always doing what they want and never doing anything for yourself."

His words ring true. He's right. Once we're done, I'll return to dancing and smiling and pretending to want to meet all those wizards and werewolves, vampires and whoever else. But I don't want that. I don't want any of them.

"You're trapped," he purrs, the low rumble of his voice making my chest pulse. "You're chained to a life that you don't want, and before you know it, some average-looking wizard will show up and tell you that he loves you. But you'll always wonder if he's lying, using you to get to your family. Yet he's your only hope because you must save them. So you marry him." He pauses, breathing into my ear, sending a flame of anger igniting down my spine. "You bear his children. You live your entire life doing what everyone else wants and expects from you until the day you die."

It's all so close to the truth, so bitterly close that anger churns in my gut like a cauldron about to boil over. The weight of this truth crashes down on me, smothering me, crushing my lungs. I can't breathe. I can't think.

Then Feylin whispers, "And your husband's name is... Edward."

Anger bright as a thousand suns hardens like a fist inside my gut. It tightens, quivering under the weight of its own power. I try to reach for it, grab hold, but the ball shifts.

And then it explodes. Light blinds me as a tornadic wind rips through my hair and clothes, bringing with it the sound of rustling trees and snapping branches.

The power consumes me, wrapping me in a stranglehold of magic that's so intense it burns my skin. After several long seconds it ever so slowly melts away, leaving me a shaking, trembling mess.

My knees give and I collapse to the grass. The light was so bright that even with my eyes closed, it still blinded me. But after a few moments I'm able to blink them open, peering through dark dots at my surroundings.

Broken tree branches lay scattered across the lawn. The grass is bent like it's been smoothed out with a giant hand. And Feylin?

He's gone.

Panic claws at my throat as my gaze rips across the lawn. There, lying about twenty yards away, face up, is the king.

"Oh my gods, I've killed him!"

My legs barely obey when I force them to run across the grass.

"Feylin!" I fall to my knees beside him. His face is motionless, his beautiful features frozen. "Feylin, wake up! Please don't be dead. Please!"

My brain's a mess, but somehow I remember that the first thing to do in CPR is check for a pulse. I press my ear to his heart and wait, listening. Very faintly, his heart drums beneath his shirt.

I raise up and touch his face. "Feylin?"

He's still not responding. Okay. What's the next step? Loosen his shirt? I pull open the collar and sit back. Next, his mouth needs to be open. As I reach to part his lips with my fingers, he stirs.

"I was holding out for mouth-to-mouth," he murmurs, his eyes fluttering open.

He's alive!

And joking.

"You dog!" I swat him. "I thought you were dead."

"You've got to work harder than that to kill me." He sits up and lazily scrubs a hand down his jaw. A second later his eyes brighten. "But you, Addison Thornrose!"

He leaps to his feet, grabs me by the arms and pulls me to him. Before I can protest, he takes me by the hips and lifts me into air. "You did it! You are something. You called the magic and you did it!"

He's beaming up at me, and I'm mirroring his smile as he holds me up in the air with my hands resting on his shoulders. For a moment we stare at each other, and it's just him and me, the two of us, and no one else on earth exists.

I want to capture this moment and memorize it, brand it onto my heart for the rest of my life.

When he slowly lowers me and I'm nestled back on the grass, tipping my face up to his, that's when it all sinks in.

"I used my magic," I murmur, wonder lacing my voice.

"You used your magic. *Yours*. No one else's, and certainly not mine since, well, you saw what happened."

My cheeks burn with embarrassment, and I duck my head. "I'm sorry about that."

"Don't be." He gently hooks his finger under my chin and tilts my face up. "You don't ever need to apologize for being you."

The way he's looking at me makes my tongue thicken and apparently forget to work, which means my only response is to nod dumbly.

He drops his mouth, and without thinking, I'm reaching for him, craving the kiss that's about to fall on my mouth.

"Feylin!" We jump apart as Ryals runs up. "What was that blast?"

He nods proudly to me. "That was Addison's magic."

The little boy's eyes widen. "You? Way to go, Addie!"

He gives me a high five and a fist bump.

When the cheer dies down, Feylin remarks casually, "Now all we have to do is figure out how to harness your power so that you don't accidentally kill someone."

30

*P*rimal emotions, Feylin tells. That's the key.

The emotions that the joining makes rise to the surface, as well as him pushing my buttons, is what encouraged my power to finally flare to life.

And how he got it to appear? Well, let's just say I'm still unpacking all of that.

For the next few days he tries to get my magic to come up —not by angering me, but by having me tap into the resource I know sits inside of me.

But we fail.

Over and over.

It's okay, he tells me; we'll get there.

In the meantime I settle into life at the castle more and more. Every morning Feylin knocks on my door and escorts me to breakfast. Ryals joins us, often telling me how he beat Feylin at chess the day before.

When our days are done, Feylin walks me to my bedroom and says good night. He lingers more and more, and I wonder, just wonder if he's waiting for me to break the barrier between us, or if he wants me to give him permission to kiss me.

But knowing the scoundrel *he* is, Feylin's probably just trying to tie me up into lusty knots.

That's the most likely answer, I decide.

As the solstice approaches along with the next ceremony, the fire ceremony, I throw myself into planning the solstice ball to keep myself from thinking about another failed ceremony.

The ball's going to be grand, with fae, witches and wizards alike in attendance. Since I'm pretending to be the woman of the castle, might as well act like it.

That's what Feylin told me one morning in his office. *Go ahead and plan the party however you want,* he said. *As far as everyone's concerned,* you're already *the woman of this castle.* He smiled at me after that, his eyes filling with an emotion that I couldn't quite place.

Or didn't *want* to place.

I imagine that it matched the emotion in my eyes as I wondered when we stopped playing pretend and it all started to become real.

Even though party planning keeps me busy, I do see my family during this time, but we skirt around talking about the bookshop, which is for the best.

So when Ophelia tells me that Zandra's come to see me, I'm overjoyed. I need a distraction from magic, from the bookshop, from all of it.

"How's wedding planning treating you?" she asks as she pours iced tea for the both of us.

"Great."

Zandra frowns, which makes a little dimple form between her eyes. "You're a terrible liar."

"Hm. Feylin says the same thing."

AMY BOYLES

She hands me a glass, and I drink it, reveling in the taste of the sugary liquid as it slips down my throat. "And how is our dear king?"

"Good." A smile pushes up onto my face. It's so wide that my cheeks start to ache. "He's very good."

She leans in. "But are you planning the wedding?"

Sweat sprouts on my palms. "Yes, of course." Total lie. "We're just trying to get through the ceremonies before we focus on it."

She flicks her glossy curtain of dark hair over one shoulder. "Fae weddings are big deals. I'm sure witch weddings are, too. But it'll all happen as it should." A pause sets in, and she sips her tea, staring at me over the rim of the glass. "So. What're you wearing to the ball tomorrow?"

Ugh. *A black gown covered in scratchy sequins hand delivered by Ovie herself* isn't an appropriate answer. "Just a black dress."

"I'm sure you'll look beautiful." She plucks a tea cake from a tray and nibbles the end. "Um. So good. Feylin's cooks are amazing."

They're not as good as he is.

She swallows the rest and lightly dabs crumbs from the corners of her mouth. "So. Have you decided what you're giving Feylin at the fire ceremony?"

I nearly spit out the tea I'm sipping. "Give him?"

"Yes. At the third engagement ceremony there's the exchanging of the gifts." The surprise must show on my face because she scoffs. "It's just like him to forget to tell you. Anyway, yes, it's usually a personal gift, something that has significance for the couple."

Good night! What do you give a king?

"Let me guess—you have no idea what to give him."

Panic, real I'm-going-to-screw-up-this-whole-thing-again angst, makes my insides wither. "I don't know what to get him. I don't have a clue."

234

She rubs my arm soothingly. "Don't worry. I have an idea."

"You do?"

"Don't sound so surprised. I've known the man my whole life. I probably never told you, but we even dated for a little while."

"You did?" Why hasn't he told me this? A barb shoots into my heart, and it takes all my strength to pick it out. Even then, it leaves a bleeding hole.

She waves her hand dismissively. "Ugh. We weren't each other's type. We couldn't get out of it fast enough."

My chest loosens as relief fills my lungs like oxygen.

"Anyway, I've known him forever. It's not fair to you that you haven't known him your whole life. You're at a disadvantage when it comes to gift-giving."

She's right about that. Since the last thing Feylin needs is for me to look like a fool at the ceremony, I greedily ask, "So, what should his present be?"

She taps one bloodred lacquered fingernail against her cheek. "There's this one book he loves. Adores—always had it on him as a kid. And I know where to find an original copy."

"But he's said that he doesn't read."

She laughs lightly and flicks her hand. "Don't tell me he's doing that whole thing again. He likes to say that, to pretend he hates reading. Trust me, that's the farthest thing from the truth."

He never seemed to be lying when he told me that. But Zandra's known him a long time, and she's right, we've really only just met. So what do I know? This *is* the same man who kept the knowledge of his cousin and previous wife from me.

I nibble the inside of my bottom lip a moment, deciding. But there's not a decision to make because honestly, not one present idea comes to mind. He's a king. The man literally has everything that he could possibly want. What could I offer him that he would take?

"This book," I ask slowly, "you say that you have an original copy?"

Zandra smiles gently. "I sure do. I'll have it delivered to you by tomorrow."

31

"Come. I have a surprise for you."

Feylin's standing outside my bedroom, his shoulder pressed against the doorframe. He's wearing a lopsided grin and looks suspiciously excited.

"A surprise?"

"Well, it won't be a surprise if you don't come with me right this minute."

I scowl playfully. "Now what kind of person only offers a surprise for a few seconds before snatching it away?"

"Ruthlessly brutal fae kings."

A laugh roars from my throat. "Okay, you've got me. I'll follow."

He takes my hand, and I shiver from the electricity that zips up my arm. I should be pulling away. I should be reminding myself that I gave my heart too easily to one man and I don't want to fall for another. But I don't do any of that.

I simply let it be as Feylin leads me through the castle and down into the village, where we stop outside of Castleview Tailors.

My gaze darts over the shop. "What're we doing here?"

He grins, open-mouthed, pearly whites gleaming. "Step inside and I'll show you."

Inside we're greeted by Daisy, the town tailor. She's a tall blonde wearing all black with a tape measure tossed around her neck.

"Well, if it ain't little Addie Thornrose. Good to see you, girl."

"Good to see you too," I tell her, still trying to put all of this together.

"Your Majesty." She half bows to Feylin. "Are y'all ready?"

He rubs a hand over his jaw. "We're ready."

"For what? What are we ready for?" *What in the world is going on?*

Daisy claps her hands, and my attention whips to the back of the shop. In the very center sits a dais cupped by three mirrors. On both sides of the dais sits a door. When Daisy claps, those doors fly open and out of each darts a silver rack filled with dresses that rustle as they fly into the room and come to an abrupt magical halt.

Daisy walks around me while I survey Feylin with a *what is going on* look.

"I pulled a few items, but now that she's here, I have a better sense of her. Maybe she'll try a few more?"

"Including the ones you already showed me?" he says, still leaving me in the dark.

"Including those," she confirms before stepping away. "Let me grab them."

I drop Feylin's hand and whirl on him. "What's going on?"

He gestures to the clothes. "This is your surprise. Pick out a gown, whatever you want, and it's yours for the ball."

My brows furrow. "But what about the witch gowns I'm supposed to wear?"

He sheepishly rubs the back of his neck. "I may or may not have pulled a few strings. You don't have to wear one."

"You what?"

He takes my hands, rubbing circles into the backs of them with his thumbs. "Addison, you are sensitive. I recognize it because fae are, too. That's why you like the clothes in your wardrobe and why you hate all the witch formals. Daisy knows how to create clothing that won't leave you itching and scratching. So." He tips his head, and warmth fills his eyes. "Let me do this for you. Try on some gowns and see which ones you love."

My throat constricts. I don't know what to say. It hits me hard what he's doing, and that no guy I've ever dated or liked or even thought that I loved has ever done anything like this for me. Part of me thinks that I wouldn't have let them, even if they'd asked.

Because deep down I've been spending my life thinking that I'm not worthy or good enough, but if there's one thing that spending time with Feylin's taught me, it's that I'm more than the sum of what I'm *not* capable of.

And it's silly, because my parents and family never made me feel like less because I didn't have magic. That was something that I placed on myself.

"So," he says, pulling me back to the present, "want to try some dresses on for me?"

Daisy raises her arms, lifting gowns that look like they're made of the softest silk. Before I can stop myself, I throw my arms around his neck. The surge of power that explodes in my body when my chest touches his is nearly unbearable, but I bite it down. At least I do until his warm hands encircle my back, shooting so much desire through me that my knees become Jell-O.

And it's right here, in this moment, that I rip down the walls that I've built around my heart. Feylin doesn't want to hurt me. He's a man of honor, unlike Edward.

"Yes," I murmur in his ear. "I want to try them all on."

He pulls away, sliding his hands down my arms and taking mine again. "You don't mind an audience, do you?"

A blush flushes my cheeks. "I'm guessing that's you?"

"Unless you don't want me to stay."

"No, I want you to see. You're treating me. It's the least I can do to repay you."

His mouth tips up as he guides me toward Daisy. "Then I'll leave you to it."

Daisy winks and cocks her head. "Come on back, let's get you dolled up."

As I follow her to the dressing room, she talks to me over her shoulder. "You know, if I'd realized a long time ago that you preferred different dresses than what your family buys for you, I would've made them."

My family'd been coming to Daisy for ages to purchase gowns. Every year we'd pile in near the holidays for our solstice dresses. But the truth was, even if the clothes were uncomfortable, I kept it to myself, figuring it was just one more way that I was different from the rest of my family.

Daisy wiggles her fingers, and three screens pop up in front of me, shielding me behind them. "Now, you remember how we do this?"

I chuckle. "I remember. Try to go easy on me."

She smirks. "Girl, with King Feylin here, I'll go as easy on you as you want."

It's only when she says it that the depth of his gesture strikes me. Feylin doesn't have to buy me a gown. He doesn't have to do anything, but he is, and he's doing it simply because he wants me to be comfortable.

"My goal," Daisy says with a wink, "is to have him looking at you with ten times more feeling than he had a minute ago."

"What do you—"

Before there's a chance to finish the question, my clothes are vacuum sucked off my body. Daisy holds up a deep violet off-the-shoulder gown that looks like it's made of butter rather than silk.

"Raise your arms," she commands.

She tosses the dress into the air. It hovers above my head for a second before sinking onto my body and zipping itself up.

The gown feels as buttery as it looks. There's not one place on my skin where a seam rubs irritatingly. This. Is. Amazing.

"Away screens." They vanish, and Daisy beams. "Why, I may have succeeded in my goal on the first try. Come on, let's go show him."

There's no good reason why my cheeks are on fire, but they are as we make our way to the viewing room. The dress fits perfectly, the hem barely kissing the floor as I walk. When we come out from the back, Feylin's lounging on a couch, his arm slung over the back rest.

He's got a magazine in his hands, and when I appear, he lifts his gaze and does a double take. His throat bobs as he absorbs every inch of me. It's not a scandalous look in his eyes. It's something...different. Something I dare not voice. But even though I can't pin words onto the emotion darting across his face, it still hits me, lodging a knot in my own throat.

And that knot, even though it's a ball of emotion, doesn't feel wrong. For some reason, everything about this moment— the way Feylin's looking at me, the fact that I'm getting to play dress-up for him—feels right.

He exhales a low whistle. "You look beautiful."

His words send a tingle cartwheeling all the way down my spine. "Thank you."

It's when I get a glimpse of myself in the mirrors that I see what he does. The deep violet offsets my complexion and highlights my auburn hair. The dress is extremely flattering, cradling my breasts and cinching at the waist. The skirt even flows in the most feminine of manners.

It's impossible *not* to feel beautiful in this gown.

"What do you think?" Daisy asks me.

One glance at Feylin and I can tell that this is the dress he loves, and surprisingly I find that I want to make him happy and give him what he wants.

"You can try on others," he tells me. "You might find something you like more."

"You may," Daisy echoes in a voice says, *but you won't.*

"I'll try on some more."

"You're already here." He leans back and drapes his arm over the couch again. "And if I'm being honest, it's good to see you dressed up. It's a nice change from the jeans and shirts."

He says it in a joking voice, but a sparkle fills his eyes.

I pick up the skirt and turn around. "Come on, Daisy. Let's try on another one."

When we're safely tucked in the back, where hopefully his fae hearing can't penetrate, Daisy magicks up the screens. "Told you so."

"Told me what?"

The dress is sucked off me and another one slips over my arms and head, bringing with it a gust of wind.

She taps her fingers on the screen. "I told you that we'd found *the dress* on the first try. This is the one he's gonna want to see you in."

I scoff. "How do you know?"

"Because darling"—she magicks away the screens and I step forward—"I know when a man's in love, and that man is desperately in love with you."

My heart stops. My mouth forms words to ask what she means, but that's when it all hits me. Feylin never had to help me find my magic, but he did. Feylin makes supper for me every night, a supper that I greedily gobble up because he can cook. Feylin's giving me a dress that'll be comfortable because he knows that none of the ones I wear ever are.

Feylin loves me? Could it be true?

But before I flirt with asking myself that question, I ask myself another. *And don't I love him?*

Because he's settled into my bones like minerals. He's become so much a part of my life that I can't imagine him not being in it, and I realize that I don't want a life that he's not a part of.

Which is when I also realize that if Feylin loves me, then I love him, too.

Which terrifies me more than anything.

32

*M*y nerves jump as Ophelia places the last pin in my hair. Voices rumble throughout the castle, and music leaks through the crack at the bottom of the door.

"It sounds like everyone's having a good time," she muses, her gray eyes shining.

My stomach clenches. "Yes, it does."

"There. Perfect."

I take in my reflection and nearly gasp. Ophelia did my makeup, drawing a sparkly butterfly in pastels over my right eye that dips down to my cheek. The effect is stunning, along with the dark eyeliner rimming both eyes.

Feylin's not going to recognize me.

"Thank you, Ophelia."

She grins. "You're welcome. Now come on. I know he's waiting for you."

I wanted to surprise Feylin with the dress and makeup, so I asked Ophelia to help get me ready in my old bedroom upstairs instead of the one across from his.

That way, he'd have no reason to pester me before the ball.

I take one last look in the mirror, admiring the violet dress that I love so much. Daisy was right. Though I tried on dresses for two hours and loved every minute of it, none of them held a candle to this one. So Feylin had purchased it and several others for me.

"For the other ceremonies," he'd told me casually.

I didn't question it. I only accepted his generosity.

Ophelia opens the door, and I squeeze her shoulder as I pass. "Thank you."

"Have a wonderful ball."

"You too."

In the Royal Court, servants join in the solstice ball. It's a celebration for everyone, and I love that.

As I sweep past her and head toward the stairs, the murmuring of voices mingled with the music become louder, and heat from all the warm bodies washes over my arms.

My heartbeat flutters like a caged bird against my ribs as I near the stairs. Gods, please don't let me trip.

I place one hand on the railing and turn with the curve of the guardrail to descend the first step.

That's when I take in the scene below. Fae, witches and wizards alike fill the grand ballroom. Torches suspended in the air cast amber light over the crowd, and a string quartet plays in one corner, the music lifting up to the heavens, where the skylights illuminate a sea of stars.

But that isn't what steals my breath. Feylin does. He's standing at the foot of the stairs, waiting for me.

He's not even enjoying his own party. He's waiting to escort me into the room.

A smile breaks out over my face as he does the same. He extends his hand as he's done so many other times, but this time feels different.

Maybe it's the caged bird in my chest. Or maybe it's all the people and the music. I don't know what it is, I only know that everything else becomes background noise as I slowly descend the stairs and take his hand.

Energy immediately throbs in my palm as my skin slides over his. His sapphire eyes warmly drink me in. "You look more beautiful than you did yesterday, and I didn't think that was possible."

I glance up shyly. "You look handsome as well."

He wrinkles his brow. "Except for that one pesky curl that always gets in the way."

It's true. I brush it back to tame it, and it stays.

"For now," he says as if reading my thoughts.

"For now," I agree, laughing.

"So. Would you like to enjoy the party that you've spent weeks planning?"

I scrape my teeth across my bottom lip. "More than anything."

"Then that's what we'll do."

For the next hour, maybe two, we dance and laugh. Feylin introduces me to everyone and anyone, and when there's time for me to take a breath, I seek out my family and catch up with them.

Blair's dressed in a shimmering silver gown with a crystal-encrusted belt and a full skirt. Her hair's pinned up and her olive skin looks golden under the lights.

Her face breaks into a wide smile. "I wanted to talk to you earlier, but you were too busy with your fiancé."

I feel a blush creeping across my chest. "Yes, sorry."

"Don't be sorry. Drink it in." She scans the crowd. "He's watching you right now."

My gaze darts from her and dances along the revelers. There, standing in a throng of lords, is Feylin. He's casually looking at me, shooting me a small smile. I smile back before turning to Blair.

She smooths her skirt. "I was worried about you. I'm not

going to lie. This whole magic thing that's between the two of y'all had me concerned. You'd just broken up with Edward, and I knew you weren't thinking straight, yada, yada, yada."

"I wasn't then." *But I am now.*

"I knew it," she says as if answering a question in her mind. "So when this magic thing happened, I begged Mama to let me stay with you, here, in this castle, but she said no."

My jaw drops as my gaze lands on our mother, who's dancing with my father. He's sweeping her across the ballroom floor, his mouth to her ear.

"Why'd she say no?"

"Because it wasn't my place to intervene. I tried to argue, but in the end I agreed." My sister slowly drags her gaze from the crowd and pins it on me. "And now I realize that she was right to let you come by yourself."

I frown, and a little divot wrinkles between my brows. "Why's that?"

"Because it's so obvious how you feel about each other. He's crazy about you, Addie, and you're obviously over the moon for him. If I'd come here, that wouldn't have happened. Your relationship wouldn't have flourished."

I nudge her elbow playfully. "Does this mean younger sister approves?"

She rolls her eyes. "Yes, it does. I approve."

My heart expands like the Grinch's when it grows three sizes. "You don't know how much that means to me."

"I'm just happy that you're happy."

"Happy Solstice, Blair. Happy Solstice, Addison."

Devlin Ross stands to our right. He's wearing a white tuxedo with a white bow tie. Of course he is. For Devlin, a black tuxedo would be too...pedestrian, is the only way that I can think to explain it.

"Happy Solstice," I say. When Blair doesn't return the sentiment, I lightly kick her.

She scoffs. "Happy Solstice. Where's your date? Or have you brought a gaggle of groupies?"

He wags a finger, chastising her. "Now, now. I am capable of attending an event by myself." He smooths a hand over his brown hair. "And where's yours?"

"I don't have one."

His eyes sparkle. "Perhaps we should be each other's dates."

"I'd rather stick a fork in my eye."

"Oh, come on now. I'm not that bad, Blair Thornrose. I'm the perfect gentleman. Ask any of the women I've dated."

"No, thank you."

But Devlin's not taking no for an answer. He extends his hand. "Solstice etiquette demands that when you're asked to dance, a lady must say yes; otherwise it's bad luck."

Devlin has her. He's right. Blair has to say yes. She inhales deeply and shakes her head. "There are so many reasons why this is wrong."

"Not the least of which is the fact that I knew I'd eventually get my dance."

She slaps her palm onto his. "But that's all you're getting."

He winks. "We'll see about that." To me he says, "If you'll excuse us."

As he steals her away, Blair looks back over her shoulder at me and mouths, *Help.*

I stifle a chuckle.

"Looks like Devlin finally got that dance," Chelsea chirps, sliding up beside me. "Wonder if she'll stick a dagger in his back once it's over."

I bark a laugh. "She doesn't hate him *that* much."

My sister quirks a brow. "She's hated him ever since eleventh grade, when they kissed behind the bleachers and the next day he was holding hands with Basheen Broadbent. I don't think she's about to forgive him now. That, and the fact that he was her magical rival in all of high school didn't help."

"No, I suppose it didn't. They do look good together, though it's the first time I've seen Devlin dance with only one woman." Our gazes lock and we laugh.

After it settles, she says, "There's a kid over there who looks like he might grow up to become another Devlin."

She points and I spot Ryals, who's found a witchling his own size to dance with. It's adorable how he's holding her hand and dancing with her awkwardly, as if he's trying to find the rhythm.

I laugh and she grins. "That's Feylin's little cousin. And speaking of him, I promised that I'd mingle with more fae."

Chelsea flourishes her hands dramatically and steps back. "Please, m'lady, don't let me keep you."

As I move into the crowd, my mind drifts back to the balls. For the first time since this all started, I don't care that there hasn't been one. I don't care that Blair, or any of the others haven't found anyone to marry. My heart's so full of Feylin that nothing else matters. As if to accentuate the point, he's suddenly in front of me, smiling down and threading his fingers through mine.

"I was beginning to wonder where my fiancée had gotten to," he murmurs.

When he says *fiancée*, a solar flare flashes through my body all the way to my toes. There's a hum in his voice, a deeper care to the word than he's used before.

"And is there a special reason why you're looking for me?" I tease. "Looked like you were having a great time with the lords."

"Please. I'd much rather your company than theirs. Come."

He tugs me to the inner circle of the ballroom, where we stop.

"What are we doing?" I ask, realizing that the fae have turned their attention to the center of the room and all conversations have stopped. Only the barest whispers can be heard blending with the music, which is a haunting, lilting tune.

The music ends and all the dancers, including Blair and Devlin, step into the crowd. She goes one way, glaring over her shoulder at him when he tries to follow.

No surprise there.

Three more couples step onto the floor, and the music begins again, only this time it's slower, more tender, full of a longing that rips at my heart.

Feylin positions himself behind me and places his hands on my hips, holding me close, possessively. He's touching me, and I love it. Ever since yesterday when I hugged him at the tailor, I've pretty much given up on the no-touching rule. I don't want it anymore, anyway.

"This is fae tradition," he whispers. "Every solstice, young couples perform the Dance of the Rose."

I tilt my chin toward him but keep my eyes on the dancers. "Dance of the Rose?"

"Watch," he tells me, his fingers tightening on my waist.

I press my back into him and feel his chest constrict. His hold on me tightens as his fingers dig into my hips, sending a ripple of pleasure diving down between my legs.

It's nearly impossible to focus on anything except Feylin and my quickening pulse.

But somehow I manage.

The couples perform a seductive dance as they circle one another, never letting their eyes stray from their partner. They come together, palms touching, before they retreat again. This happens over and over until they reach the finale—a dizzying spin with each partner holding the other as they twirl and twirl, coming to an abrupt, breathless halt.

The hall's absolutely silent, and Feylin drags me closer to him still, leaving no space between us.

In unison, each male fae summons a single red rose into

their hand. The first fae hands it to his partner, and that's when I realize what's happening.

The woman keeps a sharp eye on her lover, and ever so slowly she extends a shaking hand and takes the flower.

My hand jumps to cover Feylin's because I know what's coming. He slips his thumb over mine, offering support, comfort.

The rose, so deeply red, slowly drains of color. The crimson hue washes away, and at this point the whole room's holding their breath, waiting to see what happens.

As the red washes off, it's replaced, inch by inch, with a light sheen. Finally a golden hue erupts over the petals, overtaking them until the entire flower, from top to bottom is perfectly golden.

The crowd explodes in applause. I join them, my heart thundering against my chest. The fae man steps up to his true love and kisses her. More cheers follow.

The second couple's next. I hold my breath as the fae man offers the rose in the same way and the exact same wash of color slowly overtakes the flower.

It's golden!

Another round of cheers from the crowd.

"One more left," Feylin whispers.

At this point I'm leaning against him so much that he's taking my weight. His hands have drifted to the front of my dress, where he presses them firmly yet gently against my abdomen.

"Fingers crossed," he whispers into my neck.

My entire body's a rubber-band ball of nerves. I want to jump out of my skin from the anticipation.

The crowd stills as the final fae steps up to the woman he loves. She takes the rose, and the red slowly bleeds away, becoming lighter almost immediately.

Yes, it's going to be golden.

My fingers tighten on Feylin's, and his thumb strokes mine. His body's as tense as I know mine is. Even my chest's constricted.

The lighter hue washes over the rose quickly, as quickly as the gold did. I bite my bottom lip, expecting that any minute now the flower will turn yellow.

But then it doesn't.

The rose wilts, curling into a hulking black husk.

The crowd gasps, and murmurs of sadness wash over us as I realize that I've just witnessed the destruction of true love.

33

My heart's crushed for the fae couple. Their faces, which had been so bright and full of hope, have now collapsed, just like I'm pretty sure their hearts have.

"That doesn't mean they won't find love in someone else," Feylin murmurs in my ear, like he feels my heartbreak through my sagging body.

I tilt up my face, and my cheek scrubs against the coarse flesh of his jaw. His mouth is so, so close, looking all sexy and wanting to be kissed.

But, the couple. "But they're not each other's true love."

He shakes his head. "No, they're not, and custom dictates that this is the end of their relationship."

"Even if they love each other?"

"Even if that."

I can't imagine loving someone so much and thinking that they're my true love only to be told by some magical rose that they're not. It would crush me.

The couple takes the news with more stride than I would. They embrace before turning their backs to one another and walking away. I can literally feel them pining for each other as their feet put distance between them.

His arms around my waist squeeze lightly. "Let's get some air."

"Yes, let's."

He slips his hand over mine and tugs me through the crowd, which eagerly parts as we pass, fae and wizards alike bowing for the king.

With the other two ceremonies, even though Feylin and I were together, it didn't feel real, so the bowing didn't affect me as much.

But tonight, as people bow and look on me, I dip my head shyly, because nothing about this is fake anymore—not for me.

Feylin opens a side door and I slip out first, inhaling the sweet, warm air.

The scent of gardenias fills my nose as I step into the torch-lit, brick-lined garden. Well-manicured bushes frame the path as he steps up beside me and we slowly stroll.

"Are you having a good night?" he asks, sounding genuinely curious.

"Other than seeing a couple get a black rose, which I'm not sure I'll ever get over? Yes."

He tips his head down and shoots me a sympathetic look. "Other fae have received a black rose and lived. They will, too, though it'll be painful for a while."

"I'm sure." My gaze flicks up to meet his. "And are you having a good time?"

"Normally I hate these things." He plucks a green leaf from a bush and twirls it between his fingers. "But tonight isn't so bad. I think it's the company."

"Ah, there are a lot of good people here—Trawick, Zandra."

"That's not who I'm talking about."

A knot has suddenly stopped up my throat.

He stops and shifts to face me. I do the same, letting my gaze slowly trickle from his thighs to his waist, to his broad shoulders and finally to his, where his piercing gaze is latched firmly onto me.

"I think you know," he murmurs, lifting the hand of mine that he's holding and threading his fingers through it, "that you're the person whose company I'm talking about."

"I know."

He smirks. "Then why not just say it?"

"Because." I sigh. So many words press against my chest, a dictionary full of them. But to say them means taking risks, and the last time I risked my heart, it was shredded. But the emotion flowing in Feylin's eyes says I'm safe, nothing will harm me.

When I don't answer, he glances at our hands. "I guess the no-touching rule's been thrown out the window."

"Good riddance."

His brow lifts. "Is that so?"

"Feylin"—I can barely swallow past the baseball in my throat—"what you did for me yesterday, no one's ever done anything like that for me before. My issues—the clothes, how picky I am about food—they've always been seen as a nuisance by the guys I've dated. Even the ones who were quiet about it, I could still tell that I annoyed them. But you, you see me, and you accept me, and that means more to me than I ever realized it would.

"And even though all of this is just the effects of the joining, that's okay, and even though our situation is only temporary, that's still okay, because for the first time I've been seen, and that means more to me than anything ever has."

My heart's so big, so full and so nervous that it's knocking against my chest like a pinball. I'm staring at his throat, unable to look him in the eyes because I'm afraid of what I'll see there.

"You've given me so much, and I've given you so little."

With his free hand, he slowly lifts my chin until I'm forced to meet his gaze. His eyes overflow with emotion as he tucks a strand of hair behind my ear.

"You've given me so little?" He shakes his head. "I barely smiled before you came into my life. I don't even think I remembered *how* to smile before you arrived. You've given me deeper happiness than I've known in years. So don't say that you haven't given me anything. You've given me everything."

He glances to the sky briefly before gazing back down. "Addison Thornrose, gods help me, but I never thought I'd say this to anyone. For so long I lived in the dark. I holed myself away from the idea of loving anyone except Ryals. But you've shown me that I've been so, so wrong. Being with you these past weeks has made me realize what I was missing out on, and I never want to go back to that place again."

He rubs his thumb across my cheek so tenderly that I close my eyes.

But he's not finished. "You mentioned the joining. Yes, it ties us to one another. But even if we'd never joined, fate would have brought us together, because nothing and no one could've hidden you from me. Not even the heavens could've secreted you away. If they'd needed to, the earth and the sky would've changed places so that you and I could find one another, because from the first moment we met, I wanted to carve out a space in my life for you, and nothing on this earth or beyond would've stopped me from doing that."

My mouth falls open. No one, no one in my entire life has ever even come close to saying anything like this to me. And I know he's not lying, because it's exactly the same way that I feel. Nothing could have kept us apart, not even fate itself.

He lifts my hand and releases his fingers, pressing his palm flatly against mine. "You have changed me, and for once a fae myth is right. I didn't say it when you mentioned it, too soon and all, but we believe that a joined couple signifies true love, and I've come to believe that."

My mouth's a desert it's so dry, but I know there's one more question to ask, one more thing that'll push us to where we're supposed to be.

"How do you know?"

He spreads his fingers and threads them through mine again. His gaze is on our hands when he says, "Because if this isn't true love, then true love doesn't exist."

My chest's heaving. My skin's on fire from him, the joining, my nerves—all of it. Feylin drops his gaze from our hands and pins it on me.

And I am lost.

The hand that's cupping my face slides back to cradle my head as he dips his mouth to mine and kisses me.

The first time we kissed, it was all passion and fire, flames of heat.

This is completely different. His lips are gentle, soft, a question—will I accept his offer?

My lips part in answer, and his tongue slips into my mouth as I groan at the pleasure uncoiling inside me. He drops his hand from mine and takes my face with both his hands, holding me in a gentle promise, offering protection, loyalty, love.

He pulls back slightly, sapphire eyes overflowing as his thumbs stroke my cheeks. "You, Addison Thornrose, you have wrecked me," he whispers hoarsely before he claims my lips again.

I'm just as wrecked as him.

These kisses—as our lips touch and retreat, touch again—create a spark deep within my gut, a swell of emotion.

If this isn't true love, then true love doesn't exist. That was what he said, and every cell in my body agrees. Because it feels like my body is parched earth, cracked from dehydration, and

Feylin's a monsoon that fills every fissure, giving me the nourishment that I've craved my entire life.

Pleasure and love consume me. Feelings that I've been bottling up for weeks pour out into this kiss—pour out of him, too. Every kiss conveys something new—*I've wanted this forever. Why did we wait so long? How is it I've only just found you?*

As his lips move with mine in this dance, as our tongues meet, as shivers over shivers skate down my spine, I realize that my feet have left the ground. We're in the air, spinning in a circle of light that cloaks us in its shimmery glow.

I pull back and gasp. Feylin looks around, looks down. I do the same. We're a good ten feet off the ground. I grab his biceps, and he kisses me again, chuckling into my mouth.

"What's so funny?"

"And there's your magic. All of it. Right there. Do you feel it? Can you call it?"

I do feel it. It's a ball of light that lives in my core, ready to be expanded and pulled in at will.

I kiss him again, savoring the feel of his velvety lips against mine. I never want to stop kissing him. "Do you think I can get us down?"

He presses his forehead to mine. "Addison, you can do anything you desire. Just don't get us killed."

I throw back my head and laugh before tossing my arms around his neck and pressing my lips to his one more time.

34

FEYLIN

*F*or the first time in years, my heart's full. I'm no longer shackled to a past that can't be changed. It's freeing, this feeling, and I owe it all to Addison—whom I'm in love with. How could I not be?

"Cancel the meeting with the wizard council," I tell Trawick.

He's leaning against the wall of my study, arms crossed. My best friend gives a me a dramatic eye roll. "I already canceled it. As soon as I saw the two of you on the solstice, I knew you weren't going to shut down the bookshop."

My mouth quirks. How well he knows me. But he's right.

"I'm not going to destroy *it*, or the Thornroses for that matter." My desk's a mess, papers scattered everywhere. Gods, ever since the solstice, I haven't been able to think straight. Doing more with Addison other than kissing would *help* me think straight, but I'm not going to rush anything with her.

Not one thing.

"Where is that box?" I mumble, distracted.

"What box? You mean that red one over there?"

He points to a spot behind my head. One glance over my

shoulder and I spot the red velvet rectangle on a shelf. A sigh of relief loosens in my chest.

"Tell me that's not what I think it is," Trawick says, nodding to it.

"That depends." I clear a spot off my desk and place the box on top of it. "What do you think it is?"

He scowls. "I'm not going to say anything until you show me."

"You're my best friend." I give him a half smile. "You should know me well enough to guess."

"I'm not interested in games."

"Touchy."

"You're not being touchy enough."

My shoulders tense at his insinuation. "She's not doing anything to hurt us."

"Hurt you, you mean." He flips his hand. "Go on. Open it."

I watch him for a long beat before lifting the lid. The smell hits me first. A sweet flowery fragrance trickles up my nose, because nestled atop a pillow of black satin lies a single red rose.

"I knew it." He throws up his hands. "You're going to gift her a Golden Rose tonight."

"I am."

It feels like my heart's going to break through my rib cage, it's so swollen with love. I haven't told her that I love her yet. But I will, tonight, after the ceremony.

He rubs his face. "Feylin, do I need to tell you that you've lost your mind?"

"No, you don't."

The rose is perfect, and ready to be presented. She has no idea that it's coming, and I know it'll turn gold. There's no doubt in my mind. Once it turns, I'll propose. We'll finish the ceremonies and marry. That's the way this will go.

"You've definitely lost your mind. Feylin, her family—"

"That's over." I curl my hands into fists and just as quickly relax them. Trawick's response is understandable. For three years I've hated the Thornroses, wanted to take everything from them. It's a shock to my best friend that I've changed my mind, but he'll get used to it. "How am I supposed to look to the future if I'm stuck in the past?"

"I guess you're not," he grumbles. "But they took Tess."

Every cell in my body tightens so hard my muscles want to scream. "I know, and I'll never get over her loss. But there's another thing that I know with certainty. Addison had no part in her death, and she doesn't deserve my anger."

"So you're going to marry her? For real?"

A grin spreads across my face, and I clap him on the shoulder. "I'm going to marry her, and I want you to be my best man."

He sighs, resolved to his fate. "If that's the way you want it."

I pull him into a hug. "That's the way I want it. Now." I push him to arm's length. "I've got a fire ceremony to prepare for. If you'll excuse me. I don't want to be late."

35

—————

*E*ver since my magic finally bloomed, I've been learning how to control it by performing little tasks.

Like right now, I'm using it to lift a hairbrush off the dresser and into my hands.

"Your mother's going to be impressed," Elmore says from his spot in the mirror atop the vanity. "Have you told her yet?"

"No, but she'll know tonight when the fire ceremony works."

He smooths a hand over his wavy white pompadour. "Are you sure of that?"

"Oh, I'm sure."

And I am. I know how to release my magic and how to pull it in. The fire ceremony's going to be great. It's the least of my worries.

The one thing I am nervous about is that large blue box sitting on a table by the bed.

Elmore drops his chin onto his folded hands. "Why the long face?"

"Tonight's the exchanging of the gifts, and I'm nervous that

Feylin won't like mine, even though Zandra promised that it's his favorite."

"You should be more worried about liking what he got you." He pumps his eyebrows in curiosity. "Do you have any clue what it is?"

"No, he won't tell me, even though he's pestered me every day this week about my gift to him."

Absolutely true. Between sneaking into corners to steal kisses, Feylin's been on a mission to find out what his gift is. Goodness, for someone who leads a nation of people, he really can't take suspense at all. He's probably the type who reads the last page of a book before he starts it so that he already knows how it's going to end.

Elmore laughs. "Of course he's pestering you. He wants you to tell him, but he doesn't want to tell you. It's a tale as old as time. Come on and stand, now. Let's see how you look."

I rise and show off the deep blue dress that I'm wearing. I gave Ophelia the night off, telling her that it wasn't any trouble to get myself dressed and ready. It isn't, but I do miss her conversation.

The gown is strapless with a sweetheart neckline. I chose this color specifically because it matches Feylin's eyes, and I knew when I tried it on at the tailor that it'd be perfect for this ceremony. Yes, I could've gone with something red, since *you know,* fire ceremony and all, but why be predictable?

The sound of voices drift into the room. "They're arriving. I've got to go."

"Aren't you going to show me Feylin's gift? After all, I won't be at the ceremony. For the life of me, I can't figure out how to get into the mirrors in this castle."

"Have you even tried?" I tease.

"No, not really." He shrugs. "What can I say? I'm lazy. But come on, show me the gift before you dash off."

"Zandra gave it to me," I explain as I grab the box from the table.

His brow lifts in intrigue. "Zandra?"

"Yes, you don't know her—tall, dark skin, beautiful fae."

"Hm. There's something familiar about her name," he says with a frown.

"Anyway, the gift."

"Yes, yes. Show it to me."

A smile takes over my mouth as I lift the lid from the box and display what's inside. "Here it is. Feylin's favorite book."

A knock sounds at the door. "Miss Thornrose, the ceremony's starting."

I slip the lid back on. "What do you think?" Elmore's gone white as a penguin's stomach. "Is everything okay?"

"Yes, Addie. Look, that—"

The knocking comes again. "Miss Thornrose!"

"I'm coming!" I hoist the box into my arms. "Whatever it is, tell me when I get back. I'll see you after the ceremony."

"But Addi—"

"Don't wait up!"

And with that, I step into the hall, ready to nail this fire ceremony.

36

"You've got this," Feylin whispers in my ear.

My hand's sweating so much that I'm sure his palm's drenched. But if it is, there's no sign of it on his face. His mouth's quirked as usual in a wry smile.

A smile I've come to love.

Before us sits a chunk of ebony bloodstone. Streaks of red mar the surface in an indecipherable pattern. The rock's shaped like an egg except at the top, where it's broken and jagged, resembling a crown.

Feylin gives my hand a squeeze and nods at the stone. It's time.

I can feel everyone in the room holding their collective breaths. This ceremony's the only one that doesn't take place outside. It's being performed in the same hall as the ball, and just as many people are in attendance, all of them hoping for a successful ceremony and to watch the exchanging of gifts.

I loosen the hold on my magic, and it slowly trickles out of me. I feel it crawl across the floor and lift to circle the stone, where it mingles with Feylin's power, each of our magics circling the other in a powerful dance.

I *feel* more than see the two powers spiral above the bloodstone, his power caressing mine, mine nipping at his, until their circles become so tight that they snap together like a magnet to a refrigerator. It's only then that the power drops like a shooting star into the bloodstone.

One second passes, two, and then molten fire shoots from the crown like lava, roaring up to the ceiling.

The crowd erupts in applause. So does Feylin. He beams down at me. "See? I knew you could do it."

A sigh of relief gushes out of me, and I clap too, more in awe and surprise than anything else. My skin, which had been jumping from nerves, slowly calms, and the tightness in my stomach relaxes.

Across the hall, Blair and Chelsea do fist pumps, which makes me giggle. Dozens of fae whom I recognize from earlier events, including Zandra, smile easier. It's obvious that they can finally see the light at the end of the tunnel—that my relationship with Feylin isn't doomed.

I admit that thought unties a knot of worry in me, too.

Feylin's still smiling down at me as Trawick approaches, applauding, and nods to a table, where two boxed gifts sit—my blue one, and a rectangular red box that's Feylin's present to me.

A hush falls over the crowd as Trawick announces, "As many of you are aware, it's after the third ceremony that the exchanging of the gifts takes place. My lady," he says, gesturing with a flourish to the table, "you may present your token of affection to the king."

King. I'll never get used to hearing him called that, because Feylin doesn't seem like a king. Yes, he seems like an exceptionally powerful man, but not a king. Maybe that's because the humanity in him is obvious now, whereas when we first met, I was blinded to it.

I clear my throat and approach the table nervously. All

these sets of eyes on me make me want to run for cover, but there's no reason to be nervous. I'm just giving him a little gift is all. No big deal.

My hands tremble when I take the box and turn toward him, doing my best to forget that hundreds of people are watching what should be an intimate moment.

"For you." He takes the box and looks down at me through thick lashes as I say, "I hope you like it."

"I'm sure I'll love it." He gives me a smile that's just for me, which of course makes my heart ping-pong. Then he acknowledges his subjects and the wizarding community in attendance. "May all of you witness the opening of this gift."

His gaze shifts back to mine, and my cheeks are so hot. My stomach's fluttering as I cross my fingers, hoping Zandra was right about the book.

Feylin's eyes don't leave mine as he opens the lid. Ever so slowly he drops his gaze to peer inside.

The smile I expect doesn't come. Instead his face goes deathly white as his hands slip out from underneath the box. Because the book's so heavy the box tips as it plummets to the floor, one edge crumpling as it connects with the polished marble. The book tumbles out, sliding across the ballroom and coming to an abrupt halt two feet away from the ring of fae surrounding us.

Gasps of shock ring out across the room. Murmurs of disgust follow.

What's happening? What's going on?

The fae look at me like I'm some sort of traitor as they whisper to one another. A wave of murmurs carrying the title of the book spreads throughout the throng. Next thing I know, fae are vanishing in spirals of smoke, exiting the ballroom faster than I can keep up.

I whirl toward him. "Feylin."

He backs away, his face twisted in fury. With one wave of

his hand, everyone who remains in the ballroom vanishes—
even my family.

What have I done?

"I've sent them home," he grinds out.

"Why? What's going on?"

When he tosses his head back and laughs, it's the coldest,
most chilling sound I've ever heard. "You. Know. Why."

"No, I don't. Look, if there's something wrong with that
book—"

"Something wrong with it?" he spits. Fury rages in his eyes.
I've never seen him so mad, not even when I puked on his
shoes. "Something *wrong* with it? Tell me, dear Addison, did
you know from the beginning of this farce that you'd betray
me with that book, or was it only recently that you decided to
destroy me with it?"

My jaw drops. "I don't...I don't know what you're talking
about."

Every muscle in his face tightens as he takes an intimidating step toward me. Mist flares out around him, crawling
over the floor. "Don't lie to me."

"I'm not lying. I swear, Feylin. I'm not. I don't—"

"Understand?" he yells.

The floating candles flicker as his magic slithers over them.
His power's snuffing out the light in the room, darkening it. A
fire roars in the man-sized fireplace, but even that light's
dimming.

"You understood exactly what you were doing."

He laughs, this time bitterly, looking up at the heavens as if
for answers. Well, if he's going to get them, I'd like some, too,
because I'm confused as hell.

"You knew who I was from the first moment we met,
didn't you?" His gaze lands on me, and it's as sharp as a spear
as it rips a gash in my heart. "But you being such a good
actress, you had me fooled. And a fool is what I've been. This

whole time, while I was helping you find your magic, while I was fall"—his voice breaks and he shuts his eyes before grinding out—"you were plotting, waiting. I was ready to give you the world, but that's not good enough for a Thornrose, is it? You had to destroy me like I wanted to destroy your family."

He takes a step back, giving me room to breathe. Those eyes, which had stared at me with such warmth only minutes ago, are now as biting as ice.

"I really don't know—"

He slams his hand down on a table. "Stop lying!"

I flinch from the violence in his voice, and because of it, my voice shrivels to nothing.

"Your family's known that ever since Tess crawled into that book and *died*, I'd seek revenge. So they decided to use you to get it, didn't they? You were their tool to destroy me before I could ever destroy them."

"Destroy them?" I repeat.

My mind's working in overdrive. Tess died in a book.

Oh my gods! My hands fly to my mouth. Elmore—when I first arrived back in town, he'd started to tell me about a horrible accident that had happened, but he never got to finish. *Tess died.* Feylin's Tess died in a book, and no one ever told me. Not my mother. Not my father. Not even Blair. No one ever said one word.

As Feylin stares at me, fury still splashed across his face, more pieces of the puzzle snap in place. Feylin knew who I was all along. When he abruptly walked away from me at the ball, after I introduced myself, it was because I'm a Thornrose.

A Thornrose.

A family that he wants to destroy.

And he was going to use me to do that.

Tears burn my eyes as a crushing wave of realization crashes down on me, making my knees quake so hard that I have to steel my body so that I don't collapse. "You...you wanted to ruin my family." He doesn't answer, so I know it's true. "You were using me. When this joining happened, you were happy about it because you wanted to get back at them." I rake my fingers down my face. "This whole thing, the joining, the ceremonies, you've been holding my presence here over my family as punishment because of what happened to your wife. You..." My voice cracks as a sob escapes my throat. I have to exhale several times before the words finally come. "You only used me to hurt them."

His jaw tightens. "Then I guess we're even, aren't we?"

He's looking at me as if I'm his worst enemy, as if he hates me more than he's ever hated anyone. Gone are those warm eyes, that tender smile. I don't know who this man is. He's not the Feylin I've come to understand.

My chest hurts so much it feels like I've been hit by a boulder. All this time while I was slowly handing him my heart piece by broken piece, he was using me to hurt my family. He's just like every other man who's ever pretended to care about me in order to get to them.

I've been nothing more than a pawn in some revenge game. Our relationship was never about me. It was about my family.

A wave of nausea hits me. It's so dark in here. So dark. The air's so hot. It's stifling. My dress is cinched too tight. I've got to get out of here. I've got leave. I can't...oh gods, I can't even look at him.

Tears sting my eyes and nearly blind me as I stalk away. I just want to go, get as far from here as I can. But I'm not leaving without one last word.

I spin around to face him, taking in his tragic beauty. I thought that I loved him so much, but he never loved me back. He was pretending this whole time that I meant something. What a fool I've been.

"If I ever lay eyes on you again, it'll be too soon," I grind out before storming off.

"Addison."

His voice has changed. Don't get me wrong, it's still laced with anger, but there's another emotion underneath it. Sadness, maybe?

I pause, glance over my shoulder. "What?"

There's a heavy silence before he murmurs, "The joining. We have to break it."

That's when my heart officially cracks in two and falls into the pit that's opened in the earth.

I double over, barely catching myself from falling to the floor. Gods, he's right. If I'm going to leave here, the joining has to be broken first. How am I going to do that? I don't even want to look at him.

A long stretch of silence ignites between us. No one says a word as anger continues to roll off each of us, infusing the air with magic. Crackles of energy bite every inch of my exposed skin.

I can stay here, lock myself in a room until he finds another way to break the spell. Or I can leave and be done with all of this right now. "Fine," I reply, agreeing to end this.

"I'll have protection," he tells me, as if ensuring I don't get pregnant makes this any better.

I just don't even know what to say to that.

"Where?" he says quietly, and I know what he's asking. Where do I want to do it? Not his bedroom. Not in mine, for sure, and not here, the ballroom.

I slowly spin on my heel and stare at the floor. I can't, I refuse to look at him. "Your office," I croak out.

In a blink darkness overtakes me. Half a second later we're standing in his study. A fire's roaring, and a bearskin rug is spread in front of it.

I wait for the travel nausea to rise up, but it doesn't come. What should be a relief can't offer me any comfort right now.

Feylin steps out of the shadows, his face an unreadable cold mask. The sight of him makes a knot swell up in my throat, so I drop my gaze. His feet come into view as he stops within arm's reach. Even though I can feel his eyes on me as if they're the sun burning off my skin, I refuse to meet them.

"Are you ready?" he asks quietly.

No, I'm not ready. I'm so angry that my knees are shaking, but this has to be done, and so I swallow past the knot in my throat and prepare myself to break the joining.

37

The air stills as we face one another. The only sound's the crackling of the fire, and the only light is the orange glow that flickers on Feylin's shirt.

I'm staring at his collar. I cannot, I *will not* look into his eyes. My heart's already broken. Looking at him will only break and enrage me more.

Yes, I could tell him where I got the book, but he won't care. It won't matter, and to be honest, I'm so damn angry, so betrayed.

This—*us*, we were never real. Our relationship was always a lie.

He shifts his weight, and I'm pulled from my thoughts. Right. This has to be done.

He's obviously waiting for me to start. He's giving this to me on my own terms, and if I want it to be done, I need to get it over with.

My hands slide to my back, to unzip the gown, and then stop. No. My dress shouldn't come off first.

If this is the only time we're going to do this, even though at this moment I hate him, this will be done right.

My hands tremble as I lift them. He's wearing a silver tie, matching the flecks in his eyes. Feylin stiffens as I pull the tie loose and slide it through the buttoned collar.

I reach up to unbutton his shirt, but my fingers brush the bare skin of his throat. My entire body clenches, and the knot in my stomach loosens as desire coils in my belly.

I slowly make my way down the shirt and gently pull it from his trousers. Then I pick up his right arm and undo the cuff link before doing the same to his left, dropping both into his pants' pocket.

I slide my hands up his undershirt, admiring the dips and swells of muscles that clench under my touch.

When I reach his shoulders, the feel of his naked flesh stirs a tsunami of desire inside me, nearly making my legs fold. I grip his shoulders to steady myself as he inhales a sharp breath. His throat bobs, which gives me a small nugget of satisfaction, and with painful slowness I rake my hands down his arms, tugging off his shirt as I go.

When his shirt falls away, I take the time to admire his body. There's a small circular scar on his right shoulder—an archery accident, he'd told me. I trace it with my finger as his stomach quivers.

My fingers run down his biceps to his forearms and then to his undershirt, which I gently tug up and over his head.

My gaze drinks in his bare chest, and my eyes nearly spill tears at the sight of his beauty. He is, without a doubt, the most beautiful man I've ever seen.

And he's mine for only this moment.

Even though I despise him.

He steps closer, pressing his chest to mine, and letting me feel his erection as it strains against his pants and presses into my belly. Yes, I know how Feylin thinks, how he likes to tease.

This entire situation muddies my mind. I hate him. I want

him. I want to be as far away from his as possible, but I want him inside me at the same time.

He feels it, too. I know he does.

His finger traces the sweetheart neckline of my dress, dipping into the V between my breasts. My nipples tighten as a shiver tingles down my spine. I drag my teeth over my bottom lip to ground me.

He reaches around, and for a moment it seems like he's going to hug me, but then the sound of my zipper unwinding mingles with the crackling fire, and my tight chest tightens more.

As soon as the zipper's undone, my dress cascades to the floor, pooling around my feet. The backless bra that I'm wearing keeps a chill from sweeping over me, even though it feels like I'm exposed.

Then we're standing, half naked, both of us, in the study, and even through the crackle of lust, an undercurrent of hesitation winds through the room.

But I don't have to ponder it long because with a finger, Feylin tips my chin up, and I let him.

When our gazes collide, the air's knocked from my lungs. Pain, lust, confusion, all of it fills his eyes, same as I'm sure it does in mine.

This morning I stood on the precipice of love, and now I'm broken apart.

I don't want to think about it anymore. It's unbearable. So before there's too much time to think about what I'm doing, I push up on my tiptoes and press my lips to his.

An explosion of hurt and want and longing fill this kiss. Feylin greedily takes my mouth and gives back, his lips crushing mine as they silently scream of betrayal.

I don't know how I know this, but I do.

My arms circle his neck as he slips his arms around me and

his tongue enters my mouth. He tastes like a sunset. He tastes of broken promises. He tastes of desire.

The kiss consumes me, making passion pool between my legs, the throb of want soaking my panties.

Feylin slides his arm down to the crook of my knees and picks me up, stealing my breath. It's so much feeling. An insatiable hunger for him pricks every inch of my skin. I don't want to look at him. It'll force me to think things, to hurt. In this moment all I want to do is satisfy my need because it's overwhelming.

My mouth stays on his as he settles me in front of the fire and on top of the bearskin rug.

He starts to lay me down, but I resist slightly, not quite there yet. Yes, my body's ready, but I'm not mentally prepared for the next steps.

My tongue thrusts harder into his mouth, and Feylin moans, his calloused fingers digging into my back, which elicits a sigh from me.

I drag him down onto the rug. Yes, I'm ready. Once I'm firmly nestled atop the soft surface, he rocks back, breaking the kiss, and our gazes latch briefly before he drags his eyes to my legs, where my thin stockings are attached to a garter belt.

Yep, when I dress up, I do it right.

His breath staggers as he bends to brush his lips over the apex of my thigh, trailing to my knee, down my shin. His fingers drag over my collarbone, atop the bra and to the exposed slit of my stomach. My entire body shudders, and I can almost hear his smirk when he positions himself between my legs.

He crawls back up my body until he's right over me, his face flush with mine. My breath hitches. Feylin stares at me one, two, three seconds, and then I smash my lips to his, giving him silent approval.

He takes that approval, letting his tongue explore my

mouth greedily before breaking the kiss and tracing his lips over the swell of my breasts and onto my stomach, where he exhales, pausing, his lips hovering an inch above my skin.

Our dilemmas are the same. I hate him. Why am I feeling so much pleasure? Why do I want to *give* him so much pleasure?

The only explanation is that the joining magic's the reason why I understand how he feels, but I'm right there with him, hating myself while bliss rolls over my body in waves that wreck me inch by inch.

He pauses over my belly for a moment longer before he magicks my panties away and disappears between my legs.

Pleasure comes in tidal waves that roll up my spine and stretch over my limbs. His tongue caresses me, parting me, and my legs open wider for him. He slowly works me into a frenzy, taking his time as if to say, *See? If you hadn't screwed me over, I could've gone down on you like this for the rest of our lives.*

Or perhaps it's just my imagination.

His tongue becomes fingers, and those fingers and tongue bring me to a climax. Magic unfurls around me, wrapping me in a cocoon of ecstasy that breaks me apart in one violent shudder.

Every muscle in my body spasms before quietly stilling. My muscles become limp, and it takes a moment before I can slowly pull myself back together.

While I'm gathering all the different strings of myself, Feylin kisses my inner thigh, his tongue a tendril of fire licking my skin.

I've barely recovered from my orgasm before his mouth is between my breasts and I'm arching my back for him. His hand slides down my spine, and he unclasps the bra, pulling it away.

He sits back, the distance between us sending a chill brushing over my body. My gaze flicks to his. He's staring at me, hungrily gobbling up my naked body with eyes so dark his pupils are engorged with lust.

I rise to my knees and work my fingers slowly down his abdomen. He sighs and lifts his hands to cup my breasts. His rough finger pads graze my nipples, making the skin pebble.

I reach for his waistband. His pants are still straining from his massive erection. When my fingers brush his lower abdomen, he hisses. Now he's on top of me, gently pressing me to the rug again, and I submit as he kisses the spot at the base of my neck and works down to my breasts, where he sucks my right nipple into his mouth while he strokes the other with his thumb. A whimper slips from my mouth when he swirls his tongue over the stiff peak.

Fire and passion ignite in my core, sending a scorching blaze down between my legs. The pressure builds again, rising and throbbing as he sucks my nipple like it holds the key to life itself.

I gasp and he lifts his head, our gazes locking.

I cup his face and pull his mouth to mine, where his lips claim them, demanding all of me.

And as much as I hate him, I want to give him every single inch of skin I've got.

My fingers are on his waistband again, this time unbuttoning his slacks, unzipping them. I gently push his boxers and pants down, breaking the kiss to watch his cock bobs free from its restraints, and my mouth goes dry at the sight of it.

Truly, it's a work of beauty, the shaft long and thick, and the head larger than anything I've ever seen. Granted, I haven't seen many, but that's neither here nor there.

He eases back, much like he did in the shower, giving me time to look at him, admire his beauty. When I take his cock in my hand, Feylin closes his eyes and his breath staggers.

His eyes flutter open, and mine rise to meet him. A knot lodges itself in my throat, and I'm barely able to swallow past it. He wraps one arm around my back and steadies himself with the other while he lays me down.

The rug is soft and cushiony under my back. It's the only soft thing in this moment as Feylin positions himself on top of me, and I fold my legs around his hips and gasp when the head of his cock flirts with my opening.

I hitch a breath, and he looks up, his dark eyes, resembling liquid onyx, taking me in like he's looking into the depths of my soul.

He lowers his forehead to mine, and I shudder against the prickles of energy that skate down my spine. His nose touches mine, and then his lips brush my mouth and his tongue slips between my teeth as the head of his cock parts my flesh and drives into me.

This is the moment that the joining was made for—this moment, when two people come together as one. His first thrust is slow, deliberate. He waits while I stretch to take him, easing himself inside bit by bit until he's up to the hilt.

Then he pulls back, and with it, the intensity of the magic builds. If I'd thought that the fire and explosions pounding my skin couldn't become more intense, I was wrong.

His thrusts are surprisingly gentle, and his mouth doesn't leave mine when he fills me up slowly, giving me all of him. And I take it. I want all of him inside of me for as long as I can have him.

He moans into my mouth, and I swallow it, giving him my own moan of pleasure that he takes. The pressure builds, the desire between my legs throbbing painfully as Feylin's thrusts quicken and deepen.

I'm riding a wave of magic, of ecstasy that rises high. The power between us throbs. My entire body aches with pleasure every time he drives into me. His kisses becomes heartbreakingly tender and his thrusts deepen until I'm cracked open, my

AMY BOYLES

body splintering and shaking as I clutch him hard, my sex quivering and pulsing around his cock.

He whispers one word—"Addison."

Then he shudders and collapses onto me, both our bodies slick with sweat.

It's in that moment that the magic, the joining, the power that's held us together for weeks, forcing us to be bound to one another, shatters us apart. The wave of power overtakes me, hitting me so hard it feels like I'm being slammed against a brick wall.

It swallows me whole and everything goes black.

38

When I open my eyes, familiar wooden slats greet me. The room smells faintly of cedar from the paneling, and I inhale deeply as I pull my down duvet to my chin.

For one brief moment I'm blissfully happy. That's before all the memories from the past day slam into me like a truck going eighty miles per hour.

Pain slices deep into my chest as I relive my heart being broken into two jagged pieces. Tears prick my eyes and I slowly exhale a stuttered breath to calm and center myself. The sorrow doesn't subside. It doesn't even hide. It's right there, in my chest, tearing me apart bit by bit.

Feylin used me. This was all a game. I meant nothing to him. I was nothing more than a piece on a chessboard, my heart ready to be sacrificed for his needs.

That's the be-all-end-all truth. So now it's time to focus on other things, like—

I'm home. I'm here. He sent me away after I fell asleep. Good. I couldn't have looked in his eyes again anyway.

And since I'm home, my family has some explaining to do.

I crawl out of bed, my muscles aching (not just the ones between my legs), which is probably due to having sex on the study floor, even if there was a bearskin rug between me and it.

Luckily the king didn't magick me naked into my room. He'd had the decency to make sure that I was dressed in a camel-colored long sleeved cotton top and bottoms. First things first—put on clothes that don't remind me of the castle.

The floor's cold against my bare feet as I pad over to my closet. I swing open the double doors and find a closet stuffed to the gills in colorful dresses and gowns.

Good grief. It's all the clothes that were stocked in my room, and even the ones we got from the tailor. I slam the doors and brace my back against them, taking a few deep breaths to steady myself.

So, no closet.

After rummaging through my dresser, I find a pair of leggings and a red sweater that seems suitable enough. As soon as I open the door, I'm met with the familiar sound of bickering sisters and my father, who always tries to calm them.

"You said that you'd go with me to the concert," Finn accuses.

"Well, I'm busy that night," Georgia tells her. "Find someone else to go with."

"No. You promised."

As soon as my foot touches the last step of the back stairway that leads directly into the kitchen, all conversation stops.

My father sits at the head of the breakfast table, light hair falling into his eyes as he reads Castleview's magical newspaper. My sisters are each in different stages of eating breakfast —slathering jam on biscuits or scooping eggs onto a plate.

But like I said, all that stops when I enter the room. "Where's Mama?"

Dad clears his throat. "Your mother is—"

"Here." She enters the kitchen, black robe open, revealing plaid flannel pajamas that I kind of wished I was wearing because there's a winter draft coming in from the windows. "I'm here."

"We need to talk."

She nods. "We can do it in the—"

"Everybody out," Dad yells, interrupting her. "Girls, grab your breakfasts and let's go."

With that, he and his magical newspaper vanish, along with my sisters, who vanish in smoky poofs one at a time.

"Oh, my biscuit!" Chelsea reappears to grab a biscuit slathered in what looks like purple possum-grape jelly and stuffs it into her mouth before disappearing.

Blair shoots me a sympathetic look before she, too, vanishes in a cloud of smoke.

"Coffee?" Mama points to the carafe on the counter.

"Yes, please."

She grabs a chipped mug hanging from a wooden cup-tree and fills it, leaving room for cream. She slides it over, giving me the side-eye, before pouring her own cup.

I grab the pot of cream that sits near the coffee maker and let a good stream fall into the mug before stirring. My father likes his coffee as darkly roasted as possible. It's well-known in my family that if you're ever in need of a laxative, just ask Dad to make you some coffee, because that'll do the trick.

Which means that over the years I've learned that the best way to counter numerous trips to the bathroom post-breakfast is to temper my coffee with an almost equal amount of cream.

When my drink's good and doctored, I take a seat in front

of an empty plate. Mama takes the chair beside me, which happens to be at the foot of the rectangular farmhouse table.

"You have questions," she says, tucking a strand of blonde hair behind her ear. "But before you ask them, there's something I need to say. I'm sorry about not being here when you first arrived home. You needed me, but I was buried under alliances to shore up, and making sure that the other witch families knew that all our past agreements would remain intact."

"I know."

"But that's not all." She cuts the air with her hand. "Georgia was with me, and she's the youngest. As the eldest, you wanted that to be your place, and I knew that. But Georgia needed a distraction. Nana's passing hurt her."

"It hurt all of us," I argue.

She exhales heavily. "Your sister took it badly. She couldn't even look at Nana's body, so I said she could be with me."

I nod, silently agreeing, and take a moment to study her. It's been so long since I've sat at this table with just her that I haven't noticed the newest fine lines on her forehead, or that more crow's feet crinkle her eyes. She looks tired and worn out.

She looks how I feel.

One sip of my coffee tells me that I might have overdone it on the creamer, but better safe than sorry. "You knew about his wife."

It takes all my control not to scream the words, not to bite them out, and not to lash at her. I have to hope there's an amazingly reasonable reason why this information was kept from me.

She rubs her thumb over the rim of her mug. "I wasn't there that day, when it happened. There was someone new working, who had only been with us for a few months." She sighs and sinks back onto her chair and rubs her cheek with a hand boasting more age spots than I remember seeing before. "The queen, Tess, came, and she requested to be put into a book, one that was not in our stock. The rule is—"

"All books must be vetted." Even I know that.

She nods stiffly. "Correct. But the worker was told that I *had* vetted the book, which was a lie. From what I understand, Tess also threw her status around. So she was allowed into it."

"The book that killed her," I add solemnly.

"Yes." She gives a firm wave of her hand. "Our shop was absolved of all wrongdoing. Tess knew where she was going when she entered that tome. She knew the risks, even if we didn't. So we were not liable." Her breath shakes. "Addie, for most of my life our family has owned that shop. We are the proprietors of happiness. Never, not once has anyone been harmed. You know that."

"I do." All true.

"So when I learned about her, it felt like the world had been pulled out from under me. How could this have happened? How could someone be harmed? There are safe-guards in place."

"Yes." The books that people are allowed to jump into can be violent, but no one dies. It's a fact. "But she *was* killed, and she was his wife."

"And we never told you." Mama sighs and presses her lips into a thin line. "We let you find out the hard way, in front of a group of fae who hate our kind."

My gut clenches. "Why? Why didn't you tell me? Why did you let me go with him if you knew?"

She closes her eyes, and her grip around the mug tightens until her knuckles become white hills. "The answer to your first question is that we didn't want her death to get out to anyone that didn't need to know. It wasn't our fault, so yes, we didn't advertise what happened even though he blamed us. He blamed me because he was told that I had approved the book.

"But he couldn't do anything to punish us. He is fae. Fae govern fae, while witches and wizards govern our own kind. So there was nothing he could do but accept it."

"He didn't."

She shakes her head. "I've been heartbroken over this. When it happened, I went to Feylin. He didn't live here—*yet*. But I went to his castle, and I apologized and begged his forgiveness. This has never happened before, I told him, but his heart was so cold that he wouldn't listen, and to be honest" —she sighs—"I can't say that I blame him. There was nothing that we could do to fix this other than grovel and beg forgiveness, which he refused to give."

That sounds like Feylin. He's kind unless you screw over someone he loves, and then he becomes a furious beast. I could easily see that.

"But you never told me, not when the joining happened."

"How could I?" She lifts her hands before letting them fall with a slap to her thighs. "How could I tell you anything negative about him when I knew that you were in love?"

My heart skids to a halt. "What?"

"I was there, in the garden, the night of the ball. I heard you talking and I knew, even before you did, that you were falling in love with him."

Well, not anymore. But wait. What?

"I don't understand."

She sips her coffee. "When the joining occurred, not that there was much that could be done about it—I wanted to tell you then, so that you'd be prepared for him, you'd know what he thought about us. I was about to tell you when you disappeared, and when I saw you next, at the first ceremony, it wasn't the right time. Your feelings were already on your sleeve. So your father suggested we watch and see what happened, and the more we saw you two together, the more it seemed like you really cared for each other. His anger vanished." She laughs. "He even asked us if you could stop wearing the traditional witch gowns for your ceremonies."

My throat shrivels to dust. He did? Of course he did. He'd told me at the tailor that he'd pulled strings so that I didn't have to wear those itchy dresses.

"So I thought that you were safe, that he'd tell you in his own time." Her brow wrinkles in confusion. "And then you gave him that book."

I sink back onto the chair. "Yes. The book. I was told"—I wave my hand dismissively—"it doesn't matter what I was told. It's over. It's done with. We can all get back to our lives."

I mean that. It doesn't matter that I was tricked into giving it to him, that Zandra was never my friend. My chest aches from the betrayal, yes, but nothing I can say to Feylin will change his mind about what happened. He won't listen to me even if I show up at the castle and beg his forgiveness, and to be honest, I don't want to. He should know that I never would've harmed him. That's what stings the most—that he thinks I would intentionally cause him so much pain.

But at the same time he wanted to hurt my family and used me to do so. I'm not sure if I can ever forgive him for that.

But I'm here in my house, the one I grew up in, and my family's all around me, except for Nana, of course. If there's one thing I've learned in life, it's that family's more important than anything else.

And it's my family that's going to help me through this, because my body's raw. I ache from head to toe, gutted, unable to summon even the smallest hint of happiness. But still I force a smile to my face because I'm nothing if not Optimistic Addie. "There's something I need to tell you."

Her lower lip pouches in confusion. "What's that?"

I exhale a sad sigh, because even this can't conjure joy in my heart. "I found my magic, so I'm ready to take my place as the Keeper of the Bookshop of Magic."

39

I spend the next thirty minutes talking to my mom about my power and also explaining that if things had gone differently the night before, I would've told her yesterday how Feylin helped me summon it.

Obviously they'd already guessed that something had happened; otherwise the fire ceremony would've been an even bigger shitshow than the earth ceremony. But they hadn't dared to hope that I'd found magic.

Indeed I had.

But even with my newfound abilities, I'm still dragging my sorrow around like a piece of toilet paper clinging to my shoe. No matter how much I try shoving what happened with Feylin to the back of my mind, it's impossible to ignore the massive hole in my heart. And right now my heart's sawed wide open and bleeding.

It shouldn't be this way, because as soon as I enter the Bookshop of Magic, everything feels different.

The shop's empty; in fact most of the town is. It's barely after nine in the morning, and most of the stores don't open until ten.

Mama waves her hand, and the lights wake up, slowly brightening the store as if on an invisible dimmer. The shop looks exactly as it always does, with shelves stuffed full of books, and the smell is the most comforting in the world.

As the lights flare to life, the books awaken too. They clatter and chitter, trembling and shaking on the shelves.

It's a bit too much excitement for comfort. I step closer to my mother and farther away from them. "Is everything okay? No guard books are going to come out, will they?"

No, I never told her about the whole guard-book debacle. Better to save some dignity than none.

"No. The guards went to sleep as soon as I entered." A slow smile spreads across her face. "The other books are happy you're here."

I frown. "You sure about that?"

"Yes, this is what happened when I took over. Come." She grabs my sleeve and pulls me to an empty lectern. "Stay here."

Then she approaches a shelf, the books still grumbling. "Oh, be quiet, all of y'all. You'll get your turns. Be patient." It's literally the most Mary Poppins moment I've ever witnessed from Mama. But before she breaks into song, she runs her finger down a line of books. "Aha! There you are."

She tugs one from the shelf, and the others immediately stop chattering as she brings the book over and opens it on the lectern.

"I thought for your first time sending me into a book, that we'd do something easy."

"So you've picked the *Complete Tales of Winnie the Pooh*?"

She shrugs. "They're very friendly inside."

I stifle a laugh. Who would've thought that my mother, a woman who can literally jump into any book she wants, would prefer that she do so with Winnie the Pooh?

One side of her mouth ticks up into a smile. "The shop has

attached itself to you. The books all know you, even the guard books."

That's a relief.

"Do you feel it?"

A low hum of magic washes over my skin, caressing me slightly. "Yeah."

"Then you're ready."

I grimace, because now that I'm faced with doing what should come naturally, I'm scared to death that I'll screw it up. "How do I do this?"

She takes my hands and presses them between her cold palms. "It's easy. Call your magic, wind it around me, and drop me into the book."

"How will you get out?"

"Pull me out. The magic works the same way. You've seen me do this plenty of times."

"Yeah, but seeing and doing are two different things."

"No, they're not, my darling, not for you." She releases my hands and cups one of my cheeks. "You can do this. Are you ready?"

"Sure." Not really, but let's just say that I am. "Wait. What if something goes wrong?"

She winks. "I believe in you. Nothing'll go wrong."

At least *one* of us believes in me. But instead of voicing my worry, I push a smile onto my face. "Okay. Ready?"

"I'm ready."

I open the book to the first page and let my magic loose. It spills from me and tumbles onto the floor, springing up around my mother in a sparkling cocoon. The next thing I know, she's sucked into Winnie the Pooh.

"Oh!" I peer into the book, but she's not drawn onto the illustrations yet. I count out a few seconds and let my gaze skim the words. They slowly wobble and wave, some of them dissolving into the paper until Clara's name surfaces like a buoy popping up from the ocean.

"She's in," I screech to the other books, which shiver and stammer in happiness.

At least I hope that's happiness. Even if it's not, it doesn't matter, because I'm happy. This has made my day. My week. My year!

If only Feylin was here to see it.

If only I could share this with the one person who made it possible.

My heart squeezes so hard it feels like it's going to erupt out of my chest. I gulp down the ache. Right now I've got to focus.

"Okay, let's pull her out."

Magic unspools from me again, slithering up the lectern and spilling over the book. A second later my mother springs out and lands on her feet.

She tosses her hands into the air. "You did it!"

"I did it!"

We hug, and she's clearly elated, so I smile faintly, pathetically trying to look happy. With my fake relationship to Feylin over, it feels like I'm missing half of myself, that joy won't ever fill me again. Love was here, with me, in my heart, but it was sucked away, and I'll never get it back.

Never.

40

FEYLIN

"*W*here's Addison?" Ryals asks.

My heart squeezes so hard it feels like a hand's crushing it—slowly, painfully, deliberately, making sure that every last drop of blood leaks out before it's turned into a stump of pulp.

It's morning. What time, I don't know. I haven't even dressed. I've been lying in bed staring at the ceiling for what feels like hours, thinking about my last moments with her.

She's the last person I want to think about, but those final minutes are burned into my brain, branded like a memory that can't be scrubbed away even if they're doused with acid.

After we both climaxed, she immediately fell asleep. I stared at her for several painful moments as the joining dissolved. It took all my willpower not to shake her awake and demand to know why she'd done what she had.

But instead I sat back and drank in her beauty one last time before I magicked her and her clothes back to her own house.

Ryals knocks loudly on the doorframe, reminding me of his presence. It's impossible not to notice his down-turned lips and brow scrunched in both confusion and anger—two emotions I'm intimately familiar with, thanks to last night.

"She's gone," I tell him.

"That's what Ophelia said, but I didn't believe her."

"Well it's true. She's gone, and she's not coming back."

She's never coming back. I never want to see her face again. How could I have been so stupid to think that a witch was worth giving my heart to?

Worse, how could I have been fooled to think that it was real? She deliberately humiliated and disrespected me—in front of my subjects—when she gave me *that book.* I was taken in by love, convinced it was real.

Well, not again. Never again will I be stupid enough to give my heart away, because there's none to give anymore. Addison took it, crumpled it into a ball, and then she stomped on it, smearing it into the ground.

I yank back the covers and get out of bed, pulling on a robe that's draped over a chair.

"Why aren't you dressed yet?" he accuses.

I sigh. "Because it was a late night."

"I heard the servants whispering something about a book."

My back tightens. "It's nothing you need to worry about. Come on. Let's have breakfast."

"I already ate. It's ten o'clock."

I stop and let my head fall onto my shoulders. I can't remember the last time I slept so late. "Fine. Let's work your falcon, then."

"Things are more fun with Addison."

"Well, she's not coming back, so stop asking for her," I snap, immediately regretting it. His eyes go wide and I sigh. "Ryals, I'm sorry. I didn't mean to snap at you. I'm just...I'm sorry."

"You broke up with her, didn't you?"

I drop my gaze and stare at the floor. "You always knew she would leave. I told you that from the beginning."

"But that was before you loved her."

The shock of his words hits me like a missile to the chest. My entire body trembles as I remember how silky her skin felt under my fingertips, how her back arched when I raked my hand between her breasts.

That whole damned thing was the most confusing sex I've ever had. I wanted her. I hated her. I despised her. I lusted for her. I wanted to push her away. I wanted to thrust inside of her and feel her stretch for me.

Before my body decides to respond to my thoughts, I take Ryals by the shoulders and turn him toward the hallway. "Give me five minutes and I'll be outside." He gives me an accusing look. I know what he's going to say, so I've got to squash this before he starts to have hope. "Ryals, Addison isn't our friend. She betrayed me and my feelings for her. She never cared about us. *Ever*. She only pretended to. Do you understand?"

"But—"

"No buts." His eyes tighten and I drop my voice. "No buts. She doesn't care about us, so we shouldn't care about her. Understand?"

"Understood," he says quietly.

As he walks out the door, I realize that I meant every word, and with those words the most clarifying thought I've had all day hits me.

Time to call Trawick.

THE FALCON TAKES flight and circles the trees, sweeping left as it returns to Ryals. It sees the mouse atop the box and dives for it.

The mouse, predictably, is terrified, and tries to scurry

away. With magic, I hold it there and also hold my breath, waiting and hoping that this time, this time it'll work.

The falcon takes the mouse in its talons and lifts back into the sky. Its sharp eyes focus on Ryals, and the bird soars toward him.

My heart thunders against my ribs as the bird closes the distance between us. Right before it soars over, its talons open and the mouse falls safely into Ryals's hands.

"You did it," I shout, roughing up his hair.

"He did it," Ryals yells.

Slow clapping comes from behind us. "Bravo! Well done!" Trawick approaches and nods to Ryals. "You've done the unthinkable—taught a falcon not to eat its prey."

Ryals smiles. "If only Addie could've seen it."

My jaw tightens. "Why don't you help put the falcon away?"

"Yes, sir."

He walks off with the menagerie man, leaving me alone with Trawick.

My friend cocks his head at me. "You look like shit."

"Thank you."

"Rough night, I assume?"

I rub my hands and two chairs appear. I don't have the energy to walk to the table on the far end of the meadow.

I sit. "I don't want to talk about it."

"Fair enough." Trawick takes the second chair and drapes his arm over the back. "If it's any consolation—"

"I don't want consolation. I don't want anything."

"Yet you called me."

"I did."

He glances around the lawn. "Where is she?"

"I sent her back."

His brows lift. "Did you find another way to—"

"No, I did not find another way to break the joining."

He sighs, his shoulders falling. Then he watches me for a long minute before finally saying, "Feylin, I'm sorry. You wanted to give her that rose, I know. I know you…loved her." His voice drops. "I know how hard this must be for you."

I don't say it, but no, he doesn't know how hard this is for me. How can someone you love destroy you, and do so publicly, while smiling the whole time?

But instead of that, all I say is, "It's not hard. Not after what she did. She showed me who she truly is, and I'm better off not being with her."

"Is that why you look like shit? Because you're better off without her?"

I give him a cold stare. "She betrayed me and made me look like a fool. A fool for believing any of it was real." My body hurts so much it feels like my bones will shatter. Is this what true heartbreak feels like? If it is, I will never experience this again. "You saw what she did, Trawick."

"I did," he says slowly, "and I have feelings about it. I'm not sure they're the same as yours."

"Then keep them to yourself. I don't want to hear it. I didn't call you here to discuss how awful I look."

"Smell, too. Did you shower?"

When I give him a look that could blister his skin, he lifts his palms in surrender. "Too soon?"

I ignore his joke and push on with what I've got to say. "I've contacted the Witch and Wizard Council."

His brows lift. "When?"

"This morning. Just before you arrived."

"I assume they don't know about the broken engagement."

I thread my fingers together and tuck my hands behind my head. "What broken engagement? I never told Addison that we'd broken up."

He smirks. "So you need me to be your witness."

I drop my hands to my knees and lean forward, steeling my

heart. Pain bites into it, eating at me, ripping me apart piece by torturous piece, but I curl my fists against it. Every cell in my body screams at me not to do this, to stop, to think. But if I stop and think, I'll change my mind, and this isn't the time for weakness.

Because I want to destroy her like she's destroyed me.

One day ago, this would have been unthinkable. But not anymore. I spent weeks shifting, softening to her, but that's gone. The old me is back—the me who wants revenge.

She and her entire family are going to regret what they did.

"I called you here," I tell Trawick, "to tell you that the council's arriving soon." I glance at my watch. "Should be here in a few minutes. I want you to witness what I've wanted since Tess died. This is beginning of the end of the Thornrose family. Because when I'm through with them, none of them—not even Addison—will know what hit them."

---

41

*T*ry as I might, I can't send my mother into a book again. She smiles and tells me it's no big deal, but the reason's obvious—my family's magic is failing, and quickly.

When the rest of the employees arrive, Mama tells them that the bookshop's back on track. The magic's connected to me, and business can proceed as usual.

That should offer me some comfort, but it doesn't. While Mama stays, I feign fatigue and head home, managing to sneak into the house without anyone seeing me. Soon as I close my bedroom door, I'm under the covers and trying to get some sleep.

But sleep won't come.

That's when the tears do.

I didn't want to cry over Feylin. I didn't even cry when Edward broke up with me, and I thought that I loved him. But an ugly cry takes me over until my nose is stopped up so fiercely that I become a mouth-breather, and my eyes are so red that there's no way I'm going out in public anytime soon.

I don't go downstairs for lunch or dinner. I'm not hungry. My stomach doesn't growl once.

It's when the sun's sank into the horizon and the moon's high in the sky that faint knocking comes from the door.

If I don't respond, maybe they'll go away.

"Addie, we know you're in there."

It's Blair. She's probably got Chelsea with her.

"We're coming in."

No point trying to stop them.

The doorknob turns slowly, and Blair peeks in, a feeble smile on her face. Chelsea's right behind her, waving a tub of Tillamook Mudslide ice cream.

This is so unfair. They know I can't say no to Tillamook.

"We brought you a gift." Chelsea pulls a spoon from her back pocket and sits on the bed, as does Blair. "We had to go a couple towns over to find it, but we managed. It was the last one in the freezer case."

"Chelsea had to promise the man who was also reaching for it a date," Blair informs me.

"He was hot. We might have fun."

"If you don't ghost him." Blair rolls her eyes. "But you probably will."

Chelsea shrugs because she probably will ghost him. She opens the lid. "We let it sit out a few minutes, so it should be melted enough to eat."

When I don't move, Blair frowns. "Sit up. You've got to eat something."

"No, I don't."

"Yes, you do."

"Fine, then I'll eat it." Chelsea starts to dig the spoon into the half-gallon of chocolate bliss. "I'm going to love every bite of this."

"No, that's okay." I sit up and take the spoon and tub,

hugging the ice cream to my chest and not caring that beads of ice are crystallizing on my shirt. "I'll eat it."

Just for them, I take a bite, and it's amazing. Of course. But it's not plugging the massive hole in my chest.

Blair picks at a thread in the comforter. "I'm sorry for not telling you the truth about Feylin."

"Me too," Chelsea murmurs. "I really, really wanted it to be true love. It has to happen to somebody in this family, and when all that magic released, I thought for sure it was love."

"Nope, not love."

They look so sad, and honestly I can't be angry with them. Mama and Dad would've told all my sisters not to say anything to me about what had happened to Tess, and I understand that.

After I'm a few bites in, Chelsea says, "We heard about your magic. Of course, we saw it, too, last night. Congrats!"

"Congratulations," Blair adds, beaming.

"Thanks," I reply flatly.

They exchange a look. It's Blair who speaks first. "Addie, this is what you've always wanted. Why aren't you excited?"

"Maybe because of...you know what," Chelsea reminds her.

"Right. Well, it's still a great thing that's happened, and we want to celebrate it."

"With ice cream?" I ask around a mouthful of chocolate and fudge.

"No." Chelsea's eyes sparkle. "We've got something better in mind."

I'M STANDING in front of a rack of cast-iron skillets. These aren't your normal variety cast iron. They've got long handles and wide-mouthed pans, perfect for sitting on. There are eight of them. Wait, nine now.

One has a shiny red bow wrapped around it.

"Surprise," my sisters say in unison.

I nearly drop the ice cream, which I've been clutching like a starving dog with a bone. Anyone dares take my Tillamook and they're dead.

Tears prick my eyes. "You got me my own riding skillet?"

Blair grins. "We sure did. Want to take her for a spin?"

"Yes. Wait. I think my magic's burnt out. I couldn't send Mama into a book twice."

"It's probably built back up now," Chelsea tells me. "The least we can do is try."

I run my fingers down the rough texture of the cast iron. My whole life I've wanted one of these for myself, but I had to settle for riding double behind someone—my dad, usually.

But now I've got my very own skillet.

I set my ice cream on the back porch table and grab the long handle. It feels good, cool, but the texture gives it bite.

We take our three skillets outside, and I throw one leg over like I've done numerous times. My left hand is positioned in front of the other, and I ease back onto the flat side of the pan before allowing my magic to slowly unfurl.

It hesitantly winds around the skillet like it's feeling it out, trying to decide if the cast iron is friend or foe.

Apparently it makes a decision, because the next thing I know, I'm shooting up into the sky, zipping above the trees, the wind slapping my face and bats scattering as I race toward the full moon.

My sisters quickly catch up, laughing.

"Isn't this the best?" Blair yells.

My stomach's been left on the ground, and even though this should be amazing, it feels a bit lackluster. But they've gone to so much trouble to make me happy that I don't want them to think that this is anything but awesome.

"It is," I forcefully shout. Maybe a little too forcefully, so I rein it back in. "I feel like a real witch."

Chelsea laughs. "It's about time!"

We fly for maybe half an hour, the only bad part being when I spy the castle bathed in moonlight. My throat tightens, and I can't help but wonder what Feylin's up to, what he's done today. How's Ryals? Does he miss me? I miss him and our little family.

Blair slides up to me. "Let's go this way," she instructs, pointing in the other direction, trying to keep me from wallowing in my own pool of misery.

"Sure," I reply numbly.

A few minutes later my magic begins to fade.

"Time to turn back," Blair calls.

Hers must be dying, too.

We almost make it home, landing a few streets from our house, in a park flanked on one side by houses. It only takes a few minutes for my arm to start aching from carrying the skillet. Turns out they're easier to sit on than they are to carry. Go figure.

"That should've been longer," I say. "Didn't we use to fly longer before?"

Blair smirks.

Oh *right*. "So it's pretty bad, isn't it?"

Chelsea pushes up a smile. "It could be worse."

"Yeah, if you call having your toenails ripped out worse," Blair snipes.

"And no balls," I murmur. "Ovie said that she would start them—"

"We know," Chelsea bites out. "But Charlie kept her busy. If you remember, he showed up just before your first ceremony, which was the same day that she promised to restart them. But now he's gone, though."

"And she's in bed, crying. Yay, us," Blair says coldly.

I twist my hair around my finger. I don't want a witch ball. I don't want to marry. I have no intention of giving my heart to anyone ever again. But that doesn't mean I can't get my sisters married off.

"Look, if we're going to save this family's magic, Ovie's gonna have to get out of bed," I say.

My sisters shoot me shocked looks. "Do you have a fever?" Blair asks. "You're the one who ran off during the first ball."

"I know. But this isn't about me. It's about the Thornroses, and Blair, out there somewhere is a super hot wizard or werewolf who wants to marry you, and we need to find him."

Chelsea nudges me with her arm. "What exactly are you saying?"

"That we need to get Ovie out of her bed and back to planning witch balls."

42

Ovie needed a distraction, that's what she told us the next day, so she was happy to return to planning the balls.

"We'll focus on Blair, how's that sound?" she said.

"Sounds perfect," I told her.

So the next few days are spent with me perfecting my magical sending-someone-into-a-book abilities while Ovie plans the ball.

The day of the big event, I keep myself busy thinking about everything *other* than witch balls, or at least doing my best to. But all good things must come to an end, and the hours leading to the event eventually creep up.

"Mr. Bakerstone, how was the trip?"

An older wizard with a huge comb-over nods and smiles. "Addie, you're just about the best there is," he says in a deep Southern drawl. "Not only did you pick out the perfect book, but I enjoyed my hunt. I'd rather shoot magical animals any day than real ones."

I smile and close the Ernest Hemingway tome that I'd

selected for him. "I'm so glad. I'll put it back on the shelf for you."

As he heads toward the front door, a young woman with honey-colored skin jumps from a book. The grin on her face is so big that I can't help but grin, too.

"Mila, did you love it?"

"Yes, Addie! Oh my gosh, that book had everything I wanted—romance, adventure, a funny sidekick."

I laugh. "I knew you'd enjoy it."

"I more than enjoyed it. It was swoonworthy." She sighs dramatically. "You're the best." She grabs her hat and coat from the rack. "See you next week."

"See you then."

I close her book and add it to the one in my hands. The Bookshop of Magic was always my dream, and here I am, finally fulfilling that dream.

Mama comes over and smiles. "The ball's tonight. Why don't you go get ready?"

"You sure?" I slip the books I'm carrying back on their respective shelves. "There's still a lot to do before closing up."

She nods. "I'm sure. You've been working ten-hour days. You deserve to leave a little early to get ready. I'll see you at the ball."

"Okay." I grab my coat and slide my arms into it. "Don't be late. I have a feeling that Blair's going to meet her match tonight."

Mama laughs. "I won't be. See you there."

THE GOWN that Ovie's chosen for me, is, let's just say—

"Monstrous," Blair says, sweeping blush on her cheeks.

"You think?" I turn from side to side, eyeing the structured framework of felt that juts up from my shoulders before bending down and latching onto my back. "I don't know. I kind of like it. It has a BDSM feel to it."

Chelsea laughs. "I guess Ovie wants you to be more open to exploring that side of yourself. You know, bend over and take your spanking, Addie."

Silence blankets the room before the three of us burst into a fit of laughter. I sigh. "At least it's not too itchy."

I take one last look in the mirror. The hollows of my cheeks are shallower than they were two weeks ago. My appetite's pitiful, but if my family notices, they haven't said anything.

At least I have the bookstore. It's a small consolation for everything that's happened, but it's what I need right now. It's my anchor.

"Y'all ready?" Blair asks.

"Yeah. Let's go."

The music at the ball's sweeping as always, as a string quartet plays something that suggests romance. Blair's been dancing her head off as suitor after suitor—wizard, werewolf, vampire—have asked for her hand.

A few have approached me as well, but I've declined those offers.

Every once in a while as I'm scanning the crowd, I spot a headful of dark hair that makes my heart stutter to a stop, because I'm sure it's Feylin.

But when the crowd parts and I get a better look at the face attached to the hair, disappointment sinks in.

He's not coming. He's never coming to one of these things again.

Fine. Good riddance. I don't need love anyway.

"Having a good time?"

Ovie hands me a glass of punch. "Thank you."

"You're welcome." We're silent for a minute as we watch the dancers. "I would've waited longer to restart the balls, you know."

"I know. But with Charlie gone, we figured…"

My voice trails off, and she stares down at her full cup of punch. "Y'all figured that I'd need something to keep me busy so that I wouldn't think about him."

"Something like that," I mutter.

"He's going to change," she says quietly. "He promised. You know, gambling's a hard thing to overcome."

But he's not going to overcome it if you keep giving him money. "I'm sure it's very hard. I can't imagine."

She's quiet for a moment before she inhales a sharp breath. "Your mother tells me that you're doing amazing at the bookstore."

"Thank you. I love it. I only wished I'd found my powers sooner."

She squeezes my arm and smiles gently, her brown eyes shining bright. "My girl, better late than never."

Somehow I wish my aunt would take her own advice and dump Charlie, because later is certainly better than never in his case. But all I say is, "Good point."

The music stops. "I'm going to find Blair and see if any of these men seem like good candidates." Her gaze washes up and down me. "Try to have some fun, Addie. If not for your sake, then for your sister's."

She nods to Blair, who's shooting us worried looks. I grin widely, suggesting that I'm having the time of my life. Then I bring the cup of punch to my mouth and drain it dry. By the time I look at her again, she's directed her attention to Ovie.

I turn to head over to the punch table and come to a staggering stop. Every muscle in my body tightens into little balls of steel. My breath gets caught in my throat, and when I do manage to pull in a lungful, it stutters.

"Edward," I whisper.

He gives me a smarmy smile. "Addison, you look lovely."

"Thank you."

He strolls up as if he didn't break my heart, and as if he didn't humiliate me publicly at the very last witch ball.

When we're a couple of feet apart, I take a good look at him and for the first time notice how small he is. He's not much taller than me and thin, almost frail. He looks easy to break, which isn't how I used to think of him.

He used to hold the moon, albeit a moon that was, in hindsight, out of reach.

"Addison," he purrs, "I was sorry to hear about your engagement to that awful fae king. It's probably for the best that it didn't work out. Those fae can be so...arrogant, haughty. Don't you think?"

Look who's calling the kettle black. "They aren't once you get to know them."

He smiles, showing off that million-watt glint of his. "I'm sure. But our kind don't mix, and if there's one thing I've learned in my time, it's that witches belong with wizards."

Where is this going? "Is that so?"

"Yes, it is." He sidles up and lightly brushes his fingers over the top of my shoulder. Once there would've been sparks igniting my skin. But now there's nothing. His touch feels cold, dead.

Not like how it was when I touched Feylin.

Good grief. Stop thinking about him. You're done with love, remember?

"I heard," he continues, "that you've been busy learning how to use your magic."

Oh, I see what's going on. "Yes. I've learned it. Someone..." My throat shrivels as the words *someone taught me* nearly leaves my mouth. "I learned," I add quickly. "It was within me all along."

"It just had to be unlocked, eh?" He pumps his brows suggestively. My stomach lurches. "Speaking of unlocking things." More eyebrow pumping. "I was thinking that maybe we were too hasty when we broke things off."

"We? I didn't break anything off. You did, in case you've forgotten."

"Is that so? Are you sure? Well, I must've been out of my mind, because out of all the women here, you're the most beautiful. And you see, I miss you, Addie. You're all I've been thinking about these past weeks ever since we broke up."

It's the way he says my name that really grates on my nerves. He says it lightly, without depth, as if my name on his lips is nothing more than a ghost of a word.

It wasn't that way with Feylin.

Okay, I get it. I'm thinking a lot about him right now. But it can't be helped because—ball, Edward, horrible love—all that.

"Edward," I say, taking his tie and straightening it.

His eyes twinkle with delight. "Yes?"

He's a little breathless as I smooth the collar of his shirt. My gaze flicks from his bobbing Adam's apple to his eyes. "Edward," I repeat, "you crushed my heart, and now you're asking me to take you back."

He laughs nervously. "Well, when you put it that way—"

"Yes, I'm putting it that way because that's how it was. You broke up with me because I wasn't good enough. You told me so yourself. And you know what I've learned these past weeks?"

His gaze swishes nervously from side to side. "What's that?"

I curl my hands over his shoulders and look him dead in the eye. "I've learned that *you* aren't good enough for *me*. So no, there's no way I would ever take you back, and if I can help it, I'll make sure that none of my sisters fall for you, either."

His face pales. "Well, you don't have to be so rude about it."

I drop my hands to my sides and step back. "Yes, I'm afraid

that I do have to be so rude about it. Have a nice life, Edward. Don't let the door hit you on the way out."

With that, he huffs and storms through the crowd and, hopefully, right on out the door.

My chest swells with pride as a laugh bubbles from my throat. I wish Feylin was here to see this.

But he's not here, and I have to accept that. I'll have to settle with being proud of myself for telling Edward off, and for showing him how worthless he made me feel.

As a wobbling satisfaction flows through me, I head back to the punch table but get interrupted when the music stops abruptly.

Ovie runs into the center of the ballroom, and the couples on the dance floor part like the Red Sea. "The bookshop," she yells. "Addison! Come quickly. The shop's in trouble!"

43

I arrive to find the shop doors thrown wide open and books streaming outside, carried on a current of magic to a portal, where they disappear.

Two wizards flank the open doors, flicking their hands like maestros as they orchestrate the books out and away.

No, no, no, no, no!

I rush to the portal and pluck an armload of books from the magical current before they have a chance to disappear into goodness knows where.

When I'm loaded down, I throw myself in front of the wizards. "What are you doing? What's going on?"

The wizard on the left looks at me and sighs like he's thinking, *I don't get paid enough to deal with this.* "We're shutting it down."

My heart plummets. "Shutting it down?"

"Yes. Now get out of the way, or we'll be forced to arrest you."

I scoff. "On whose authority?"

The second wizard rolls his eyes. "On the authority of the Witch and Wizard Council."

My heart, which is currently lying on the ground, flops over. "What?"

"Now, move," the second wizard snarls. "This is your final warning."

"You can't do this."

They exchange a look, and the first one shakes his head as if wondering how he got stuck with the job of dealing with the hysterical witch in front of him. When he turns to me, his face sinks with pity.

"Look. Your mother's already trying to talk to the council, but there's nothing you can do here unless you can convince *him* to change his mind. And I doubt you will."

"Him, who?"

The other wizard thumbs over his shoulder. "Back there."

My gaze sweeps past them, and that's when I see him. Even though he's standing in shadow, I would know that silhouette anywhere.

Feylin.

An electrical pulse flares down my spine at the sight of him. Shadows gobble him up, and it's impossible to tell if the darkness is from the lack of witch lights or if it's leaking from his very soul.

Either way, fury wraps around my body and pulls tight. He can't do this. He can't shut down the shop.

Still clutching the books, I charge between the wizards and head over.

Blair intercepts me, grabbing my sleeve. Her gaze flicks worriedly to Feylin. "Mama's trying to stop this. Don't do anything stupid."

"I'm not waiting for her. If we don't do something now, they'll have all the books gone by the time she gets here. I know what I'm doing."

I don't but that's not important. I shrug off her hold and storm over.

He stands in shadows like he's become them, and his aura's so dark that it steals my breath. "Feylin, what are you doing?"

He doesn't answer, but anger rolls off him in waves of energy so thick that it's suffocating.

"You will talk to me!"

I charge up, stopping only feet away. He lifts his head and takes a step forward. The shadows slip off as he steps into a pool of light.

It's the look in his eyes that makes me stop breathing. Those eyes, which once held a world of softness in them, are now as hard as diamond-encrusted daggers.

I swallow past the watermelon-sized knot in my throat. My fingers tremble as they clutch the books harder to my chest. There's nothing but malice in his gaze as he drinks me in, noting the way my hair's piled on top of my head before his gaze flicks to the dress I'm wearing.

It must look like I jumped right back into the dating circuit as soon as we ended things, ready to find a husband.

It only deepens the betrayal in his eyes.

"You can't do this," I manage, doing everything to keep my voice steady. "I know you hate me. But you can't close the shop. It's my family's livelihood."

"They should have thought about that before they let an innocent die."

"It was an accident. Feylin, you've got to—"

"Believe you?"

He stalks forward, his feet eating the cobblestones that separate us. A wall of his magic slams into me. It's thick, stifling and steeped in betrayal, rage. That same rage burns in his eyes. When he stops in front of me, our chests are so close that they nearly touch. I'm forced to bend my neck just to keep eye contact.

A muscle in his jaw feathers as he glares down at me. "Why should I believe you?"

The anger in his eyes glows hotter than a galaxy of suns. Every argument that I have slips from my mind as fury burns in him. My tongue's in knots. There are no words to counter the rage that's wafting off him in thick, smothering sheets of magic.

Before I can answer, one of the wizards approaches. "We've got what we need. You can do what you want."

Feylin nods and slips past me.

"We'll be taking those." The wizard grabs the first few books in my arms before there's a chance for me to stop him. When he reaches for the last one, I clutch it to my chest as if my life depends on it.

"No. You can't have it."

"She's not giving up one of them," he calls to his partner.

The other waves him off. "As long as it doesn't get destroyed, I don't care what happens to it."

The wizard drops his hands to his hips. "I guess that solves that. You can keep it."

Without another word, he walks off.

His words replay in my mind. *As long as it doesn't get destroyed.* What does that mean?

And that's when my gaze latches onto Feylin. He takes a position dead center in front of the store.

My gaze slashes right. The portal's closed, but hundreds of books still line the store's shelves. The wizards didn't take all of them.

I glance at the book in my arms and my body shudders. It's the *Book of Ruin,* an ancient and dangerous text. It's rare. This is the only copy.

Realization hits me hard. The other books that I was holding were probably rare, too. Which means that what's left in the shop are the common, everyday books.

Pieces of the puzzle click together.

The wizards now stand off to the side, watching Feylin,

who lifts his hand. That's when cold dread pools in my stomach.

He's going to burn it to the ground. It's the only way for him to destroy the magic that makes the store capable of letting people into the books.

Before my logical mind has time to tell me that what I'm doing is stupid, I fling myself in front of the bookstore. "Stop this, Feylin! You've got what you want. The store's closed."

His next words grind out of him. "Move, Addison."

"I won't." I lift my chin defiantly. "If you're going to burn it, you'll have to burn me, too."

"You need to move," he says again, his voice steel.

Everything about him is hard—the muscles clenched in his face, the tight line of his shoulders. He's not willing to give an inch. Well, neither am I.

"No. I'm not going anywhere."

"For the last time—"

"No! You'll have to destroy me, too!"

"Very well," he murmurs.

He lifts his left hand, and before there's time for me to react, magic wraps around me, pulling me from the doorway and slinging me through the air.

"Feylin, no!"

I call on my own power, or try to, but he's locked it away. There's no way to stop the magic that drags me from the bookstore, holding me tight. I try to dig my heels into the ground, but they trail along the cobblestones as I'm pulled twenty yards away and held in place.

All I can do is watch in horror as magic erupts from Feylin's palm, creating a spiral of power that jumps into the bookshop.

The world's still for a moment before a great *whoosh* sounds from inside the shop. Thick fingers of fire smash the glass windows and flick like a giant tongue from the doorway.

The store has burst into flames.

The fire's so hot, and it eats at the inside of the shop so fast that within seconds I know it's all lost. It's all gone. Every book, every bit of magic that made the store special, is destroyed.

Feylin's magical hold on me loosens, and I collapse onto my hands and knees, sobbing. I'm crying for all of it—what happened the night of the fire ceremony, the joining that forced us apart, my broken heart, how Feylin looked at me like I'm nothing more than a stranger. All the agony that's been tearing my heart apart these weeks flows out of me onto the cobblestones. I was right never to want to love. All it does is destroy your heart and your life. It's not worth it. Loving isn't worth it.

As my shoulders quiver and my stomach clenches, I dare another look at the shop.

My gaze lands on Feylin. He's turned around, staring at me. My breath hitches as his dark eyes absorb me. And then, as quickly as our gazes latch, he vanishes, leaving my family, and me, destroyed.

44

The next day, there's nothing left of the shop except for a charred and smoldering skeleton. The fire was self-contained and burned itself out over the course of an hour. But there wasn't anything to save by the time it finished sweeping through the store.

Brittle, charred beams crunch under my feet as I make my way inside.

Mama bends over and picks up a piece of paper that's mostly burned, though a square of it is untouched by the fire.

She sighs. "It's all gone."

My father hugs her to him. "We'll build something else, Clara. Something better."

She gives him a feeble nod, but I know what she's thinking. The shop's been in our family for years. What else can we do? What else do we know?

My sisters shuffle through the mess. Tears streak down their cheeks, and they threaten the do the same to mine, but I curl my fists every time a tear threatens to pop out from under my lids.

I can't scrub the image of Feylin's last look at me from my

mind. His expression was unreadable, but there he was, watching me, gloating, probably, elated that he'd finally done what he'd wanted all along—to end us.

An arm wraps around my shoulder. I glance up at my father, who squeezes me into his side. "Come on. Let's get this mess cleaned up, and then we'll plan on making a better future."

"Sure," I tell him.

But there isn't a better life after this. Only a few weeks ago I was promised a better one, and that got ripped away, just like the next one will be.

FEYLIN

ray smoke curls into the sky. It almost looks like fog in the early morning sun.

Almost.

I don't know how long I've been standing in this window, staring out, watching the destruction I've wanted for years.

Revenge should feel good. I should be rejoicing, but the pit in my stomach is even bigger than it was before.

An image of Addison hunched over the cobblestones, light slashing across her back as she sobs, slips through the mental barriers that I thought were well established when it comes to her. After all, I didn't give an inch when she begged me not to destroy the shop. There wasn't even the temptation to hesitate. She's nothing as far as I'm concerned.

Then why won't that damned picture of her crying leave my head? *Because it was the* way *she sobbed.* The thought penetrates my mind before I'm able to stop it.

She wasn't crying just because of the shop's loss. It was because of something else, something more.

Me. It was because of me.

"Majesty?" My gaze flicks to the doorway, where Ophelia stands with a tray. "Your breakfast."

I shift my weight from one hip to the other. "You can place it on the desk."

She nods and enters, taking in the rumpled blanket on the couch, the empty whiskey glass on the side table, and last night's dinner that still sits untouched atop my desk.

She moves that tray aside and puts down the new one. I turn back to the window.

"You have to eat," she murmurs.

"I will when I'm hungry," I grumble.

Ophelia's steps are fae-silent as she walks back to exit the room. I feel the shift in energy before she pauses at the door.

When I glance over, she's staring out the same window that I am, watching the smoke trickle to the heavens.

"Majesty, I know it's not my place, but…" Her gaze slashes to the open rectangular box sitting atop my desk. The golden rose, still perfectly red, sits inside, waiting to be taken by someone. "I know you may not want to hear this, but I don't think Miss Thornrose planned for what happened at the fire ceremony."

I grind my next words to dust. "Then what do you think she meant, Ophelia?"

She fidgets briefly before clearing her throat and gaining the courage to go on. "I can't imagine that she would ever have hurt you, and may I say that when she was here, you were, for the first time since I've known you, happier than you've ever been. Not that you weren't happy with the late queen. You were. But with Miss Thornrose there was a lightness to you that I'd never seen before. And for what it's worth, the night of the solstice was the happiest that I'd ever seen both of you."

Her words make my throat dry.

"She loved you very much," Ophelia adds.

And it's those words that cause a shift in me, that make my heart tighten so hard it might explode.

Addison loved me? I rip my fingers through my hair. Of course she loved me. She got her magic the night of the solstice when I all but told her that I loved her. And I did love her. It's a lie to deny it.

The floor falls out from under my feet.

What have I done?

I've taken everything from her family, and I did it all because I couldn't let go. For so long I've held on to my anger, and now I've got my revenge. The bookshop's burned to the ground, never to be reopened.

And how do I feel about it?

Even worse.

Ophelia's right. With Addison, I *was* different. I was, dare I even think it—*happy*. I was able to push thoughts of Tess aside and let them go. Fury didn't have the same stranglehold on me that it used to.

But I gave all that up. For what?

Because she betrayed me, I remind myself.

"I'll go," Ophelia says.

She leaves, and the only sound is the crackling of the fire.

Until it isn't.

"Oh my goodness, you don't know how long it's taken me to figure out how to get into this thing. Ugh. I thought three lifetimes might pass before I got out of that stupid compact and into a more suitable mirror."

I'm staring at the one mirror in my study, and the reflection isn't occupied by me. There's a man in there—a man with a white pompadour that's almost a foot high.

Am I imagining this? "Who are you?"

The image clears his throat and grabs the lapels of his jacket. "My name's Elmore, and I'm a friend of Addison's."

I cock my brow. "A friend?"

"Yes, a friend. Someone you need to talk to."

"And why's that?"

"Because there's a lot you don't know about that last ceremony."

Doubtful. "There is?"

"There *is*—starting with, Addison was set up."

Set up? I cross to the mirror and stare at Elmore for a long beat before saying, "Tell me everything."

46

We get most of the bookshop cleaned up, but it's still charred to a crisp by the time we leave for the day. I don't sleep well that night, and the next morning, as soon as the light seeps into the sky, I pull on a sweater, tug on a pair of old boots and head outside into the backyard.

Two homemade swings dangle from the giant oak that eats up most of the grass. I sit in one and swing idly back and forth, trying not to think about...anything, really.

Which is impossible. The place is destroyed, and it's all because of me.

"You look lonesome."

Blair makes her way down the stairs, a long braid swept over one shoulder. She sits in the swing beside me and glides back and forth.

"I guess I am."

We're quiet for a minute before she says, "It's all gone."

Just hearing that makes my shoulders fall. "I'm sorry. It's my fault."

"How?" She looks up from the ground, where she's been

slowly digging a hole with the toe of her shoe. "How's this your fault?"

"If I hadn't given him that book—"

"Addie, no. Just stop. You didn't know what that book meant when you gave it to him. None of this is on your shoulders. We should've told you."

"But I didn't tell him how I got the book. That I was tricked into giving it to him."

"He wouldn't have listened. He was too in love with you and too shattered. Because it hurt him so much."

Her words strike me. "What?"

My sister pushes off and swings back and forth slowly. "Just what I said. Feylin loved you too much to listen to you." She sighs. "That's why he burned down the bookstore."

I scoff. "No. He did it to get back at me."

"Yeah, because he loves you."

"Stop saying that."

"Why?" She shrugs. "It's true. He's hurting because of that love. And you love him, which obviously he doesn't know or else he wouldn't have done what he did."

I rise from the swing. "What are you talking about?"

"Come on. It's so obvious." She scoffs. "Feylin destroyed the store, and even though it sucks—because it does—it's because of his feelings."

"I hope this isn't supposed to make me feel better, because it doesn't."

She shrugs. "It's just an observation."

I plop back down on the swing. "Burning it down was his plan all along."

She frowns and comes to a stop. "If that's true, then why didn't he do it earlier? Why'd he wait?"

"Well, because…" Why didn't he do it earlier? We spent weeks in each other's company while he tried to figure out how to get my magic to flourish. He could've done it then.

He could've done it at any time.

But he didn't.

Realization hits me like a semitruck. "Oh my goodness! He loved me!"

"And probably still does," she says, smiling sadly. "But the question is—do you love him?"

"Of course I don't…"

As she watches me, my voice trails off. I'm angry at him, yes. Furious? Yes. But even with all of that, Feylin's still the only man who ever accepted me just the way that I am. When I was with him, I felt whole, complete, and without him, I'm a hollowed-out shell.

My eyes widen because I'm realizing what's been staring me in the face. I still love him. Even though I never said it outright, that doesn't make it any less true.

"I do love him," I tell her. "I was so…different with him. I could be myself and not worry about him being annoyed because of my picky eating habits or that most of my clothes are itchy."

"Did you ever say it?"

"Well, no. But neither did he."

As all these thoughts ping-pong in my head and I allow myself to feel what I've buried in my heart for weeks, I realize that I don't care that Feylin destroyed the bookstore. He didn't mean it. He was trying to say was that he's in pain, and hurting, and loves me. And he doesn't know how I feel about him because I never told him.

If anyone needs to hear that he's loved, it's Feylin—the broken king who, for so long, carried his burden of responsibility quietly, and who, out of all the people that I know, needs to hear that he's loved.

Will it make a difference? Probably not. He may still hate me. But that's okay, because he needs to know how he completed me. Even if he slams the castle door in my face when I'm done, it'll have been worth it.

I jump out of my seat.

"Where're you going?"

I spin around and puff up my chest. "To take a shower, and after that, I'm going to tell the man that I love exactly how I feel."

47

FEYLIN

"Zandra, you came quickly."

Her cherry-red lips twist into a sorrowful frown. "Feylin, I'm so sorry about what happened. I never thought that Addison could be so cruel." She brushes her fingers across my collar. "How are you?"

"I'm...managing," I reply, struggling to find the right word.

I wave her to the stuffy brocade couch. It's the one place of furniture that I never sit on. It's a leftover from my father's office, who kept it because it had been passed down from his father.

She sits with a heavy sigh and crosses one glossy black high-heeled foot over the other. "I'm so glad you called."

"Can I get you something to drink? Water? Whiskey?"

"Whiskey would be great."

I ignore the fact that it's eleven in the morning and pour her two fingers. She takes the tumbler from me, being sure to slide her hands over mine before topping the gesture off with a slow lick to her lower lip.

"Thank you."

"You're welcome." I sit in the plush leather sofa across from her.

"You're not going to sit beside me?"

"No, I'm too angry."

"Yes," she agrees. "Like I said, I never thought Addison would do something like that. She seemed so nice." She tsks. "But after all, she's a Thornrose. What did I expect?"

"Exactly." I curl my hand into a fist and tap it against my thigh. "I'm just glad that I found out sooner rather than later the kind of woman she really is."

Zandra spreads her hand over her chest. "Exactly. Thank the heavens. In my opinion you've done yourself, and all of us, a favor. That woman never could've been our queen."

She leans forward, letting her blouse fall open to expose her cleavage.

It's all I can do not to roll my eyes. "You know, Zandra, ever since Addison left, I've been thinking about my friends."

Her eyes light up. "Yes?"

"And how you're one of them."

"Absolutely." She bows her head. "I am but your humble servant."

Spare me the theatrics. "I've always known that, but lately"—I rise and cross to her to sit; she scoots closer to me—"lately I've come to realize what I've been missing my entire life."

Her eyes dance with delight. "Is that right?"

"Yes. You remember how I didn't want to marry Tess at first."

"How could I forget? We'd only broken up a little while before then."

"Yes." I take her hand—the one that's not clutching the whiskey in a talon-like hold. "And I've come to see that I was wrong to end things between us."

"Oh?" She smiles as warmly as a serpent. "Do you think so?"

"I do. Zandra, we belong together." I caress her face before dropping my hand and rising, turning away from her. "But I'm torn. You've always been there for me. Your friendship means so much."

"It does?"

"How could I have been so blind? Tess and I were never as close as us. She was assigned to me, and I did my duty in marrying her. But luckily you were there the day that she died, and you were able to tell me everything that happened. But honestly, deep down—and I hate to admit this—"

"What, Feylin, what is it?" The desperation in her voice is so thick that I can nearly smell it.

"Tess and I, we were never a good match. We only tolerated each other at best. I wasn't miserable, but I wasn't far off, either. We were roommates more than anything. Which is why there was never a child."

Zandra sucks in a breath.

"And even more so, I'm relieved that Addison's gone." I laugh bitterly. "Can you imagine *me* being with a witch? What a joke. She did me a favor when she gave me that book. Now that I think about it—two favors have happened. Tess died, and Addison tried to humiliate me. I could've done without the humiliation, but things worked out the way that they did for a reason. If only there was someone to thank for all of it."

"It was me," she yells.

I whip around and Zandra's holding the glass, standing up, her expression a mixture of hope and confusion. "What did you say?"

Her face contorts with worry but also glee as she floats over. "It was me, Feylin. I gave Addison that book. I knew she wasn't right for you." She tips back her head and chuckles. "How could a king, a fae at that, marry a lowly witch who's only claim to fame is that her parents own a magical bookshop?"

I exhale a gusty sigh. "I know. I married wrong the first time. And to think, I almost repeated the past by wedding someone so wrong for me. Tess was bad enough, but Addison? I would've been miserable. I'm glad they're gone from my life." It takes all my will to clutch her arms and squeeze them. "Thankfully you're here. What I wouldn't give to turn back time and make up for all that we lost. I wish…"

I drop my gaze, and Zandra's voice is soft when she says, "What do you wish, Feylin?"

I hesitate. "I wish that I'd never married Tess. It was a mistake. I hate to say it, but that book did me a favor."

It's soul-crushing just to say it. Never mind how my insides have withered throughout this conversation.

But Zandra doesn't wither. She blossoms as her lips curve into a devilish grin. "What would you say if I told you that Tess's death wasn't an accident?"

I tip my head to the ceiling in relief. "I would say, thank you. I wish I'd known sooner."

She walks her fingers up my arm to my shoulder. "I planned it."

"Impossible."

She grins slyly. "Feylin, we both know that Tess didn't understand what you need. She was thrown into the marriage just like you were. I could tell that you didn't love her, but you couldn't leave her, out of respect for your parents. Your father arranged that marriage in case you hadn't settled down by the time you turned thirty. When your thirtieth birthday arrived, I thought for sure that you'd ask me to be your wife. But when you broke it off so that you could fulfill your father's arrangement, I was crushed.

"But I watched you and Tess together. There was some affection between you, but it wasn't what *we* could have had. And obviously there weren't any children, so you couldn't have been doing it. So yes, I took it upon myself to save you."

I want to punch a wall. "Please, go on."

She shrugs nonchalantly. "So I hatched a plan. I don't know why I'm telling you this. Maybe I'm tired of holding on to all of it. But you deserve to know, and you've said what I suspected all along—that you never really loved Tess."

Stay on track, Zandra. "But your plan."

"Yes." She swigs the last of the whiskey and places the tumbler on a nearby table. "I told Tess about this wonderful place I'd heard about—a shop where you could jump into the books. I'd been before and knew that they had strict rules, but I have charm and few can tell me no." She smirks, so proud of herself. "So I picked a book with the most violence and the most fun. I convinced her that we'd be safe, and I made her promise not to tell you what we were doing. When we arrived, the worker didn't want to use our book. He made some excuse about only vetted novels. But all it took was a few smiles and pouty lips to convince him that the owner had said it was okay. I mean, I'd come so far. I wasn't about to let some lowly wizard ruin my plans.

"And on top of that, Tess was all-in. I'd already promised that she'd be safe. We'd only do the harmless chapters." Her lips part in a grin fit for a piranha. "But I lied." She shakes her head. "I don't know why I'm telling you this," she repeats.

"Please continue." I grab the empty tumbler and drop another finger of whiskey into it. "Don't stop."

She takes a sip and smiles. "Like I said, I lied to her. But not completely. At first everything *was* fun and easy." Her jaw flexes. "But I'd loved you since we were children, and Tess didn't deserve you. She couldn't even give you an heir. I could," she says bitterly. "If I was given the chance."

I stroke her cheek. "Of course you could."

Her wistful expression hardens before her gaze flicks to mine and her jaw softens. "So I pushed Tess into her death. I made sure we crossed paths with the darkness, and I let her be killed while I remained hidden. Every safety that could've been placed on the book was turned off, and she died alone while I watched. When I knew she was gone, I ran out of my hiding spot, smeared some of her blood on my face to make sure it looked like I'd been wounded too, and then I signaled for us to leave the book. Of course, everyone was appalled at what had happened, and it wasn't hard for me to blame the wizard who'd let us into the story in the first place." She shakes her head and scowls. "When it was done, I thought that you'd be so happy. I thought for sure that you'd come to me for comfort."

I squeeze her shoulder. "I had to look sad, you understand."

Her lids flutter in surprise. "Of course. She was your wife."

"I remember how you cried."

"I *was* sad. Tess had been a good friend." She shoots me a stern look as if this will convince me that's true. "But now there was nothing stopping us from being together; yet you didn't come for me."

I graze my knuckles over her cheek. "It was a mistake, one that needs to be rectified."

Hope alights in her eyes. "Starting when? Feylin, I'm more than ready to be your wife. You understand my loyalty. I've killed for you—sort of. I would kill for you again. If you'd gone through with that marriage to Addison, she would've died, too. But she was too stupid to even know what hit her when I delivered the book. She deserves whatever punishment you gave her for that."

I brush a loose strand of hair from her eyes. "Do you really mean that?"

"Of course."

"And do you think that anyone who defies me should receive whatever punishment I give them?"

"You're my king." She bows. "Of course I do. Anyone who defies you should be punished severely."

A slow smile spreads over my face. "I'm glad you feel that way. Guards!" The door opens and in streams a line of men bearing weapons. "Take this woman prisoner and throw her in the darkest pit we have. Give her just enough food to keep her alive."

Their hands curl around Zandra's arms, and she struggles against them. "What are you doing?"

It takes every bit of restraint not to destroy Zandra with my bare hands. "You killed the woman I loved. You destroyed her for your own gain. Tess was a good person, and you destroyed her because of the evil in your heart. You baited Addison, who knew nothing about what had happened to the late queen." I pick up the tumbler. "And you should always be careful when you allow a king to make a drink for you. You never know what sort of talking magic he might pour into it."

She stares at me for a moment before tipping her head back and laughing. "My father'll kill you for this. You have no proof."

I cock a brow. "Really?"

"It's your word against mine."

"Huh." I spin around. "Trawick, you here?"

He dissolves the glamour that hid him and steps away from the wall, arms crossed, glaring at Zandra. "Heard the whole thing. Sounds like someone's going to rot in a cell for the rest of her life. Unless she's hanged, of course. Do we still do that?"

I shrug. "We could make an exception."

"And I'm here, too," Elmore says, appearing in the gilded mirror. "Sounded like quite the confession to me."

I nod to the guards. "Get her out of my sight, and make sure I never see or hear her again."

As they drag her away, Zandra struggles to break free. "No, Feylin! I was just kidding. I didn't do any of it! Don't let me rot in a cell!"

Then she's gone, her screams echoing in the hallway as she's taken to what I hope will become her final resting place.

With that done, I rub my hands together and say to Trawick, "The Witch and Wizard Council?"

He nods. "That should be taken care of."

"All right. Then there's only one thing left for me to do. Elmore, you're on."

He nods. "Got it."

And quick as a wink, the image inside the mirror disappears.

48

*T*he castle's right up the hill. All I have to do is knock on the door and tell Feylin how I feel. He deserves to know. If he chooses to kick me out on my rear end after that, it's fine.

But at least I'll have told him the truth.

I'm about to charge up in a pair of black leather boots with fresh heels (should I rethink this?) when Blair's voice grabs my attention.

"Addison, come see!"

"What?"

She rushes to me, the tails of her long cardigan flapping in the breeze. "Just come. You won't believe it."

"But I—"

She grabs my arm and tugs. "That can wait. This can't."

I'm not so sure about that, but I relent and turn toward the village.

We've just reached the dead center of Castleview when I stop. The doors to the bookshop are wide open. It looks brand-new, like it wasn't burned to the ground only days before. And all the books?

"They've been replaced," she whispers. "We've even gotten the rare ones back."

A tear falls down her cheek. Tears are about to stream down mine, too. "What happened?"

"Feylin," she whispers. "He contacted the council, and he fixed it, Addie. He restored it along with the magic."

"Impossible."

She shakes her head. "Not impossible. Not at all. See for yourself."

I cross the threshold and see that it's true. Every book's back, and they're all in their place. It looks like the fire never happened. Even the charred smell is gone.

My mother, hair pulled into a low ponytail, rushes out from the back, beaming. "Feylin fixed it!"

"But why?" I wonder. "Why would he change his mind?"

"I don't know, but I suspect that you have something to do with it."

It feels like an arrow's hit my chest and burst into flames. I don't know how to react to this. I'm grateful, yes. But it also seems like the great King Feylin decided to show us grace, and so that's what we got. It feels unearned, almost like he's proving that he can show kindness when he wants to.

"Why didn't he come and tell us himself?" I whisper.

"Oh, look at the time," Mama says. "I've got...somewhere to be. Blair, I need you with me."

"Right." My sister squeezes my shoulder as she walks past. "I wouldn't think about it too much. Just be grateful. And you don't mind watching the store for a few minutes, do you?"

"Well, I guess—"

"Great. Thanks!"

They each shoulder their purses, and before I can say another word, they're out the door, letting it slam shut behind them.

Just as I take a breath and let Feylin's gesture seep into me, a voice calls my name.

"Addison!"

My face breaks into a smile. "Elmore!"

I whip around to see him looking very serious, brows pinched, in the brass mirror that rests on a side wall.

I sprint to him. "Elmore, I'm so sorry. I must've left you in the castle. I completely forgot."

He quirks a brow. "Until just now?"

"Um. Well. A lot's happened." It's a terrible excuse, but the only one I've got. "I'm really sorry."

"It's fine." He waves his hand with a flourish. "Listen, while your sister and mother were here, a boy went into a book. He's been gone awhile, and I'm worried about him."

"What are you talking about? They didn't say anything about that."

"They must've forgotten to tell you. But he's inside, and his time should've been up a minute ago. He's not out yet. You've got to go in and get him."

"What?"

Elmore shoots me a stern look. "You've got to enter the book and pull him out. We need to know if he's okay. Look, it's someone you're friends with."

"Who?"

He swallows. "Ryals."

My heart skids to a stop. A literal, huge stop. "Ryals? What's he even doing here to begin with?"

"He snuck out. You'd talked so much about going into books that he wanted to try it for himself." He shoots me a stern look. "That's what he said, and of course Feylin would never agree to it, even if he has dropped his charges with the council against the store and all that. So the boy came, and your mother let him in. You've got to get him out and make sure he's okay."

My rational mind is blaring huge alarm sirens at me. Why did my mother leave? Why'd she let Ryals go into a book by himself? Where is she? How could she have forgotten such an important thing?

While that's going on, my mind's also telling me that there's no way that my mother would've ever placed Ryals into anything dangerous. She probably stuck him in *Winnie the Pooh*. But even if that's the case, if anything happens to Ryals—Tigger gets rabies and bites him, Pooh Bear loses his mind and goes feral—if anything were to happen to Ryals, I'd never forgive myself.

"Where's the book?"

Elmore points to one open atop an onyx lectern. "There."

"I've never thrown myself inside."

"Just picture yourself diving in. That's how you do it," he explains. "It's the same as projecting another person into the story, except you're focusing on you."

"Okay."

There's no time to even read what book Ryals is in. It doesn't matter. Either way, I'm coming for him.

I close my eyes and release my magic. The power slithers around me tightly, and the next thing I know, I'm springing from my spot on the floor and being sucked down, down, down.

I land gently on an uneven surface. I blink my eyes open, half expecting nausea to come but not surprised when it doesn't. It seems I'm cured of my travel sickness. Probably has something to do with a certain fae king.

But back to the book. In front of me lies a sprawling meadow dotted with wildflowers. At the end of it sits a charming stone cottage. Smoke curls up from a chimney, and outside, two young women carrying baskets and wearing clothes from a different century approach the house.

There's a small brook, and a black carriage slowly rolls up to the cottage. I've been in this book before, but it's been years.

It's Jane Austen.

"Pride and Prejudice," comes a low-timbred voice from behind me.

My spine snaps tight. At the same time my bones ache and my heart squeezes to the point of bursting.

I exhale a shaky breath and slowly turn. My legs are limp as wet noodles, and I'm surprised that they don't collapse. My face immediately heats as my gaze lands on Feylin.

He's wearing his usual—dark jeans, white button-down shirt. His eyes brim with emotion. And in his hands is a red rectangular box. I recognize it as the one from the fire ceremony.

My heart's in my throat, taking up all the space so that I can't speak. I wouldn't know what to say, anyhow, so it's a good thing when he talks first.

His beautiful full lips quirk slightly. "I'm sorry that I brought you here on false pretenses."

"Ryals?"

He cocks his head toward the brook. Sure enough, there's Ryals, knee-deep in the water, turning over rocks.

My chest loosens. "I'm glad he's safe." Feylin starts to say something, but I hold up my hand. "Wait. Whatever you're going to say, there's something that I need to say first."

He nods, waiting. But of course the elaborate speech that I'd planned instantly vanishes from my head. I can't remember one word of it, so it looks like I'll be winging this.

Also, watching my fingers while I fidget with them seems like a great idea. "Thank you for giving my family back the bookshop. I—I understand why you shut it down. That doesn't mean that I agree with it, but thank you for returning it to us."

He doesn't say anything, and I'm beginning to wonder why

he's even brought me here. But there's still more to say in my mind somewhere, so I force it out.

"We spent a lot of time together, and I'm sorry about what happened at the fire ceremony. You didn't listen to me then, and I don't know if you'll listen to me now, but I didn't know about Tess dying in a book. My family didn't tell me the whole story until I got home. If I'd known—"

A swell of emotion hits me hard, and the words become a clot that jams up my throat. I manage to swallow past it and start again. "If I'd known what happened to her, I never would've given you that gift. It was Zandra. She gave it to me."

"I know."

I've been staring down this whole time because it's impossible to look at someone while pouring your heart out. But when he says that, my gaze jump up.

He says it again. "I know that she fooled you."

My heart, which has been beating as fast as a racehorse's, somehow manages to accelerate. "Yes, but anyway, there are things that I never told you. I...I love you, Feylin." His throat bobs when I say it. My palms sprout extra sweat. "I should've told you before, and maybe none of this would've happened. But I do love you, and I think I've loved you since we first met. When you took me to the tailor, I knew for sure, and I'm sorry that I never said it. I regret that I never did. It's funny"—I run my fingers through my hair—"people think you're cold-hearted, but I know the truth. When you give short responses or narrow your eyes, I know that you're trying to figure out if a thing is best for your subjects. I love how when something's really funny to you, your eyes dance with laughter. I love that only a very few people, including me, know that you love a good joke, and that you have a sense of humor, and most of all, I love how you're completely selfless. You put your entire kingdom before your own needs. And I love you for all of it. And my one regret is that I never told you, because if anyone deserves to know that they were loved, it's you. Because you've had so much taken from you, that you need to hear how much you're cared for."

He rocks back on his heels and exhales a breath so deep that his shoulders fall. "If I hadn't come here to do what I'm going to, that speech would've convinced me."

I chuckle nervously, no clue what he means.

He steps forward and offers me his hand, which I take hesitantly. When my palm slips over his, I don't expect to feel the same bite of power that the joining always provided, and I don't. But there's no denying that a different fissure of electricity has replaced what once was. It winds around my spine and grabs my heart in its clutches. It's comforting yet also energizing.

I tip my face to his, and he looks down, closing his eyes briefly. "I'm sorry that I didn't listen to you. If I had, we could've avoided all of this. I should've—" He winces, stops. "You wouldn't have hurt me. I know that. *Now*. And I also know the truth—Zandra tricked you. Not only did she do that, but she also played a role in Tess's death. It was Elmore who helped me see that."

"Elmore?"

"He came to me."

Oh, so that's where he's been. "He figured out how to escape the compact?"

He laughs. "Yes. Of all the things for you to be worried about, that's the one?"

"It's an important detail."

He smiles, making the corners of his eyes crinkle. "I've done so much wrong in this." He turns my hand over and kisses the inside of my wrist, which makes tingles cartwheel down my arm. "I'm sorry about the bookshop."

"You restored it."

He nods. "I hope you can forgive me for burning it."

341

"Only if you promise never to do that again."

"I do." He exhales as he sweeps his thumb over the back of my hand. "Right now I have a chance to do something right. Addison—" His voice breaks.

My heart's beating wildly against my ribs because it feels like something big is about to happen.

"Addison," he starts again, "you are my everything, and you were before I ever admitted it to myself. I've loved you longer than I know, and I wasn't lying when I told you that if this isn't true love, then true love doesn't exist. I love you so much it feels like my heart's going to explode. I love you with every last breath that I have. I love you. I love you." He presses his forehead to mine. "I love you."

I don't even have my own breath as I take in what he's saying.

He pulls back, drops my hand and lifts the lid of the box. "If I'd given you this gift first at the fire ceremony, I doubt that any of the rest would've ever happened."

He tips the box so that I can see that inside lays a perfect red rose. My brows wrinkle as I put two and two together. "Is this a Golden Rose?"

He pulls it from the box and extends it in offering. "From me to you."

Part of me doesn't want to take it. I want to live in this perfect moment, where we've each admitted that we love one another. Because if I take ahold of that flower and it turns black, then we have to walk away from each other. Forever. I can't do that. Not now. Not when we've come so far.

But at the same time I want to know that what we feel for each other is true. Because ever since he told me the story of the rose, I've wanted—no, *needed* him to gift me one so that I could prove to myself and to him that our feelings for each other dive deeper than some joining or strange twist of fate.

This is destiny, and I've known that since…well, since right after I puked on his shoes.

It's that thought that spurs me to reach for the flower, trembling hand and all. Every muscle in my body's twitching from anxiety. Yet peace blankets me because I intuitively know what lies on the other side.

My fingers brush his as they curl around the stem. I clutch it in a stranglehold, cinching my breath and watching with my heart in my throat as the crimson begins to wash away and is slowly replaced by—

"Gold," I whisper.

"Gold," he murmurs as he slides his hand across my cheek and pulls me into a kiss.

That kiss shatters every last sliver of anger that I might've been holding on to. In one sweeping kiss all that confusion and fear is replaced with love.

And with that love, magic pours out of me, circling us and wrapping the two of us in a powerful embrace.

When we separate, Feylin brushes his mouth over my forehead. "There's one more thing."

I cock my head in worry. "What?"

He pulls back, eyes sparking. "Will you marry me?"

49

"Where's the bouquet?"

Blair's eyes widen. "Don't you have it? I don't have it."

"Chelsea?" My panic level's sitting at one thousand percent. "Where is it?"

She grimaces. "I thought you had it. You're the bride."

I swish one way and then the other, searching the room. Since the wedding's at the castle, I'm getting ready here, so the room's an explosion of flowers and chiffon and champagne and, for some reason, jewelry.

Feylin apparently opened up some jewelry vault and pulled everything out of it, leaving millions of dollar's worth of diamonds for me to choose from to wear. There are necklaces dripping with emeralds, sapphires, pearls. There are even stones that I don't recognize.

But none of that matters. What matters is that we're getting married, and that I can't find my bouquet. It's not like I can substitute a diamond bracelet for a bouquet.

Or can I?

No. I can't.

"Where is it?" I'm about to pull my hair out. "Seriously."

Blair pushes a pair of emerald studs into her ears. "You can just magic up a new one."

"No, I can't. That has our golden rose in it."

Of course I'd kept the rose. What kind of question is that?

The door opens and Ophelia enters. Her hair's up in a loose bun, and she's wearing a sea-foam colored dress that suits her.

She's also holding my bouquet.

"Thank goodness!" I rush over. "You are a godsend. Thank you."

She smiles. "You're welcome. I found it outside and knew you'd be missing it. Are you ready?"

I grin. "I am."

"They're waiting for you."

Chelsea drains the last of her champagne. "Time to rock and roll, sis."

I take one last look in the mirror and smile. The pale pink dress is everything that I've ever wanted in a wedding gown. It's all chiffon and grace, with delicate lace straps and a bell skirt. And it's one dress that Feylin hasn't seen me in, though I took it on Daisy's authority that he would, indeed, be blown away by it. If my sisters' and mother's reactions were any indication of how he'll react when he sees me, I've chosen correctly.

I exhale and take the flowers Ophelia hands me. It's a simple bouquet of white roses with one golden rose in the middle. "Okay. Let's do this."

Blair and Chelsea lead the way. My mother stands at the head of the stairs, waiting. My sisters keep going down the steps as Mama greets me, Blair giving me one last smile before disappearing below.

"You're the loveliest thing I've ever seen," she says.

"Thank you."

My mother pulls me into a tight hug before pushing me to arm's length and letting her gaze survey me from head to foot. She sniffles, magicking a tissue that she dabs at her eyes.

"You have turned into a beautiful woman, so full of grace and kindness. I may have been worried about Feylin at first, but he loves you, and that's what matters."

I squeeze her elbow. "I wouldn't be standing here if it wasn't for you and Daddy, for how good of parents you've been."

She cringes. "Except for when we kept important details from you."

She means Tess. I hitch one shoulder in a shrug. "You did what you believed was best. That's what we all do at any given time."

"I suppose so." She presses her lips together and smiles. "Your father's waiting."

"Let's not keep him wondering where I am."

She escorts me to the foot of the stairs, where my father stands. He kisses my cheek. "You look beautiful."

"Thank you."

I slip my hand through the crook of his elbow as my mother gives me one last smile and sweeps past us, heading outside, where the guests and Feylin wait.

Dad cups one hand over mine as he leads me to the open doors. "You'll always be my little girl."

I rest my head lightly on his shoulder. "I wouldn't expect any less."

He chuckles. "It's a big day."

"The biggest, and I'm ready for it."

It's absolutely true. I'm more than ready. It's been six months since Feylin proposed, which means six months of only seeing him during dates. No, I didn't move into the castle, though he asked me about a million times if I wanted to. I've stayed with my family, helped keep the business thriving, and even had a few dates with Feylin in a book now and then.

Before he'd ever jumped into *Pride and Prejudice,* he'd sworn to himself that he would never, under any circumstances, ever go into a book. Intuitively I knew that, which made his gesture more meaningful because he took the leap to prove how much he cares about me.

And I'm about to leap, too.

We've reached the doorway, and now the lawn's in view. Chairs lay sprawled across the grass, and every one is filled with fae, witches and wizards alike. Our communities have come together, which I think makes me the proudest of all.

The sunlight pierces my eyes only momentarily. When the sharpness fades, I see him. My groom stands at the altar, a huge smile on his face. My heart races at the mere sight of him.

This is real. I've found the love of my life, and he's mine, all mine.

My father walks me down the aisle and hands me over to the king, whose gaze hasn't left mine since he spotted me.

But before Dad goes, he says, "I know you'll take good care of her."

"With my life, sir," he replies.

Then I take Feylin's hand and he whispers, "You look beautiful. I almost didn't recognize you."

My brow lifts. "Would that have stopped you from marrying me?"

He smirks, silently saying *as if that would've stopped me.* "Your light can't be hidden beneath clothes. You shine like a star, Addison Thornrose, and I love you."

"I love you, too."

My heart's full then, and I barely even hear a word that the priest says as he begins the ceremony.

WHEN THE PRIEST announces that we're married, Feylin leans down and kisses me sweetly. When our lips part, he murmurs, "My queen." My lids flare wide and he chuckles. "Get used to it. You're going to hear that a lot."

Before I can reply, a surge of magic rips through me. My gaze darts to my mother, who nods. I've done it. I've brought back an ounce of our power. There's still more to do, more sisters to marry to ensure that we're able to keep all our magic.

But before there's a chance to think more on that, I'm swept into a celebration that features music and food. Fae dance with witches. Wizards dance with fae. Our people mingle, and my heart balloons with pride.

The dancing and eating last well into the night. I barely have a chance to talk to Feylin as lords and ladies alike greet us, giving their blessings and welcoming me as their new queen.

Queen.

I'll never get used to that.

It's when the festivities are finally winding down that I say goodbye to my family. Feylin escorts them to the door as I spot Trawick.

He's just finished talking with a lord and approaches me. He's wearing a dark three-piece suit and is growing a beard that suits him. He didn't come with a date, which surprised me, as Trawick's a beautiful fae man.

"My queen."

I smirk. "You don't have to call me that."

"It's my duty and privilege," he says, a note of truth ringing in his voice. His gaze slashes to Feylin, who's still with my family, before landing back on me. "I've never told you this, but I'm happy he's found you. You're exactly what my friend needed, and I'm honored to serve you both."

"Thank you."

He kisses my cheek. "May your union be blessed."

I thank him again and he leaves. My family's left, too, and it's when Feylin turns to me, his eyes brimming with emotion, that Ryals drags himself over.

"I'm tired. I need to go to bed."

Feylin smiles. "Piggyback?"

"Yes," he moans.

I laugh as Feylin bends down, and Ryals climbs onto his back. We drop him off at his room, and the boy says, "Addie, will you tuck me in?"

His request plucks one of my heartstrings. "Of course."

I magick some pajamas onto him and pull back the covers of his bed. After he's slipped in and the duvet's tucked under his chin, Ryals rubs his eye.

"I'm glad you're going to live with us."

I kiss his forehead. "Me, too. Now get some rest. I'll see you in the morning."

"Okay."

He's snoring lightly by the time I reach the hallway. Feylin threads his fingers through mine and shuts Ryals's door. We walk in silence to his bedroom, but when we stop, it's outside of my old room, the one across from his.

My gaze washes from one door to the other. "What are we doing here?"

He rubs the back of his neck sheepishly. "Open it and see."

I quirk a brow. "Nothing's going to jump out at me, will it?"

He rolls his eyes. "Do I have to answer that?"

"No." I giggle and turn the knob. As the door slowly opens, my breath hitches. The room—the one that'd been mine, full of all kinds of feminine beauty—has become a blend of Feylin's masculine taste and my own softness.

The walls are painted a light gray, and the accent colors are a deep navy with touches of pearly white here and there, softening the edges. There are pictures of my family, of the two of us together, of Ryals. Feylin's clearly done everything that he can to make sure this room feels like a space for both of us.

Words choke in my throat. "Feylin..."

He smiles. "You like it?"

"I love it."

I throw my arms around his neck and kiss him. He greedily kisses me back, his arms sweeping around my lower waist. We've been really, really good these past months, doing everything to temper our lust for one another. Why? Well, neither of us has said as much, but—

He breaks the kiss and glances down at me, his eyes full of tenderness. "Finally we get to do this when we're not angry with one another, and when we're not confused."

That's why. Because we wanted our emotions to be aligned to the right place, and they are.

He pulls me inside and kicks the door closed. Every touch as he unzips my dress is light as a feather and imbued with a fire that sizzles down my skin. No, our touches no longer have the joining magic behind them. They have something different. It's a deeper emotion, an electric spark that makes every touch sweeter as his fingers caress my shoulders on their way to tug down the straps of my dress.

The gown falls away, and I step out of it. We don't break eye contact as I unknot his tie and let the fabric slip through the collar.

Energy buzzes between us, supercharging the air. I tip my face up to his, and his mouth falls on mine. His kiss is slow, patient. Mine is, too. I work my way down his shirt, pushing buttons through holes one at a time until I've reached the bottom.

He shrugs out of the shirt, leaving an expanse of naked chest before me. I run my palms down the swells and dips of his body, losing myself in his beauty.

I lightly touch his scars, recognizing those on the outside of his body and those on the inside, and acknowledging how all of them have brought us to this moment.

He kisses me again, and his tongue sweeps over my bottom lip, taking me by surprise and making a shudder sizzle down my spine. It feels like a switch's been flipped. What started as a kernel of desire has swelled to become full-on *want*. I want more of him, all of him.

Our tongues collide, and it seems like he wants all of me, too. I wind my arms over his neck and coil the tips of my fingers around his hair.

"Addison," he moans into my mouth.

"Feylin," I reply.

Our kisses deepen as I quickly unclasp his belt and unbutton his pants. I hear them fall to the floor, and Feylin presses his body against mine, letting me know how much he wants me. I can't get enough of his hard masculinity, and I don't mean his erection. I mean all of him—the beauty that is my husband.

He's a work of art beneath my palms, like he's been sculpted from marble and given life. There isn't one imperfection on him.

"You are so beautiful," he whispers.

"I was just thinking that about you."

He pulls back and looks down at me, smiling. "I think you've got me beat."

I tip my head back and laugh, and he drops his mouth to my neck, nuzzling his way to the base of my throat. My muscles go limp as he pulls my bra away and my hard nipples scrape against his bare chest.

"There's only one piece of clothing left," he murmurs in my ear.

I grin. "It's all you."

He smirks before pressing his mouth to mine and tracing

his tongue across my bottom lip. Then he kisses his way down my breasts, taking each nipple in his mouth in turn, which makes a moan rip from my lips.

The tip of my breast falls from his lips before his tongue swirls over the nipple. His mouth leaves my chest and grazes down my stomach to my waist.

He kneels before me and drags his teeth to the thin band of material at my hip. He clamps his mouth over my panties and tugs them down a few inches before his fingers slide up my thighs and pull them the rest of the way off.

"While I'm down here," he breaths into my skin, "there's something else I need to do."

"What's that?"

He tips his head back and meets my gaze. "Make you come."

The look in his eyes is enough to make me explode right there, but he winks and rises quickly, lifting me into his arms, which elicits a surprised screech from me.

Before I know it, I'm on my back atop the bed and Feylin's at the edge, kneeling. Heat pools between my legs as he lifts my leg over his shoulder and eases his fingers into me.

"You're so wet," he says with admiration.

The first thrust makes my entire body shudder. "Oh no," he says in a devilish voice. "You're not coming that quickly. I want this to last."

And so he slowly brings me to the brink, masterfully working me with his fingers as he sucks my clit. Every time I get close, he eases back until I'm begging for him to let me feel release.

"Only if you're sure," he teases.

"I'm sure."

And then he uses his tongue alone, pushing me to the edge of ecstasy. The pressure builds in a huge wave, pulsing between my legs. Then I'm split apart, breaking into a million pieces as my back arches and my body clenches around his tongue.

When the wave breaks away, I'm left breathless, sweaty.

But I'm not done.

Feylin appears beside me, fist tucked under his head. "Tired?"

I shoot him a skeptical look before pouncing on top of him. He rolls onto his back, laughing.

I nip his nose. "Not tired."

"I see. Then I've got a job for you." He lifts my hips and slowly eases me onto him. I take his length all at once, and his breath hitches, eyes widening.

I lean down and whisper in his ear, "Looks like I'm full of surprises."

"You are that, my queen."

We come together slowly, deliberately. We don't rush this. We take our time, keeping eye contact and holding one another as we climax together, our bodies shuddering and quaking at the same time.

When we collapse on the bed, moonlight spilling in through the windows and splaying over our bodies, Feylin brushes a strand of hair from my sweat-slicked forehead.

"If this isn't true love," he whispers.

Taking his hand, I kiss his knuckles. "Then true love doesn't exist."

He pulls me to him, tucking me under his chin. "And I've got a golden rose to prove it."

50

EPILOGUE

SIX MONTHS LATER

"*I*t's not done yet," I tell Feylin.

He rakes his fingers through his dark hair. "How long do these things take? Can't we use magic to hurry it up?"

His impatience makes me smile. "When you're finding out if you're pregnant, wouldn't you like it to be *right* rather than quick?"

"No."

I roll my eyes. "Ten minutes." I place the stick on the bathroom counter. "You can wait that long, my king."

He grumbles something unintelligible as I sweep past him. "Come on. Let's eat supper. I'm sure Ryals is waiting."

It takes several seconds before Feylin rips his gaze from the stick and follows me down the hall.

"I don't know why we can't use magic to make it go faster," he grumbles.

"For someone who has a lot of patience, you really don't have any."

"I'm full of patience," he argues. "Just not when it comes to this."

"Noted."

I take his hand and beam up at him. His tight jaw slackens as he smiles back. "I'm just nervous."

"I gathered that." I hug his arm. "There's nothing to be nervous about."

"We're only talking about guiding a new life."

"You're going to be a great father."

He taps the tip of my nose. "You'll be a better mother."

I drop my head onto his arm. It doesn't quite reach the top of his shoulder, which is fine by me. I've always loved how opposite our bodies are—his so big, mine so...*not.*

"Thank you."

He kisses my head. "You're welcome."

We're about to turn into the dining room when a commotion comes from the front hall. Feylin stiffens. "Stay here."

He charges to find out what's going on, but there's no way I'm going to let him go alone. I've got magic. I can defend myself if I have to.

I'm at his heels in an instant, to which he grinds out, "I thought I said—"

"I know what you said. I didn't obey."

He curses but only replies, "Stay behind me."

As soon as we round a corner, we come face-to-face with—

"Nana."

Blood drains from my face.

My grandmother doesn't seem to notice my response as she casually brushes dust off her shoulders like if it's no big deal that she's dead. And here. In the castle.

She looks exactly the same as she did in life—curly silver hair piled high on her head, full makeup, and dressed to the nines.

She straightens the tall collar of her black brocade gown.

"What a trip. Didn't think I'd ever get here. You have no idea how hard it is to travel when you're dead."

"Nana."

I literally just keep repeating the word because I can't think of anything to say. Feylin's hand is on my shoulder, squeezing it, pulling me back from the proverbial cliff I stand on.

She appraises my husband proudly. "So this is the man you married. You did marry him, didn't you?" she eyes Feylin with satisfaction. "Yes, you married him. I can tell."

I clear my throat in the hope to knock some sense into my brain. Nana is here. Nana is dead. Nana is here.

"Feylin, meet my grandmother, Rebecca—"

"Nana will do," she interrupts. "I'd love to hug you, but being dead and all, I can't make any promises that it'll work."

Feylin doesn't miss a beat. He bows deeply out of respect. "It's a pleasure to meet you."

"The pleasure's mine. Any man who can bring out Addie's magic has a special place in my heart." Nana glances up and around the castle. "You've married a king, Addie. I give my blessing."

"Th-thank you."

"Now." She crosses her arms and narrows her eyes, getting down to business. "There's still more work to do. The rest of your sisters have to marry, and I'm looking at Blair." She tips her head in thought. "What's the name of that man she thinks she hates?"

"You mean Devlin Ross? You want to set them up?" When she nods, I laugh. "Good luck. She despises him."

"Not when I'm done with her she won't." My grandmother strokes her chin, and with a twinkle in her eyes adds, "Welcome to matchmaking by the dead. Now. Let's get started."

Thank you so much for reading HOW TO FAKE IT WITH A FAE. I hope you loved Addison and Feylin as much as I do. Their story was a joy to write.

You can grab Blair and Devlin's story, HOW TO OUTWIT A WIZARD, by scanning the code below.

Lucky for you, Addie's story isn't finished yet. There's a BONUS SCENE, one that answers the question of whether or not a little plus sign popped up on the window of the pregnancy test.

To get your scene, you have to sign up for my newsletter. Don't worry, I won't spam your inbox. I only email when I have sales, new releases, or other fun things going on.

If all that sounds good to you, click **HERE** to grab your scene and receive my newsletter.

You can also touch base with me by joining my Facebook group, Amy Boyles's Cozy Coven. Click HERE to join.

ACKNOWLEDGMENTS

Books do not exist in a vacuum, and HOW TO FAKE IT WITH A FAE is no different. First, I'd like to thank God for all the blessings that He has bestowed in my life, leading me to write this book being one of those.

Thank you to my plotting partners-in-crime: Bambi Crivello, Jean Hovey, and Stephanie Jones, who helped shape the very beginnings of FAE.

A big thank you to Lea Ann Schafer for being one of the first readers and telling me when I needed to dive deeper. You have an editor's eye and I'm so very grateful.

Eryn Scott, your detailed insight was spot-on, and your love of all things romantasy is so much fun to be around. Maybe one day I'll convince you to write one with me.

Huge thanks to my local librarians, Alex and Sarah, who were fantastic alpha readers. Thank you both for cheering me on.

Thank you to all my writer friends who agreed to read an early copy of this book. All of you are such an inspiration. I'm grateful for connecting with every one of you.

Big hugs to my existing fan base for going on this journey with me. Your love and support of my work is a blessing, and one I don't take for granted.

Lastly, much love to my family for putting up with my Saturday work-days and my early nights (when you're up at 4 am, it's hard to stay up past 8 pm). Much, much love to Mark, Harper, and Briar, plus Leo the Pug.

ALSO BY AMY BOYLES

OTHER SERIES

A MAGICAL RENOVATION MYSERY

WITCHER UPPER

RENOVATION SPELL

DEMOLITION PREMONITION

WITCHER UPPER CHRISTMAS

BARN BEWITCHMENT

SHIPLAP AND SPELL HUNTING

MUDROOM MYSTIC

WITCH IT OR LIST IT

PANTRY PRANKSTER

HOME TOWN MAGIC

WITCH APPEAL

WHITE MAGIC AND WARDROBES

RESTORATION RUNES

LOST SOUTHERN MAGIC

(Takes place following the events of Southern Magic Wedding. This is a Sweet Tea Witches, Southern Belles and Spells, Southern Ghost Wrangles and Bless Your Witch Crossover)

THE GOLD TOUCH THAT WENT CATTYWAMPUS

THE YELLOW-BELLIED SCAREDY CAT

A MESS OF SIRENS

KNEE-HIGH TO A THIEF

BELLES AND SPELLS MATCHMAKER MYSTERY

DEADLY SPELLS AND A SOUTHERN BELLE

CURSED BRIDES AND ALIBIS

MAGICAL DAMES AND DATING GAMES

SOME PIG AND A MUMMY DIG

SWEET TEA WITCH MYSTERIES

SOUTHERN MAGIC

SOUTHERN SPELLS

SOUTHERN MYTHS

SOUTHERN SORCERY

SOUTHERN CURSES

SOUTHERN KARMA

SOUTHERN MAGIC THANKSGIVING

SOUTHERN MAGIC CHRISTMAS

SOUTHERN POTIONS

SOUTHERN FORTUNES

SOUTHERN HAUNTINGS

SOUTHERN WANDS

SOUTHERN CONJURING

SOUTHERN WISHES

SOUTHERN DREAMS

SOUTHERN MAGIC WEDDING

SOUTHERN OMENS

SOUTHERN JINXED

SOUTHERN BEGINNINGS

SOUTHERN MYSTICS

SOUTHERN CAULDRONS

SOUTHERN HOLIDAY

SOUTHERN ENCHANTED

SOUTHERN TRAPPINGS

THE ACCIDENTAL MEDIUM

WITCH'S BLOCK

POISONED PROSE

SPELL, DON'T TELL

SOUTHERN GHOST WRANGLER MYSTERIES

SOUL FOOD SPIRITS

HONEYSUCKLE HAUNTING

THE GHOST WHO ATE GRITS (Crossover with Pepper and Axel from Sweet Tea Witches)

BACKWOODS BANSHEE

MISTLETOE AND SPIRITS

BLESS YOUR WITCH SERIES

SCARED WITCHLESS

KISS MY WITCH

QUEEN WITCH

QUIT YOUR WITCHIN'

FOR WITCH'S SAKE

DON'T GIVE A WITCH

WITCH MY GRITS

FRIED GREEN WITCH

SOUTHERN WITCHING

Y'ALL WITCHES

HOLD YOUR WITCHES

SOUTHERN SINGLE MOM PARANORMAL MYSTERIES

The Witch's Handbook to Hunting Vampires

The Witch's Handbook to Catching Werewolves

The Witch's Handbook to Trapping Demons

ABOUT THE AUTHOR

Hey, I'm Amy,

I write books for folks who crave laugh-out-loud para-normal romance and cozy mysteries. I've got a Pharm D and a BA in Creative Writing.

And when I'm not writing, I can be found reading or binge-watching a K-drama. If you have any suggestions on good K-dramas, I will take them!

If you want to reach out to me—and I love to hear from readers—you can email me at amy@amyboyles.com

Happy reading!